Createspace Print Edition - April 2013
ISBN 978-1484100530

Cover Art by Bethany Vargeson Copyright 2013

http://www.valnon.org

EVENSONG'S HEIR

Book One of the Songbirds of Valnon

By L. S. Baird

SHARYN: SING TO BRING HEAVEN DOWN! L. S. BAIRD 2013

For Joy, who knew it all along.

The streets of Valnon had not been planned by a sane man. In fact, the idea that Valnon had been planned by anyone, regardless of mental faculties, was a notion that strained credulity. Valnon had simply happened wherever it took a notion to do so. The buildings had long since outgrown the island beneath them, and now spiraled up and out in fantastic spumes of walls and bridges, while the roads twisted over the island's surface like a skein of yarn that had become entangled in the rocks. The result was a city clinging precariously to a high perch above the waves, festooned on the white rocks like some gaudy colony of barnacles.

Opinion was divided on who or what had caused the confusion. Some of her citizens said her streets were built on the fragments of ancient Hasafel's roads, roads that once lead to other islands now drowned beneath the sea. Others called the roads a result of St. Alveron's fancy, or of Antigus the Terrible's arrogance, or the aimless wanderings of a large number of unknown and sorely underestimated sheep.

Either way it's utter bollocks, Nicholas Grayson thought, glaring through the chilly downpour at a shuttered tavern that should have been the cheesemonger's on Eastgate Road. Sheep, saints, and tyrants had all left Valnon centuries ago, and at that moment, the city's haphazard byways existed solely to thwart him on his business.

It had been months since he had last felt rain on his skin, and longer still since he had been in the upper streets. Grayson's home was a humble room above the Silver Pearl, a quayside tavern that sat beneath the vast cavern roof of Valnon's Undercity, and neither rain nor snow ever burdened its eaves. But the beer was tolerable, the bed was comfortable, and Grayson had taught himself he did not need the sky. He saw a slice of it well enough every day through the great, gaping stone mouth of the Undercity harbor, and he thought himself as content as a man could only be in his grave. Only the jarring familiarity of that name, written in that left-tilting hand, had roused him from his Undercity tomb and set him walking the rainy surface streets at this ungodly hour.

Rouen, the letter had been signed, though Grayson knew that was no longer the man's name. He was Kestrel now, Lord Kestrel the Temple Preybird, and next in line to be High Preybird. The full list of his titles, current and past, would have quadrupled the length of the letter. But he had signed his letter with the only name Grayson had ever called him. On the seal beside his signature, a lark held an orb encircled in its wings. It seemed to curl in on itself as though in pain, and the numeral that should have appeared between its wingtips was a smudge clotted with the wax from several recent messages. The parchment was ink-spattered, the letters hasty, brief.

Nicholas,
Come quickly. I need you.
-Rouen

Fourteen years had passed, with no word. Grayson wasn't even sure how Rouen knew how to find him. But then, Rouen was not the boy Grayson had left behind all those years ago, and all of Valnon was at his fingertips. If the Preybird Kestrel desired Nicholas Grayson, then Nicholas Grayson he would have.

But it was for no Preybird that Grayson had come up Darkmarket Road, out of his dry shadows and into the downpour. Rather, it was for the Songbird that Rouen had once been. In those days Grayson had entertained no longing without russet hair and a Lark's sable; he had dreamed of oaths, of devotion, of honor. Those things meant little enough to him now, but for Rouen, Grayson would go. Fourteen years later, the ends of the earth were not too far to journey for that name.

Of course, his odds of getting to the ends of the earth were pretty slim, as Grayson couldn't even navigate a city block with anything like success. He was back at the closed tavern again. He swore in a way long and loud and rarely heard in such a respectable part of the city, as the rain sank through the padding of his brigandine and pressed, chill and damp, against his skin. Grayson suspected the building was shuffling around when he wasn't looking, determined in some demented fashion to block his path. The surface was not like the Undercity, where there was little space to tear down and rebuild with frequency, and no weather to wear down the walls. On the surface of Valnon's island, change was inevitable, fourteen years was too long, and Grayson had to admit that he no longer knew the way. If he could reach higher ground, he could look for the Temple's spire, but at his current rate he'd be more likely to wind up at the bottom of the harbor. There was nothing for it but to backtrack once again.

He turned around and instantly sank to the ankle in an overflowing gutter. Grayson shook his waterlogged boot and scowled at the stream, certain now that the whole city had some private grievance against him. The city baths, perhaps feeling that the deluge an insufficient amount of nastiness, had flushed their tanks for the night. It was a small consolation that the rain had already scoured away most of the daily filth, and the water held nothing more offensive than the incongruous, ghostly flutter of rose petals. Grayson blinked at them dumbly for a moment, wondering if his eyes were playing tricks on him. The petals in the gutter were no ostentatious crimson or pink from a noble's garden, long out of season now. They were silver, tinged at the edges with deep purple, crisp and fresh as tiny coracles bobbing on the current. Evensong roses bloomed until long after the first frost, and only in the Temple gardens. The water soiling Grayson's cloak hem was from no common city washtub.

With the urgency of a hound at last on the scent, Grayson spun around and took three brisk strides towards the source of the flow. He did not get much further. With his eyes on the gutter and his hood pulled low against the rain, the wild clatter of running footsteps penetrated his ears too late. Grayson looked up, yelped an unheeded warning, and collided full-on with a tall, hooded figure. The impact was enough to jostle them apart on opposite sides of the walk. The stranger staggered back further through gutter water, reeling off-balance with a gasp of pain, barely able to keep his feet. His cloak gaped for a moment, revealing a glimpse of his tunic beneath. Under his shabby cloak he was wearing enough pearls to choke every whore in Darkmarket. He did not pause, he only clutched the stained fabric closer around him as he gathered himself up to keep running, without a word of excuse or apology.

"Here, now!" Grayson began, snatching the man's shoulder and hauling him back. He was already fed-up with everything Valnon's surface had to offer, and that included inebriated, overdressed noblemen. "Just where d'you think you're--"

"Help me," said the voice of the man under the hood. It was a refined voice, but not that of a drunken nobleman. Its peculiar timbre sent a shudder of recognition down Grayson's spine. The stranger clung to him with a hand that was not a child's, or a woman's, though his voice was sweet enough to be either. His gray velvet cuffs were soaked with rain and too much blood to be his own; a thin wash of crimson stained the tails of the silver birds winging their way up his sleeve. On his finger, a bright circle of wings glinted in the flicker of distant lightning, undimmed by the gore. The stranger started as the thunder retorted among the city spires. Desperation fractured the music in his voice; beneath the cowl there were blue eyes ringed white with terror. "Please, in the name of the saints, I beg you--"

"How--" Grayson began, but he was interrupted by a burst of firelight from across the square, a pale orange echo of the lightning. The stranger flung up a hand as though to ward off a blow, and shrank back into the shadows behind Grayson, turning his head from the light.

Boot-heels rang between the close buildings, hot pitch sizzled on the wet paving-stones, and dark figures detached themselves from the alleyway. Grayson's hand instinctively went to his sword. It was a plain thing; there were no wings on the hilt or vows along the blade, but it was more than serviceable. The strangers were an unpleasant knot of ruffians in muddy leathers, and they drew up short at the sight of Grayson. There were four of them, with torches that hissed and spat in the rain. Most kept one hand inside their cloaks. Grayson eyed the men, weighed his odds, and found them in his favor.

"Good evening," Grayson said, evenly. "Is something amiss?"

The man in front flashed a yellow smile in his weather-tanned face. If Grayson was an unexpected component in the situation, he was quickly accounted for. "Ah, nothing that need detain you, sir. Though I see you've caught our runaway thief for us, you have. We're much obliged. Hand him over and we'll be on our way."

"Thief?" Grayson echoed, raising his eyebrows. "I'm afraid you must be mistaken."

"Hardly," the man said, pointing with a dirty fingernail. "That boy there just took six crescents off me in the tavern round the corner. He might have swallowed the evidence, though. They're known to do that." His companions shared a rough laugh and some knowing motions of their elbows. "Best let me look him over, mate."

Grayson had to struggle to keep the distaste off his face. The surface had changed in more ways than simple architectural arrangement. "This young man has been in my company now this whole evening," Grayson said, "and I paid well for the privilege. I assure you, his fee at the Swallowtail is far more than the six crescents you mislaid." At this, the stranger leaned up against Grayson in a passable imitation of expensive affection. *Either that,* Grayson thought, *or he's dying.*

The man, however, was not convinced by the display. "That one's no whore," he spat, as though the stranger in gray velvet was something much worse.

"I'll wager he's not a thief, either," Grayson returned, his tone a level warning that would have made wiser men retreat. "And I'll thank you to be on your way, gentlemen." He turned to leave with the young man still on his arm, hoping he could keep his feet long enough for the two of them to get away. Grayson did not think the boy's trembling was entirely from fear. They had not gotten two steps away before their escape was thwarted by the sound of steel scraping free of its scabbard, and a half-circle of serrated blades closed around them. The ruffians' swords were single-edged things, a foreign make too elegant for their owners and all too familiar to Grayson.

"He's ours is what he is," the first man snarled, jogging the Thrassin cutlass in his hand, "and we'll have him, and you'll not keep us from it."

Grayson rolled his eyes heavenward, in combined annoyance and supplication. At his side, he felt the young man go tense. "Stay back," Grayson murmured. He did not wait for an answer, or for the men to advance. With one hand he shoved the boy away from the crowd, with the other he ripped off his heavy, rain-sodden cloak and hurled it right into the path of their attackers. It landed on them with a satisfying smack, and Grayson plowed into the confusion it caused.

It was hardly a pleasant chore, but it was a quick enough one. They were the sort used to slow and unsuspecting prey, and Grayson was neither. Their illegal blades were new to them.

Grayson had crossed his sword with Thrassin steel often enough to know its strengths and weaknesses, the best techniques to make the most of the swords' cruel design, but his enemies had no such advantage, and it cost them. Grayson's blade tore through the rain, through hasty defenses, through flesh and bone. The torches fell to the streets, smoked briefly, and drowned, rain drawing its dark curtain over the street once more. Aborted cries of pain bounced off the closed shutters of the inn, and the water in the gutters ran dark with blood, infusing the rose petals with a sinister blush of new color.

Grayson looked down at the bodies strewn across the street, and frowned. He mopped back his dripping hair, and toed the body of the leader. His backhand was getting sloppy, Grayson thought, eyeing the torn jerkin and the sprinkling of cheap mail rings scattered on the road. He'd have to work on that. Grayson wiped his sword on the soggy twist of the dead man's cloak, picked up his own, and turned around to see just whom, exactly, he had rescued. "Look, glad as I am to lend a hand, I am in something of a hurry, so if you would just..." Grayson got no further. He was alone in the street. Sheathing his sword, he shot off in pursuit of the fleeing stranger.

It wasn't much of a chase. Grayson had half-forgotten Valnon's streets, it was true, but the man he was following had no more concept of his surroundings than a rabbit. He hesitated at the mouths of alleys Grayson knew for dead ends just by the rubbish heaps outside them, he would reel, bewildered, in the brief cobblestoned opening of a market plaza. Grayson caught him by the elbow before he had gotten three blocks away.

"Bloody hell, boy! I said stay back, not make for Iskarit!"

"Unhand me!" He was tall, but he was no fighter, and his struggle to wrench his arm from Grayson's grip was almost comical. Grayson had a very good idea already of what kind of creature he had caught, but how had he come to be lost and alone in the empty streets of the city, bloodied and scared, with his colors covered by a common sell-sword's cloak?

"What happened to, *Help me in the name of the saints?*" Grayson asked, jerking the young man a little closer. "And for the love of Grace, quit screeching. Those admirers of yours might have friends, and I'm in no mood to kill anyone else for free this evening."

The young man went utterly still. "*Screeching*?" he repeated in tones of deep offense, forgetting to struggle.

"Well it sure as hell wasn't Evensong," Grayson hissed, and was met with the stony silence of an insult too bruising for any retort. "Now hold still. I don't want to hurt you. D'you think I would have bothered saving you if I did?"

"I'm worth more alive," he answered, but there was a quaver of fear now in his voice. Grayson knew that he had probably just imagined all the things that could be done to him without killing him, and if he had any creativity at all, they would not be pleasant.

"Depends on who's trying to catch you, doesn't it?" Grayson dug in his belt and produced a crumpled scrap of parchment, which he brandished in the boy's face. "You recognize this seal, don't you?"

"That's Kestrel's!" There was a flash of relief in the blue eyes beneath the tatty cloak, but it quickly turned to suspicion. "How did you get that? Who are you?"

Grayson stuffed Rouen's letter away again. "I'm somebody who hasn't gotten a thank-you yet for saving your life," he said, and was a little mollified by the scandalized expression he got in return.

"Let go of me," the young man said, his voice ghostly, all the color draining from his face. He began squirming again, and though he was weaker than ever, there was a frantic desperation to it that made him even harder to hold. Grayson's amusement evaporated. He didn't think his tone had been quite that threatening.

"Listen," he said, as gently as he could manage while trying to restrain his flailing prize. "Hold still! We both need to get back to the Temple. We'll have better luck together, right?"

"I can't go back," he answered, and something in his face made Grayson realize the young man was no longer aware of him, or of the rainy street, or of anything save the hands restraining him and the private horror in his mind. He was shivering like an exhausted horse. "I don't know the way. Where am I? Boren--in the garden--I can't--" He broke off with a soft little cry and put a hand to his face, as though to fend off visions too horrible to bear. A second later his knees buckled underneath him, and Grayson staggered under his sudden insensate weight. His head rolled back limply, and the cloak slid away from his face.

He was perhaps twenty at the most--it was hard to tell with his kind--but his hair was the bright silver of the rose petals in the gutter. Platinum feathers winked from the tips of his collar, chiming as the rain hit them. Grayson knew a Songbird's devices, but he had never before seen one dressed in the grays and lavenders of Evensong. Over the musty smells of blood and waterlogged silk there was a faint odor of rich censer smoke clinging to him, his skin perfumed with rare fragrances that had been drizzled into baths of carved alabaster. Grayson's pulse tripped with the certain knowledge of what he had found, far from the shelter of Temple walls where he belonged.

The young man in his arms was the Dove.

Grayson had often imagined returning to the Temple. In younger days, he had thought of turning up on the last Dawning of Rouen's term as Lark, to lay defiant claim to the heart Rouen could at last freely give. But in the end, Grayson had stayed in the Undercity where he belonged. At the time, it had been five years since their parting, Grayson was no longer the man he had been, and Preybirds did not consort with sell-swords.

Since then the fancies had been more fleeting, but they still struck from time to time. Grayson would go to the Temple for Noontide, or for Canticles Eve, or to see the miraculous Dove: the first Songbird in three hundred years to claim that title. He would go and ask after Rouen. Or he would go and then leave, without lingering, to say to himself he had done so.

But he never went. Even if he had, no entrance could have been as dramatic as the one he had not planned, bursting through the Temple doors and into a ring of bristling prentices' spears, the dripping and unconscious Dove of Valnon in his arms. It took a good deal of protest on his part to convince them that he was not the kidnapper himself, and that he was there on express request of the Preybird Kestrel. The furor was not assuaged until a tall man in emerald robes strode into the atrium, his black hair like a war pennant and his eyes blazing.

"Haverty! Put that thing down until you're certain you need to make use of it. That goes for you too, Tolver. All of you, get back to your positions at once, until you're called for." Fourteen years had only sharpened Hawk's angular features, and there were very few threads of grey in his hair, not near as many as his age merited. His blood was foreign; Shindamiri or the like, and there had been a scandal some decades ago when he had been cut for a Lark. Rumor had it that some outside the Temple's walls--and inside of them-- did not take well to an outsider being one of Valnon's Songbirds, much less his becoming High Preybird and right-hand of the Wing himself.

But Grayson's memories of the man had nothing to do with his narrow eyes and the caramel tint of his skin. There was only the recollection of a stern fairness overwhelmed by crushing

13

disappointment. Grayson shifted the Dove's weight in his aching arms, and tried to not feel so completely diminished. It was as though he was eighteen and disgraced again under the High Preybird's stare.

"Truly, I did not think that you would come," Hawk said, in greeting. He reached out one long hand and rested it against the Dove's pale cheek, his relief evident as he felt warmth beneath his fingers. "Much less that you would aid us before we could even ask it of you. Where did you find him?"

"He mowed me over in a street near--well, it used to be the Sword and Sparrow years ago, I've no idea what it is now. He had some troublemakers after him. Undercity hires, I'd say, but none I knew."

"I will send out some Godswords at once to find them and dispatch them--"

"You needn't," Grayson interrupted, and was himself once again, a capable man long years away from boyhood's failures. "Unless you wanted someone to cart the corpses away."

Hawk raised his eyebrows, his mouth thinning. "I see," he said. "Though it does make them difficult to question." His black eyes flicked briefly to the prentices. They were standing like carved stone, faces impassive, but straining for all they were worth to hear the conversation. "Enough of that for now. This is no place for discussion, and the Dove needs attention. If you would be so good as to bring His Grace, and come with me."

Hawk gestured with one voluminous sleeve, and billowed towards the sanctuary with the clear expectation that Grayson would follow. He made a sharp turn to the right, just short of the bolted sanctuary doors. Grayson went after him up the stairs, noticing the prentices flinch as he passed them by. Grayson knew all too well what they were thinking: the outrage of an Undercity mercenary walking bold-faced into a passage reserved only for Temple Birds, wearing sharpened steel on his hip, his unholy hands on the Dove's body. Only fully-vested Godswords were permitted to carry swords into the presence of Songbirds, and then rarely. Even the prentices that guarded the Temple were forbidden any blade longer than an eating knife, their halberds allowed only because the amount of wood far outweighed the steel tip. As for touching their Songbirds, even casually, that was entirely out of the question.

Yet Grayson followed in Hawk's wake, his boots leaving muddy prints down the immaculate marble floor, his rain-soaked clothes spattered with the blood of recently dead men, the Dove's head heavy on his shoulder. And the High Preybird did not so much as bat an eyelash at the sacrilege. Grayson could hear the prentices whispering as soon as they deemed Hawk out of hearing. He wondered if any of the young Godswords-to-be knew of his name, or his reputation, or his disgrace. If so, it was still unlikely they would know him on sight, and somehow that thought was not comforting.

The Temple's walls flickered by, silent mosaics and lush hangings, the soaring stonework of Valnon's greatest architects. It was a treasure-box, a coffer for the finest jewels, beautifully made and securely locked at all times. And yet the most precious prize in its keeping was the one Grayson carried in his aching arms, wrapped up in a ruffian's stained cloak.

"If I may," Grayson began, in the hush that those corridors always seemed to demand, "Might I inquire as to how--"

"I'm sure you have many questions," Hawk said, cutting him off. "And I'm afraid I haven't the time for proper answers. If you wish explanation, it will have to wait."

Grayson made a face at the High Preybird's back. Hawk's authoritative tone had lost none of its potency in the intervening years.

"I will say," Hawk continued, unexpectedly, "that I take it by your speedy response to Kestrel's message that you are currently without an employer?"

"Employers come and go, in my line of work," Grayson said, and his voice had more bitterness than he intended. "But I have none at the moment, no."

"Good," Hawk said, with a brief glance over his shoulder, and did not elaborate further. They passed in silence through the halls of the Temple Birds, and Grayson could not look too closely at the shadows in the cross-corridors. Temple lore was rich with ghosts both horrible and benevolent, but all the ones Grayson saw were of himself.

"Here," Hawk said at last, unnecessarily. Grayson knew the steps to the Songbirds' private chambers--knew them far better, in fact, than any outsider ever should. They opened up onto a circular, domed room, where a bathing fountain murmured silkily to its pool. In a recessed sitting area, low tables and divans lay curled up around a glowing brazier like drowsing cats. Three arched doorways were hung with curtains of precious beads: purple, crimson, black. Grayson had never before seen the amethyst doorway. In his day, the Dove's bedchamber off the Solar had sat as empty as a cenotaph, the entrance sealed with a heavy marble slab.

Hawk swept the beads to the side, holding them back for Grayson to enter the Dove's chamber. The bed was a round cushion on a raised dais that echoed a Songbird's exalted pedestal in the sanctuary. Four great elephant tusks served as bedposts, riddled into lace by delicate carvings of birds and vines, curving overhead and joined in the center by an elaborate lamp set with purple glass. The light it cast was dreamy and mysterious, its filigree sides scattering ornate patterns on the velvet coverlets. The Dove made a soft noise as Grayson put him down on the bed, and as he lay there in his soggy, blood-spattered grays he looked like nothing so much as a dead bird in the bottom of a magnificent cage.

"He was conscious when you found him?" Hawk asked, feeling the Dove's wrist for his pulse, smoothing back the pale shadows of his hair.

"Yes, and talky enough. But he passed out shortly after. Felony weed, isn't it?"

"Mmm." Hawk's fingers danced over the Dove's collar, undoing the pearl buttons of his tunic. "Not enough of it. They underestimated a Temple Bird's body weight and gave him too little. I daresay it saved his life, but not as much as you did."

"Ah," Grayson said, unsure what to do with the praise of the High Preybird. "I was only passing by--"

His protests were interrupted by a wild clatter of beads from the doorway. A Songbird stood there, by his build (all long bones and chest) and his age (barely twenty) and his colors, which even in his sleeping pants and tunic were the flaming golds and reds of Noontide. The state of his hair said everything about the poor quality of his night's sleep, and when he saw the Dove he charged forward as though propelled from a siege engine.

16

"Willim! You've found him! Is he all right?"

Hawk folded his arms in his sleeves, pursing his lips as though he was trying to turn a smile into sternness. "Ellis. You should be asleep."

"I should be inhuman if I was!" retorted Ellis, mounting the raised platform, and putting one knee down on the Dove's bed. Once convinced Willim was still alive and breathing, he curled over his still form with a relieved noise, still clutching the Dove's unresponsive fingers. "What happened to him? His hands are like ice. Are you going to leave him lying here in these wet things?"

"Naturally," Hawk answered, acidly. "I thought we should compound his troubles with a case of pneumonia. He's only been in the Temple for half a measure, Ellis. If you insist on being here, then make yourself useful and fetch him some warm clothes. And for the love of St. Lairke, do not shout. Dmitri will have blood if he's woken at this hour."

"*He* didn't have any trouble sleeping," Ellis said, with some vehemence. "Heartless son of a--" The Thrush of Valnon broke off as he at last noticed the stranger in the room. His eyes swept Grayson from boots to cropped blond hair, doubled back to the sword, and went wide.

Hawk made an exasperated noise. "Ellis, this is Nicholas Grayson, an Undercity swordsman of some repute and responsible for the safe retrieval of our Dove. Grayson, this is His Grace Ellis the Thrush of Valnon, fiftieth of his title, and I'll thank him to fetch Willim some clothes, like I asked, before he takes a chill. There will be plenty of time to ogle at a later date."

Grayson smiled wanly at Hawk's summary. "I am honored, Your Grace," he said, with a bow to the Thrush. "Unfortunately I do not often have a chance to visit the Temple for Noontide, but I knew your predecessor, Alexander. Word in the Undercity is that you do St. Thryse proud in his place."

"The forty-ninth Thrush is now the Preybird Kite," Hawk said, with a meaningful look at Grayson that said, quite clearly, that sellswords were not to go about calling Temple Birds by their common birth names. "And I believe I've asked you twice now, Ellis."

The Thrush of Valnon was still staring at Grayson as though he had just dropped down from the moon. "I--you--yes, yes of course," he said, with some difficulty. He glanced once more at the worn pommel of Grayson's sword, and at the blood on his gloves, and then hurried over to the Dove's clothes-press to retrieve dry garments.

"It's just as well the boy can sing," Hawk sighed, "or else I would have grave concerns for his future. Tell me more about these ruffians you encountered. Were they Vallish?" Hawk stripped the Dove out of his tunic, revealing bruises and scratches from his misadventure, as well as the glint of platinum hoops strung through his nipples and his navel. Grayson took a sudden interest in a flight of ivory wings on the bed-post as Hawk unceremoniously divested the Dove of his wet finery.

"They had Undercity accents," Grayson answered. "One of them might have been from the Northcamp, or somewhere in the mainland. Sailors, by the look of them, and probably privateers. I'd say they were locally bought. They had Thrassin weapons, but none were too sure of them."

"I suspected as much." The counterpane rustled as Hawk pulled it up over the sleeping Dove, a tenderness in his hands that was equal to the stern tones of his voice. "I think we can leave the Dove in the Thrush's care, for now." Hawk moved around the side of the bed and caught Ellis at the step, his arms full of clothes. "I would be grateful if you would stay with Willim tonight, Ellis." Hawk patted the Thrush's shoulder. "He'll probably sleep through the night, but send one of the prentices for me if there is any change. I'll have Dmitri relieve you if Willim has not woken after Dawning, and he can tend to his injuries then. You'll need some sleep yourself before your hour."

Ellis nodded, his face torn between disappointment and relief. Alone, he could care for the Dove's needs without being concerned for propriety, but Grayson suspected he was sorry to lose the chance to listen to Hawk and Grayson discuss things further.

Grayson's last glimpse of the Dove was of him lying white and still against cushions of violet silk. His platinum jewelry stood out starkly against his pallor, blue veins traced inscrutable glyphs under his skin. His eyes were dark-circled, bruised-looking, and his unusual hair gave him an age his face did not echo. There were more tales of a Dove's ill-fortune than there would ever be rumors about old Temple scandal, and looking at Willim there, Grayson believed every one of them.

"Will he be all right?" he asked, suddenly guilty for the rough nature of his rescue.

"He needs rest, more than anything," Hawk answered. "He might not look it, but he's sturdy. Ellis will watch him like a mother falcon over her eyas, I assure you. I'll have the Temple Physician look over him in the morning." He passed through the beaded curtain and Grayson, resisting the urge to look back at the Dove again, followed.

"I must apologize," Hawk said, when they were once more out into the passageway. "You are not a hound to be whistled for, and yet you came at our call, in spite of how the Temple treated you all those years ago."

Grayson's face felt as transparent as glass; he longed for the ability to shut it up like a reliquary. "Rouen," he said, and tried to keep his voice from breaking on a name rarely said, "knows that I will always come if he needs me."

"Yes, and I fear we have used that to bring you here." Hawk stopped, his head bowed. "The Temple asks for your aid, Grayson. You have every right to refuse us."

"Rouen asked for my aid," Grayson replied, softly. "And I came." There was an uncomfortable pause in the corridor, and Grayson's throat worked to force out words he had not been prepared to say. "...May I see him?"

Hawk studied Grayson's face. "He is waiting in the portrait room," he said, at last. "I don't expect I need to show you the way."

Grayson did not trust his voice, he shook his head instead.

Hawk exhaled slowly, as though preparing to sing. "Good. I must report to the Wing about the Dove's condition. I will join you there shortly. Please be so good as to tell Kestrel that Willim is safe."

"I will," Grayson promised, and watched as Hawk went back the way they had come, turning down a side-stair and vanishing. Grayson was left in the lamp-lit corridor, to walk alone down a path he had trodden a thousand times over in his dreams.

It was no long distance to the portrait room. Three turnings, that was all, to a more public section of the Temple. It was a place where there were fewer boundaries of occupancy, where Songbirds could meet with Temple outsiders without violating the strict tenets of their terms. It was a place for important meetings, for reunions, for justice. Grayson had no pleasant memories of it.

The room had not changed, looking as though Grayson had last passed through its door yesterday. It was still dark-paneled, somber, and more oppressive than the older areas of the Temple. On the far wall, the huge painting of Saint Alveron hung as it had for time out of mind, his stern face and belling robes overshadowing all that went on below him. It was a painting designed to make the observer feel insignificant, and Grayson knew from experience that it was extremely effective at doing so.

The man standing beneath the gilt frame showed no concern for the saint looming in paint above him. He had his back to the door, and was bent over a table littered with parchments. Messages and maps were scattered across the tabletop and around his boots, his hair was straggling out of its ribbon, and a guttering taper at his elbow threaded unnoticed beeswax beads down the table-leg. For a man forbidden the arts of war, and prohibited to wear a weapon of any sort, he bore a striking resemblance to a harried general in the field.

"I've just gotten word from Raven," he said, without bothering to turn around. The quill he was using stuttered on the parchment, spraying a mist of ink across his letter. He sighed, and deliberately dipped it into the inkpot again, his white knuckles showing the effort it took to retain his patience. "He says that Boren is alive, for the moment, but he does not expect him to last the night and does not wish to leave his side. You'll forgive me if I took the liberty of writing to Jerdon for his advice. Raven is knowledgeable enough in the ailments of Songbirds, but he is ill-equipped to deal with a blow from a Thrassin blade. Those wretched things flayed poor Boren open to the bones. It's only out of sheer obstinacy that he's held on this long."

All of Grayson's imagined greetings failed him. It was here that they had been together last, fourteen years ago. Here, that they had been given no chance for farewell. He had half-expected to find the Rouen of the past waiting there, seventeen years old and still in a Lark's sable, his kohl smeared with tears. To the man he had become, all Grayson could manage to say was, "...You chose blue."

The Preybird Kestrel narrowly avoided upsetting his inkpot.

He spun around, his breath coming up short and failing to become words. For a moment they stared at each other, weighing the differences time had placed on them. Grayson supposed that he must look as much a stranger to Rouen as Rouen did to him, the two of them refurnished houses: unfamiliar at first, but with the ghosts of their past selves still lingering somewhere in the architecture. Belatedly, Kestrel put his fingers to the cobalt tunic he wore.

"Yes, well," he said in strained tones, and then swallowed. "Kestrels traditionally have a shade of blue for their Preybird colors, and I--I have always been fond of the color." He stopped, frowning to himself, as though after hearing them aloud he deemed the words too foolish for the occasion. "...I thought you were Hawk."

"A man I am unlikely to be taken for at any other time," Grayson said, and summoned up a smile that was not long for the world. The atmosphere of the room was too heavy for it, and Grayson let it fade. "Hawk sent me ahead, to let you know that the Dove has been recovered unharmed. He's gone to inform the Wing."

Kestrel sagged against the table, one hand over his face. "Merciful Alveron," he breathed. "I hadn't even dared to hope. How did he make it back here?"

"A stranger came to his aid in the streets."

"And here I thought Valnon had no kindnesses left," Kestrel said, raking back his loose hair. "I was certain we had lost Willim for sure."

"Luckily, his kidnappers were incompetent," Grayson said, peeling out of his gloves. "They did not drug him enough, and he was able to run."

Kestrel laughed without mirth. "Indeed? Well, *that's* not a mistake anyone from Thrass would make. They use their eunuchs in the gladiatorial ring." He caught Grayson's curious look, and waved it away. "But never mind that now." Kestrel reached for the cup and ewer resting half-hidden among the parchments. The wine sloshed as he poured it, betraying his nerves, but he filled the cup and held it out to Grayson. "Here. You look drenched. Come and stand by the fire."

Grayson crossed the room and took the wine Kestrel offered,

trying to pretend it was from a stranger's hand, taking care that their fingers should not touch.

Kestrel arched an eyebrow at a fresh blood-spatter on Grayson's sleeve, the mark left by Grayson's messy final blow. "...You need to work on your backhand," he said, folding his arms. "You could have said you were the one who saved Willim."

"I could have. I wanted to see if you would guess." Grayson took a grateful swallow of the wine. It was sweet and delicate and certainly more expensive than Grayson's last ten bottles put together. "You're right enough about his attackers. They were Vallish, but I doubt they'd ever darkened the sanctuary door for reasons of faith. They had Thrassin weapons, but they weren't the Ethnarch's men. What's being played at here, Rouen? And what of Commander Boren? The Dove mentioned him as well, but his drugs got the better of him soon after."

"I fear Boren's soon for Hasafel," Kestrel said heavily, and began searching in his papers. "For some time he has been the Songbirds' personal guard. Thrass grows more openly belligerent with every passing day, and it has made the Wing cautious." Kestrel sighed. "I wish he had not been proven right so quickly. Boren was found this evening--yesterday evening I should say--in the Songbirds' private garden. He was badly wounded, with this stuffed in his teeth." Kestrel had found what he wanted, a parchment inked with sharp letters, one edge stained dark with blood. Grayson recognized the formal Thrassin script at once. "Willim was nowhere to be found. That's when I sent for you."

"It's a ransom note," Grayson said, putting the cup down on the table to better study the parchment. "A rebel group demanding the immediate withdrawal of the Godswords from their occupation of the border, and the opening of negotiations to return Thrass to sovereignty."

Kestrel drummed his fingers on the table in a quick, precise cadence. "That is what we are meant to think," he said. "I know full well how quickly things are unraveling in the south, and yet I have no reason to think that Thrass has a damn thing to do with Willim's abduction, except that someone wants very much for us to be convinced it does."

"Southern blades, yet no sense of how to use them, a mistake with felony weed no Thrassin agent would make, much less the

Shadowhands they'd like us to think they were. And--" Grayson ran a finger down the ransom note, and paused at the crease of the parchment. "Thrassin rebels would not drag the tip of the pen so," he said, bending close to examine the letter. "Their language is written from left to right, the stroke order from top to bottom. This is Thrassin in a Vallish hand."

Kestrel leaned against the table, his smile fond and sad. "God, Nicholas," he said. "What a waste the Temple made of you."

Grayson did not trust himself to look up. "At the least, I hope I have not made a waste of myself. I take it you called me here because you need a replacement for Boren? Are there no other Godswords to be had? Or are they too costly to spend?"

"Both. When was the last time you saw a full cavalry unit in Darkmarket Garrison?"

Grayson's fingertips went to his sword, smoothing the worn metal of the hilt as though looking for something misplaced. "I don't make a habit of frequenting the garrison, Rouen."

Kestrel followed the motion of Grayson's hand and flinched, as at the twinge of an old wound. "I suppose not. It's just as well that few know just how thin our forces are in the city. Commandant Ransey left for the southlands this fall with most of them in tow, and those to be rotated back to the city have not yet arrived. At this moment, Valnon is perilously vulnerable, Grayson. The Godswords who remain here are little more than old soldiers, prentices, and wounded recovering from their injuries. Few of them are ready for pitched battle, and there are none I feel can be trusted implicitly. Enlisting the Queensguard is out of the question, they're little more than blades for hire and besides, the Crown would never abide the imposition. My options are sadly limited, Nicholas. But the Dove must be protected at all costs. Will you help us?"

Grayson stood up and cracked his spine, considering. "Surely you would not blame me if I refused?"

"I would not, no. Hawk said it was unlikely that you would even come at all." Kestrel's laugh was musical even in its irony. "As a matter of fact, he owes me twenty-five crescents and a bottle of Alfiri red, now."

Grayson slapped his gloves against his thigh, undecided. "Tell me about this Dove of yours," he said, at last. "I won't be hired to protect a foolish, spoilt Songbird with more privilege than promise. My sword comes at a price these days, but I have the freedom to turn it down. I am sworn to no Temple, to no duty but my own."

"Yet you went to war in the southlands anyway," Kestrel countered. "Even after you were cast out of the Godswords."

"For money, Rouen. Not for faith."

They stared at each other, and the distance between them yawned far wider than a scant three feet of polished mahogany table. They had not yet sorted out how to bridge it when the door creaked open to admit a tall figure, hooded in deep red velvet that masked the better half of his face. Though the cut of his garb was simpler than that of any Preybird, and his thin lips parted in a gentle smile, he radiated a kind of quiet power that dwarfed even that of Saint Alveron in his gilded frame. Kestrel made a startled noise in his throat and bowed; Grayson, his heart seized by the painful grip of memory, could not move.

Hawk stepped in after the man in red, and the door's rarely-used bolt slid home into its socket. "The Wing," he announced, "wishes to offer his personal thanks to you for your assistance this evening."

Grayson remembered himself at last and bowed, willing away the recollections of their last meeting. "Your Grace," he said, hoarsely. "It was pure chance that I encountered the Dove tonight, nothing more."

Lateran XII, Wing of the Temple and the single most powerful man in Valnon, had to be at least eighty. Rarely did he leave his rooms, preferring to interact solely with Hawk, and due to his advanced age, little question was made of the practice. But the smoothness of his voice was as sleek as that of a new-minted Preybird off the dais only yesterday, the angles of his jaw were supple and firm, his step certain, his back straight. That Temple Birds were a vain lot who aged well was a noted fact, but the Wing seemed to take that tendency to a new and discomfiting extreme. "I don't put much stock in pure chance, Nicholas fa Grayce," Lateran said, and as it had done fourteen years ago, the man's voice wiped any doubts from the minds of those present. There was power there, it was true, like the faint echoes of Evensong, and Grayson knew it was not something within the grasp or understanding of an ordinary man like himself. Still, even with those honeyed vowels, he could not help but flinch at the sound of his old name.

"Your Grace, forgive me, but that is not my--"

"What's to forgive, fa Grayce?" The Wing asked, amused. "Or do you intend to argue with me?"

Grayson shut his mouth with a snap. "No, Your Grace."

"I thought not," the Wing concluded, and settled into the chair nearest the fire, his back to the flames, throwing his figure into even greater shadow. "But as you wish, Grayson, if you prefer. We are greatly in your debt, and yet I fear I must ask for even further assistance."

Kestrel coughed softly. "It would seem," he said, "that Grayson has little interest in protecting our Songbirds."

"Let the man speak for himself, Rouen," Hawk said, and it was Kestrel's turn to fall uncomfortably silent.

"Rouen is right," Grayson said, spreading his hands in apology. "Your Grace, I'm sorry, but I have no place in the Temple now. Being here is painful for me, as I'm sure you can understand, and my presence would do nothing but stir up scandal and bad memories. Surely there are swords far more able--and less tainted-- to do the service you require, without bringing further shame upon Rouen--" Grayson's voice cracked, he reached for his cup of wine and swallowed some, unnerved by the Wing's impassive silence. "...and further shame upon the Temple."

"I have never known you to bring shame upon anyone," the Wing said, softly, "And rarely have I known anyone else so worthy of the name you have been forced to put aside. But that is all by the by. You are correct, of course, and it is a pity you could not serve publicly in Boren's place. However, I'm not asking you to be the Dove's formal guard." He leaned forward, and his smile made his eyes flicker in the depths of his hood. "I'm asking you to kidnap him."

Grayson choked on his wine; Kestrel made a strangled noise of surprise.

"Excuse me?" Grayson said, when he could manage.

The Wing waved one ringed hand in airy dismissal. "Your reputation makes you unsuitable as a guard for a Songbird, it is true. But it also makes you ideal as a captor of one. Don't misunderstand me, Grayson. The task I propose is extremely dangerous, and should you fail, even my efforts might not be enough to save you. But I am presented with a situation too precarious for leisurely action. I must get the Songbirds safely away from Valnon with as little fuss and delay as possible. I would rather have them kidnapped by you than by those who actually mean them harm."

Grayson remembered his cup before it could slip from his fingers. "So you know who is behind the attack tonight?"

Lateran XII raised one thin shoulder. "I have suspicions that I fervently hope are untrue. What matters is that the Songbirds, and Willim especially, are seen tomorrow during their hours, which must be sung and done as though nothing was amiss. Afterwards, during Dawning the next day, you will need to make off with them as quietly as can be managed. I can get you out of the Temple and into the Undercity without detection. From there, you will travel away from the city with an escort I have arranged. Officially, notice will be put round that they have taken a slight fever due to the change in seasons, and as a precaution they will not be singing until at least Canticles Eve. It's hardly uncommon for this time of year."

"The ruse will distract the Songbirds' attackers on the outside, and keep their attention on the Temple," Hawk explained. "And they will be out of reach of any enemy that might come from within. The delay will give us time to root out the source of the trouble. Meanwhile, you will take them under the city through the tombs, to our contact in the Undercity."

"And if it all goes wrong, and I'm strung up for high blasphemy against the Temple, you can't get involved with saving me, correct?"

The Wing's mouth tensed; it was not a smile. "To do so would reveal too much of our plans, and alert our enemies."

"You ask Grayson to risk his life in such a shameful fashion?" Kestrel was appalled. "After what the Temple has already done to him?"

"Sparing his life once already, you mean?" Hawk answered, giving Kestrel a narrow look.

"He was innocent!"

"No, he was only equally as guilty as *you* were." Hawk's sharp retort landed on Kestrel with the force of a blow. "No one will force him to accept, Rouen. This is no trial."

"No," Grayson broke in, swallowing back the sour taste the wine had left in his mouth. "It is not. And to be honest, Your Grace, I fail to see why I should bother risking my life and the small bit of honor I've wrangled for myself for the sake of three spoiled boys."

"You speak poorly of young men you have barely met," the Wing demurred. "But you are wrong to think we would not offer just compensation for your efforts." He lifted his head, the light sliding easily from his hood, resting in a blood-red droplet upon his ruby ring of office. "Aid us in this, and I will see to it that not only are you given the rank you deserve, but once more made fa Grayce in the scrolls of your family line. I could not prevent the words you spoke in trial fourteen years ago, or halt the damage made in the recklessness of youth. But few now in the Temple remember those days, and still fewer care. Do us this service, and I will grant full exoneration from your crime."

"It was no crime," Kestrel breathed, little more than a stirring of air between his lips, but Hawk shot him a look and the younger Preybird went still.

"What do you say to my offer?" The Wing leaned forward slightly, his eyes fixed on Grayson's. "Would you be Lieutenant Nicholas fa Grayce, Godsword of Valnon, and lend us your arm as the holy knight of the Temple you were destined to be? Or will you leave now, with your invented name and your invented shame, to go back to the Undercity and sell your blade to the highest bidder?"

Grayson's throat worked soundlessly as he fought the tight grip of longing in his chest. He had never allowed himself to dwell on what-ifs or could-have-beens; he had banished the dreams of younger days for the cold embrace of the Undercity. It was not the life he had been born to or desired, it was true, but it was a good life all the same and far better than some. He had money enough for comfort and work that rarely troubled his sleep. And yet, and yet...

"I can think of one who would remember, and who would care," Grayson said at last, in a rasp that wine would not soothe. "Rouen spoke his name when I first came in the room." He lifted his head to meet Kestrel's gaze, the Preybird's fine brows drawn together in something like anguish, for a moment a perfect echo of the heartbroken boy Grayson had left behind. "Raven would not be soon to forget those days."

"You think I cannot contain one Preybird?" Lateran said, and Grayson thought his tone too light, his response too quick.

"I think he was once High Preybird, and I would be a fool to think his demotion had nothing to do with my trial." Grayson's eyes were hard. "At the time he said he would not be satisfied until the day of my execution. I doubt the years have softened his heart towards me."

"Leave Raven to me," the Wing said, and there was a danger and a power to those words that Grayson had no desire to cross. "I handled him well enough at your trial; I flatter myself that I have not lost my touch. If you doubt me, however, you are free to refuse my offer."

There was a strained silence, taut as the skin of a drum. The fire hissed to itself, and Saint Alveron studied the scene through leaping shadows. Grayson stroked his thumb over the lip of his wine cup, worrying his thumbnail at a nick in the silver rim.

"Full exoneration?" Grayson asked, at last.

The Wing was too politic to smile at his certain victory. "I will personally scrape the trial history from the parchment in the archives."

Grayson set the empty cup on the table, precisely in the center of the forged ransom note. "I would want to hear them sing, first," he said, cautiously.

"Of course." The Wing dipped his head. "It would be our pleasure to have you as our guest at hours tomorrow. Have we an agreement, then?"

Grayson's eyes narrowed. "Captain," he said. "And not behind a desk at some backwater outpost, either. Shock Cavalry, if you please, and with the finest ton of horseflesh under me that the garrison's stables have to offer."

"I told you he wouldn't settle for Lieutenant," Hawk murmured, startling Kestrel into a smile.

"Captain it shall be," Lateran said, warmly. "It's done then. You shall abscond with our Songbirds, and I shall do away with your past." He rose, and held out his hand for Grayson to accept.

"Provided they can sing," Grayson said in reminder, taking the Wing's hand in his own, and bowing over his ring.

"Oh, I should have no doubts about that, Captain fa Grayce," Lateran said, with a tiny smile as Grayson's lips brushed his ring. "No doubts about that at all."

3

Willim woke in a sweat, his limbs still twitching with a blind, animal panic. For a moment the terror of his dreams retained its hold, but then the darkness resolved itself into familiar shapes: the arch of his doorway and the silvery pool of his mirror. It was the smallest hour of the night. The candle bowl at his bedside sent up a thin curl of smoke, an ember still clinging onto the wick. Diffuse moonlight filtered in from the windows, cutting white wounds through the shadows. He was safe in his own bed, and all else he was willing to call nightmares and nothing more.

But that did not ease the fear as it should have. Something was wrong. Almost always there would be music in the Temple, even if only a lone Laypriest singing the midnight hour. But Willim's room had the hush of the sanctuary before song. It was deathly cold, and he was not alone.

Someone was moving around in the solar, coming closer to the doorway with every dull thud of Willim's heart against his ribs. It was not the familiar footfall of a flock boy coming in to relight his brazier, nor the comforting presence of a Preybird on his midnight rounds.

Willim looked to the door in expectation, but no one came. Only something invisible, something that stirred the curtain of beads in his doorway, making them clink and sway. The cold grew intense. The water in the glass by Willim's bedside sparked with tiny blossoms of frost, and Willim's breath misted in front of his straining eyes, but he saw nothing. The bead curtain went still, while the distant, musical chiming continued.

Willim knew the sound as well as he knew his own breathing. It was the jangle of a Dove dressed for his hour in St. Alveron's holy armor, the strands of pearl and fine chain drumming softly against the platinum cuffs and collar. Willim wore the Dove's Temple dress every sundown for Evensong, and it was, at that moment, locked up securely in its trunk at the foot of his bed.

Whatever Dove of Valnon had wandered into Willim's room, it was not one of flesh and blood.

Willim had heard the tales, of course. They cooled the sweltering summer air in the flock boys' dormitory, whispered breathlessly from pallet to pallet in the dark. They could be sometimes coaxed from Kite, who swore he had seen him the last night of his term, before Willim sang at the trials the next morning. Rumor suggested that even Kestrel had had encountered the second Dove's ghost, but he would not speak of it.

The ghost's path never changed, from the lowered dais to the Songbirds' chambers. Always he went from the dais, never towards it: the last walk from his last Evensong, unfinished in life. Flock boys rushing to the privy in the night sprinted past empty corridors in fear of meeting him. Old Preybirds blamed him for everything from unnatural weather to overturned inkpots. Down in the archives, the Preybird Osprey grumbled that if the man's music and his memory had been honored properly, perhaps his soul would stay put in Heaven's choir where it belonged.

In truth, no one living knew the real reasons. They only knew that when Valnon was restless, Eothan walked.

"Go away," Willim breathed, or tried to. No sound came out of him, and in some distant, unfrozen part of his soul, he was glad. Who was he to dictate to the invisible? What could he understand of the second Dove's grief, what did he know of a sorrow that could drive a man from his grave? Never before had Willim met his predecessor, dead for three hundred years, and he had been content with that. Some had said that perhaps Eothan was pleased that there was a new Dove at last, and he would no longer wander. There had been no confirmed sightings of the second Dove's phantom since Willim had been cut ten years ago, and reports from the flock boys invariably turned out to be nothing more spectral than the shadow of a broom handle at a slant, or a Laypriest's robe flapping at an open window.

But the thing in Willim's room was none of those things, as it passed through a shaft of moonlight and stole all the illumination from it. It was first a fog of air and darkness, then it pulled itself into a form, a half-circle flicker of platinum collar and the shaken shadows of black hair. A white oval lifted, sharpened. For a moment the figure was whole and clear and nearly human. The black pits in the face were not the sunken hollows of death, but the expansive, out-flung wings of a Songbird's ceremonial paint, ornate with a full twelve years' service. Blue eyes burned within that cage, eyes full of grief enough to fuel Willim through a thousand requiems. He choked on the second Dove's sorrow, he drowned in the relentless tide of Eothan's pain. Willim squeezed his eyes closed against the horrible vision, and prayed for St. Alveron to deliver the second Dove from his bondage, and the third Dove from his presence, but Eothan's cold drew closer. Even with his eyes shut, Willim could sense him there, standing beneath the curved ivory arches of Willim's bedposts, eyes blazing and hungry, chill fingers outstretched to touch Willim's shoulder. He was a fingerbreadth away, he was a whisper of frost on Willim' skin, and then he was five cold fingers closing on Willim's arm. With a yelp of panic Willim lashed out at the second Dove's phantom. For a ghost, Eothan was remarkably solid when struck, his curse vivid.

"Lairkeblood! Haven't you been enough trouble already?"

Eothan vanished, the moonlight transformed to purple-tinted sunlight, and Willim was awake. Reality asserted itself in the shape of the lamp above his bed, in the distant strains of Noontide, and in the pinched, infuriated face of the fiftieth Lark of Valnon. Dmitri stood at Willim's bedside, one white cheek rapidly blossoming crimson where Willim had struck him. His sleek blond hair was unusually tousled, and the lack of his habitual kohl made his narrow gray eyes seem oddly large, even when he was scowling. That, at least, was as it should be: Dmitri was almost always scowling.

Willim stumbled on the aborted start to several questions, still trying to untangle himself from his dream and his sheets. He got nowhere, distracted by a stinging pain from a cut on his left arm, which Dmitri was cleaning with ruthless efficiency. The ghostly cold he had felt was nothing more eerie than soapy water. "Dmitri, what the--when the--ow!"

"Ugh!" Dmitri flung his sponge into the basin on the nightstand, in disgust. "If only you sang as poorly as you speak. We'd all be spared a lot of trouble in your keeping."

"That hurts." Willim yanked his arm away from Dmitri, but Dmitri, with all the bedside manner of an irritated mother bear, yanked it right back and reached for the salve jar.

"Hold," he said, in no uncertain terms, "still. Raven's busy, so if you want patching up, you'll have to do as I tell you."

"What in God's name do I need patching up for?" Willim tried to remember anything about the night before, but he could not. Not saying goodnight to Boren as he did after every evening's game of queensperil, not undressing for bed. The night was a blank, and Boren remained in the garden, bloody and glassy-eyed beneath the nodding heads of the silver roses. Hands came out of the darkness, Eothan formed himself from the shadows, and Willim's memory fractured with the sharp report of cracking glass. His head throbbed. He put his face in his hand. "How did I get here?"

"You were carried here," Dmitri retorted, as he slathered the pungent salve over Willim's cuts, "In the arms of an Undercity sell-sword, with your head full of felony weed and looking like something found wedged in a sewer grate." He clicked his tongue at another cut he had missed. "Look at the wreck you've made of yourself. You must've tried to run *through* the rose lattice, rather than around it. Have you no sense at all? I'm surprised you didn't hop right into your kidnappers' arms."

Willim was still struggling with the deluge of information. He latched onto the largest chunk of debris and clung to it. "I was *kidnapped*?" he repeated. His arm twitched, but Dmitri had a good grip on him now, and kept his hold.

"Of course you were kidnapped! What could be more of a bother to us all?" Willim did not think wound salve had to be applied with such vigor, and he flinched as Dmitri slapped on another dose. "The whole Temple's in an uproar. It's been disastrous. Flock practice cancelled. Rehearsals thrown into utter chaos for the rest of the week. Prentices hissing at each other like a new breed of gossiping viper. Hawk has at least seven new silver hairs, I counted them during Dawning today. Do you think there's not enough work to be done, with Canticles coming up?"

Willim swallowed past a sick feeling in his mouth. "Where is Boren?" he asked.

"He was taken to the infirmary after Kestrel found him in the garden," Dmitri said, releasing Willim's arm at last. He wrung out the sponge in the basin, and it seemed to Willim that he was taking a long time over it, chewing on something before saying it. His jaw was tense, his pale brows drawn together, giving his constant frown a kind of trepidation that did not suit him.

"And?" Willim prompted. Eothan's presence lingered in the back of Willim's mind, and he braced himself for the worst.

The Lark of Valnon studied the water dribbling from his fingers, then he rested both hands on Willim's bedside table, his head turned away. "Willim," he said, and even if he had said nothing else, it was enough for Willim to know, his heart plummeting. "...Boren is dead."

Willim stared at Dmitri, and then at the mountainous shapes his knees made under the coverlet, all without seeing them. He tried to swallow, but couldn't manage anything more than a gulping sound. His dreams congealed into an ugly truth and worse memories, ones he could not simply call the dregs of nightmare. "...When?" was all he could manage to say. "Last night?"

"No. Just after Dawning this morning." Dmitri looked Willim full in the face for the first time, and Willim realized why the Lark of Valnon had avoided the usual thin line of kohl to darken his fair lashes. The redness around his eyes was not from anger. "He never really had much of a chance, Willim. They set on you both, and cut him to shreds. I'm surprised he lasted as long as he did. He never woke up." Dmitri picked up the basin, its pink-tinged water sloshing. "Raven wants to look you over, once he's done cleaning up Bor-- the infirmary. So don't go far." Willim and Dmitri looked at each other for a long moment, until Dmitri, blinking hard, said, "...I should go rinse this."

He left without another word, his strange brand of mercy giving Willim the chance to curl into a ball in his coverlet and weep, in private.

Willim was still there ten minutes later when there was a soft knock on the arch of his door, and the curtain of purple beads rattled aside.

"Willim? Are you awake?"

It was not Raven, with his hard, prodding fingers and rheumy stare, but Ellis, still resplendent in St. Thryse's copper, fresh off the dais after singing Noontide. The last few notes were still vibrating in the sounding vents, and Ellis' ribs heaved. He must have jumped off the dais before it was fully down, and run all the way back to check on Willim.

Willim smeared his hand across his eyes, and blinked at Ellis. "You're already done?" he asked, trying to keep his voice somewhat normal. He wiped at the damp patch on his pillow. "I can't lie around like this. I promised Hawk I'd finish writing that lament for Hasafel today. He wants it for Canticles Eve, and saints have mercy if it's late." He looked around for his clothes, remembered that he hadn't undressed himself the night before, and dragged his sheet around his hips as he got to his feet. He was talking too fast and too much, and he knew it, but he could not make himself stop. "Sorry I wasn't awake to help you with your dress. Do you want me to help you put it away?"

"Willim," Ellis began, his brown eyes soft with worry behind the intimidating pattern of his paints.

Willim stepped up to his dressing-table, rooting through the drawers for a clean clout. "And I've got sket practice with Kite this afternoon! Dammit. Maybe I can distract him into just talking gossip, I haven't practiced those intervals, and I'm terrible at playing sket anyway, not like you, so it's no loss..."

"Willim," Ellis said again, and Willim at last got a glimpse of himself in his mirror. His hair was wild, his face hollowed with sorrow and lack of sleep. Wrapped up in his sheet, he looked like a corpse that had staggered from its niche, trailing its winding-cloth behind. He was nearer to the second Dove's specter than to the living third Dove he was supposed to be, and his protests died in his throat. He sank down onto the stool, defeated.

"...Boren's dead."

Ellis hugged himself, his copper bangles clinking. "I know. Kestrel came to tell us this morning, after Dmitri finished Dawning."

"It's my fault," Willim said, digging the heel of his hand into his eye, as though to drive out the images that had lodged there. "It all happened so fast. When they came at Boren, I couldn't even cry out for help. I just stood there." Willim brought his fist down on the table, and his tribute jewelry rattled out of its glass boxes, rings spilling onto the floor and turning in tiny futile circles, bracelets jangling into a heap. "I just stood there while they cut Boren down, and then when he fell I just wanted to run away, just wanted to--"

"Willim." Ellis put his hand on Willim's shoulder, and the hot metal of his copper cuff was as warming as a summer day. Willim turned towards him, pressing his face into his best friend's bare stomach. The sobs shuddered out of him, raw and unmusical, and he clenched his fists in the vivid silk drape of Ellis' Temple-dress. Ellis let him cry, smoothing Willim's hair with his ringed fingers, humming a soft melody that Willim, in his grief, could not place.

It did not take very long. Willim's breathing evened, no longer hitching in his chest every time he exhaled. He still held on to Ellis, but without the desperation of a drowning man clinging to an overturned hull.

"Let it out," Ellis murmured, kneading Willim's back. "You'll feel better. I went down to the instrument room and howled all over Kite this morning. You can't see it with my paints, but my eyes look like I've been rubbing leeks in them, and my voice was nearly wrecked. I had to have three cups of anise tea to keep from croaking right through Noontide, and even with that I had to fake a few chords. I should get you some. Have you had anything to eat?"

Willim shook his head, pulling away from Ellis' gentle grasp. "No. I haven't even been awake half an hour yet and I really need the privy."

Ellis laughed in the relieved way that comes after mourning, and let him go. "All right. Get into the bath when you're done, and I'll get out of this. Hawk will kill me if he catches me still in it. I'll be out to join you in a minute."

Willim did not intend to get involved with a full soak in the bath, but after splashing under the fountain, the steaming water of the pool was too inviting to ignore. Willim waded hip-deep into the pool and sprawled against the marble ledge. Now that the first wave of grief was past, small physical pains were letting themselves be known. The hot water stung in his cuts and pulled the ache from his muscles, penetrating the thick, stuffy pressure behind his eyes.

"Will you be all right for Evensong?" Ellis asked, sloshing into the pool and capsizing half the flotilla of rose petals on the surface. The glory of St. Thryse had been packed away for tomorrow's Noontide, and he was once again only plain, brown, square-handed Ellis, with his rumpled hair and sensible concern. "You look terrible."

"I feel terrible," Willim answered, and slicked back his hair. "But I'm not going to miss Evensong. Boren's pyreboat will go tonight, won't it?"

Ellis shucked water off his wet arms, nodding. "That's what Kite said. Tonight at sundown, full honors from the garrison, and he'll have his name sung at Requiems tonight. They're calling the cause a sudden affliction of his heart, rather than announce that ruffians were able to snatch you right out of our garden. It would make the Temple look bad, and might give other people ideas."

"A sudden affliction of the heart," Willim repeated. "Makes it sound like he died of a case of infatuation."

"He was old enough that no one will ask too many questions."

"It's an insult. He was a warrior, and he died a warrior's death." Willim gently prodded one of the rose petals, it sank at his touch. "I could write him a song, but... it seems so useless."

Ellis' smile was sad. "You know Boren would be thrilled at the Dove of Valnon writing a song for him. He was such a humble fellow. He didn't like any fuss. Just delighted that he was allowed to look after us, and play peril with us, and teach us all those old Godswords' marching songs behind Hawk's back. An old hacker, he used to say. No good for anything but... keeping all his armor... filled out." Ellis scrubbed at his face as though he'd just realized he had missed a spot of paint somewhere. "...dammit."

"I never thanked him." Willim felt the tears burning behind his eyes again. "Not for anything."

Ellis swallowed a hiccup, and tucked his knees up to his chest. "Me, either."

They listened to the soft drip of the fountain, the clatter of a flock boy's footsteps in the corridor below. Somewhere in the distance a Preybird burst into song, the melody flowering from one of the sounding vents and then vanishing as the singer moved away from the perfect, fleeting acoustics of some cross-corridor.

"That's *Naime's Lament*. Kite's on his way to ensemble rehearsal with the little ones." Willim shook himself out of his stupor. "I've only got an hour before sket practice."

"Oh, forget sket practice. I really doubt he's expecting you, Willim." Ellis sank down next to Willim, and wiggled his outstretched toes above the surface of the water. "We're to have a new bodyguard, of course. After this, we'd damn well better! I'm half afraid to go to the privy alone, and it must be worse for you."

Willim hadn't even gotten around yet to being scared for himself, but Ellis' announcement made him shudder. "A Godsword?"

"Probably. Kite didn't know who it was to be. He said Kestrel's been too scarce to ask him about it, and Osprey hadn't heard anything from Hawk. Seems like the higher birds are keeping their beaks buttoned."

Willim stared up at the ceiling, but the dome was obscured behind writhing tendrils of bath steam. They tangled up among the lamp-chains, as convoluted and evasive as Willim's thoughts. "Boren was killed for me." Willim splashed out of the bath, ignoring the protest from his aching body. "I want some answers, even if I have to go ask the Wing himself."

"Hrm." Ellis pattered his fingertips on the edge of the bath. "Maybe you could get them from that Grayson fellow."

Willim paused, towel dangling from his fingertips. "Who?"

"Grayson," Ellis repeated. "The man who rescued you. He's still around, he was in the balcony with Kestrel for Noontide just now." Willim continued to look blank, and Ellis added, "How the hell did you think you escaped and got back here last night? Just bashed the bastards in the head with a frypan and trotted back on your own?"

"I don't know!" Willim answered, feeling beleaguered. "I don't remember *anything*, Ellis."

"You'd remember Grayson if you remembered anything," Ellis said, with meaning.

Willim rolled his eyes, roughly scouring the towel over his hair. "Obviously I wouldn't, since I don't. Did he have an extra head or something?"

"No, but he was the most memorable thing I've seen around here in ages." Ellis twisted a finger in his ear. "I wouldn't mind being kidnapped to have him carry me back up here, that's for certain."

"You're worse than Kite," Willim said. He threw the towel at Ellis and tugged on his shirt and slippers, struggling with the soggy lacings of his breeches. He had not been very thorough with his drying-off. "You shouldn't go around making lewd comments about sell-swords. You'll give Raven an attack."

"We should be so lucky," Ellis answered, yanking the towel off his face. "Otherwise I'm afraid he'll live forever. ...Where are you going?"

"I'm going out to the garden. I want to look around."

Ellis erupted up out of the bath, alarmed. "But-- they haven't cleaned it up yet! You don't want to go out there now, Willim, it's a mess--"

"I know," Willim answered, pulling his over-tunic off the bench. "That's why I'm going. If Raven comes looking for me, tell him I'm fine. The last thing I want now is to be poked at and told how I don't deserve my colors."

The Thrush of Valnon made an extremely un-saintly face. "If I wanted prunes, I would have them sent up on my breakfast-tray." He hovered half-out of the bath, looking as though he'd prefer stay indoors. "Do you want me to come out with you?"

Willim shook his head. "No. Thanks for everything, Ellis, but I just want to be alone for a while."

It was cold outside, and dank with the temperament of autumn's less-cordial side. Willim's breath plumed in the chill, his skin gave off faint vapors of warmth from his bath. The steps down to the garden were covered in colored shards of broken glass from the shattered lamps, and the fountain on the wall had been wrenched from its moorings. Willim dimly recalled crashing into it as he fled, and his ribs ached at the memory. The queensperil table sat in the shadows, and Willim could see some of the pieces scattered along the floor of the colonnade. The rain had washed away most of the blood, but under the shelter of the arbor roof, dark smears of it remained, enough to turn Willim's stomach. One flat patch of grass beneath the roses was black and gummy where the Godsword had fallen, and it was there that Willim first saw the stranger.

It was a man perhaps Kestrel's age, and he was no Preybird or Laypriest, or even a Godsword. He was dressed in well-worn leather brigandine, and wore his short blond hair swept straight back from his brow, like a soldier. In the fading garden, under a gray sky, the stranger's crimson cloak seemed to be the only color in the whole world.

Willim knew that he should turn back and tell Ellis, that he should raise some sort of alarm. But instead he remained where he was, clinging to a column behind a skeletal weeping cherry. Surely, he thought, no kidnapper would be so preoccupied with a patch of grass, nor would he sit in the Songbirds' garden in the middle of the day. Willim watched as the man ran his fingertips over the ground, examining every heel-gouge, every crushed leaf, searching the torn grass as though he had lost a favorite boot-buckle there.

Apparently satisfied with his survey of the garden, the stranger got to his feet. By Willim's estimation they were almost of a height; a considerable accomplishment for a man who had not been cut for a Songbird. He had none of a Songbird's long build and powerful torso, making it up in the impressive set of his shoulders. Against the sky his profile was clean and appealing, yet something about it stirred an uneasy familiarity in the back of Willim's mind.

"It would do you well to show more caution, Your Grace," the stranger said, still looking down at the trampled grass. "Especially after last night. I could have had your life three times already, if I wanted it."

Willim started, then shoved away from the column and stepped down into the garden, glass crunching beneath his shoes. He would not cower. "You don't look much like an assassin," he answered. "But if you were, you would be dead before you made it out of the Temple at this time of day. The halls are full of prentices, and you would have no escape but through the main nave, or past the Godswords' training grounds on the south end of the Temple." He waved one hand at the Temple rooftops, their steep terraces an untenable terrain mounting up to the dizzy height of the sanctuary's spire. "Unless you somehow learn to fly."

The stranger chuckled, and toed over a chunk of turf. "If I was a Thrassin zealot, my life would be a small price to pay for the violation of my enemy's most precious treasure." He looked up at Willim at last, and his eyes were the blanched, clear blue of a midwinter sky. "And," he continued, "if I was a Songbird of Valnon, I would take a moment to examine the mosaic of the seven larks across from the Preybirds' tower stairs. In doing so, I might discover an old passage through the aqueduct that would take me-- or anyone--from here to the kitchen garden without passing by the nose of a single Godsword, prentice or no."

Willim felt his ears burn. "Who are you?" he demanded.

The man shrugged, resting one hand on the hilt of his sword. "I'm a friend of Rouen's." It took Willim a moment to place the name, and his confusion must have shown in his face. "Your Preybird Kestrel," the stranger clarified. "He wanted my advice about the visitors you had last night."

"I take it then that you are *not* a Thrassin zealot," Willim answered, tartly. "And as such, you make yourself quite bold by being here unescorted."

"I've already made myself quite bold by saving your life, Your Grace," the stranger said, with a narrowing of his eyes that might have been the beginning of a smile or a scowl. "And in light of your ill-temper, I'm willing to deduce that you have no memory of our last meeting. Surely, the Dove of Valnon would be more gracious to his rescuer."

Willim's blood went from hot to cold with no warning, his fractured memories at last coming together. Somewhere in the jumbled confusion there was an image of the tall stranger's face, a rain-filled gutter, and the reek of quenched torches. "You?" Willim managed, in strangled disbelief. "You are Grayson?"

He nodded. "Most recently, yes."

Willim stood up straight, making full use of his height. "I would think the man who saved me would have the manners to introduce himself properly at the start."

"If you think that," Grayson said, his smile much more in evidence, "then you do not know me very well. But I expect that will change. We should have plenty of time to get familiar in the coming days."

Willim glared, as baleful as St. Alveron in his painting, and he summoned all the frozen wrath of Heaven in his voice. "*Explain yourself, sir.*"

"Sorry, I don't make a habit of it." Unmoved by Willim's display, Grayson strolled up to the edge of the colonnade, and bent down to rescue one of the queensperil pieces from the gutter. "Do you play, Your Grace?"

Willim deflated like a spurned peacock. He folded his arms in an attempt at retaining his composure, not willing to be baited into further losing his temper. "I do. Most evenings, when people aren't trying to murder me." He forced himself to look at Boren's empty seat by the peril board, and then at Grayson. "What of it?"

"Hrm." Grayson jogged Willim's lost consort piece in one hand and studied the board. The peril set had been a tribute gift from the Queen for Willim's first Canticles, and was worth the ransom of several of her number. "You played with these, didn't you? The crystal ones, not the ivory."

"Boren's side was ivory," Willim answered, glancing askance at the board. He refused to ask how Grayson knew which pieces were his, but Grayson spared him the trouble.

"I thought so." Grayson placed the piece back among its fellows. "You can't have won much. You're too protective of your Preybirds." Grayson nudged the pieces around, rearranging the pattern of Willim's interrupted strategy. "You cannot protect your whole flank all the time and still win the game. You must expose your pieces to some risk."

"I won often enough," Willim snapped, more irritated by Grayson's cunning peril skills than by the deft summation of Willim's losing streak. Grayson didn't answer, still musing over the game board. "He's certain to be captured that way," Willim said in rebuke, as Grayson placed one piece in a position of hopeless vulnerability.

"That's true. But in order to win an unwinnable game, you must accept two things." Grayson sat down in Willim's abandoned seat, and fished the Queen out from under the bench. "First," he said, as he placed her back into position, "accept that your men would not be on your field unless they were committed to your cause." In Grayson's fingers, Willim's Preybirds traded places with his Godswords, keeping the more powerful Godswords in reserve. "Second, accept that your moves will take the lives of your men, regardless of what your moves may be. You must learn to manage the measure of that loss. You must make your enemy bleed harder and faster than you do, but you will not escape it unscathed. For victory, sacrifice is required. That is the first rule of war. " Grayson pondered the layout of the board, and finally swapped Willim's consort for one of the discarded prentices. "There. You see?"

Willim looked at the board, and considered the moves available to his opponent. Crystal would lose half his forces to Ivory, it was true, but Ivory would be in peril in three moves and queensperil in five, bogged down in his own large force and giving Crystal the victory that had so often eluded Willim.

Grayson smiled at the comprehension on Willim's face, infuriating Willim all the more. "If you want to learn how to fight a war while being forbidden to carry a blade, Your Grace, you could do a lot worse than learn how to play dirty peril."

"I never said I wanted to learn the arts of war," Willim said, with an arch glance that would have done Dmitri proud. "I am a Songbird of Valnon, and such things are beneath me."

"Good thing they aren't beneath me," Grayson returned, coolly. "Or else you would be dead or worse right now."

"I would be dead or worse if I didn't eat every day," Willim shot back, "but you don't see me stirring my own pot of porridge in the kitchen."

"I don't." Grayson rose from his seat, and all the friendliness was gone from his face. "And I might like you better if you did. You're a spoiled little creature, like I suspected, and as proud as the only cockerel on a farm. Quite frankly I found you more personable when you were unconscious. I'm not sure I should be sticking my neck out for you again."

"No one is asking you to," Willim said, brittle.

"On the contrary." In the place where Grayson's smile had been, there was now a kind of grim danger that chilled Willim's blood. Grayson cocked his hip to the side, resting his hand on it in such a way that his sword, once discreetly covered by his cloak, was fully visible. The scabbard was worn and stained, the wire and leather grip shiny with use. He was a man who killed for a living, and he was extremely competent at his job. "The Wing himself has asked me to risk life and more for you, Your Grace," Grayson continued, "and I am as yet undecided if you're worth my trouble. Lucky for you, I like the looks of my reward better than I like your temper." As swiftly as it had appeared, the glimpse of the sword was gone, and Grayson was only an insolent, bored idler out-of-place in the garden. He glanced up at a pair of sparrows squabbling on the edge of the garden wall, and scratched at his cheek with one finger. "There is one condition left, of course, and that is your talent as Dove of Valnon. It's well and good to be arrogant if you've the skill to back it up, but only just. And if you prove to be less than your title, I promise you will not have to endure my presence any longer." Grayson bowed at last, and even in Willim's annoyance he could see the precision of it, the concise, martial gesture of a man who showed no other signs of such good breeding. "Rouen tells me I will not be disappointed. I trust that's the case. Good day, Your Grace--and my condolences about your loss." Grayson gestured slightly to the peril board, as though he was talking about the game and not Boren's death. Then he turned on his heel, as crisply as a Godsword marching in parade, and left through the side door on the opposite side of the colonnade. Willim was left with no company but the bruised roses, and his own equally wounded pride.

4

"I take it you've met our Dove properly at last?" Kestrel asked, with only the smallest glance away from his cluttered desk. "And from the looks of you, formed an opinion."

"I have." Grayson poked a finger into the lattice covering Kestrel's window, rubbing at the fog on the pane beyond. "I found him to be arrogant, short-tempered, judgmental, and entirely too spoiled for my liking."

"Hrm." Kestrel had a tiny smile playing around his lips. "Did you."

"On the other hand," Grayson continued, as he looked through the clean spot he had made on the window, and frowned at the distant spires of the Palace, "He is also intelligent, quick-witted, and straightforward. Not to mention he's still terrified by what happened to him, yet he marched right back into that garden today to face it. Lesser men might have stayed away longer before daring that. A spoiled Temple darling might even have waited until the garden was cleaned, so as to blot out the memory, but no. He was there for a good hard look at the blood, I saw it in his face." Grayson scooted aside a sheaf of old letters on the window seat, along with the cat sleeping on them, and sat down. "And he has a faint glimmering chance of becoming a decent queensperil player, if he can start thinking like a mercenary and not like a Songbird."

Kestrel steepled his ink-stained fingers above his desk. "You like him."

"Do I?" Grayson asked, wide-eyed. "It's the first I've heard about it."

"You don't bother assessing queensperil skills on anyone you don't intend to play," Kestrel said, drawing a thick fold of parchment from one of the pigeonholes on his desk, and unfolding it. "And you don't play people you don't like. So I'm glad to hear it. I'd hate for you to have a charge that got on your nerves."

"Did I say he didn't?" Grayson mused, with mock-thoughtfulness. "I must have left that bit out. Rouen, the boy gets on my nerves."

"After Evensong tonight," Kestrel said, ignoring Grayson's commentary, "It will be your responsibility to get the Songbirds out of the Temple. My task will be to prepare them for the trip." Kestrel unfolded the parchment, revealing a partial map of the Undercity tombs. They were for the most part a vast, uncharted maze, and only little pools of cartography had been plumbed by the occasional treasure-seeker or historian. On Kestrel's map, several of the more complex chambers had little fold-out flaps with red-inked lines of closer detail, but more than a few passages trailed out into blank parchment, their terminations unknown. It was still a finer chart than Grayson had ever seen. Kestrel made a satisfied noise and folded it again, adding it to a leather satchel on his desk.

"Evensong? That's earlier than the Wing said."

"He feels it better to speed his plans. While you're at Evensong, I'll tell Dmitri and Ellis what's afoot for tonight. I'd rather they didn't know any sooner, and it'll be easier to convince Willim to go along if I've already gotten the other two on board. Willim's stubborn, but he'll yield to Ellis' better sense eventually. And he will never be seen to shirk something Dmitri is doing, and Dmitri would sprint to the moon for me should I ask him."

"How cruelly you use those who adore you," Grayson said, with only a little bit of teasing to blunt the edge of his words.

"Practical," Kestrel demurred, "but hardly cruel, Nicholas."

Grayson arched a brow, and Kestrel cleared his throat, continuing briskly, "Once Willim is off the dais, I'll fill him in. He'll still have a few hours to prepare. It's Boren's pyre-boat tonight, and so the dais will be going up empty at midnight for his requiems."

Grayson removed the white cat from his lap for approximately the eleventh time in five minutes, and brushed at the fine coating of hair on his breeches. "What's the music schedule to do with anything?"

Kestrel pulled a number of tapers from a box and added them to the bag. "You'll see. What matters is that you have the Songbirds with you and meet the Wing by the Dovecote an hour before midnight. He will guide you from there."

"You can't tell me anything else?"

Kestrel made a sour face. "I can't tell you what I don't know, Nicholas."

"Wing hasn't seen fit to fill you in, has he?"

Kestrel's shoulders went rigid in a way that Grayson found all too familiar, though it had happened much more often when Rouen was a prideful little Lark. "The Wing tells me what I need to know, and that is all." He made a show of checking the contents of the bag again. "If I were to learn any more, I might be in danger if our plans fail. Hawk trusts the Wing, and I trust Hawk. That's enough for me."

"You know, for a moment there I almost believed you." Grayson gave up and let the cat remain, butting its head against his belt-buckle and purring with the velocity of a spinning mill-stone. "Let me know if you manage to convince yourself."

"Dammit, Nicholas," Kestrel breathed, his shoulders slumping again. "I am trying, here. I had hoped the Wing would set you to finding out the Dove's attacker, not this. But I cannot argue with His Grace. I owe him so much."

"For letting you stay in your colors all those years ago?" Grayson made a brief appraisal of Kestrel's left hand, callused in a way not caused by the use of sket or quill, and his eyes followed the faint, hard line of an object concealed beneath the azure drape of the Preybird's cloak. "Or because he overlooks your hobbies now?"

"I worked hard for my skills," Kestrel grumbled, adding a few more items to the bag, and testing the weight. "And I paid a heavy price for them. I'm not about to give them up, Lateran's orders or no."

"It's good to know you're still a diligent pupil."

Kestrel's eyes flashed with something like his old arrogance. "I expect I could best my teacher, now. Pity we've no time to try it."

"Pity," Grayson said, but he was smiling. "Perhaps sometime when I'm not courting a charge of High Blasphemy. Again."

"Oh," Kestrel said, with an airy wave of his hand, "What's another three counts?"

"Not much, I suppose." Grayson leaned over to add the tin of wound salve Kestrel had forgotten. "They can only execute me once, after all."

"And then," Willim continued, grinding up his mica powder as though Grayson's head was under the pestle, "he had the nerve to imply that my singing might not be equal to Kestrel's praise."

"He certainly knew where to bleed you," Ellis said, unable to stifle his grin. "You know only Dmitri can get away with insulting your singing."

Willim glowered at Ellis through a mask of half-finished Temple paint. The pattern of dots and whorls around his eyes had grown more complex with each year of his term, spreading wings of kohl around his eyes. Normally, Willim took to his paintwork with bored precision, making it a perfect replica of the unique tenth-year pattern recorded under his name in the Temple archives, but his recent hardships had inspired his hand to a kind of controlled savagery. Framed in the gleaming lace of his ceremonial paint, Willim's usually unremarkable eyes were the stark blue of a vengeful saint. "That's because I ruined Dmitri's life the day I out-sang him at the trials. I could write him a song-cycle of praise in my own heart's blood and it wouldn't be enough to redeem me in his eyes. The least I can do is let him complain about my talents, and we both know it's not true."

"The truth is you're just annoyed Grayson got the last word." Ellis threw open the trunk at the foot of Willim's bed. Inside, the holy armor of St. Alveron rested in indentations of purple velvet. The jewel-encrusted platinum collar and cuffs gave off a powerful aura of ancient ritual and--with somewhat more potency--the smell of metal polish. The armor required less care than St. Thryse's copper, which needed weekly buffing to maintain the proper shine, but Kestrel had still ordered the Dove's dress especially cleaned that afternoon. Ellis whistled at the sight of it. "I hope Kestrel gave the flock boys extra honeycakes for this. You'll strike the whole sanctuary blind when the light hits you."

"*Good*," Willim grumbled, dusting his wet kohl with the mica. "I hope Grayson's in the front row."

"Glad as I am to see you getting your spirits back," Ellis said, grunting as he pulled the broad gorget from the trunk, "it is possible that you didn't really catch Grayson at his best. He seemed genuinely concerned for your well-being last night, and he did carry you all that way, in the rain."

Willim swore. His hands were still unsteady, and he had smudged the careful sheen of safflower rouge on his mouth. It made him look like he had been beaten, and he had a vivid flash of Boren's face, blood pouring from his nose and mouth. "He probably wanted a reward," he said, groping for his sponge to repair the damage.

"I didn't hear him asking for anything. And Hawk acted like he knew him rather well."

"He said he was Kestrel's friend, not Hawk's." Willim stopped, slewing around on his dressing-table stool. "Actually, he said he was *Rouen's* friend."

Ellis' eyebrows got the better of him. "Did he, now. That's rather... intimate."

"I thought so, too. I haven't ever heard of Kestrel having a lover out in the city, have you?"

"There's that doctor, the Queen's physician. But I don't think that's anything more than friendship." Ellis shook his tousled hair out of his eyes. "If he does have one though, pray it doesn't get to Dmitri! He's waiting to pounce on Kestrel the moment our term is over, and if some sellsword gets in the way this close to the finish, it won't be pretty."

"I think Kestrel has more sense than to throw over Dmitri's devotion for some understreet bastard."

"What about an understreet bastard with extremely good shoulders?"

"Never," Willim countered, standing. "Not even if Hasafel should rise again. Hand me my cuffs, I'm late."

"Not so late that you don't have a moment for a good looking-over," came a new voice from the solar.

Startled, Ellis dropped Willim's cuff with a loud clang. Blocking the doorway of Willim's chamber was a craggy, white-haired Preybird in thunderstorm-blue damask, his cold, pale eyes glittering like those of a carrion-bird scenting battle. He leaned on a polished ebony staff capped with his namesake in silver, its wings upraised. It was a crutch, for a leg prone to rheumatism, but he bore it like a scepter of rule. Willim felt his gut twist.

"Raven," Willim said, something that was not greeting. Rather, it was like announcing the presence of something poisonous to others present and unaware, lest they tread on it unsuspecting.

"Your Grace," Raven returned, equally cool. "It is such a relief to see you about and well."

"Doesn't he ever knock?" Ellis hissed, picking up the cuff and closing the empty trunk. "I know there's no door, but still."

"Quite well, actually," Willim said briskly, snapping the cuff into place around his forearm. "Thanks for coming to check on me, but I'm sure you already know, I have no time for it now." Willim rose from his seat, proud and serene as marble. "If you'd like to look me over, it will have to wait until after Evensong."

"I'm so pleased you can tell your physician what can and cannot wait," Raven said, his velvety voice only a little rough with age. He caught Willim by the arm as he attempted to go by, his hand like an iron vise. "But I fear your capability to sing Evensong is for me to decide. If it makes you miss your hour, then you should have come to see me earlier."

Willim's eyes flickered. Raven knew Willim was not to go down to the infirmary alone after what had happened, and he had deliberately waited until it was almost sunset before coming to check on him. Inside, Willim shuddered with outrage, but somehow it was easier to close that up around Raven than it had been for Grayson. Raven was a familiar antagonist, and Willim had had more practice with him. "I don't think you wish to keep me from my holy duty," Willim said, his painted eyes hooded. "Least of all when a brave man is dead in his pyreboat for me." He pulled his arm from Raven's grasp, shoving the bead curtain aside as he left the room. "But I'm grateful for your concern."

"I am concerned," Raven said, with a sincerity as genuine as an almond-paste cockatrice. "I'm concerned for your state of mind. I would not want the strain to affect your nerves. I tried to persuade the Wing to excuse you from the dais tonight, but he insisted it was up to you. I had hoped you might have better sense. You've been through a great deal in the past day."

"None of which has the least bit to do with my lungs," Willim said, making a grand show of gathering up his train. "And I'm not so overwrought that I'll swoon off the dais mid-song. But should I develop a sore throat, you'll be the first person I'll call."

"Do not be so blithe when you speak of falling, Your Grace," Raven answered, placing a lark-ringed finger to his breast in a show of rightful trepidation. "Not while the platinum you wear is polluted with the blood of your predecessor. It was still there, blackening the settings when it was resurrected for your use years ago. They cleaned the gems that showed it, but I imagine Eothan's stain sleeps still beneath the pearls." Raven's pause was calculated, worse than a flock boy's before announcing that whatever dreadful tale he was telling took place in *this very part* of the Temple. "Be careful you do not sing his taint down on yourself, and share his cursed fate."

Up to that point, Willim's annoyance with Raven had been at a distance, somewhere low on the list after his irritation with Grayson, his urgency to get to the dais, and the deeply-buried shame of his cowardice the night before. But Eothan's ghost persisted in Willim's memory, a sad and lonely figure, a Temple Bird mute in death. With a day's distance, Willim felt no fear, only pity. Raven's comment brought Eothan's pain swiftly to the fore, beyond any petty grievance of Willim's. He whirled on his heel, leaving Ellis scrambling to keep up with the long end of Willim's drape.

"What do you know of Eothan?" Willim's voice was not loud, but the power of his title was behind it, and it rang in the close space of the doorway. There was a terse, dangerous edge to it that surprised even himself. "You have no right to malign a Dove of Valnon, no matter his fate. In doing so you scorn St. Alveron himself. Do you dare such blasphemy?"

Ellis' eyes had gone wide with shock, and even Raven was startled. Whatever he had intended to provoke out of Willim, it was not holy wrath. But he recovered quickly. Raven's lined face went still, his eyes hard and calculating. "You only prove my point for me, Your Grace," he said, with a bow so shallow it was only a centimeter away from mockery. "Doves are, on the whole, doomed to bring ruin on themselves and all of Valnon. I tried to warn the Wing the day you sang at the trials, but he would not heed me." He shook his head, and the regret in his voice was raw, honest. "Don't speak to me of blasphemy, I know full well what amounts to it, and I strive to avoid it. Though I advised him against your cutting, and in the end refused the task myself, the Wing would not be moved, and ordered you and your Songbirds to be cut by a common surgeon. Ill-omened, my boy. Hardly a rite worthy of St. Alveron."

"St. Alveron," Willim reminded him, "had his cutting at the hands of Antigus' torturers."

"And after his torment, and his bloodletting, and his song, he wished for no such pain to his heirs." Raven looked at Willim a long moment, as though there was something else he wished to say. Willim didn't think he had ever seen such an expression on the Preybird's face. It was gone before Willim could put a name to it, and Raven swept past them down the stairs. "Sing to Bring Heaven Down," he said, tossing off the traditional phrase as though it were an insult. "Though I hope it does not crush us all in the process. Good evening, Your Graces."

"Thryseblood," Ellis whispered, as Willim snatched back the length of his drape, and the thump of Raven's staff diminished down the corridor. "What in hell made you go at him like that? Are you insane?"

"Maybe," Willim said, hurrying out the door, and not waiting for Ellis to catch up. "And if Eothan was too, it was probably some old piss-pot Preybird that drove him to it."

"Yeeees," Ellis agreed, with hesitation. "But everyone knows Eothan was mad. And he drowned half the Undercity--"

"Eothan didn't drown anyone!" Willim shouted, and then at once relented at the sight of Ellis' flinch. "I'm sorry. I just don't think Raven likes Doves, any Doves, at all. And he doesn't know anything about Eothan. He wasn't like that. He couldn't have been. He just looked--" Willim realized what he was saying and began walking again, busying his voice with humming scales instead of letting it run away with itself.

"Merciful Alveron," Ellis breathed, as all the color drained out of his face. "Have you *seen* him?" He shook himself, and hurried to catch up to Willim's long stride. "Willim! Did you see Eothan?"

"After a fashion," Willim admitted, with reluctance. Ellis had the tenacity of a lobster, and would not be shaken. Once he knew something, the whole Temple knew it, and the last thing Willim wanted bandied about among the Laypriests was that the Dove was seeing spirits. "But it was a dream," Willim stressed. "He didn't *appear* to me, not the way you're thinking. You were by my bedside all night, and Dmitri afterwards. If Eothan had really walked into my room, one of you would have been there to see him, too."

"But... the second Dove," Ellis said, paling. "God. Willim, maybe you *should* stay off the dais tonight--"

"Don't you start singing Raven's tune!" Willim stopped walking long enough to catch Ellis' shoulder, turning him so their eyes met. "Listen to me, Ellis. I don't want a note about this out. It was just a bad dream, that's all. So nothing to Dmitri, and for the love of Alveron, nothing to Kite or anyone else. If Raven catches word of this he could get me off the dais with it. No one's seen Eothan for ages. Let's keep it that way, for Raven anyway."

"He's an old bird with no claws." Ellis shrugged, but he looked back over his shoulder before continuing, in a whisper. "He hasn't had any real power for years."

"He's got enough that he could turn me out of my colors and blame it on ill health. All he needs is an excuse, and I'm not about to present him with one. I don't care if I'm missing a leg; I'll never let on to him that I can't stand and sing my hour. Swear on it, Ellis."

Ellis looked unhappy, but he raised his hand level with his eyes, so his ring of office glinted in the lamplight. "I swear," he sighed, "by Thryse's wounds, and by the foundations of Hasafel, and Alveron's left nipple, and by whatever else you want."

"I don't care what you swear by," Willim said, flashing Ellis a look. "Just don't say anything. It's never an easy thing to convince someone you're not a lunatic. Raven would declare me unfit for the dais, and then that would be that. He has only to hint that I could fall off."

"Don't even say that! Not after... Promise me you'll be careful tonight, Willim, all right?" Ellis had real fear in his eyes as they reached the gate to the lower dais chamber. The Thrush of Valnon, the shining light of Noontide and all the glory of the day, had a palpable fear of the dead and the uncanny. Omens did not come easily to him, and as a result, they were a matter to be respected.

"I can't be careful it the sun goes down without me," Willim said. "Hurry."

Ellis unlatched the gate, and they descended the steep ramp to the base of the dais pillar, located in an ancient, rough-walled chamber beneath the sanctuary floor. There was no glitter or finery there, save on the dais itself, and over the centuries the lamps had left long black streaks up to the narrow aperture in the ceiling.

"Made it!" Willim said, stepping into position. The dais pillar, when completely lowered, was only a short, circular step capped with precious tesserae. "Fix my drape, would you? I'm not about to let Grayson be smug about anything, from my singing to my trappings." Above them, the grate in the sanctuary floor winked away, carried off by flock boys preparing for the service. Willim could hear the murmur of the crowd, and his jaws ached with the sweet promise of his song, as at the flavor of some delicious, tart fruit.

"I don't think he'll have any complaints." Ellis creased the drape into deep folds, fanning around the top of the dais. He did not usually bother with formality, installing Willim on the dais with a jaunty wave and a shorthand "sing down." This time, either knowing it was Boren's Evensong or to counter Eothan's ill-omen, he pressed the hem of Willim's drape to his lips and bowed deeply, as the lowest of the Temple Birds to the highest. "Sing to Bring Heaven Down, Your Grace," he said.

There was no time for Willim to answer; the dais shivered with potential beneath his feet. Willim took a deep breath and exhaled it out again in song, carrying Ellis' somber smile with him as the dais turned him slowly upwards towards his destiny.

5

Grayson's seating for the Songbirds' hours was a perch up in the dome of the sanctuary, nestled in one of the balconies on the highest level. They were often empty, save on festival days, when as many people as possible needed to crowd into the Temple, and the otherwise capacious floor seating was insufficient. They were a challenging climb and less comfortable than the padded stone benches below, and the view of the dais was not quite as close. They had not been originally sculpted for seating, after all, but for sound.

A conical shell of a chamber, with hollows and arches of marble flourishing between its wooden ribs, the Sanctuary was a vast instrument. For a Songbird's true talent was not just in the singing of his hour, but in the conjuring of his echo-chords, the ghosts of his previous notes lingering and reflecting back at him to form intricate harmonies, creating a music nearly infinite in its layers. The rising dais both lifted and turned the singer upon it, multiplying the melodies a hundredfold, creating an invisible choir from one mortal voice. It was said that in Hasafel, the great Temple of Doves had been three times over the magnificence of the one St. Alveron built, and a single note sung just so there could linger for hours, folded back and forth upon itself until it was utterly spent.

But for Grayson, the mechanics of Valnon's sanctuary were complicated enough. Kestrel had once tried to explain the process to Grayson--about the precise distance of traveled sound, about absorption and reverberation, about the pauses required by the singer--all the mathematic angles involved in the singing of a Songbird's hour. It gave Grayson a headache then, and the thought of it still did. At the time, Grayson's only counter had been to launch into a discourse of advanced military strategy, but it hadn't done any good. Kestrel had *wanted* to know about that.

Some things Grayson understood in practice, even if not in theory. Draperies of thick velvet were arranged to muffle certain echoes, or pulled aside to extend others. For Dawning they had been black, raised in select spaces to focus the pure, piercing soprano of the Lark of Valnon, to dampen the echoes before they became shrill. For Noontide, the crimson drapes had been placed to enhance the Thrush's warm resonance. Now the flock boys worked diligently at the violet bunting, hauling on ropes and rigging with all the industry of the Godswords' navy, arranging the panels in some arcane manner to best flatter the Dove's Evensong. When the work was completed, the rigging was concealed behind the curtains, so that the Temple was draped in soft streamers of color as though streaked with paint, the folds touched here and there by brilliant flecks of sunlight through the western window.

Grayson took his seat in the balcony just as the flock boys twitched the last tassel into place, and he watched as they hurried from sconce to sconce, lighting candles that the fading light would soon make into a necessity. He had watched the ritual for Dawning countless times, standing watch at the sanctuary doors before they were opened to the public, lending a hand now and then when some task of preparation was too much for a flock boy. It was from their ranks that the Songbirds were chosen, boys who were foundlings or gifts of tribute from noble houses. They labored in the Temple's service until their voices broke, unless they were chosen for the higher calling of the dais and the song of the saints. Afterwards, the adventurous could join the Godswords (whose lowest age of apprenticeship was, not by chance, the oldest age permitted of flock boys), while those still inclined to music or Temple life joined the Laypriests. There were few of the flock who did not return in some form to the Temple, with either sword or quill to its service, drawn to its music like the long-lost child to his mother's lullaby.

Grayson had never served in the flock. He was sent to the Temple and straight into the prentices at age twelve, to learn some measure of self-discipline, to become skilled in the use of a blade, to waste some youthful energy in the city, and most of all because it was simply what a fa Grayce did. Whether or not they returned to the holdings in the Northcamp was up to them; Grayson's mother had daughters enough to keep their exalted bloodline steady, and at least one of Grayson's brothers had already wandered off for exploits unknown. As sons of a famed line, their options were few: return to the family holdings, marry into a lesser family to bolster its standing, or go on to an illustrious career in the military. Grayson was disinclined to marriage and had never fancied life in the family brewery, haggling over the price of hops and grain, but neither had he intended to cut his traces in such a disastrous fashion. Barred from the Godswords, already his last resort, and utterly cast off from his family, Grayson had been hard-pressed to find employment for himself. Lateran XII might be a man of great mystery and great power, Grayson thought, but it would take nothing less than a song straight from St. Alveron's lips to give Grayson welcome in his family halls again. And all that remained of St. Alveron was the third Dove of Valnon to sing his Evensong, carrying his eternal wound and his unearthly song up to the sky for the sake of his saint.

"Let's see what you can do, little pigeon," Grayson muttered, and folded his arms, waiting to be impressed. He knew enough of Songbirds to not be moved by them solely for existing. They were men much like any others, save for the peculiar construct of their physiology and their isolated lives of musical training, and those things no longer held any especial awe for Grayson. All their glory was in their paints and their performance, and while it was extraordinary, Grayson was hesitant to call it miraculous. Skill and talent were worthy enough to earn Grayson's respect, and needed no mythical gilding. Kestrel had once been hailed as the greatest singer of Dawning since Saint Lairke himself was on the dais pillar, and Grayson had loved him beyond the scope of reason. If this Third Dove of Valnon could best the heartbreaking perfection of the Rouen in Grayson's memory, he would be worthy of the devotion he received. If not, so be it.

The grate over the dais opening was gone; the sunset turned the purple glass of the western window into the burning heart of an orchid. With a brassy peal, the Evensong bell resounded through the sanctuary, disturbing the scores of doves roosting on the outside of the spire. Their winged shadows flickered against the glass of the west window, and after the velvety heartbeat of their flight faded a thick silence filled the sanctuary.

Grayson held his breath, unaware he was doing so. It had been long years since he had last prayed, and his faith was as bedraggled as his name, but some kernel of it still remained. It was a longing to believe, a wordless desire for something beyond the gritty reality of his existence. From somewhere deep inside himself he sent out a plea into that rich stillness. *Be who they say you are. Be a song worth my life. Be the Dove of Valnon.*

As though in answer, from some unknown distance beneath the Temple, there came a Voice. Ghostly at first, it soared upward from the prison of the sanctuary floor, gaining strength with each measure. Already it had begun the lowest echoes, already the harmony began to vibrate in the stones. It looped and rolled over on itself and its ends met, like a drizzle of pale honey pouring back and forth into a whole golden pool of unspeakable beauty and perfect clarity. It rose as the sun set in the west: St. Alveron's hymn, the Song of Heaven, a tremendous music that grew and expanded at its singer's will, as much as the tide swells below the beckoning moon.

Long before the rising dais lifted the singer into the sanctuary, long before the light struck fire from his armor and his amethysts, long before there was Willim's thin flesh to wrap around the song, there was the Dove: Alveron on earth again, incarnate. Gone was the arrogant young man Grayson had met in the garden, gone was the confused and frightened boy he had rescued in the rain. He was a vessel for his song, the holy heir of Alveron and of Hasafel, and it was not paint or platinum that made him so.

Grayson's jaded spirit made a reflexive attempt to fend off the full realization of the Dove's power, but his defenses were shattered at once, as a shield of blown glass under the onslaught of a mace. Disarmed, he crumbled willingly before its glory. The Evensong went beyond music, beyond the flimsy enclosure of words like talent and skill. It cut through Grayson as light through a storm-driven wave, saturating him with it, and leaving him broken on an unfamiliar shore.

Later, it would occur to Grayson that he never actually said yes to Rouen's proposal. After the Evensong, Grayson simply assumed that he would give his all to the Dove's service, as much as it was assumed that the sun would rise and set each day. At the time, Grayson could only watch the dais lifting the Dove high into the sanctuary, as his song closed like a fetter around his heart.

When the dais had drawn level with him and the Dove was framed in the window, Grayson turned his face away. It was an instinctual respect for the otherworldly, as his ancestor Grayce had bowed down in awe before the song of his saints. For Grayce and his men, that moment of reverence had spared their lives.

For Grayson, it spared the Dove's.

A glint of light splintered in his eye, refracting in the prism of the tear Grayson had not yet blinked free of his lashes. Its source was a slim device resting on the lip of the balcony nearest him, a thing that to the uneducated might seem to be a child's toy crossbow. Grayson took it in in a flash, as lightning paints a sudden afterimage on the eyelid. He saw the cinnabar designs inlaid in the stock, he saw the ebony hand carved to hold the drawn-back string. He saw the sensuous curve of the bow, and he saw the slender needle nestled in the channel, its barbed point trained on the unobstructed target of the Dove's heart.

It was not enough to kill--the dartbows of the Shadowhands were not so coarse. They were made to incapacitate, to deliver a swift dose of toxin that would stop the nerves, but not the mind. In the days of his power, the Ethnarch of Thrass had fancied nothing so much as a good execution, and the signature weapons of his elite guard had made certain that his enemies remained alive for them. But for the Dove of Valnon, even a slight graze would be enough to make him lose his balance. The dais was now at its full height, and to fall from it would be death.

Grayson did not hesitate to consider his actions. The Evensong had washed caution and self-care right out of his veins. He leapt onto the ledge, put both his hands on the smooth marble pillar between the two balconies, and swung out into the open air of the sanctuary, landing in the next balcony over before either the Dove or his supplicants had a chance to notice.

The assassin noticed, however. Draped in a Laypriest's white robe, the hood masking his face, he switched targets at once, from the Dove's heart to Grayson's. The needle plinked harmlessly on Grayson's brigantine, but Grayson had plenty of skin exposed for another try. The assassin made a swift gesture and the string was latched again. Another needle was already in the chamber; it could fire up to ten before needing to be reloaded.

Hampered by the narrow space, unable to draw his sword, Grayson went for the assassin's wrist and grasped it with bone-crushing pressure, trying to force him to drop the dartbow. The man hissed in pain, but his oath was lost in the echoes of the undisturbed Evensong. Without warning he twisted to the side, and something tore through the air. Grayson had a fleeting impression of silver wings before his vision exploded in black flowers of agony. He had been struck across the cheek with something heavy and cold. Heat flowered over Grayson's face, blood spattered in a dotted arc across the other man's robe. The assassin wrenched himself free and took aim again, and not at Grayson.

Grayson blinked past the pain and his own fogged vision, and lunged for the other man. The dartbow grated on the edge of the balcony, jostled by their struggle. Up close, the musical twang of the bowstring was like a counterpoint to the Dove's Evensong, the carved black hand clicking down as it released the missile. The assassin shoved Grayson away. Beneath the robe he was wiry and well-built, and Grayson's balance was still addled. He had a glimpse, but no more, of a pair of watery blue eyes, alight with cold intellect and smoldering fury. It was enough for Grayson to know his enemy by name.

"You!"

"Catch him or catch me," Raven hissed.

Grayson looked out into the sanctuary, and his heart was seized with sudden fear.

The Dove had stopped singing. His echoes still sounded throughout the chamber, and the audience had not yet realized there was trouble. But Grayson, on eye-level with him, could see the shimmering line of blood trailing down from the Dove's arm, the mist of confusion across his eyes. Already he wavered on his exalted height, his jeweled sandals sliding towards the lip of the dais.

Raven fled, his distraction successful. Grayson let him go, and snatched a handful of the purple drapery instead. The Evensong began to fade, as the crowd at last concluded there was something wrong and fell to uneasy murmuring, as the Dove of Valnon tilted, like a falling star, towards the deadly embrace of the earth.

Grayson jumped away from the balcony and into the empty air, praying the fabric would hold, praying the saints were watching over their Songbird. He swung out towards the dais in a wide arc, letting the fabric slide through his hands so that he would be low enough, close enough...

A woman in the audience screamed, her voice piercing the last echoes of Evensong, and the Dove of Valnon landed across Grayson's arm with force enough to pull his shoulder from its joint.

The impact was numbing, the weight of Willim and his holy armor considerable, but Grayson held on. His hands bled, burned by the velvet, the sanctuary spun in a nauseating circle around them as the drapery swung backwards. The fabric tore at the strain, jerking twice and then dropping the Songbird and the sell-sword down into an ignominious pile in the back row of seats.

And Grayson still did not let go.

Willim was alive. The thought came to him at a distance, through radiant clouds of confusion and streamers of light. They dissipated abruptly, leaving Willim in an uncomfortable sprawl on the sanctuary floor, his drape hopelessly tangled with a length of tattered curtain, his headpiece askew. His extremities buzzed with sparkles of pain, and a large shadow blocked the light. Willim blinked. The shadow was Grayson, blood shining in streaks from his cut lip, a curiously-shaped red imprint on the side of his face.

"There's a bird on your cheek," Willim said.

Grayson bared his bloody teeth in a grin. "Glad to hear it," he said.

Willim was about to argue that he wasn't addled by whatever it was that had just happened, there really was a bird-shaped mark on Grayson's skin, but the clamor of mail and boots disrupted his thoughts. They were quickly encircled by a ring of prentices, their halberds making a pointy forest in the middle of the sanctuary. At their lead was Petrine Tolver, one of the few female prentices in the Temple. Willim knew her, a daughter of one of the lesser city houses, whose elder sisters had also been oathed Godswords. He thought of her as being a little short on personality, but compared to her current brisk demeanor, she may as well have been a court jester before.

"You are to come with us at once," she said, glancing at the prentices in the aisles. They were busy escorting the citizens from the sanctuary. Most of them had already dispersed, urged on by the prentices' spears. The empty dais pillar was already cycling back down again, sinking into the floor as though nothing had happened.

Grayson looked at Petrine in annoyed astonishment. "Who are you to so order your Dove? He may be injured, he shouldn't be moved until--"

"*You* are to come with us at once," Petrine repeated at

Grayson. "You are under arrest for attempted assassination of the Dove of Valnon. Surrender your weapon and yourself upon the saints' mercy, or resist and be met with your immediate death. It is entirely up to you."

Grayson's throat was suddenly haloed with the silver leaves of spear points. Slowly he lifted his hands, as his sword was ripped from his belt by one of the prentices, his armor patted for more weapons.

"Wait a moment," Willim began, forcing himself up on his bruised elbows. Every inch of his skin hurt. "Grayson has already saved my life twice, he's not about to--"

"Forgive me, Your Grace," Petrine interrupted, her green eyes like little chips of flint. "But it is very likely you aren't thinking clearly at the moment. Please let us look after your safety."

"How dare you--!" Willim tried to sit up, but something went wrong in his limbs and he didn't quite make it. He managed to get to his knees, but Petrine and Grayson were ignoring him.

"This is a terrible mistake," Grayson said, resigned.

"I think not," Petrine answered. "Your reputation is not unknown in the Godswords' halls, Nicholas Grayson. You could do very little that would shock me."

"I suppose that's true," Grayson said. "But while you're wasting your time with me, the real assassin is getting away."

Petrine's smile was neither very happy nor very nice, but it was knowing. "That is the idea," she said.

Something went quiet in Grayson's face, and for some reason it caused all the muscles of Willim's belly to draw taut.

"I'm sorry to hear that," said Grayson, in a voice that sounded every bit like he meant it. "And I'm equally sorry about this."

"Save your apologies--" Petrine began, but she had not realized that Grayson was apologizing not for anything he had already done, but for what he was about to do. Grayson's hand flashed up and caught the end of one of the halberds aimed at him, shoving it backwards and into the jaw of its holder. The prentice's head went back with a snap, Grayson wrested the halberd from his limp hands, and swung it wide to knock the other ones away. Only Petrine had the clear-headed determination to lunge forward; the others hesitated. Grayson caught the point of her spear in the haft of his stolen one, shattering his own weapon to uselessness and forcing Petrine to shake the splintered haft loose from her spear.

"They're with Raven!" Grayson shouted, hauling Willim to his unsteady feet and pulling him along the nearest aisle. The empty seats flickered by on either side of them. "Run!"

"Raven?" Willim repeated, then recalled the mark of the bird on Grayson's cheek, as though he had been struck hard with the silver ornament on a certain Preybird's staff. The tension in his gut turned to icewater without a moment's warning, and he ran.

"Flank them!" Petrine shouted, not near as far off as Willim would have wished her to be. "Block the exits!"

Galvanized by her command, the other prentices rushed to do as they were told. From all over the Sanctuary bolts were sliding home, first in the Sanctuary main doors, then the balcony steps, then the back entrance used by the flock boys.

"There's no way out," Willim gasped, as they skidded to a halt in the middle of the Sanctuary. The dais was down, leaving a gaping hole, and the prentices began a slow advance towards their quarry, tightening around them like a wire snare. "We're trapped."

"Don't let them slip through!" Petrine called.

Grayson's eyes swept the Sanctuary, from the dome to the floor. "*For those who shan't in Heaven dwell, there's room to spare in Hasafel.*"

"What do Heron's *Idylls*," Willim said, irritated by Grayson's sudden literary turn, "have to do with anything--" He broke off, alarmed, as Grayson grabbed him around the waist as though he was nothing more than a jewel-encrusted sack of meal. "What in the hell are you doing?"

"Saving you, I hope," Grayson said, and hurled them both down the dais pit into the black maw below.

6

The world fell away around Willim, his knees and stomach fluttering with the sudden realization of his own gravity. The lower part of the dais was not even a full story below the floor of the sanctuary, and Willim had not gotten over the shock of the fall before it was over. He and Grayson were lying in a tangled heap atop the lowered dais pillar. Willim's emptied lungs struggled for air even as he flailed to get his limbs free.

"Quick, on your feet," Grayson said, trying to disentangle himself from the yards of dove-colored train. He ended it with an oath and a tearing sound, ripping away most of Willim's hip-mantle. Tiny pearl beads clattered around his boots in a priceless rain. "They'll come down right after us. Are you hurt?"

"No," Willim gasped, though his shoulders were raw where they had scraped the walls of the pit, and his ribs ached from the pressure of Grayson's hold. "I'm fine, but the prentices, how could they--"

"They've made their choice." Grayson's eyes flashed as the light from the sanctuary flickered above them. "Get back!"

Willim heard the tooth-aching sound of armor dragging on stone, and a single prentice dropped down from above. Grayson was unarmed, but he still had the Dove's mantle in one hand, and the hem was heavy with embroidery and beads. Grayson snapped the length of fabric forward like a whip, catching it around the man's neck, and then shoved him forward again. The prentice's boots caught on the raised lip of the dais, his head cracked on the stone wall, and he slumped unconscious to the pedestal. Willim drew back in horror as his broken nose oozed blood in a thin cobweb over the cracks of the dais mosaic. His name was Dervis, Willim remembered. As a flock boy, he'd been good at the sket, but he couldn't sing a note.

"Go!" Grayson tossed the twist of bloodied fabric away and snatched up the prentice's spear.

Willim glanced back once before he obeyed. "Is he dead?"

"He'll live, but we won't if we stand here gawking." The iron gate to the dais passage squawked open, and Grayson waved Willim through. They had emerged into an oddly silent Temple, all the musical echoes muffled out of it, as though wrapped in felt. The sounding vents had been closed. The silence made Willim feel sick and dizzy, even more than the lingering effects of fear and poison. Grayson waved his spear point down the corridor. "Quick, get to your rooms. Rouen should be there already."

"What's going on?" Willim asked, pressing one hand to the stitch in his side. He had been breathing from the top of his lungs, and he chided himself for letting fear affect something as instinctive as his breath control. "How was I hit on the dais? Did Raven attack you?"

"Not now," Grayson said. "Rouen--"

The Preybird's old name was overlapped by his new one, as a scream of unspeakable anguish tore through the air, in a voice Willim barely recognized as Dmitri's.

"*Kestrel*!"

Grayson, already running, broke into a flat sprint. He reached the steps to the Songbirds' rooms two strides ahead of Willim, who was hampered with the weight of his trappings. By the time Willim scrambled up the steps after him, the doorway was mostly blocked by Grayson's shoulders, and he held out one arm to keep Willim from going in any further. It kept Willim back, but it did not obstruct his view, and he almost wished that it had.

The divans had been knocked aside, their cushions sliced open and oozing feathers in a slow snowfall, the delicate carvings chipped and splintered. Dmitri's books had been trampled, torn pages littered the floor. And sprawled halfway in the fountain was the limp and waterlogged figure of a blue-cloaked Preybird, his auburn hair matted with blood and a spreading crimson shadow tinting the water around him. Dmitri knelt beside him, his arms wrapped around Kestrel in a protective embrace. A longknife lay bloody and discarded some distance from Kestrel's left hand, and even further away were several prentices, incapacitated but still alive, bleeding all over the brightly-colored rugs. More prentices, uninjured but breathing hard, had moved in to take the place of their wounded companions.

"Willim!" Ellis was held in the firm grip of two burly prentices, his tunic torn and his nose bloodied, but otherwise whole.

"Your Grace," Raven said cordially, from the middle of the

room. "How good of you to join us."

Ellis yanked his face away from the prentice trying to stifle him. "Are you all right? Raven's been saying--"

"I'm fine," Willim said. "But Kestrel--"

"Oh, he'll probably live." Raven made a gesture, and a pair of prentices wrenched Dmitri away from Kestrel's body, while a third hauled the Preybird out of the bath and left him in a soggy wad by the steps of the fountain. He was breathing, but just barely, his hair plastered over his face. "I daresay he was holding back to keep from wounding any prentices too badly. Luckily, they lack similar finesse. Soft-hearted idiot." Raven scowled down at Kestrel, and at the pink-tinged rivulets he was dripping on the marble steps. "Look at you. I was a fool to think you deserved a place at my side, as my proper heir."

Kestrel shuddered, opening one eye. "Why?" he wheezed, with an unsteady grin. "Because even as Lark I had more sense than to accept a place in your bed?"

Raven's expression went from mocking to ugly; he made a swift motion with his staff and Willim could hear Kestrel's ribs crack. Kestrel curled into a ball, coughing little flecks of blood onto the floor.

"Get away from him!" Dmitri shouted, as the prentices struggled to keep their hold on him. "Raven! You bastard!"

"Not to mention," Raven continued, to Kestrel, "but you've nearly spoiled Dmitri beyond any use, and he's the finest thing to come to the dais in decades. Unlike his fellow birds." Raven swept an arch glance in Willim and Grayson's direction. "But the Dove should be a part of this, as well. Come in, Your Grace, and bring that bit of Undercity refuse with you."

Grayson tightened his grip on his halberd, but Petrine and her fellow prentices had caught up to their quarry, mounting the steps behind them. Willim and Grayson were caught, and this time there would be no escape down a convenient hole.

"No," Willim whispered, and rested his hand on Grayson's for a moment. "There's too many." Grayson nodded after only a second's hesitation, and lowered his spear. Willim slid past Grayson, and lifted his chin in defiance at Raven. "I expect you have a good and lengthy explanation for this outrage," Willim said, to Raven. "Considering how much you like to hear yourself talk."

Ellis laughed, but he was the only one, and it was brief and nervous.

"So," Willim said, "I suppose I can ask you just what the hell you're doing?"

Raven lifted his eyebrows and tsked. "Such coarse language, Willim. Exactly the kind of unfit behavior that sadly typifies Temple Birds these days. Petrine, get them in here. We're going to have a chat."

Petrine's forces closed on the doorway, and a gloved hand fell on William's shoulder. He gave a look of reproach to its owner, a young prentice who murmured an apology and would not meet Willim's eyes.

"I hope you know what you're doing," Grayson said, as the spear was wrenched from his hands, and the Songbirds herded onto the one divan that was still upright.

"Not really," Willim admitted.

"Report, Petrine."

Petrine snapped a salute in Raven's direction. "We've taken Osprey and Kite in the archives, Sir. There was only a minor scuffle and they surrendered in order to prevent any bloodshed in front of the flock."

"More likely Osprey was worried for his books," Ellis muttered.

"And Hawk?"

Petrine's brow creased under her coif. "He... resisted, sir. But we subdued him in the end."

Raven nodded. "Good enough. Get him in here, and keep it quiet."

"Kestrel needs his wounds seen to," Willim said. Raven's lip curled, as though to prepare a retort, and Willim added, "As do your prentices. You say the Temple lacks civility, Raven. But I've yet to see that you have any of your own."

Raven scowled, but tipped his staff in Petrine's direction. "Wait. Bring me one of the Laypriests with some herb-lore in his head. I don't care which. Preferably one too stupid to make trouble, but that describes most of the herd."

Petrine bowed and hurried off to do as she was told. Willim thought he heard Dmitri breathe out a tiny word of thanks, but when he looked at the Lark next to him, his face was still a hard mask of fury.

The apologetic prentice bound Grayson's hands as he stood at spear-point behind the divan, and Raven tapped his staff impatiently on the floor. "I had no desire for it to turn out in this manner," he said, a note of regret in his voice that was actually sincere. "I dislike you, Willim, but I feel it's hardly your fault for your predicament. You did not ask to be Dove, after all, and others convinced you that you were worthy of it."

"My voice makes me worthy of it," Willim said. Somehow, defending his position from Raven's insults was almost comfortable footing. The familiarity of it eased the fear a little; the words, often said, came easily. "I sang at the trials, and I succeeded. I was offered the dais, I accepted the wound of my saint. I don't see what makes me unworthy."

"My dear boy," Raven breathed, exasperated. "That's exactly the point. You cannot be worthy of Alveron. No Songbird can be. Much less some muddled-blood orphan from the priestess' abbey in the Undercity. Your song--while technically good enough, I suppose--is only a fluke. Eothan was a similar disaster, and I would think the Temple should have learned its lesson then. But lest you think me too petty, this has very little to do with you personally. No, in this case you are little more than a token on a game board, and a powerless one at that." He mused for a moment on his staff's ornament, turning it so the wings caught the light. "I find I am left no choice but to start a war, and a proper one. Not this wasteful skirmishing on the border, not this endless series of armistices and concessions, to be made and broken over again like flawed pots. You were to be a martyr, Willim. The Dove of Valnon, stolen away by agents of the Thrassin Ethnarch. The people would demand war, and the Wing would have no choice but to give it to them." He brought his staff down hard, chipping the edge of the step. "Your one opportunity to be of some use, and it was ruined, as so many things are, by none other than Nicholas fa Grayce."

"I try," Grayson said, modestly.

Raven whirled on him. "Well in your trying, you have forced my hand. I was going to spare the Dove's life. I had already accepted the offer of the Iskati Empress to purchase him and keep him safely in Iskarit. But your interference yesterday spoiled that.

Still, I tried to warn Willim from the dais tonight. But by Willim's insisting on singing Evensong, I was obliged to take matters into my own hands. And once again, who is in my way but Nicholas Grayson." Raven took a moment to smooth his hand over his hair, struggling to keep his anger in check. "But from the ashes of lofty plans comes opportunity, they say. Lest you think me too cruel, there's still a chance to settle this without further bloodshed, and even for most of you to come out of it alive." Footsteps sounded in the corridor, and Raven lifted his head, his eyes going bright. "Now, we will see if you have the sense to accept it."

Petrine stepped down into the Songbirds' solar, dragging with her a young, wild-eyed Laypriest. He had straw-yellow hair that was just barely grown out of boyhood's brevity, and fear made his face the color of milk. Willim did not know his name, but his face had a vague air of familiarity, part of the white-robed blur that the Laypriests tended to become.

"This one claims to know something of medicine," Petrine said. "Though he tried to take it back when we wanted him to come with us. Will he do?"

Raven gave a curt nod. "Tend to the prentices' injuries," he said, "and then mop up this Preybird. One note out of tune from you and I'll have you whipped until you bleed, do you understand?"

The Laypriest flicked his pale eyes in the Songbirds' direction, but he was too frightened to leave them there for long. "Yes, Your Grace," he whispered, and hurried to do as he had been told.

In his wake, another two people entered the already crowded room. Hawk, save for his rumpled robes and bound wrists, could have just stepped out of Canticles rehearsal. But his calm expression could not hide the overpowering waves of displeasure he gave off, an aura enough to make even the most indifferent flock boy mind his sharps and flats. For escort he had a well-built prentice with a pleasant face and hair that was neither fair nor dark. If nothing else, he was remarkable for being absolutely unremarkable, and Willim could not place his name. Raven spared him the effort.

"Haverty. Is everything under control?"

"Alder Haverty," Ellis whispered, next to Willim. "That bastard, I spent an hour talking about Alfiri riddle ballads with him yesterday, and he never let on he was planning on turning traitor."

Alder showed no reaction, though he could not but hear Ellis' words. "The Laypriests and flock boys are all quiet, as are the younger prentices, and they've assured us they won't make any trouble. Kite and Osprey might be more difficult, but right now I've got them under guard in the archives."

"Good enough," Raven said. "Any further sign of the Wing?"

Alder shook his head. "Hawk led us to his rooms and didn't interfere with our search. From the looks of it, he fled not long ago."

"Then we shall have to carry on without him," Raven said, not sounding very disappointed at the prospect. "Let's get on with business. Sit down, Elloren, and stop your glowering. Your face will stick that way, if it hasn't already."

Hawk's mouth twitched, as though the insult of his birth-name was the last in a large pile of final straws, but Petrine put a chair upright for him, and he sat in it.

"I suppose you think you've won, Jeske," Hawk said to Raven, returning disrespect for disrespect. Willim had never heard anyone, not even Osprey, call Raven by his birth-name.

"Won?" Raven shook his head. "I've hardly begun. In the past few decades, my work has been piling up on me. The Ethnarch has spent his time far more wisely than we, building up his rebellion, forging alliances, while Valnon has sat, smug and sanctimonious, pretending there is peace. How many Godswords have died in the past year alone, from skirmishes on the border? Skirmishes that I might add would not exist at all, if Valnon would reach out with her full might once and for all."

"The Wing does not condone unnecessary war--" Hawk began.

"The Wing has fled!" Raven shouted back. "He is nothing more than a febrile old man, too senile to be of any use. You've had his strings round your fingers for years, don't dare pretend otherwise. And you, with that cold Shindamiri blood of yours, it's a wonder you don't have scales and a tail. You'd never do anything to make your position precarious, or interrupt the smooth ascent of Kestrel into place behind you. You've had Valnon neatly tied up for years now, luxuriating here, content and spoiled, while Godswords die for this mockery of peace. Unnecessary war! Was it unnecessary then for Petrine's sisters to die?"

70

Petrine sucked in a little breath, but if she felt the eyes of those present turn to her, she did not acknowledge them, keeping her gaze steady on Raven.

"And what of Locknally's father?" Raven continued, waving at another prentice. "Felled not six months past? What of all the fathers, and sisters, and brothers, and friends, and lovers? They are all dead now because you and your puppet of a Wing lacked the fortitude to engage in outright war." Raven paused to take a deep breath, nostrils flaring. When he spoke again, it was in a calmer voice, but with no less passion. "We may bear the wounds of our saints, but it does not make us less men unless we, in indolence, choose to be so. Our saints were men of conscience, of action, and when their blood was spilled, it was hot upon the very ground where we stand. With every generation of Temple Birds after mine, I have seen that blood wane and grow cool. I will stand for it no longer."

"So that's how you coerced the prentices to your side," Hawk said. "By manipulating their grief. You think the Wing does not despair over every life lost? You think he relishes this situation?"

"I wouldn't know," Raven replied. "I've rarely had the pleasure of chatting with him without you looming nearby, save upon the occasion he relieved me of my place as High Preybird--the position you now occupy. And that exchange was remarkably brief. I wonder how much of that was your machinations, as well?" He studied Hawk's closed face for a moment, but it gave him nothing. "At any rate, I am not a coiling Northern serpent, like you. I coerced no one, I did not sway them or scheme for their hearts. Petrine came to me, Elloren. Broken-hearted at the death of both her sisters in one battle, a battle fought when we should be at peace. She begged me for some herb, some draught, to ease her grief. I could have poured sleep upon her sorrow. Instead, I urged her to make it her strength." Raven turned to his subordinate, and his expression of pride was galvanizing. Her shoulders went back further, her chin lifted. "Look at her now. When did you last see such confidence in a Godsword's eye? Not since the days of Queen Renne, Heaven keep her soul. Coerce them? Why, I had to turn some of them away. They want this war, and they would be the ones to fight it, and to win it. So why deny them?"

"Valnon is not a nation of conquerors," Hawk shot back. "And if you think we are, then it would behoove you to study the song-cycle of your saints with a bit more care."

"Nor are we a nation of cowards. Saint Alveron sought to form a model country ruled by faith, where might was discarded in favor of reason and peace. It is a lofty ideal, but only an ideal, and one that can sustain itself only in fantasy. Such notions did not save Hasafel from the tread of the infidel's boot, they will not save us. We cannot make the same mistake, or we will sink like our city of old." Raven turned at last to the captive Songbirds. "And whether the Dove of Valnon shall be listed among the fools of his kind, or the wise, remains to be seen."

The room had grown dark as Hawk and Raven argued, with no flock boys coming to light extra lamps, and Willim had not been watching the Preybirds. He had been distracted instead by the fair-haired Laypriest as he moved from prentice to prentice in the shadows, tying up wounds and advising the application of poultices, murmuring words of comfort and receiving expressions of surprised gratitude in return. When he reached Kestrel, his care was all the more tender, fetching a discarded cushion for the Preybird's head, searching out the worst wounds among the many smaller ones. For a long time he whispered to Kestrel, and eventually got words in response to his queries. When the Laypriest was satisfied, he approached Grayson to inspect the side of his face, mottled purple now where Raven had struck him. The prentices guarding Grayson warned the Laypriest back with their halberds, and the startled Laypriest fell down behind the divan in his haste to bow apology, landing on the floor with a clatter.

"Leave that one to bleed," Raven said to the Laypriest. "Are you finished?"

"The Preybird needs more care than I can give him here," the Laypriest stammered, knotting up his hands in his wide sleeves. "He should be taken to the infirmary."

Raven's answer was a sour frown. "He does not leave my sight until this business is concluded," he said.

The Laypriest bit his lips, nervously. "Then... he should at least have proper treatment for his wounds. I do not have enough salve for his injuries, and he needs binding for his fractures."

Raven sighed. "Fine. Two of you, take the Laypriest down to the infirmary to get what he needs. If he tries anything, thrash him

72

for it."

Two of Petrine's prentices escorted the Laypriest away, leading him out the door with a firm hand on each arm.

"Now," Raven said, eyeing the Songbirds. "Your Preybird has been seen to, so perhaps we can get on with things."

"Your hospitality is overwhelming," Dmitri growled.

Raven shook his head, sadly. "Dmitri. We used to be such good friends during your flock boy days, when you assisted me in the infirmary. Affection makes fools of us all from time to time, but I thought you had more sense than that. There's no need for you to lose your colors. It's long been my plan to see you become High Preybird as you deserve. I know how it must chafe, to be second to such common rabble as our Dove. But with your help, we can overcome this ugly chapter in Temple history."

For a split second, Willim thought Dmitri would agree. He made no secret of his resentment, denied the future power and the current glory given most Larks, forced into second place by the rarity of Willim's talent. But Dmitri was in all things constant, not only in his bitterness at being second Songbird, but in his unwavering love for Kestrel, and his nature knew nothing of forgiveness. His answer was prefaced with a withering stare of contempt. "I will spit into your pyre one day, old man," he said, as icy as a midwinter morning with no Dawning. "And I'll go to my own before I do your will."

"Correct me if I'm wrong," Willim said to Raven, "But I don't think he's interested in your offer."

"A pity," Raven said, looking at Dmitri and then away in revulsion, as though he was the badly rotted corpse of a beloved friend, "but hardly disastrous. The flock this year has been promising, and replacements can always be found. In that case, Dmitri, the Dove will have the deciding of your fate, as well." Raven focused his attention on Willim, and for a moment there was nothing in his face but resignation and weariness. It was not unlike the look he had given Willim only a short while earlier, urging him to forgo his hour.

Was he trying to warn me? Willim wondered to himself. *Does he truly feel he has no choice in what he does, and wanted to give me a chance to escape?* For a second, Willim was moved to something like understanding. But then Willim heard Kestrel's soft groan of pain, and the brief window of empathy was shuttered and barred. Raven's actions were unconscionable, regardless of his motivations.

"I cannot expect you to comprehend this, Willim," Raven said, "as so little of the outside world is permitted to reach the ears of Songbirds. But the skirmishes on the border have sapped the strength of the Godswords now for years, as a leech beneath a warrior's armor. Had we crushed it in one stroke, there would be no need for this. But when the war ended, the Wing accepted a surrender that was far too favorable to Thrass, when he should have eradicated them, as they would be all too willing to do so to us. I offer you this one chance: to rise beyond your existence of happenstance, to be elevated to a rank that quite honestly is more than you deserve. Valnon will go to war in your name, in the name of the third Dove, and Valnon will at last be the indomitable empire it always should have been. We are mightier, more learned, more civilized than any other city in the world. It is time we behaved as such. And you will make it possible, you the last Dove, you more glorious in your abbreviated term than you would ever be in your full one. Be the stone for Valnon to step upon to rise higher, and even Hasafel will look pale beside our glory."

"It's a pretty speech you're making," Willim said, trying to push away the rising nausea that Raven's words inspired, "for one that's meant to convince me I should let you murder me."

"I said nothing of murder." Raven looked offended at the very suggestion. "Boy, if I just wanted you dead, I'd have poisoned your tea long since, or slit your throat in the bath. I have loftier goals than mere murder. My actions tonight were merely the hasty result of alternate plans, And to be honest, I think it's to the better that Grayson stepped in. I think with his aid, we can set things right far more easily." From his robes he drew out a thick fold of parchment, spreading it open on the teakwood tea table in front of the Songbirds. The glass dome above the bathing pool was black now with full night, and at Raven's gesture Petrine brought over a lamp and set it down on the table, revealing the parchment's dense blocks of text, more obtuse than five treaties put together. Some sections had been recently scraped clean, and re-written. Willim saw Grayson's name squeezed into a few places, awkward as an enjambment. Raven had already placed his signature and seal on the bottom, and there was space there for the imprint of another ring. "This was intended for the Wing's signature, but as he is gone and your authority technically supersedes even his, you will do."

"Your offer is extensive," Willim said, glancing at it. "Suppose you just hum the refrain for us?"

"It is simple enough." Raven pressed his knuckle to a relevant paragraph. "You and the other Songbirds shall vanish, as Alveron and his kin, to some suitable location far enough away that your legend here may flourish unbothered by fact. The Empress of Iskarit was delighted at the acquisition of one Songbird, I should think her beside herself at the prospect of having three. Should you like, I can even send your Preybirds with you." He gestured at Grayson. "Though I will need to have the head of this nameless bastard, as he made such an ideal scapegoat of himself this evening. As for the rest of you, nothing would please me more than for the lot of you to be gone from Valnon forever. You will be free to retire in luxury in Iskarit, or somewhere else if you prefer, where you may while away your lives in pleasant diversion."

"Delightful," Ellis muttered, sullen. "I can practice my orange-peeling skills."

"I hardly think the Empress would require such rare pets to so menial a task as peeling their own fruit," Raven said, ignoring Ellis' sarcasm. "Truly, I offer you nothing but a life of comfort and quiet luxury. Your labors as Temple Birds will seem like heavy burdens by comparison."

Willim looked at the contract until the letters blurred in front of his eyes. "And in exchange, we leave you to make whatever mess you please of Valnon and the Temple, correct?"

"If by a mess, you mean a restoration to its proper place, then yes." Raven was almost pleading. "Be sensible, Willim. This whole thing can be nothing but a rest in the measure. Last night was frightening for you, I understand. But those men wished you no lasting harm. They were only the delivery-men."

"They killed Boren," Willim said, in retort. "three upon one, with Thrassin swords and with open delight. And you ask me to trust you after that? After all this?"

"I ask you," Raven answered, with narrowing gaze and a cooling of his previous warmth, "to do as you are told."

Willim let his anger flare and sink within him, banked to

coals, unvoiced. "And if we refuse?"

"Ah," Raven's face fell in disappointment. "Well then, my boy, I'm afraid we will have to speak of murder. Yours, specifically, and the public execution of Grayson and your Preybirds for their unseemly plotting with him. Your Lark and Thrush will be sold as common pleasure-slaves, and you, Willim, will be horribly mangled by the Shadowhands, by the order of the Ethnarch. We'll have to leave you recognizable for your pyre, but only just. We'll need plenty of froth among the populace, and misguided as they are, they do adore you. I require a spur for my war, Willim, but it needn't be a gilded one. I can make do with a bloody one just as well."

Willim's throat was dry. Even when he was kidnapped in the garden, even when he wavered on top of the dais, never had his own death been laid out in such blunt terms before him. Is this what Eothan's appearance had truly meant, that morning in his dream? Was Hasafel's gate already yawning open to admit his soul?

"Don't give in to him, Willim," Ellis said. His laugh was pitiful, too bright. "I imagine it'll at least be interesting being a pleasure-slave. We'd get out of our celibacy two years early, anyway."

"And Kestrel would rather die than see the Temple in your hands," Dmitri snapped, glowering under his mussed hair. "As would we all."

"No," Willim said. "I can take responsibility for my own fate, but not for the fate of my Songbirds, or my Preybirds..." Willim's gaze flicked to Hawk, who had his head bowed, and then to Kestrel. He almost jumped in surprise. Kestrel, when last he looked at him, had been leaning against the edge of the bath, as though overcome with the pain of his injuries. But now he was staring hard at Willim, his eyes bright and alert, his face intense.

When their eyes met, he made a little gesture with his hand, just the slightest tip of his fourth and first finger. Willim knew the motion, though it had been a long time since it had been directed at him. It was a command to the chorus, a signal to adjust pitch slightly to flatter the main melody line sung by a soloist, or to better accommodate the acoustics of an unfamiliar venue. It was to sing not as written, but on instinct, to lie for the sake of a finer performance overall. *False music.*

Willim could not comprehend its meaning, not at first. Was Kestrel telling him to go along with Raven's plan? To lie? Or was it something more subtle? Was Kestrel the one lying, not as injured as he pretended to be?

Kestrel made an impatient motion with his toe, and Willim at last noticed that while there was still a bloody imprint on the rug where it had lain, Kestrel's longknife was gone. His heart thudded heavily against his breastbone, and he understood.

"But you leave me little choice," Willim said, as though his pause had only been deliberation. "I cannot consign the innocent to death, Raven."

"Not like the Wing, apparently," Raven sighed. "He does it every day."

"It is to spare the innocent that the Wing stays his hand," Grayson said, speaking at long last. His face was dark with anger, his eyes hard. "Have you seen war, Preybird? You have not. Certainly not war as Thrass makes it. This war of yours will give you glory, but not the kind you seek. Valnon would win, in the end, but we would triumph over a land of corpses. Thrass would gleefully blunt our swords with their own children and elders, all for the sake of their holy cause, their impurgerable nation. In fact," he concluded, his mouth twisting with disgust, "they're very much like you."

"I don't recall asking your opinion," Raven replied. "Nor would I ask the opinion of a man whose disgrace gives him little in the way of moral high ground."

"I'm content that I'm not a murderer," Grayson returned, unmoved.

"No, only a sell-sword, which is so much better." Raven made an exasperated noise. "Charming as this is, I grow tired of it. Your answer, Dove. Death for you all or life in exile?" He snapped his fingers, and Petrine hurried to bring him a quill and ink. "Your signature and your seal, and you will be escorted to your boat at once. I'd rather you didn't linger, I've much to do and I've wasted too much time already."

Willim picked up the quill. It was the one Ellis had been sharpening earlier, when Willim came back from the garden. It was a swan wing feather, trimmed to a tuft on the end as Ellis liked them, and yet it felt as heavy as lead in Willim's hands. He looked again at Kestrel, but the Preybird was once more unconscious or feigning it well. Hawk's face was unreadable, distant. Only Grayson would meet Willim's eyes, Grayson, who faced death with either choice Willim could make. Willim remembered how, only hours ago, Grayson had mentioned risking his life for Willim. His cut face was an earnest reminder of how seriously he took that duty, painted in vivid color down his jaw, staining his collar. Blooded already, and for a Songbird whose behavior towards him had been anything but grateful. And yet his face showed no fear, no hesitation. For a moment they were the only two people in the room, in the whole world, and the terrible choice between them was laid out as simply as the red and black diamonds of a queensperil board.

Grayson's lips moved slightly, and though Willim did not hear, he knew what had been said. The first rule of war: *For victory, sacrifice is required.*

Willim dipped the quill in the ink. The lamplight flashed on it, tracing an arrow's point of fire on the tip. All the days to follow that moment built up under Willim's breastbone, as the first breath of a song not yet begun, and Willim made his choice.

"Peril," Willim said, as calmly as though he and Raven had only an idle game between them. He had only a second to see the comprehension in Grayson's face, and then he turned and drove the sharpened quill deep into the flesh and bone of Raven's outstretched hand.

Raven shrieked with pain and surprise, recoiling in agony as Willim kicked the table over, shattering the lamp onto the floor. Raven's treaty ignited with a soft gasp of combusting parchment, and the room erupted into chaos.

Grayson rolled away from the blow of his startled guard's halberd, sweeping the man's feet out from under him and diving under the divan where the Laypriest had fallen earlier. When he came up again a second later, Kestrel's longknife was in his bound hands. Petrine made for Grayson at once, but in doing so, she neglected to take note of Hawk. The Preybird leapt up from the chair, his bound hands struck her in the back of the head with a sharp crack, and she dropped like a stone. "Go!" Hawk roared, kicking his chair into the path of the next guard. "Take them and go, Grayson!"

"What of you?" Grayson shouted back. "Rouen's in no condition to--"

The prentice rushing towards Grayson was felled unexpectedly by a broken chair leg, and Kestrel, standing over him, shot Grayson a look of complete exasperation. "Dammit, Nicholas, this is no time to be chivalrous!"

"We won't just run--" Dmitri began, but Kestrel gave the Lark a violent shove, both to encourage him to get a move on, and to move him out of the way of another prentice's blow.

"Do as you're told, Dmitri!"

"That's right," Ellis agreed, pulling Dmitri after him through the melee. "Better part of valor, and all that. You'd be a terrible bed-slave anyway."

"Come on!" Willim waved them over to the door, as Hawk's chair shattered against another opponent and splinters plinked on Willim's holy armor.

"Stop them!" Raven screamed, clutching his wounded hand in a bloodied twist of his robes. "Kill them if you have to!"

With a grunt of effort, Grayson at last got his knife through his bonds. He shook the ropes away as he herded the Songbirds towards the steps. The doorway was blocked by one prentice only, the rest of them occupied with Kestrel and Hawk's surprising skills in hand-to-hand combat. Alder Haverty stood on the top step, his halberd barring the way.

"I don't want to kill you," Grayson said, in a low voice. "So just get out of the way, boy."

"I can't do that," Alder said, but he loosened his grip on his halberd, and his eyes were touched with a faint smile. "It wouldn't look convincing enough."

Grayson blinked, and then his smile mirrored the prentice's. "If you say so." Before Willim could even begin his question, Grayson's fist swept up and caught Alder right above his belt buckle, doubling the boy over his arm.

"That's better," Alder wheezed, with the remnants of air left in his lungs. For a second his eyes were fixed on Willim's. "The Wing... waiting for you. Dovecote... Hurry." He slid to the floor in a heap, and then rolled slowly down the steps with a deafening clamor of mail to land, unmoving, at the bottom.

"Convincing," Willim said, as they stepped over him and fled down the corridor. "Is he on our side?"

"*Was* he on our side, I think you mean," Ellis said. "Not sure I would still be after that punch."

"Even if they want a holy war, I can't imagine many prentices condoning harm to a Songbird to get there." Grayson paused at a cross-passage, his arm out to keep the Songbirds back, but all the halls were empty. "I noticed more than a few hesitating tonight, and not for lack of skill. I suspect not all of Raven's converts are as devout as he thinks."

"Raven's no fool," Dmitri put in. The front of his tunic was still rusty with Kestrel's blood, and he studied it with a little frown. "But he will use the tools that come to hand."

"They were earnest enough when they went at Kestrel," Ellis said, with a shudder. "Phew, he had me scared. Acting of that caliber belongs in an Apocrypha Cycle! I thought he was really hurt."

"He *is* really hurt," Grayson said, and made no effort to conceal the pain in his voice. "He bought our escape at a high price, and it is not a gift we should squander. This way, hurry. They won't hold them off for long, and if they catch us, they will to worse to us than they have done to Rouen."

Willim swallowed past the sudden constriction in his throat, and ran until knives of pain slid through his ribs, his thoughts a whirl of fear and urgency. Kestrel could not die. It was beyond comprehension. He did not know what hope or allies were to be found at the Dovecote, but he prayed for the vengeful phantoms of Alveron and his kinsmen saints, with Grayce's horsemen arrayed for battle behind them. When he saw that the only person waiting at the alcove was a lone Laypriest, his disappointment was acute.

"Friend or foe?" Grayson demanded, brandishing Kestrel's longknife. "Which are you?"

"I would think you'd know that by now, Nicholas fa Grayce." The stranger lifted his head, revealing himself to be none other than the young Laypriest Petrine had brought to tend the prentices' wounds. He was not cowering now, and his eyes were bright with a cunning that had been entirely absent before. Willim felt a sudden pang of alarm for the fates of the two prentices that had been with him. "I hope that by taking up the weapon I left you, that means you have agreed to my proposition. Let's hope we all live long enough to see you get your reward."

Grayson stared at the Laypriest, at the knife in his hand, and then at the Laypriest again. He looked as though there were several things he wanted to say, but none of them quite managed to get out.

The Laypriest reached up to cast back his hood, and in so doing, the lamplight flashed on a heavy ring on his forefinger, the large ruby carved with the shape of a curled bird. Willim knew the ring, as he had seen it glinting beneath a sleeve of crimson velvet on the day he sang for his title at the Trials. Never before had he seen the face of the man who wore it.

"You are the Wing of Valnon," Willim breathed, the certainty only wrapping the man further in mystery, submerged beneath the deluge of a thousand questions there was no time to ask.

"Hardly the febrile old man of Raven's imaginings, hmm? It has been of the greatest use to me, and to my Preybirds, to be the exact opposite of what is expected of me." Lateran XII reached out with his long Songbird's fingers to touch the bruise on Dmitri's temple, the dried blood beneath Ellis' lip, the vivid scratch that Raven's needle had left on Willim's arm. The Wing stepped back, satisfied with his inspection of the Songbirds. "Battered, but not broken. Much like our plans."

"You intend to follow through?" Grayson asked. "Even now?"

"We have little other choice." He turned to Grayson, and now his voice was low, urgent. "Raven intends to keep as many pretenses of normal Temple activity as he can manage, and that will be your way out. He has closed the sounding vents, to keep the noise of his coup from spreading, but he will soon have them open again. You must be as quiet as possible until you are out of the Temple. This exit will open at midnight, but do not hesitate. I don't know when you may have another chance." The Wing spared a smile for his Songbirds, and it was somehow bracing. He extended a hand to Willim, some unnamed emotion flickering across his face as his fingertips lingered, not quite touching the warm metal of Willim's collar. Willim took a breath and the Wing looked away as though startled, curling his hands back in his sleeve and turning to Grayson. "Take them to Jerdon in the Undercity, by whatever means you can manage. You may trust him as you would Heaven's own emissary. Wait there for my instructions."

"Your Grace," Grayson said, in obedience. "I will do all I can."

"What about Hawk and Kestrel?" Willim said, trying to keep his voice calm in spite of his fear. "And everyone else?"

"You must trust me to look after them." Lateran glanced back down the hallway, his face intent. Willim wondered how he could have ever thought the man an idle young Laypriest, much less a fool. There was a Preybird's competence to his every gesture, and his lush voice had not only the beauty of a man cut for the dais, but the wisdom of one many years from it. "Quickly, there is no more time. This is your way out."

"Here?" Ellis asked, in patent disbelief. "The Dovecote?"

The Wing had the audacity to wink. "By now you should know, Ellis, that not everything in the Temple is what it seems."

The Dovecote was nothing more than a decorative alcove under a staircase, a little nook covered in mosaic to imitate its agrarian namesake. Doves rested in their nest-holes, protective over half-hidden eggs, and everything from the blue sky in the distance to one falling feather was a flat imitation of life. It was a good place to sit and hear hours without being in the sanctuary, and Willim had spent a good deal of time on its circular bench. Never once had he thought it held any secret, and yet when the Wing reached up and brushed his fingers over the tiles, the doors in the mosaic swung inward with a rasp of stone, more real than ever expected. Beyond them was not the country meadow advertised beyond the ceramic-tile windows, but a steep stair leading down into darkness.

"As a matter of fact," Lateran XII concluded, "I can't think of much in the Temple that is. Go, fa Grayce. I leave them in your hands."

Grayson bowed his head to the Wing and plunged down into depths. Dmitri followed, his face unreadable. Ellis was much more hesitant, ducking through the opening only when the Wing offered him an encouraging little wave of his hand.

"I don't want to run away again," Willim said, as Lateran turned to him expectantly. "This place is my home, it's everything I know. I can't let Raven have it without a fight."

The Wing of Valnon smiled. "You've given him a reminder he

82

will not soon forget," he said. "And it was hardly a coward's gesture. The hour of your song will come, Willim. You should know that a Songbird only lifts his voice when the time is right."

"And he should shut up and wait in the meantime," Willim answered, with a frown.

Lateran laughed, an unexpected sound, and it more than anything shook the chill of fear out of Willim's bones. "Yes, though it should sorely try his patience." He rested one hand on Willim's hair, briefly, and his face grew serious. "Whatever you face in coming days, know you are capable of meeting your destiny. Trust your intuition, and no matter what, keep your Songbirds safe as best you can. You are their Dove. They will look to you."

"I can't protect anything--" Willim began, feeling his fear draining away into panic.

"Raven is right about Songbirds in one respect, Willim. You are only helpless if you choose to be so." Lateran took Willim by the shoulders, his grip was firm and warm. "While you and the Songbirds live, Valnon endures. This Temple is merely a building. It is your song that makes it sacred. No colors or trappings or oaths will ever change that." From down the corridor there was a muffled shout, a clink of armor. The Wing of Valnon touched his face to Willim's bowed forehead and then ushered him to the first step. "Follow your song, Willim. It will not lead you astray. Farewell."

Willim turned on the top step as the doors closed again, and Lateran drew his hood up over his head once more. Willim had only the faintest glimpse of wheat-colored hair before the thin thread of light snapped and he was alone in the darkness.

7

For a long moment Willim stood alone on the steps, unable to see anything in the black. From somewhere below him there was a rasping noise, and a click, and then light blossomed up from a lantern in Grayson's hands. It was only a single flame reflected in three panes of caged glass, but it might as well have been the sunrise to Willim. Something like relief uncoiled in his stomach, even as the warmth of the Wing's hands slowly faded from his bare shoulders. Grayson held the lamp up until its light splashed over Willim's toes, and then he waved at Willim to hurry down and join them.

The steps ended in a narrow passage, old rock that had been left unfinished after it was chipped out of the heart of Valnon's isle. Like the dais passage, there was no adornment, and no lamps. Brackets that might once have held torches now hung crazily from their moorings, rusted and forgotten. The roof was stone, low and claustrophobic.

"There are supplies for us here," Grayson whispered, pointing to the satchels Ellis and Dmitri were wearing. "Rouen prepared them for you earlier today. Don't lose it."

Willim nodded, more because he did not trust his voice than out of a desire to keep silent. The leather bag Grayson pressed into his hands was well-made and serviceable, but lacking any device or embellishment to mark it or its owner as belonging to the Temple. Willim wrapped his arms around it and shivered as the cool leather pressed against his belly. Whatever else was inside, he hoped there was a change of clothes. He was wearing little more than jewelry, and the tunnel was cold.

Grayson waved them forward, and they left the staircase behind. The passage sloped downwards, twisting so that the blackness soon nipped at Willim's heels, and he very quickly lost any sense of direction. The passage did not branch, nor did it widen, and after ten minutes' tense walk, it ended at a blank wall.

Ellis sucked in a breath that almost became a noise of indignation, but Grayson made a sharp motion with his hand and the Thrush bit back on his oath.

"Here we wait," Grayson breathed. "I advise you to rest, and sleep if you can. We have a long journey ahead. I'll wake you when the way is open."

"What if it doesn't open?" Ellis whispered, voicing what Willim himself had been thinking, not relishing the idea of a slow death in the dark.

"Then you'll still have had a nice nap," Grayson answered, with a shrug. He looked at Willim, and Willim had the impression that Grayson was actually seeing *him* for the first time in hours, not as an object to protect, or as the fallen avatar of a saint, but as a man, cold and exhausted and hungry and scared. His expression softened a little. "There should be spare clothes and food in your bags. Change, and take off or conceal anything that will mark you as Birds of Valnon. Your jewelry, your colors. Hide your armor in your bag, Willim. It will be heavy, but I don't want to leave it here for them to track us." Grayson sat down with his back to the Songbirds and his face towards the darkness of the path back to the Temple, and busied himself with cleaning Kestrel's longknife.

Willim's fear of dying forgotten in the dark turned into a fear of being discovered by Raven at a dead end, and he turned his attention to the contents of his pack for distraction. Folded on top were doe-skin breeches and a plain white shirt, as well as a cloak whose brownish-gray wool was closer to a true dove's colors than anything Willim had ever worn during his service. He stepped outside the circle of lamplight and removed his armor, the padding on the underside of his collar damp with sweat. The clothing Kestrel had chosen fit well, but the common cut of the fastenings was strange to his unsteady hands, and he stabbed his finger on the cloak-pin. He was grateful to be done as he traded places with Ellis, and sat down to lace up his boots. Ellis emerged from the darkness a moment later, looking strange in dun-colored linen, and Dmitri was equally odd in dull blue. Between the three of them they wrapped up St. Alveron's armor in the tattered remnants of Willim's drape, dispersing it between their packs so none of them would have the full burden of the weight. Willim stripped away his jewelry, including signet of his office, with the dove curled around its amethyst, and the third numeral set with pearl between its wingtips. He stared at it a long moment before he stuffed it quickly into the bottom of his satchel. It was not the loss of finery that disturbed him, but the unexpected and vast uncertainty as to who he was without it.

Willim had seen sulphured apples and bread in his bag, but the sick emptiness in his middle was a long way from being hunger. Ellis, never one to let anything put him off meals, picked listlessly at one of his honeycakes. Dmitri simply put his head on his pack and lay down, his gray eyes staring out at nothing.

Willim wanted to say something to them, some words of encouragement or comfort. He especially wanted to give Dmitri his thanks for standing up on the side of the Dove, but the Lark of Valnon would not meet Willim's eyes.

The silence was as thick as the close air. Willim looked at Grayson's hands as they worked at the stubborn blood caked on Kestrel's knife, thinking of the Wing's words. He had called Grayson a fa Grayce, as had Raven. But surely such a thing was impossible, or a mistake. Grayce was the first Godsword, the protector of St. Alveron. His line was famed and respected, and though there were few involved in Valnon's government, they were without question the bluest blood in all of the Northcamp. If Grayson was really one of them, what was he doing as a common-named sell-sword? His name alone should have put him in the Godswords, in a gold-studded gorget at the head of his own command. Willim tried to get a good look at Grayson's face, but he was a sketch of light and dark patches in the lamplight, blurry and indistinct.

The minutes crawled by, each one bringing another question Willim could not answer, and did not know how to ask. Finally he closed his eyes, and rested his head back against Ellis' shoulder, wondering how on earth anyone could be expected to sleep in such a situation.

A loud grumble of moving stone woke him up, hours later. His first panicked thought was that Raven had somehow forced open the doors to the Dovecote, but as he shoved away the dregs of sleep he realized it was coming from the wrong direction for it to be an attack. In the lamplight, the surface of the dead-end wall was moving. As Willim stepped forward he could see that it was slightly curved, bending out towards them. It shimmered like polished glass, worn smooth from centuries of motion.

"I know that noise," Dmitri said. He looked haggard, but alert.

Willim wondered if he'd slept at all.

"The dais is rising!" Willim said.

"Midnight!" Ellis said. "The dais is going up empty for Requiems, and this is the base of it!"

"Then this is the way out the Wing mentioned." Willim reached out his fingertips and brushed them against the moving stone. It made enough noise in its turning that whispers seemed unneeded now. "We must be deep under the Temple, below the sanctuary, below the dais chamber. I never knew this was here."

"I don't think anyone did," Grayson admitted, in a little grunt. "Not even Rouen. And I thought we knew more of the Temple's hidden passages than anyone."

"It would take Raven more than a few hours to shut down the dais mechanism," Lark said, with a keen look at the spinning stone. "It is a complex thing of water and steam, and would require stoppering up all the pipes in the Temple, for the baths and the cisterns and the kitchen ovens. Small wonder the Wing knew the dais would still rise for Requiems. But I'm not sure how it is meant to get us out."

"Not through this gap here." Ellis bent down to peer at the base of the moving pillar. A darker shadow winked in and out by his toes, inching higher with every slow turn of the dais, chewing at the floor of the tunnel. "Unless... d'you suppose it's cut all the way through, and further down?"

"I suppose just that," Grayson said, in grudging admiration. Only then did Willim realize that Grayson had felt every bit as unsure about their escape as the Songbirds had. The opening was now as high as Ellis' knee, but impenetrable as an ink-stain on stone. "Damn clever."

Willim watched the pillar vanishing into the roof of the chamber, thinking about the dais rising silently in the sanctuary above. Was anyone to witness its ascent? Or was the sanctuary deserted, empty of everything but echoes and the shattered remains of the Temple's order? He shuddered, not only with dread, as a cold draft seeped out of the hole and lifted gooseflesh over his skin. Poor Boren deserved a better send-off, but he was an old soldier, and he could find his way to Hasafel without a requiem to point the way. Willim would sing for him later, for his own sake if not for Boren's.

"Not the escape route I would choose," Grayson said, as he handed Ellis the lamp. "But I'll take it. Ellis. You know the timing of the dais better than I do. Can you let me know when you think it'll be near its apex?"

Ellis rested his fingertips on the turning pillar, grateful for something to do. "It shudders about six measures before locking into place," he said. "I'll wait for that."

"Good." Grayson turned next to the Lark, who was standing just outside the circle of lamplight, his face tilted away from its beam.

"Dmitri," Grayson said, and the Lark made no noise of protest at the over-familiar use of his name, or at the equally forward hand upon his shoulder. "The wounds Rouen took were grave, but they need not be mortal. He's a strong man, and he has every cause to bear up through this. You must do the same. The Wing will look after him, and despair will only sap your strength."

Dmitri swallowed, his lips parting as though he would speak, but in the end a tight little nod was the only answer he gave. Satisfied with this, Grayson turned at last to the Dove. Willim tensed, waiting for orders or advice, but Grayson only shrugged at him.

"Well! I suppose I'll have to wait to hear the rest of Evensong," he said, with a little smile. "But the first part was enough to convince me that you certainly can sing. And play a cunning game of peril with Raven, as well."

"I owe you an apology," Willim said, hugging his cloak around him. "My behavior today, in the garden--"

"You owe me nothing," Grayson said, too quickly. He might have said more, but Ellis called out that the turning dais was slowing and would soon stop. Grayson took back the lamp as the dais reached its apex, settling down in its foundation with a heavy thud that reverberated in the close space. Bored through very base of the pillar was a rough, narrow doorway, veiled in ancient cobwebs. The breath that sighed out of it was stale and dusty, and the space beyond it was a black emptiness. Grayson poked the lantern into it, but the light seemed reluctant to go very far.

"Where does it go?" Willim asked.

"If I had to guess," Grayson said, inspecting it, "it goes through the catacombs."

"We're going through the *tombs*?" Ellis said, and Willim was grateful he had been spared asking it himself. If Grayson had said that the door opened onto hell itself, he would have been little surprised.

"Better to walk among the dead than be one of them, Ellis." Grayson jerked his head at the doorway. "Go on. I'll go last. It's only open as long as the dais is at its peak, so no dawdling."

Ellis' answer was a faint whimper. Willim knew he hated close spaces only a little more than he hated dead things, so he kept a supportive hand between the Thrush's shoulder-blades as they edged through the dais. For a moment Willim felt suffocated, with Ellis creeping along in front of him and Dmitri pressed in behind, and his lungs ached with his own shallow breaths. At last they were out, and Ellis fell forward with his hands on his knees, gasping. It had taken only a few seconds to pass through.

"I know the dais stays locked in place for a quarter hour," Ellis said, drawing a shaky hand over his clammy brow. "But I just knew we were going to wind up stuck in there."

"It'll be solid enough if they think to come looking for us," Grayson said, lifting his lamp. "And by then we'll be long gone. We should be able to make good time, now."

"Good time to where, exactly?" Willim asked. They stood in a round, empty chamber, its walls daubed with faded frescoes. The pallid faces staring back at them were archaic, the figures full of rigid gestures and hooded eyes, the once-smooth plaster splintered by cracks and sparkling encrustations of minerals. Thin needles of stone covered the ceiling of the chamber, formed by the slow drip of water from the surface. It felt far older than Valnon, and deeply unwelcoming. Space for the dais had been cut out of the wall, and though it had occupied the spot for six hundred years, it protruded from the pre-existing paintings like a newly-broken bone from the flesh.

"That's a very good question," Grayson said, stepping down into the only doorway out of the chamber, a low arch painted with faded red blossoms. He held a map close to his face, studying the cramped blocks of burial chambers. "If I'm reading this right, we should come out into the Hall of the Heavens with little over an hour's walk. Let's go."

At first there was no sign of Valnon's dead in the passage,

save for the mummified shape of some long-expired rodent slowly turning to dust on the floor. Ellis wondered aloud if their travels would take them through the oldest passages, and not the tombs themselves. "After all," he finished hopefully, "this passage doesn't look like it was made to be a tomb."

"It probably wasn't," Dmitri said suddenly. He was eyeing the walls with keen interest. "Antigus didn't know how to build anything, only how to scavenge what his betters had left behind. He found these sunken chambers and turned them into slave warrens, because that's what he needed. Then they became tombs, because that's what the Undercity needed." He cocked an eye at a worn mosaic above them, a chipped peacock peering over the lintel. Like the frescoes beneath the dais chamber, it looked as though it had not been meant to exist underground. The floor under their feet had once been laid with tiles of marble, now broken and obscured beneath centuries of dirt. Dmitri brushed his fingers over the space the peacock guarded, an alcove that might once have looked out onto open sky, not rock. "The Temple closed the tombs after the last quake, saying they were unsafe, but it was an excuse. Alfiri-style pyreboats had become popular, and there was no room left underground. By then even the oldest chambers had been filled, the ones from before Alveron's time. You can only stack so many skulls."

"Trust you to know all the ghoulish history," Ellis muttered, and they fell to mild bickering about Dmitri's grim taste in reading material, and Ellis' lack of taste in pretty much everything.

But Dmitri's words sank into Willim's thoughts, which were already morbid in spite of the dearth of bodies. *Before Alveron's time*. There was a time before the saints, and before the Temple. In the history of Valnon's island, the Temple's rule was only six centuries, a mere blink of an eye compared to Hasafel's millennia of glory. Should the Temple fall, should the Songbirds vanish forever, it would not matter to the rocks. The ruin of the Valnon Willim had known would sink down to the sea, like Hasafel had, to be beaten to sand by the endless march of time. He ran his fingers over the dusty lip of the alcove, wondering who had once stood there, what view he had looked out upon. The successes and failures of his life were nothing now. Did it matter, really, what became of Willim, when a fleeting few years would bring a similar

90

end to him and all he had done?

Eothan's face flashed into Willim's mind, all black paint and sorrow, and he shuddered and hurried to catch up to the others. He was still alive, after all, his blood still ran warm in his veins. Whatever kind of creature Eothan was now, he was a powerless thing, an echo, and Willim had no desire to join him.

To Ellis' dismay, the catacombs soon lived up to their name. The narrow tunnel gave way to a vaulted room, the first in a nest of linked chambers, all piled to the roof with a snarling tangle of bone piles. Skulls lay heaped in yellowed pyramids, their gaping eyes staring with blank indignation at the intrusion of the living, each jawless mouth gnawing vacantly on the pate of those below.

"You have to admit, the patterns are almost charming," Grayson said, sweeping the lantern light over one pile of quilted skulls in a large burial chamber, the femurs stacked in martial chevrons. "A shame the quake made such a mess of things." The stacks nearest Grayson were orderly, but the opposite half of the chamber was tilted at a crazed angle, and a deep fissure had lifted up the central crypt on the floor like a sundial's stile. One door led out on an upper level, another was three feet down on the other side of the crack. Bones disrupted by the quake had rolled into every corner of the room, slowly crumbling, indifferent to their displacement. Grayson placed his lamp on the ledge of the crack, and hopped down. "Stay put, you three. I'll check our direction."

"Eugh," Ellis said, lingering by the relative tidiness of an empty loculus. "Did they have to build everything on top of the tombs?"

"Everything in Valnon is right on top of the catacombs," Grayson said, examining the vacant plinth of a soul-marker. Its former tenant, a black marble figure carved in the garb of a Songbird, lay broken on the ground below, flung from his perch in the violence of the second Dove's earthquake. His gilt collar and cuffs were mottled with tarnish like mortal decay, his dusty eyes stared up at nothing. "There was nowhere else. No one's been buried in them for centuries, and they're naught but bone, now. They'll do you no harm, Ellis."

Ellis did not look entirely convinced. "When we were flock boys, Dmitri told me that the ghouls would reach through the privy grate and feel ankles to find the plumpest boy to snatch. I didn't eat for a week, and I was scared to death to take a piss. Hawk was livid when he found out."

"I think he was more livid about you replacing Dmitri's privy sponge with a sea-urchin," Willim answered, leaning wearily on a wall full of crypts, plaster epitaphs caved-in on their occupants. An hour before, he might have been squeamish about it, now he was only tired.

"You have to admit, he deserved it," Ellis flashed a knowing grin at the Lark of Valnon in the doorway of the chamber. "Right, Dmitri?"

Dmitri, sullen and wan, looked right through both of his fellow Songbirds to Grayson, still kneeling by the broken remains of the soul-marker. "Do you even know where we are?"

Grayson stood, dusting his hands off. "Right on track," he said. "The Hall of the Heavens is just ahead, and from the bridge there it's only three passages over to the old road."

"By whose definition," Ellis said, a short walk later, "is this called a *bridge*? "

Grayson lifted his lantern higher, but that did not change the unsettling view in front of them, nor the dubious expression on his face. "By someone with an over-optimistic opinion of architecture," he said. "But it's what there is, so we'll have to use it."

True to its name, the Hall of the Heavens was a glorious chamber, even in ruin. It rose upwards into darkness, but from the shadows far above, flecks of gilt mosaic twinkled like stars in the light of their lamp. Tier upon tier it was filled with doors to other passages, some humble, some as ornate as a palace gate. Soul-markers stood at intervals between them, their black arms pointing out ways long-forgotten by the living. It was the great crossroads of the old Undercity, the hub of a city now given over to the dead. In spite of its glory, the chamber was lacking in one crucial detail: there was no floor. Bits of paving and rock clung to the edges of the room, a jagged lip around a chasm that went down an unknown distance. Water muttered and gurgled in the deep somewhere far below them, and it sent echoes through every gaping doorway. Threaded across the emptiness was a bridge of sorts, made of a thick, single twist of rope. Once it had boasted smaller rope railings, but these trailed down into the emptiness below, broken and frayed. Willim felt his stomach quail with fear at the sight of them.

"No." It was Dmitri that said it, but his voice was so unlike his usual haughty tone that Willim almost didn't recognize it. The Lark of Valnon was as white as plaster, his dusty hair clinging to the sheen of sweat on his face. "No," he said again, and then, "I can't."

"I don't like it either, but it's the only way across--" Ellis began, in friendly commiseration, but Dmitri snapped him off.

"Don't get patronizing with me! I said no, dammit! I'm not going!"

"Well you can't stay here forever--" Ellis started again, more angrily this time.

"You'll only get me on that accursed thing if you drag my corpse over it," Dmitri said, lifting his chin in a show of his typical defiance, but both his voice and his hands were shaking. "I said I can't, and I won't."

"You're afraid of heights?" Willim said, surprised out of his own fear. He didn't know Dmitri was capable of being afraid of anything, but Dmitri's scowl was answer enough. "But you're a Songbird! You ride the dais every Dawning--"

"The Lark of Valnon is not afraid of heights!" Dmitri shouted, his voice ricocheting around the chamber. Something faltered in his face, and he looked away from the bridge. When he continued, his voice was thinner than that of the most nervous flock boy at trials. "...I'm only afraid of falling."

"Then we should find another way," Willim said, without a moment's consideration. "Surely there must be one."

"I don't need your pity," Dmitri started, but Willim shook his head.

"It's not pity," he said. "You refused Raven's offer tonight, when you probably had more cause to join him. I won't forget that."

"It didn't have anything to do with you," Dmitri said, with mild surprise that Willim could think of him doing otherwise. "I am a Lark of Valnon. I would not disgrace my colors by siding with a traitor."

"All the same, it's a favor I'm glad to return," Willim answered, and turned to Grayson. "It's decided, then. We'll find another way."

"It's not decided at all," Grayson said, shoving his map back into his belt. "I'm in charge of this little expedition, in case you've forgotten."

"And I am the Dove of Valnon, and these are my Songbirds," Willim retorted, his ringing echoes expertly squashing Grayson's. "In case *you've* forgotten."

They glared at each other like two fighting cockerels in a dirt ring, each waiting for the first move that would excuse bloodshed. Willim knew Grayson was probably exasperated with him, knew he was acting like the spoiled Songbird Grayson had accused him of being. But that didn't matter. Rival or not, Dmitri was one of Willim's own, he and Ellis all of the Temple he had left. He would not push that aside to side with an outsider, no matter if he was good at queensperil or not.

"Maybe we could try going around the side?" Ellis suggested, into the terse, silent battle of wills. "There's some flooring left."

"It'll never hold us all," Grayson said, ripping his eyes from Willim's with one parting glower. "One of us might make it across before it crumbles, but not all of us. It's a wonder there's any footing at all." He waved his lantern along the lip of the hole, and its light revealed a broad archway a several yards away along the curved ledge. "But since *His Grace* insists, we'll have to try it. That way has some promise, though I shouldn't be surprised if we all plunge to our deaths."

Dmitri gave a violent shudder, closing his eyes, and Willim said, "We'd be more likely to do that on that scrap of worsted you're calling a bridge."

"Fine." Grayson stripped off his pack and his cloak, then hefted his lantern again. "I'm going to scout that door over there and see if I can find a way around, but I don't expect to find one. Don't come after me until I come back. There's no need to heap any extra weight on our path before we have to. I've got two hours' worth of oil in my lamp. If I don't find anything in the first hour, I'm coming back, and we're taking that bridge, Dove of Valnon or no. Is that clear?"

"We shall wait here," Willim said, with a regal tone that he hoped was as infuriating as he meant it to be. Grayson didn't want to use that bridge either, Willim would have bet St. Alveron's platinum on that.

Grayson shot him a look that was unapologetically filthy. "You do that."

"Haven't got anywhere else to be!" Ellis sighed, collapsing onto the stone floor like some sort of long-legged campaign furniture with its pegs removed. The spare lamps that were in their packs were simple affairs, a folding frame of lightweight horn panes with a socket for one candle, and Ellis set one up in a clear spot on the floor. Its puddle of tawny light didn't seem to reach very far. "Be careful, will you?"

"I'll be back shortly," Grayson said, with a heavy sigh, "I suspect we're the only live things within leagues of here, but should you have any trouble, call for me. Sound carries well here, and I know how loud you can be." He gave them all the most cursatory of bows, and then stalked off to the other side of the chamber. His lamp was a wavering globe of light as he sidled along the narrow ledge, it flared up in the open space of the arch, and was soon gone altogether. Willim sank down into the light cast by their humble candle, wondering if he'd done the right thing.

"You know, Willim," Ellis said, speculatively, "I begin to think you *like* arguing with him."

"You don't want to take that damnable bridge either, and neither do I. Nobody sane would." Willim hugged his knees up to his chest. Now that they weren't moving, it was cold. "Not even Grayson."

"You're too much alike," Ellis grinned.

"You take that back this instant!"

"Not a chance, Your Grace." Ellis said. "He's just got a stubborn streak, just like you. You put him into place rather neatly, but I think it was for show. He's a sell-sword, so he must like taking orders, or I imagine he'd do something else."

"He's not a sell-sword because he likes taking orders," Dmitri said, with meaning.

"Oh really?" Ellis said. "And what do you know about him?"

"More than you two do, apparently," Dmitri said, and refused to say any more. He curled up on his side, either asleep or doing a good imitation of it, and Ellis eventually got tired of prodding him when he saw he would get no satisfaction for it.

"I hate to admit it," Ellis yawned, "But I think our Lark has the right idea. I can't keep my eyes open." He gave Willim a wistful look. "But I suppose we ought to stay awake and wait for Grayson?"

"Go ahead and sleep," Willim said. The argument had gotten his blood going, and though he was tired, he knew he was a long way from sleeping. "I'll stay up."

"You're a saint," Ellis said, cuddling up to his pack. "Wake me up if you want to trade, all right?" He was snoring within three measures, his mouth open, looking as comfortable as if he was still in his crimson-sheeted bed in the Temple. Willim was left alone in the empty Hall of the Heavens, with the silent figures of the soul-markers and the patient dead all around him.

8

Grayson stalked down the new passage alone, telling himself that it had been the right choice to separate from his charges, and he had done so for logical reasons, not because he wanted to step back before he choked the living daylights out of the Dove of Valnon. Just when Grayson thought Willim had gotten over his pampered Temple helplessness--that bit with the quill in Raven's hand had been absolutely brilliant--he had to go and turn into a spoilt bird again. Which made it all the worse that he was right. The rope bridge was a disaster waiting to happen, and Grayson would not have been comfortable leading a team of Shindamiri acrobats across that span, to say nothing of three exhausted Songbirds.

The truth was, they were not the only ones exhausted. Grayson's aching shoulder had not recovered yet from catching Willim off the dais, and it felt swollen and tight under his armor, stabbing him with little needles of pain every time he moved it. Dislocated, he thought, resigned. And he hadn't helped it by pulling that trick with the halberd in the Sanctuary, and then Willim had landed on him rather hard when they fell down the dais pit. Their escape from the Temple had fetched him a few more wounds to garnish the main dish. Grayson was a professional, and he could carry on for quite some time yet and was still good for another hot fight or two, but his patience was threadbare, and the slow oppression of the tunnels sapped his strength. They reminded him too much of smaller, dirtier holes bored beneath the fortress of Kassiel on the border of Thrass, and he shuddered with memory. No, he did not blame the Dove for standing by his companions, nor did he blame the Lark for his fear. He would be just as glad as they to reach the civilized parts of the Undercity, where the roof did not press down so close, where the air smelled of the sea and the marketplace, not of age and dust and death.

But a large part of him still wanted to throttle Willim. Grayson knew the feeling all too well and didn't like it at all. When he'd first met Rouen, they'd gotten into a shouting match within five minutes for much the same reasons, and it was obvious how that had turned out. It was not a mistake he planned to make over again. No matter the beauty of the Dove's song, or his fearlessness in the face of danger, or his loyalty to what he held dear, or the way his eyes shifted color when his arrogance faltered. That was a path far more perilous than any in the Undercity, a thread of silk across a chasm with no bottom. Grayson would not be tempted to cross it, certainly not while he was the Dove's protector. So he told himself, more than once, as his shoulder ached and spiders scurried from the light of his lantern.

The passage, in spite of its ornate doorway, had very few branches. Grayson poked his lantern into a few side rooms, finding only low chambers overcrowded with bones. Many of them had their inhabitants scattered in pell-mell heaps. They had been tossed aside, either by looters who were long since as dead as their quarry, or by tremors that had gathered skulls and tibiae into unmoving pools at the ends of lopsided rooms. The lintels of the chambers bore names in old tiles and chipped plaster: The Architect's Hall, the Vault of Scribes. Graffiti on the walls heaped anarchist scorn on members of the city council ten generations gone. But nothing spoke of another route past the Hall of Heavens. Still, Grayson pressed on, though a growing sense of unease filled his mind. Though he paused once or twice to check his map, it was no use. He was far from any charted passage.

The silence was oppressive, even more than the roof of the tunnel close overhead. He was glad for the scrape of his boots on the stone, the cadence of his heartbeat, the creak of his armor. For a fleeting moment he thought to hum a marching tune, to dampen the ringing in his ears, but the tunnels twisted the notes weirdly before he got through a measure. They came back to him as a different melody, thin and eerie. At first he thought the Songbirds must be singing, half a mile back in the Hall of the Heavens, to while away the time. But the melody was coming from the black coil of tunnel ahead, and growing closer with each step Grayson took. He was not a man easily unnerved, but as the notes budded into words, twining around Grayson like a clinging vine, he found it harder and harder to keep his hand from his knife.

Starling, my darling, the Temple is falling
Pyre-smoke spills in the sky,
and who should come creeping, with nary a greeting,

but a man with a life made of lies?

"Who's there?" Grayson called, and his voice scattered the melody into nothing. The silence pressed against Grayson's ears, furry and heavy, and the darkness throbbed outside his lantern. "Show yourself!"

For a full minute Grayson stood waiting, and then another, but the music was gone, as was its maker. In its absence something brushed Grayson's face, only the tiniest stirring of air, cool and fresh. Somewhere ahead of him there was an opening, and a large one. His heart rose. It was possible he was close to a main passage, perhaps one that bordered on some Undercity tenement. Unscrupulous landlords were known to knock down backing walls to expand their holdings, while those without permanent housing made themselves comfortable squatting among the dead. Grayson had probably heard some old soul looking for a place to sleep, and had terrified him with a strange light and a voice from the depths.

It was good reasoning, Grayson thought, but it did nothing to rid him of the cobwebs prickling over his skin. The singer's choice of words had been a little too familiar for comfort. But if there was danger in the tombs, beggars or robbers or worse, he would root it out before it threatened his charges. Kestrel's knife bare in his hand, he dove forward into the dark.

The tunnel spilled open a few yards ahead, turning into a long, vaulted chamber lined with epitaphs. Grayson's lamp, long confined to smaller space, spread its light as far as it could, touching dimly on ornate crypts. Grayson started, thinking he had intruded on a room full of sleeping men. But the figures in repose upon the biers were made of stone, their features cracked and dusty, their coverlets of cold alabaster. This too was a tomb, but a tomb made to mimic a warrior's hall, with shields painted into the plaster, and braziers in the shape of a twist of spears at an encampment.

Beneath Grayson's boots, a large mosaic was full of cavorting horses, their riders wearing circular gorgets, a black-haired swordsman at their lead. Grayson swept his foot over the writing, clearing away years of undisturbed dust. The lettering he uncovered was not Vallish, or even the tongue of ancient Hasafel. It was the language of the people of Antigus, and it had been laid down by those forced by the lash to speak it in lieu of their own. Yet there was no grudge in the use of it here. The men in the crypt had been of Antigus' clan, they had spoken his language, but they had been buried as men of Valos. Grayson's grasp of the glyphs was tenuous; the language had been deliberately forgotten by many. But he knew the name in the center of the mosaic, the one above the dark-haired horseman, the same one carved deep upon the threshold of his ancestral home.

Grayce, son of Greisil, whose sword was God's, for Alveron and his Kin.

Grayson stood in the Hall of the Horsemen, burial place of the first Godswords, and the tomb of his Patriarch. For some time he was too dumbfounded to move. Only the spluttering warning of his lamp sent Grayson out of his reverie. He walked past the crypts to the side, their names sparkling at the corners of his vision. At the center dais, he set his lantern down at the foot of Grayce's tomb. It was a huge rectangle of marble, its sides engraved with images from Grayce's life. Grayce himself was carved in repose on the lid, the rigid locks of his hair flowing over his stone pillow. He was missing his nose and three of his fingers. The hilt of his sword had once been broken off, but it had been replaced in its socket, only a little loose now for its misadventure.

Grayson looked down into the face of his ancestor, feeling he should say something. The air was impatient, expectant. Grayson had not yet sorted it out when someone else spoke for him, a mocking sing-song that hardly suited the occasion.

No flowers brought for fallen knights?
Indeed, it is a sorry sight.
Your shame and lamp alone you bear
No garlands for the sleepers here
I would have thought you'd know your place
Oathless, empty, and once fa Grayce.

The last line of the song breathed itself out against his ear, as close as a lover's sigh. He whirled; there was nothing there but a seething ring of darkness pressed up against the contours of Grayce's tomb.

"I do not discourse with shadows!" Grayson shouted, louder

than he meant to. His voice echoed over and over again in the vault, fleeing down the halls. "Show yourself! How do you know who I am?"

His answer came back to him on his own echoes, now far in the distance beyond the chamber door. It was a new melody, no less sinister. And yet the voice was sweet, as sweet in its way as the Dove's, or as the new mother's over her sleeping babe's cradle. It was a Temple Bird's voice, but wilder. The singer was a man cut for his music, and his song slid like a knife-edge down Grayson's spine.

Oathless blade, as Grayce's was, the day that Heaven fell.
Nameless knight for third of Doves, drowned deep in Valnon's
*   hell.*

Why come you here? What do you seek
Among these sleeping bones?
Or would you bid these mute mouths speak
Of dust, and dark, and stone?

"Your tricks do not impress me," Grayson retorted, to the not-empty-enough crypt. "I'm not afraid of you."

"Then you are a fool, Nicholas fa Grayce."

The voice came from behind him again; Grayson turned to face it. There, perched on Grayce's tomb, was the singer. He was older than the Songbirds, but Grayson reckoned him to be younger than Kestrel. His body was as lean as a soul marker's, bare to the waist, his hair black and chaotic as it tumbled past his shoulders. Around his neck and wrists were masses of necklaces and bracelets, glinting with cheap glass beads and fragments of chain, oyster-shells polished until they shone like pearls. He wore no sword at his belt, only ragged silks in grays and lavenders, but his fingers were tipped in cruel, sharp curls of silver, like talons. In them he cradled the broken sword-hilt of Grayce's effigy. His trappings jangled like a troupe of belled jugglers as he leapt down from the tomb and into the shaking circle of lamplight, and yet Grayson had not heard the least whisper of his approach, only his singing.

"Who are you?" Grayson demanded. "And I want an answer,

not a riddle-ballad."

"I am called Starling," he announced, dropping Grayce's sword hilt back into its socket, where it landed, perfectly centered, with a dull explosion of sound. "Guardian of the dead, singer of songs, finder of lost things." He bowed, with a flourish of claws and rags and unkempt hair, and tilted a razor-edge smile at Grayson. "And you--are lost."

"I can find my way back to the Hall of the Heavens." Grayson kept his knife high. Starling was unarmed, but he looked like a madman, and Grayson did not care for the claws he wore. They stirred a memory in the back of Grayson's mind. Hadn't he seen Rouen wear them once? Yes, years ago, on Saints Night. Rouen had had sung the Lay of Hasafel in a freezing midnight sanctuary, with all the lights in the doused save for one shivering candle. He had worn archaic braids and silver bird-claws, as Thali would have done the night he sang Heaven's justice down. Songbirds did not usually wear the talons, as they were a holy weapon of old, but the singers in the Hasafel's Temple had been trained in their use, long before the coming of the sea.

"Did I say you did not know the way out of the tombs?" Starling tossed his head in contempt. "No, I said that you were lost. Your ship is sinking fast, you cannot bail out the entire sea. Your past seeks to overcome you, the water is rising. You cannot fight it as you are. You do not even know *who* you are."

"I know who I am," Grayson answered, banishing memories of Rouen until they were drowned as deep as the lost city of Hasafel. "I am Nicholas Grayson, and I seek a way out of the tombs."

"For you and for your charges left behind," Starling said in a gentle reminder, as though the Songbirds were a hat Grayson had forgotten to put on before going out. "You are not alone, I know. I've watched you. You and your little flight of lost birds."

Kestrel's knife flicked upwards to Starling's jaw. To his credit, the man did not flinch. "How much do you know of them?" Grayson demanded.

"More than there is time to sing," Starling answered, with a little shrug. "But save your knives and threats. The price of my song is high; I will not sing for my enemies."

Grayson mulled this over, wondering if that meant Starling

would not tell anyone he had seen the Songbirds. Grayson's task was too important for maybes. He would have to ensure Starling's silence, one way or another.

"Ahh," Starling said, watching Grayson's face. "And now you are thinking of becoming my enemy. That is unwise, even for a fool like you. Would you make harm when you could have help?" Starling's sharp fingertip traced over the carved letters on Grace's sword, pulling up tufts of dust and making a grating sound on the stone.

Grayson studied the man's rags, slowly lowering the knife. There was careful deliberation in his choice of ribbon and trinkets, Grayson could see that. "You sport the colors of the Dove," he said. "Do you hold him dear?"

"Do you?" Starling's mouth quirked up in a wry smile.

"If you do," Grayson pressed, "then you should aid me and my companions."

"Colors can deceive. A canny wolf wears stolen fleece, and lies low unseen in the fold." Starling tilted his head to study Grayson, as calculating as a raven. His fingers drummed along the edge of Grace's tomb, tapping out a melody only he could hear. "Whose colors do you claim, Nicholas fa Grayce? Those of the Lark you lost? Or of the Dove that needs you?"

"I no longer have any right to that name." Grayson wasn't even sure how Starling knew to ask the other questions, much less how to go about answering them. "It was forfeit, along with--"

"No man can take a name from another," Starling interrupted. "No man can force a name on one who does not wish to keep it for himself. Even Songbirds choose to be what they are, they are not simply *chosen*. Hide behind your banishment if it pleases you, but do not make so bold as to deny your birthright at the very feet of your ancestor. Not even the dead could stay mute at such offense."

"I meant no offense. It is for my offense that I no longer have my name--"

"No!" Starling made an abrupt gesture, his pointed fingers slicing through the air. "Your lack of honor is more honorable than those who kept theirs. Ask the Temple black-bird who cast you out. He fears you. He remembers. He knows the truth. You have let him name you: Grayson, sell-sword, no one. What name would you have your Dove call you? Beloved Godsword, as Grayce was to Alveron? Or do you call yourself unworthy, and so doing give your Dove a common blade with no more loyalty than a whore's bought affection? Is that all you can offer your Dove?"

Grayson felt his defenses shuddering, as they had in the wake of Willim's Evensong. There was a music in Starling's voice even when he was not singing, and it bit deep into Grayson's scars, making them as fresh as new wounds. "He is not my Dove," he said, and could not look at the sleeping face of his ancestor.

Starling arched one black brow. "Then whose Dove is he?"

Grayson wasn't sure how to answer that. "He... he is Valnon's Dove--"

"Valnon's Dove!" Starling spat, his eyes suddenly blazing. His claws shrieked down Grace's effigy. "What does Valnon know of Doves? She has broken them all. If you would see this one safe to his destiny, he will need the sword of Grayce himself to shield him. Can you draw it? Are you worthy?" Starling's hands closed over the stone sword on the tomb, marble fractured with time. The winged hilt was in his hand, his fingers twined around the chipped remnants of Grayce's.

"Grayce's sword has surely gone to dust by now," Grayson said. "And that one you hold is no use to the living. I did not come here to--"

"I don't give a single bastard's damn for why you think you came, fa Grayce." Starling vaulted over the tomb and caught Grayson's knife-hand in his armored fingers. Grayson could not wrench it away. He was held as much as his blade was, pinned by the cold light of Starling's eyes. Everything else seemed to dim around him, swallowed whole by the tomb's increasing darkness. "My charge here is a higher thing than your mercenary pride. Would you save your Dove? Would you save yourself? Grayce knew his duty." Starling's eyes flashed, he lifted the heavy stone hilt high above Grayson's face. "It is time you knew yours."

The lamp went out.

9

Willim had spent little of his life alone. His earliest memories, as a boy in the flock, were of sleeping on a straw pallet next to Ellis in a room with a score of other boys. They had learned together, bathed together, eaten together, performed together. Being a boy of the flock was to be a mere particle in a whole, a single voice in the choir, and of very little individual note. Even in times of great change, as when he was made Songbird, he had not been alone. His cutting had been done in the presence of his fellow Songbirds, the blood of their oaths mingled together in the bathing pool. They had slept that night together on his bed in the newly-opened Dove's chamber, Kestrel and Kite quietly watching over their successors, all of them passing the hours together on the way to new names and a new life. Though as Songbirds they were kept apart from others, the partitions of the Temple only gave the illusion of isolation. Sounding vents carried music and snatches of conversation, subtle reminders of the other Temple dwellers around them. It was a comfort, a hum in the background no longer heard, save for the jarring moment when it suddenly ceased.

Sitting in the dark in the Hall of the Heavens, Ellis and Dmitri asleep at his feet, Willim felt very much alone. It was not quiet, as the chamber was noisier than any other they had passed through so far. The water at the bottom of the chasm shushed softly to itself, and the countless invisible doorways each breathed a distinct sigh, like a distant audience in a darkened amphitheater. More than once Willim lifted his head, thinking he had heard a snatch of melody far away, or the nearby whisper of his name. It was the realization, time after time, that there was nobody there, perhaps not for miles, that made his heart ache for companionship, for the sound of an ordinary conversation in an adjacent room.

More than once he thought to wake Ellis, or even Dmitri, but he scolded himself for being selfish. He envied them their sleep, even though he knew it was only brought on by weariness and grief. He had said he would stay awake, and he would. Grayson would not come back to find him sleeping. But the longer Grayson was gone, the more Willim felt his energy draining away, until his head nodded above his knees, and the lantern doubled in his fading vision.

The voice of the chamber crew dull in his ears, muffled by a soft, liquid sound like rippling fabric in a swift breeze. It was maddeningly familiar. Willim's exhausted mind at last fumbled over the image of a thousand beating wings, the cooing wave of a flock of doves taking flight from the Songbirds' garden. But the only birds in the underground were the three sitting around the lamp.

I'm so sleepy I'm hearing things, Willim thought, at arm's length from himself. *I wish I'd wake up.* He forced himself to focus his gaze on the lantern, but as he beat back the tide of sleep, the noise only intensified. And with it came an acute sensation at the base of his spine: the disquieting and unmistakable feeling of being watched. At last Willim lifted his heavy head, turning to look at an upper entrance to the chamber. There, beneath the fractured stone lintel of a door half-blocked by rubble, the second Dove of Valnon stood staring back at him.

Willim's jolt of shock was enough to wake him from any dream, but Eothan remained, as solid as the walls around him. He wore his full Temple dress--the very same Temple dress Willim had hidden in his satchel--but Eothan's holy armor was pristine and gleaming in the dark, his drape touched with silver light. His face paint was a complicated maze of designs, the lacy, unfurled wings of a Songbird in the last year of his term, and as crisp as though freshly-applied. Blue eyes shone within that inky mask, but it was not the luminous gaze of the undead or the insane. The madness of Willim's cursed predecessor was nothing more than a slow tide of sorrow, drowning Willim as deep as Hasafel itself. Eothan was perfectly still, and though every bell and bangle of his trap was as mute as the dry skulls in the catacombs, there was music vibrating at all his edges.

Willim did not know how long they looked at each other. Time had fallen out of cadence with itself, as harsh and jangled as a tuneless choir. Eothan said nothing, inscrutable under his paint, and then he turned and walked deliberately out of the chamber. Willim was on his feet and up the stairs after him before the edge of the second Dove's drape vanished around the corner, his weariness forgotten and the startled voices of his companions lost to him.

Eothan was always twelve steps out of reach. His measured pace kept Willim at a run, following the ghost down unknown passages of the dead. Faint illumination hung around Eothan's tousled black hair, glinting off his platinum. It splashed in dim waves over the worn faces of soul-markers, it made the empty-eyed skulls roll their sockets in curiosity as the second Dove passed them by.

Willim trailed after the ghost in pursuit, through the meanest bone-pit, through vast underground gardens flecked with distant galaxies of crystal, along streets and byways long forgotten by the living. Eothan's pace never slowed, he never hesitated. Willim turned after him into a narrow passage lined in glistening black rock, and suddenly found himself utterly alone in the dark. Eothan had winked out like a sinking candle, and Willim was left with nothing but his blistered feet and aching limbs, and the sound of his own harsh breathing bouncing back at him.

He turned in place, bewildered and panicking, and was instantly dazzled by the harsh orange glow of Ellis' lantern crashing over him. He flung his arms in front of his face as Dmitri and Ellis ran to a stop in front of him, winded and flushed.

"What the devil are you playing at?" Dmitri demanded, taking Willim roughly by the arm, forcing the Dove to look at him. His scowl relaxed when Willim blinked back at him, his voice softening. Only then could Willim see how very frightened he had been. "Lairkeblood! You've led us for a chase!"

"Phew! I'm glad you stopped," Ellis gasped, massaging his ribs. "We yelled and yelled after you, and you never so much as twitched. I thought you'd gone mad or elf-shot, one."

"Maybe I have," Willim said, uncertain. "But surely you saw him too?" One look at their faces--Ellis' worry and Dmitri's disgust--told him otherwise.

"Saw who?" Ellis wanted to know. "All I saw was you taking off like all the hounds of Antigus were at your heels. If you hadn't made such a racket getting up we'd still be asleep and none the wiser."

"I--" Willim began, and looked back at the corridor. "I thought I was--" He trailed off, no longer certain of what he had seen. Eothan, if it had been Eothan, had brought him swiftly to nothing more enlightening than a dead-end passage. "I don't even know," he admitted.

"Well we certainly don't," Dmitri retorted. "Do you even know where we are anymore?"

Willim's silence said everything that needed to be said. They were hopelessly lost in the labyrinth, and Willim was the one who had led them there, far beyond the sweep of any soul-marker's arm.

"I lost track after four turns," Ellis admitted, his face bleak.

Dmitri swore with an obscenity and inventiveness Willim would have admired had the situation been different. "There's nothing for it. We'll have to try and backtrack. Maybe we left enough marks in the dirt. Though I shouldn't be surprised if we don't live to find our way out."

"I'm sorry," Willim said, more miserable than he thought it possible to be. Was Eothan so eager for companions, that he would lead them to a slow death? Defeated, Willim slumped back against the wall, and then jumped back again at the sound it made. It was not the opaque thud of stone he had expected, but a sweet hollow echo, as full of promise as an empty sket belly.

"Did you hear that?" Ellis said, brightening underneath the heavy mantle of his fatigue. "There's something back there!"

"Probably just another passage on the other side," Dmitri said, and shoved Willim's pack into his arms. "Here, I'm tired of carrying your share. Let's go, Ellis. If I'm going to wander aimlessly until I die, I'd rather get on with it."

"Now hold on, hold on," Ellis said, running his hands over the wall. "There's something funny about this bit."

"Yes," Dmitri snapped, "It's exactly as amusing as every other wall down here. Don't go looking for some miraculous exit, Ellis. Things like that only happen in song-cycles."

As if insulted by such doubts, the wall gave a violent shudder under Ellis' fingertips. A tongue of rock withdrew into the cavern floor and revealed an uneven rectangle of dim light. Startled, Ellis yelped and took several steps back away from it. At once, the opening slid shut again, enclosing them in rock once more.

Ellis gave Dmitri a look so loaded it would have been criminal for a civilian to possess it after dark. He swelled up to deliver a lovingly-crafted "I told you so," but the Lark did not give him the chance.

"Counterweighted," Dmitri said, with a little tsk of surprise, looking down at the floor. He took a few deliberate steps forward, and one section of stone sank an inch lower than the rest of the cavern floor, incised into a neat square beneath his boot. The thin panel of rock slid down again, obligingly. "Clever," Dmitri admitted. "Probably centuries old, and still works. I wonder why it's here?"

Willim blinked at the gray space beyond the doorway. It was not the lightness that compelled him, but the air. It hit the three of them in a cool wave, fresher than anything that had filled their lungs for hours. They stared at each other like sleepwalkers suddenly wakened.

"Listen!" Ellis said, seizing Dmitri's hand, and was just as quickly shaken off. "Do you hear that?"

"Horses," Willim said. The sound was distant but distinctive, iron-shod hooves on cobblestone. "We must be close to an opening somewhere, leading out onto an Undercity street." He looked back down the tunnel, hoping for the ruddy glow of Grayson's lantern. There was nothing behind them, not even Eothan's ghost. "We've found a way out, but I have no idea how to get back to tell Grayson about it."

"Or how to return here if we did find him," Ellis added.

"You're forgetting something," Dmitri said, and moved off the trigger. The slab of rock slid upwards into its socket once more.

"Dmitri," Ellis cautioned, eyeing the door nervously, "it's rather elderly, for a mechanism, and it's probably only meant to do that so many times."

"We can't all go out at once," Willim said, realizing what Dmitri meant by the demonstration. "Someone has to hold the door open."

"If we're going out it at all," Dmitri answered. "If we do, Grayson may never find us. If we don't, we'll starve down here." He folded his arms, looking for all the world like Kestrel when he posed a particularly thorny question of musical theory. "So, Dove of Valnon, what do we do?"

"Sorry, any reason you're asking me?" Willim snapped, shaken out of a frantic contemplation of their options, all of them few and none pleasant.

"You outrank us," Ellis reminded Willim, in a small voice.

"Fine time for you two to admit that," Willim grumbled. "You never paid any attention to it before. Let me think." Irritating as Grayson could be, Willim owed him his life, several times over. Even if he didn't, no man deserved exile under the tunnels. "Could Grayson track us in the dust, do you think?"

"Possibly," Dmitri admitted, with a shrug. "Most of the passages we went through had a dirt layer, and we weren't exactly delicate in our pursuit. He could certainly tell where we went from the Hall of the Heavens, since we were in such a scramble to follow you."

Willim hefted the weight of his bag, and inspiration struck him with more speed than it ever had for a composition. "I have it," he said. "Dmitri, you weren't a Temple foundling, were you? You've lived out in the city with your family before coming to the flock."

"Yes, until I was six, and it was on the upper level." Dmitri made a face. "For all the good that does down here."

"It's better than what I've got, or Ellis," Willim said, balancing his pack on his knee and digging through the contents. "You're the best chance we have of getting to this Jerdon fellow the Wing told us to meet. Maybe if you can get us to the right part of the Undercity, we can find our way to him."

"Why didn't you just say that?" Dmitri asked, in utter exasperation. "He lives off Gerod's Rise on the southwest terrace wall of the Undercity. I've carried Kestrel's outgoing letters down to the Laypriests before. He corresponded with Jerdon quite often."

"Saints," Ellis breathed. "I never thought I'd be glad you're such a dammed snoop."

"They were addressed on the *outside*," Dmitri demurred. "If I was a snoop, I would have opened them and read them."

"And we're all sure you didn't do that," Ellis retorted.

Dmitri, very wisely, did not respond.

"I honestly don't care if you were going through Kestrel's letters, or his linen-press," Willim said, pulling St. Alveron's heavy collar out of his bag. "Can you get us there, Dmitri?"

"I suppose," Dmitri allowed. "I can hit the right area, at least."

"Good. We'll find him, and if Grayson hasn't tracked us by then, we'll come back with this Jerdon fellow and find him ourselves. Here, get my Temple trap out of your bags and put it on the trigger. I'll stand on it, and you two go out." Willim put the collar on the counterweighted section of floor, and the opening cracked a grudging half-foot. "It'll slow down the door and leave a gap at the top. Hopefully it's enough for me to slide over."

"You're just going to leave St. Alveron's armor here?" Ellis said, aghast.

"Dmitri said this door hasn't been used in years. Nobody will know to look for it, and my armor's probably safer here than with us." Willim took the cuff Dmitri handed him, and added it to the pile. "And it'll tell Grayson where we went, and how to follow us."

"Not bad," Dmitri said. "When I asked you what you wanted us to do, I never really expected you to come up with anything."

"*Thanks*," Willim said. "Is that the last of it, Ellis?"

"Yes," Ellis said, buckling his bag again. "At least cover it up with your drape, Willim."

"No, I want it to shine if the light hits it. There." Satisfied with his arrangement, and that the door had opened over halfway at the weight of the armor, Willim traced Jerdon's name in the dirt around the stack of jeweled platinum. Once he finished, he added his own weight to the trigger for Ellis and Dmitri to go through, then let his armor hold the door down enough for him to slither through the gap after them.

Once on the other side, Willim felt as though he had just escaped the womb. The texture of the darkness around them was different, the air charged with the energy of other heartbeats. They were in a narrow passageway with stairs leading up out of one side, and it was from there that the breeze came. "Hoods up," Willim said, pulling his own close around him. "Without our colors and our paints, most people in Valnon won't know us, and only Raven knows we're missing. With any luck we're boring enough to avoid notice."

"Ellis is, and I can make do," Dmitri said grimly, "but that hair of yours makes you look like a pearl on a paving-stone. I suppose you could pass as a distant cousin of one of the fa Ranseys. There's dozens of them and they all have your coloring."

"Maybe you are one of them, Willim," Ellis said, brightly. "Someone had to dump you on the Priestess' Chapel when you were an infant."

"Likely without looking back," Dmitri said, as Willim mulled over the curious prospect of his own origins. "The young bloods of the fa Ranseys keep half the Undercity brothels in business; they probably have more bastards than they have summerhouses on Lake Clarie."

Willim's fleeting notion of having noble blood was effectively squashed. "It hardly matters now," he said, with the briskness of a flock boy sweeping dust beneath a rug. "Dmitri, we're in your hands. Try not to get us caught or killed, will you?"

"I'll do my best," Dmitri said, and vaulted up the stairs. A short, steep walk brought them to a rusted iron grate at the end of an alley, the pronged bottom spanning a dry gutter full of old trash. It was the sort of place easily overlooked by people indifferent to Valnon's tunnels and sewers.

"Locked?" Willim asked, as Dmitri rattled the latch.

"No, just old." Dmitri put his shoulder to the grate, and it opened with an annoyed squawk of hinges. "Put out the light, we won't need it here." Dmitri led them out of the alley and into the street beyond. They had emerged into a quiet residential district, with many-storied houses built up against the side of the cavern. The streets were wide and well-kept, but empty, to Willim's relief. Even under the safety of his hood, he felt exposed. It was well past time for any civilized business in that corner of the Undercity. The bottom-floor shops were all dark, and the streetlamps illuminated only empty cobblestones and shuttered windows. Willim would have preferred to slink along from shadow to shadow, like a thief, but Dmitri took his path right through the most well-lit areas, his chin and shoulders back, radiating an air of confident resolve.

"Will you two quit skulking around back there?" he demanded, once the alleyway had been swallowed up by the perpetual twilight of the Undercity. "I've never seen anyone acting so suspiciously. Just pretend you're walking from our rooms down to the archives, and no one will look at us twice."

As though to prove his point, a pair of well-fed gentlemen rounded the corner ahead of them, their path lit by a hired lamp-bearer. They were engrossed in their own conversation about the exorbitant going rate for tufted wool and the equally high cost of the boys at the Swallowtail. Dmitri passed right by them with an indifferent nod, got a gruff good evening in return, and nothing more.

"See?" he said, when they had moved beyond the merchants, "It's simply a matter of looking like you know what you're doing."

Dmitri paused at a side street, studying the signpost. "Looks like we're on the right side of the Cavern, but we'll have to take the scenic route around to avoid Fishmarket; I'd rather not end my days raped and robbed and stuffed into an offal barrel."

"You make it sound so enticing," Ellis said, with a shudder.

Dmitri did not set an idler's pace. The street he took descended in a sharp zigzag down from the wall of the cavern, and the landscape changed quickly. The houses were lower now, but closer together, and the second stories protruded so far over the first that they often met overhead. Eventually the Songbirds were enclosed in a passage made by the connected buildings, the wooden eaves overhead hung with placards offering tailoring and jeweler's shops. Willim, in spite of his anxieties, could not suppress a certain flutter of excitement. Never before had he walked freely through the streets of Valnon, never before had he passed anywhere unnoted and unnoticed. The thrill of his own anonymity was as intoxicating as the feeling of freedom.

"Where are we?" Ellis whispered, as though the place demanded silence. In truth, there was a lingering, late-night bustle to the neighborhood, with lamps glowing from upper windows, the muted noise of conversation as the residents worked into the night. From one upper balcony came the sound of someone playing the sket, and a young woman in a maid's smock smiled at them as she put out a plate of scraps for the cat. The air smelled of lamp oil, hot charcoals, and fish stew.

"Dmitri," Ellis persisted, tugging the Lark's sleeve. "I asked you a question. Where are we?"

"This is Gemsplit Close," Dmitri said, sounding bored. "It's the best of the Closes. Most of the mid-level craftsmen and merchants live here."

"I like it here," Ellis said, smiling back at the maid and making her blush. "It's homey."

"You would think so," Dmitri said, with disdain. "Try to pick your feet up, will you? We're crossing over into Saint's Walk, and I'd as soon get through it as fast as possible."

"Phew, are you a rotten tour guide," Ellis grumbled, but he matched his pace with Dmitri's as they crossed over a bridge and down into an area much brighter and louder than the one they left behind.

"Saint's Walk is the pleasure district," Dmitri said, in a surly tone not at all likely to disprove Ellis' claim. "The gaming-houses are here, as well as the better brothels in the Undercity. Nobles come down here for their entertainments, then go back to their households above. If we had purses, I'd advise you to keep them inside your cloaks. As it is, don't linger. Lingering can cost you, here."

"Doesn't seem to me like a place a saint would frequent," Willim said. Though built much like Gemsplit Close, almost every door and window on the street was lit and open. A dozen different songs mingled together in the air, with a regular percussion of laughter and the occasional roar of drunken merriment.

A swinging sign caught Willim's eye, sporting a fanciful bird nipping its own tail feathers, its plumage all the colors of the rainbow. *The Swallowtail*. It was the brothel the fat merchants had been complaining about. Ellis had been distracted by more than the sign. A woman was watching them from the balcony just above it, her gown a layered drape of vivid silks beneath her openwork metal bodice, each color more sheer than the last, all flattering the rosy glow of her skin. Her hair was the color of old gold, and her eyes were on the three Songbirds. When the other two followed Ellis' gaze to her, she broke into a smile that melted over them like warm tallow.

"Good evening, Gentlemen. First time on the Walk?"

"Uh, n-no," Ellis said, his eyes whipping over her, from her white throat down to the slipper dangling off her foot as she swayed one bare leg on the railing. She was wearing a trinket of copper and garnets around her ankle; the Thrush's colors for earthly prosperity, for the full radiance of the sun. Willim thought she hardly needed the help.

"We've been down here... a few times," Ellis went on.

"Ellis," Willim hissed, in warning.

"Oh, well," the Madam said, for there was no longer any doubt as to what she was, ruling over her bright house like an incandescent queen, "You haven't been coming to my house, then. And if you've not come to the Swallowtail, lads, you've not done the Walk."

"I don't think we can afford..." Ellis began, and Dmitri seized his arm.

"Ellis. For the love of Lairke. Shut up."

The woman laughed. "Well, you're not the first young men to come to the Walk and wind up with only the lining left in your purses." She bent down as though to get a better look at them, and Willim was concerned that her bodice was not up to the demand. Ellis' eyes were on the verge of falling out of his head, and the madam was on the verge of falling out of everything else. "But if you wanted to earn some coin," she said, with a calculating gleam, "I'd be willing to take you in. I've the most honest contract in the Undercity, and board and room included."

"We're hardly to the point of selling our virtues on a plank for base gold," Dmitri said under his breath, as he dragged Ellis away. "But we'll keep it in mind."

Willim managed an apologetic farewell to the madam as he left, turning just in time to see the slim figure of a man join her on the balcony. He was dressed in only his breeches, wine glass in hand. Even at a distance, Willim could see the lace of scars across his body, including one that slid down over his face, nipping off the end of one eyebrow. His red hair looked bloody in the lamplight, his eyes as cold as the heart of the sea. They pinned Willim in place briefly, and in that moment Willim felt as though the stranger had turned him inside out and scraped every last secret off the inside of his skin. He hurried through the crowd to catch up with Dmitri and Ellis, who was having difficulty shaking off the encounter.

"That dress was something else! You could see all of her--"

"If you say one more word, Ellis," Dmitri said, "I will kill you."

Ellis shut his mouth. Somehow, Dmitri didn't leave any doubts as to his sincerity.

"Did either of you see the man with her?" Willim asked, glancing over his shoulder. The streets were busy with revelers and idlers, and none of them gave the Songbirds more than a moment's attention.

"I only saw that we've wasted enough time already," Dmitri said, and the subject was officially closed. All the same, Willim felt the stranger's eyes on him long after they had left Saint's Walk and the Swallowtail behind.

Dmitri was in no mood for further distractions. He herded his fellow Songbirds through the streets with the single-minded determination of a juggernaut, and if Willim or Ellis so much as paused by a shop window, they were quickly treated to the scathing edge of the Lark's tongue. In this manner the gaiety and lights of Saint's Walk quickly vanished behind them, and the overhanging stories of the Closes soon gave way to wide avenues lined in elaborate lamps. Houses sat back from the streets behind stone walls, their tops trimmed in the blackwork lace of thief guards, their gates showing glimpses of courtyards flowering with trees made of agate and glass.

The only thing that marked their passage was a dog sleeping on the steps just inside one of the gates, as it thumped its tail hopefully but did not budge from its post. But still Willim felt followed, and Dmitri did not need to urge them to keep up the pace, even though the road rose steeply now and Willim's legs were aching.

"I know," Dmitri said, when Willim cast a searching glance into the empty street behind him. "Someone's following us."

"What?" Ellis started to turn as well, but Dmitri hissed a warning to keep him from it.

"Act normally. I'd rather we didn't let on we knew. It's why I didn't say anything before."

"How long has he been behind us?" Willim asked, fighting the urge to look again.

"Since Saint's Walk," Dmitri admitted. "This is one way to get back to the surface from there, so it's not odd that there'd be foot traffic coming the same way, but I doubt anyone with pure intentions would bother hiding himself so well. He doesn't want us to notice him."

"Then how did you know he was there?" Ellis demanded.

"Because unlike you two, I was paying attention to my surroundings instead of gawping at them." Dmitri sighed through his nose, exasperation not quite managing to conceal his unease. "We're almost to Gerod's Rise, and that's patrolled regularly by Queensguard. He wouldn't try anything there."

"I don't think he's going to wait that long," Willim said. The red-haired man from the Swallowtail's balcony emerged from the darkness behind them, the cockade in his hat casting a ragged crown of shadows around his face. He met Willim's eyes and smiled like a fox in a dovecote, feathers and blood around his jaws. Willim felt again as though he really should have stayed in bed, or possibly in his cradle.

"Run," Dmitri commanded, sprinting off with the same grace and speed he displayed in his festival-day dancing. He took a sudden turn down a narrow, dark side-street behind one of the houses, skimming over discarded bottles and heaps of apple-peels, leaving Ellis and Willim to follow as best as possible in his wake.

Willim, however, had not been born under a dancing planet. He edged around a stack of barrels that Ellis had skirted with ease, but the sleeve of his tunic snagged on the rough wood. It spun him off balance, nearly sending him to the ground. Ellis caught him at the last moment, but the delay was enough to narrow the distance between them and the stranger. Their pursuer was close enough for Willim to see the glint of his green eyes, and his outstretched hand grazed Willim's shoulder.

"Get the hell off!" Ellis shouted, and kicked the barrel over, sending a slurry of fetid-smelling rubbish out into the alley.

Willim heard the man curse, heard the ripping sound of his own sleeve, and heard Dmitri calling them from somewhere above. The alley opened out onto a bright, empty courtyard, and a tumbrel sat parked beneath a low wall. Willim did not have a chance to ponder the convenience of it, or the gap in the fanciful iron spikes on the wall above. Dmitri swarmed up and over it, leaning down to catch Willim's hand and haul him up.

"He's just going to follow us," Willim gasped, halfway over the wall with his boots scrabbling for purchase.

"The hell he will," Ellis answered. He jumped onto the tumbrel, kicked the brake, and caught Dmitri's outstretched hand as the cart rattled down the steep street, right towards their pursuer. Willim caught a glimpse of the man's startled face before the cart collided with the barrels in the alley. He did not see if he emerged from the chaos, as Ellis shoved Willim hard on his backside and all three of them fell over the wall, landing with a discordant crash on a slippery pile of charcoal.

"You call *this* being hardly noticed?" Ellis exclaimed, dusting his coal-blackened hand on his pants.

Willim's only answer was a ragged cough. His lungs were full of coal dust, his heart thudded painfully from their near escape, and he had landed badly. He sucked in a wheezing breath to retort, but it all escaped him as a door opened somewhere beyond the darkness of the coal-pile. The brightness was blotted out in the middle by a tall, indistinct figure, throwing a long shadow out across a perfectly-manicured stone courtyard.

"Well, that's that," Ellis said, in despair. "Unless our resident brain can come up with some way to convince this fellow we aren't trying to rob him blind."

Dmitri could only shake his head as the figure drew closer.

"Well then!" the stranger said, in a clipped, cultured accent that placed him as a denizen of exactly nowhere in particular. "It's well past time you got here, Your Graces. I was beginning to worry." The figure stepped into the street-lamplight, resolving into a long-faced gentleman in a green Iskati tunic and gold spectacles, his brown ponytail doing its level best to escape its ribbon.

Dmitri started to his feet with a cry of recognition. "Jerdon!" he gasped, his perfect voice made raw with relief.

The queen's physician bestowed a benevolent smile on the Lark of Valnon, then put one hand to his heart and bent forward in a penitent's bow. "Indeed. I don't believe I've had the pleasure of introducing myself before, and certainly not to the Dove and Thrush. They were rather drugged when last we met, and it was hardly an occasion for small-talk."

"When last we met?" Willim asked, struggling to rise. The realization that they were in no immediate danger had left his limbs feeling rubbery and uncooperative.

"Ah," Jerdon said, offering Willim a hand up, and slapping some of the coal-dust off Ellis' shoulder. "A matter of professional duty, Your Grace, nothing more."

"Jerdon performed the surgery of our office when Raven refused to do so," Dmitri explained, as the doctor bobbed his head in an apologetic manner. "Kestrel told me. He spoke of you often."

"So you know what he looks like?" Ellis was dubious.

Dmitri answered Jerdon, instead. "I've seen you at Dawning with Kestrel, in the east end of the sanctuary."

"So that's how you knew me," Jerdon said, a bit of pleased color coming up into his face at being recognized by the Lark. "But I do not think we should confine our dear Preybird to the realms of past tense just yet, any more than I should confine my guests to

118

standing in a dank courtyard." He sidestepped the coal pile with the deft indifference of a street acrobat, and caught the Thrush's elbow in one hand and Willim's in the other. "Come in, come in. You'll forgive me for saying so, of course, but I must confess that the lot of you look rather worse for the wear."

Willim supposed that Jerdon's house was typical for a well-to-do Undercity dwelling, but it was nevertheless an exotic locale for a Songbird who had spent nearly his whole life inside the Temple's walls. Willim could not get his eyes all over the place fast enough, as Jerdon breezed through the foyer. The front door of the house and Jerdon's offices lay adjacent to each other, and Willim caught a glimpse of shelves lined with herb-jars. Jerdon's surgeon's tools hung on hooks on the wall, their menace not subdued by their tidy polish. The house had for its back the very bones of Valnon itself, built right against the cavern wall. The stairs to the second floor split along the landing to accommodate a great fin of black stone that thrust into the house like the prow of a ship, lending the civilized environment a certain air of savagery. Its surface was highly polished, and the veins of marble shimmered in the light of dozens of silver filigree lamps. On the first floor, beneath the stairs, an open doorway revealed the reflections of candles on water, and Willim could hear the gentle splashing of a bathing pool. Directly opposite was the entrance to a banquet hall, and it was here that Jerdon led his bedraggled guests. There were no windows in the room, but the chamber walls were painted in a lively fresco to suggest rolling hills and vineyards instead of the cold confines of the Undercity. It was not empty.

"Grayson!" It was not the first thing Willim intended to say, but it was the first thing that came out. Grayson sat at a long, low table amid piles of floor cushions, the remains of a late meal scattered on the table. He had his shirt flung over one bare shoulder, the other was bandaged and purple with bruises. Beside his plate was a moldy old chunk of marble, carved in the shape of a sword-hilt. Grayson's expression on seeing the Songbirds standing there whole in the doorway was not one of betrayal at being left behind, but of dumbfounded relief. He managed to get it off his face fast enough, but Willim was nevertheless grateful.

"I think I asked you to stay put," Grayson said, trying to fold his arms, but wincing with pain.

"And I think you said you'd be back in an hour," Willim retorted, but unable to put the resonance in it that he wanted. Relief had quenched his indignation, and he felt his legs wavering under him.

"Now now, none of that," Jerdon cooed. "You're all here, though you did take a roundabout way, and that's what matters. I found Grayson unconscious in a heap on my back stoop, neatly delivered, no more than an hour ago. Though I admit, when I learned he was alone, I was concerned for your safety. I sent my snipe out to look for you, and I'm afraid she will be quite put-out to find you've gotten here before her."

"How did you get there?" Ellis said, in some confusion. "We left him miles behind us, on the other side of the Undercity!"

Jerdon fluttered his sleeve at Grayson, dismissively. "There are quite a few characters that live beneath the city, Your Grace, and it seems Grayson ran into the most interesting of them, that is all."

"You make this Starling out to be no more than a fire-juggler or writer of morality plays," Grayson said, affronted.

"Starling?" Dmitri repeated. "The ghoul of the tombs? My mother told me tales of him to make me obey when I was a boy. I thought he was some invention of hers."

"Oh, he's real," Jerdon said. "Though not technically a ghoul, and in spite of popular tales he probably cares very little whether or not you eat all your dinner, or keep your chamber tidy. He is a simple tunnel-dweller, though perhaps a bit mad."

"I still say he's dangerous," Grayson growled, rubbing a tender place on his forehead where he had been struck, hard, with the stone hilt of his ancestor's sword.

"There are worse dangers," Jerdon said, before turning back to the Songbirds. "I do apologize." Jerdon wiped his spectacles on one of his sashes. "I have a few ways out of my house, you see. The stone in my hall backs onto long corridor which leads to a hidden door. Through that is a passage further into the tombs, and a hidden door that leads to a grate on the far side of the Rise."

"Hidden door?" Willim said, weakly. "Leading to a grate?"

Dmitri groaned. "You mean if we'd found the door on the other side, we would have taken it straight here?"

"Is that how you got out of the tombs?" Jerdon blinked

owlishly at them for a moment. "What a fascinating stroke of luck for you! Yes, I suppose you would have had a shorter walk, and come out through the section of cave wall you saw in my foyer." Jerdon beamed. "But I expect you enjoyed your little stroll through the Undercity. Quite a treat for three cloistered Songbirds, hmm?"

"Treat!" Ellis exclaimed. "We were almost knifed by some scarred-up ginger bastard in a cockaded hat!"

Jerdon and Grayson exchanged an inscrutable look.

"Hm," Jerdon said, after apparently sorting through several responses and deeming that one the best to be had. "Well, compared to the rest of your evening, I suspect it was an adventure hardly worth the mentioning. And now that we're all here, perhaps you'd better tell us just why you took off without waiting for your bodyguard to come with you. Tea?"

10

Willim found the weight of sleep a heavy burden to shed. Every time he pushed it away, it tumbled back over him again, submerging him in half-dreams and keeping him in the warm shallows near waking. In such a place, the fear and fire of the Temple's fall was a distant memory. The smell of hot food at last dragged him into consciousness, and he fumbled for the strength to sit up. Voices murmured above him, indistinct.

"Grateful as I am for your aid," Grayson was saying, his irritation barely tempered with chagrin, "I don't fancy the thought of that madman knowing about the Songbirds' escape route. If Raven's men were to find him, they would find us, and in short order. That back door of yours only has secrecy as a defense, and Starling knows about it. I'm going to go look for him just as soon as I can--"

"And abandon your charges here, to a man you trust even less?" It was Jerdon's distinctive voice, matter-of-fact over the clink of a teapot. "Now, don't make that face at me. I know full well that my connections to the crown are hardly reassuring to you. I could swear my loyalty to the Temple until I was blue, and it would do little to convince you."

"Your insistence that Starling is trustworthy is even less convincing."

"I said nothing of the sort. What I said was that Starling is a gibbering lunatic. He is not a man you set out to find. He is a man that finds you. But he leads more out of the tombs than he leaves in, and he only murders looters. Moreover, his devotion to the Temple is nothing short of zealotry. You heard his singing?"

"I did," Grayson admitted, grudgingly.

"Then you already understand my point. The grand bazaar of Iskarit might see five slaves castrated in an hour; it does not make them Songbirds. For a man to do such a thing to himself, and then to have the music to go along with it, to abandon all civilized life for the sake of his own art and the catacombs' acoustic marvels..." Jerdon's shrug was audible. "Such a man would not be the sort to idly blab information for something as mundane as money or status. Even if Raven knew to look for him, he would never find him; even if he found him, he would never get sense out of him. Only Starling knows what Starling will do, and he's as mad as the sea is deep."

"I'd still rather he hadn't seen us."

"Then you will forgive me for saying, Grayson, but if that were so, odds are good you and your charges would at this hour be in a very perilous position."

"More perilous than the one we're already in, you mean?"

"My dear fellow. We have all three Songbirds, safe and warm and whole, and Raven does not. That's quite good for before breakfast. And speaking of which, I think our Dove is stirring."

Willim pushed himself up on his elbows, and blinked at his surroundings. He had fallen asleep shortly after he sat down at the table. His explanation of Eothan's ghost had been vague at best; he was exhausted and didn't relish the idea of sounding insane. Instead he said only that he had seen a stranger in the passages and followed him, but he wasn't sure anyone had bought his tale. Grayson and Jerdon were both shooting him curious looks over the breakfast dishes as he rose.

"Care for something to eat, Your Grace?" Jerdon asked.

"Yes." Willim sat up carefully. He had slept solidly, but his whole body ached. "If Ellis left any food for me, that is."

"He did rather put it away this morning," Jerdon said brightly, plucking a clean teacup from the tray and filling it. "But after your long walk last night I can hardly say I'm surprised. He and Dmitri are in the baths, and I expect you'll want to join them as soon as you've eaten."

The tea Jerdon served was as sweet as any sold off a stand in Iskarit, strong enough to stand a spoon in and lightened with a good deal of cream. Willim thought he'd never tasted anything so delicious in his entire life. He emptied the cup at once and Jerdon, as though expecting this, poured him another right away.

"How are you feeling, Willim?" Grayson asked. He had been in the baths as well; his hair was still damp and the wound Raven had made in his cheek was not so terrible now that it was cleaned.

"Hungry," Willim said, tugging the bowl of porridge closer. "But otherwise nothing worth mentioning. What about you?" Willim raked his eyes over Grayson's collection of bandages, a far more impressive set than the few scrapes Willim had acquired.

"You're far more injured than I am."

"I'm afraid your friend here misuses his body most grievously," Jerdon answered, before Grayson had finished opening his mouth. "Dislocated shoulder joint, sprained wrist, enough cuts to make a paper-lace screen out of himself, and that lovely pair of lumps ruining his good features for the moment. You really must take better care of your bodyguards, my boy. You've only just gotten this one."

Willim tallied Grayson's injuries and felt a pang of remorse. He looked down into his teacup, but the only reflection he saw was the memory of Boren's battered face. "I'm sorry," he said. "I seem to be too rough with them."

"That's enough, Jerdon," Grayson warned. "Firstly, I'm his kidnapper, not his bodyguard, and secondly, I'm responsible for the wounds I take, not the Dove."

"Willim," Willim said, in soft reminder. "You shouldn't be calling me anything else right now."

"Well," Jerdon relented, "that much is true. We're a long way from Raven's ears down here, but there's no need to be careless. And now that the kidnapping bit is done, I think *bodyguard* is quite a suitable title. Or would you rather be called his keeper?"

"I'm not sure I'd want the keeping of him," Grayson said, but lightly, to get a rise from his charge.

Willim only prodded his spoon at a lump in his porridge, uneasiness taking most of the edge off his hunger. "Do you think they're all right? Hawk and Kestrel and the others?"

Grayson inhaled to reply, the answer hesitant on his face, but Jerdon's easy confidence overrode the swordsman's caution.

"I am certain that they are still alive. They are more canny and capable than most give them credit for. Kestrel is not the only Preybird with sharp talons beneath his feathers, and I expect Raven will soon learn that his fellows can rend and tear as well as any of their namesakes." He topped off Willim's tea again, and nudged the plate of honeycakes a little closer to Willim's reach. Whether by chance or design, the action made Jerdon's large ring flash in the lamplight. It was a cabochon of mirror-black onyx framed in silver wings, opulent enough to have once been Temple tribute. He was, as many scholars were, a devotee of St. Lairke of the Dawning, the Lark's saint. In Valnon, much could be gleaned about a man based on which Songbird he favored, and just how prominently that devotion was displayed. Willim was comforted in spite of himself.

"We are at a slight tactical disadvantage at the moment, but as Grayson here will tell you, it is possible to win a game of peril with only two pieces left standing. Difficult, yes, but quite possible." Jerdon tipped up his spectacles, a fond smile on his thin face. "I realize you may feel utterly without allies, my boy, but you have more than you think, and they are formidable."

"Formidable allies," Grayson said, planting his elbows on the table. "Such as?"

Jerdon smiled, evasive and serene.

Grayson shook his head. "I wouldn't accept your hospitality at all, to be honest, except that we are here by the Wing's order." His eyes narrowed in as much a smile as in suspicion. He was not to be swayed by anything so superficial as a display of Lark-tribute. After all, it was a former Lark that had betrayed them. "But I wonder if half of what you say can be trusted."

"My dear sir, that is a truly generous compliment," Jerdon said, with a bow. "Most of my colleagues would insist they cannot trust *anything* that I say. And now, Willim, if you've finished your breakfast, I'll show you to the baths."

With a last glance at Grayson (and shrug of indifference from his bodyguard) Willim followed the physician into the main hall.

"I wished to put you up in guest rooms, but alas, Grayson tells me you're more defensible if you're all kept in one place," Jerdon explained. "But I don't wish you to think of my home as your prison, only as a haven. Make yourselves as comfortable as you can, though I know your hearts must be greatly troubled by what you have endured. I cannot tell you how sorry I am that you've been forced to this exile." For a moment Jerdon's face had a look of such heartache that Willim wondered how even Grayson could doubt him. Jerdon shook himself, and his cheery, unrevealing smile was back in place once again. "At any rate! The privy is there under the stairs, and mind you, the water comes right up from the sea and is very cold. Don't mind the occasional shrimp. Help yourself to the library, it is upstairs and to the left along the landing. If you take the door to the right it will lead you up into my modest little garden, but I would let your guard dog know first if you plan to go out. Just as well, it's beastly weather today."

"You have a garden?" Willim asked, stunned. "Underground?"

"Ah," Jerdon raised one long finger. "Living smack up against the cavern wall does have its advantages, my boy. I'm sure you'd hardly call it a garden, compared to what you have in the Temple, but it's a bit of sunlight and fresh air, and more than once I've been glad for it. I'll be delighted to give you a tour in a little while. But first I'm sure you'll want to freshen up." Jerdon swept aside a curtain of clinking beads, the sound a memory of Willim's own chamber in the Temple, and gestured Willim through the door. "It would be impolite of me to linger. I fear you may not have the privacy you knew in the Temple, but I shall endeavor to respect your boundaries as holy Songbirds. I trust you will find the baths adequate."

Willim thanked him, though Jerdon was already on his way back to Grayson, and stepped into the baths. While not as ornate as the ones in the Songbirds' chambers, they were quite a few steps above adequate. The frescoes on the walls made it seem as though the narrow space was triple its actual size, filled with other bathers and fanciful pools in the distance, an illusion so complete that Willim was at first unsure of the room's actual dimensions. A warm mist swirled around the single real fountain in the middle of a triangular pool. Ellis sat on the ledge beneath it, his head back in grateful abandon as the water drummed down on his skin.

Dmitri had already finished his ablutions, and was dressed in borrowed clothes of cream-colored linen. He looked strange and ghostly, sitting on one of the cushioned benches with a solitary game board in his lap. His hand hovered forgotten over the pegs, his eyes staring through the wall as though he sought to reach through it to wherever Kestrel was. When Ellis spoke, he started, and the peg in his hand clattered loudly onto the floor.

"Ah, so the Dove of Valnon yet lives!" Ellis vaulted off the ledge with a splash, and sloshed through the waist high-pool to Willim. "I don't know what devil took your nose to lead you here, Willim, but I'd like to thank him. This is an exile I can endure."

"Let's hope we don't have to endure it long," Dmitri said in irritation, bending over to rescue his lost game-piece. "Every moment the Temple sinks deeper into chaos."

"There's not much we can do about that," Willim said. He shed his clothes with a noise of relief before plunging into the pool to scrub the smell of soot out of his hair.

"Dmitri," Ellis announced, with an air of great ceremony, "doesn't quite trust our host."

"Really?" Willim dipped his head back to slick his bangs out of his eyes. "Even though he's Kestrel's friend, and he favors St. Lairke? You were glad enough to see him last night."

"Last night I was just glad to be alive," Dmitri said, "But if he truly favored Saint Lairke, then I would have seen that ring pass through my tribute box at least once during my term."

"Maybe it's an heirloom and he didn't want to risk you keeping it," Ellis argued. "There's no guarantee that a Songbird will let the Temple sell back tribute once he's done with it."

"We'd be up to our ears in baubles if we didn't," Willim put in, "but not everybody knows that. For all you know, Dmitri, that ring was tribute for Kestrel, or Hawk, or for some other Lark way back when. Just because he didn't send it to you doesn't mean he doesn't adhere to Saint Lairke, or that he isn't loyal to the Temple--"

"It's just a feeling I've got," Dmitri said, looking more irritated than ever. "And you don't have to imply that I'm jealous just because he values some other Lark higher than me. I know full well there are plenty of Temple patrons who think it's ill luck for a Lark to be blond, or who liked Kestrel's coloratura better than mine. Jerdon's Kestrel's friend, and he's risking his own life to keep us here. I'm just saying, I think he's hiding something."

Willim clattered in the soap jars, unleashing a soft cloud of clove and cassia scents. "Well he certainly doesn't have to divulge his life secrets to us. If it's true that he did our cutting, then he's right that he's not likely to hurt us."

"Our cutting was ten years ago." Dmitri jammed the last peg into the puzzle board, marking out the finished pattern. "A good deal can happen in that time. It only took a day for Hasafel to fall, an hour to bring the Temple to ruin, and a second of my foolishness may have cost Kestrel his life."

"Not this again." Ellis looked down at a floating lime slice, unable to find an answer for Dmitri's seething guilt. "Kestrel told us to run when the prentices attacked us in the Solar," he explained to Willim in a low voice. "Dmitri wouldn't leave him."

"He can't blame yourself for that, Dmitri, " Willim said.

"He can, and he's been doing an exceptional job of it for the last hour." Ellis flung up dripping hands in surrender. "Maybe you can talk some sense into him, Willim, but I think it's a task even St. Alveron would quail at."

"I promised myself I would be of some use to him," Dmitri said bitterly to no one in particular, his hands white-knuckled on the edge of the bench. "And what have I become? No better than a hostage prince to be rescued. I deserve neither Kestrel's care nor his bloodshed." Dmitri turned and stalked out of the chamber, the proud line of his back somehow fragile.

"...It's a shame about our oaths," Ellis said, when the Lark of Valnon had gone to stew in solitude. "One good hard tumble would do wonders for that one's temper."

"Be my guest, if you want to try him. But I'd rather keep what I've got left of my privates, thank you." Willim eyed the swaying curtain of beads. "Say, Ellis."

"Mmm?" The Thrush of Valnon stopped lolling in the shallows and looked over at Willim. "What is it? You've got a funny look on your face."

"It's about Grayson," Willim began, hesitantly.

Ellis' smile turned impish. "Are we still on the subject of good hard tumbles?"

Willim pulled one arm through the water, dousing Ellis and his insinuations in a soapy wave. "It's about his *name*, idiot. The Wing called him fa Grayce. So did Raven."

"Huh." A lime slice had gotten stranded in Ellis' hair from Willim's tidal wave; Ellis picked it out and flung it over his shoulder. "He did, didn't he? I suppose I wasn't really paying attention at the time."

"Why would a man named fa Grayce be a common-named sell-sword in the Undercity?" Willim persisted. "He should be an officer in the Godswords. He's talented enough."

"Maybe he didn't want to be a Godsword," Ellis answered.

"If he wasn't a Godsword, he'd still be a fa Grayce." Willim sighed. "I wish Dmitri hadn't gone. He knows something about it, I'm sure."

"*I* know what really happened."

Ellis and Willim both started at the unfamiliar voice, Ellis squelching off of the submerged ledge of the pool in his haste to turn around. Sitting on the bench Dmitri had abandoned was a

128

young girl with red-black hair, her tight Iskati vest gaudily embroidered and her dusky arms lined in gold bangles. Her eyes, when she looked up at the two Songbirds, were a startling green. "It's old gossip, of course, you couldn't get a crescent for it on the street. But I heard Jerdon and Kestrel talking about it once, oh, ages ago." She waved one arm with a musical chime, as thought to indicate some time in dim centuries past. "They were pretty drunk at the time. How are the baths?"

"Who are you?" Ellis demanded, flattening belly-first against the side of the pool in the hopes of retaining some shred of dignity. "What are you doing here?"

"That's nice," the girl answered, tartly. "I live here, thank you very much, and it's my baths you're using. I filled them myself this morning. I'm Rekbah."

"Are you Jerdon's daughter?" Willim asked, trying not to stare. The occasional female prentice in the Godswords was usually an immobile figure on guard, swathed up in regimental tunic and armor. But Rekbah was no cold soldier, and though her assets were modest, they were generously displayed.

"Maybe I'm Jerdon's mistress," she said coyly, stretching her belled ankles, the slit side of her pants revealing the firm curve of her calf.

Ellis was unmoved. "Jerdon must fancy them young, then. You can't be a day over fifteen. If you're his mistress, I'm his chamber-maid."

"And very pretty you'd look in an apron, too." Rekbah swatted Dmitri's game board at Ellis, sending the pegs rolling on the floor. "Not that you have anything left to cover up!"

"You're the one ogling us," Ellis answered, flushing. "We've got enough to put in a codpiece, and if you hadn't noticed that by now, then perhaps that doctor of yours ought to examine your eyes!"

Rekbah's response to this was a careless toss of her head and an oath in Iskati; Willim thought it something of a mercy that neither he nor Ellis could understand it. She stomped out of the baths with her chin high and her bells jangling, and Ellis subsided back into the bath, his scowl enough to set the water steaming.

"What's she even talking about?" he grumbled, in exasperation. He made an emphatic gesture at his hips. "This water is transparent, isn't it?"

"I think she saw plenty enough to know just where to strike you back," Willim answered, trying for Ellis' sake to keep his smile under control. "You shouldn't have let her bait you." Willim tilted his head at the curtain, the strands of beads still clinking with Rekbah's turbulent exit. "I suppose she's Jerdon's snipe."

"Rude little snit, snipe or no." Ellis surged up out of the bath, as though trying to convey the extent of his wounded pride in the sheer distance of splashed water. "And as soon as I get dressed, I'm going to find her and give her an ear-full she won't soon forget. I--" Ellis drew up short at the bench, looking around in consternation. "...Wait. Where are my clothes?"

From the doorway of the bath chamber there was a peal of girlish laughter and the bright chiming of fleeing footsteps. Willim would have found Ellis' defeat more comical if Rekbah hadn't been so thorough as to take *his* clothes, too.

11

Rekbah was in the dining room once Ellis and Willim returned from the baths, having found their clothes hidden behind one of the decorative agate plants in the hall. Sitting next to Jerdon with both his and Grayson's full attention, she was in the midst of a report on all the morning's gossip from the Undercity. Dmitri, feigning his disinterest, was curled up with a book of Shindamiri erotic poetry he had found in Jerdon's copious and varied library.

"...Obviously, Raven could not come out with the fact that he's let all the Songbirds slip from his grasp," Rekbah was saying. She glanced sidelong at Willim and Ellis, arching her brows and making a little moue of displeasure that they'd managed to find their clothes so quickly. "According to all the news I've heard, they're supposedly being kept safe inside the Temple until their would-be abductor has been captured to face justice."

"Which would be me," Grayson said, rubbing his finger over the polished surface of Jerdon's table. "Knowing most of my contacts in the Undercity are the sort with negotiable loyalties, Raven wants to set them after me for a reward. Once he's pared my options down to the trustworthy minimum, he can then turn them over one by one until he's found us."

"Fortunately, he doesn't know about me," Jerdon said. "And I should like to keep it that way as long as possible." He turned to Rekbah. "Excellent work, my dear. But enough about our enemies. What news is afoot regarding our friends?"

Rekbah was sober, all the previous mischief gone from her face. She pulled a fold of coarse paper from her bodice, its corners torn where it had been yanked from a public notice board. "Raven may pretend that he still holds the Songbirds," she said, "but according to this, he actually does have Kestrel."

Willim skimmed the notice, feeling his gut twist as though he would be sick. It was an enumeration of Kestrel's supposed crimes against the Temple and the Songbirds, including his conspiracy with the missing sell-sword, Nicholas Grayson. Buckled next to the list of his charges was a single, heavily-inked phrase: *Subject to the Justice of Heaven.* Kestrel's crimes had been deemed to be against the Temple itself, and the trial would be held privately, by the acting High Preybird.

"Raven wouldn't dare execute a Preybird," Ellis breathed, but Willim was thinking how little there was beyond Raven's daring. "And even if he would," Ellis continued, his voice shaking as though he had been thinking the same, "the city would never stand for it."

"The city is divided," Rekbah said, bangles clinking as she clenched her hands on her knees. "Kestrel is well-liked by those who like him, but he does not suffer fools, and there are fools aplenty who have been on the short end of his temper over the years. They would relish the downfall of one they think is too blue-blooded, or too powerful, or too involved in the affairs outside the Temple. Even some on the city council would look the other way. His mother is a powerful member of the ruling houses, and allowing Kestrel to fall would be a strike against her." Her face scrunched up with dismay. "A Preybird piece will often be thrown away for the sake of a Queen."

"Indeed," Jerdon said, looking at Grayson. "And Kestrel's record is hardly sterling. Raven was clever to put Grayson's name up next to Kestrel's. He knew it would bring up old memories. Old scandal is soon forgotten, but it can be quickly recalled when we would least like it to be. Disbelief and dismay give way to suspicion. And then when you consider that Kestrel spent an inordinate amount of his free time down here in the lower city, consorting with ship-captains and foreign agents and doctors, of all people?"

"What scandal?" Willim asked, frustrated that Jerdon would speak of it so casually, while they knew nothing. "What's Grayson to do with Kestrel's past?"

"It hardly matters now." Jerdon tilted up his glasses. "It's plain knowledge that Raven hates Hawk more than he does Kestrel, but he wants them both cleared out of the Temple, and Kestrel is by far the plainer target. His past is more easy to exploit, and he is closer to the Songbirds. Take out Kestrel first, and Hawk's elimination will be easier. Dangle Kestrel's life by a thread, and he may yet draw the Songbirds out of hiding. Raven is a fellow physician, you see. He knows how to prioritize the injuries he sees in his patient, what to suture first and what to mend later. He thinks the Temple wounded, and if it needs bleeding, if it needs amputation, he will do it. Whatever it takes to keep what he views as healthy, and eliminate what he feels is diseased."

"Like me, and the Preybirds, and Boren." Willim glared at the notice, wishing he could burn it to ash with his very rage. "Boren was killed to remove me, and now Raven works his way through the rest of his surgeries. I won't stand for this. The Wing will not stand for it."

"That's all well and good," Ellis said. "But it's Kestrel's neck that will bleed for us all first."

"Let me go back to the Temple," Dmitri said, and Willim started. He had not even heard the Lark approach. "Raven wants me installed as High Preybird; I can tell him I've reconsidered his offer and will join him if he drops Kestrel's charges."

"Out of the question," Grayson said, taking the notice from Rekbah and skimming its damning lines. "After Jerdon has contacted the Wing, we will make plans accordingly. But until then we wait here."

"I fear I must agree," Jerdon said, his clear brow knotting in consternation. "Without a doubt, we must do all we can to aid Kestrel, but placing you in danger in his stead will accomplish nothing."

"On the contrary. I can give Raven's takeover a semblance of continuity and credibility. It will be enough to delay Kestrel's execution, and I will be an ally for us inside the Temple." Dmitri's countenance was as unforgiving as an effigy, and he would not look at Willim. "You need not send the others."

"I'm not going to run away and hide while you fling yourself on something as weak as Raven's mercy," Willim said.

Ellis voiced similar protest. Dmitri said something unkind about Ellis' limited usefulness for anything other than singing Noontide, Ellis' indignation was sharp and certain, Willim said Kestrel's life was the more pressing matter. For a moment the Songbirds bore more resemblance to a trio of squabbling pigeons than to their namesakes, but Grayson scattered their arguments before they could degenerate into further insults.

"Enough!" Grayson threw down the notice of trial on the table, managing somehow to look like an entire fortress with the boiling lead ready to pour. "I am charged with your protection, and I'm afraid that does not include letting you walk back into the Temple and right into Raven's clutches. You heard the Wing's orders last night, and you'll abide by them."

"So we just run away and hide." Dmitri's face flushed with color. "Does Kestrel's life mean nothing to you?"

Grayson's head came up quickly, his jaw taut and his eyes full of warning, but Dmitri barreled on, tossing his hair back out of his eyes, his voice relentless.

"Clearly, it does not. If not for you, he would not be such a ready target for Raven. You sullied his entire career with your base passion, you subjected him to public humiliation unthinkable for any Songbird, you very nearly had him stripped of his colors, and all because you hadn't the honor to keep your cock down until his term was over--"

"Dmitri!" Jerdon slammed his hands down flat on the table, hard enough for the crack of his ring to go off like close thunder in the stone-lined room. His veneer of idle sophistication was gone, replaced by a smoldering authority. "That's quite enough from you. You are a Lark of Valnon, and such behavior is utterly unbecoming of you and of your saint. Grayson is absolutely innocent, and you have no idea what he has suffered for Kestrel's sake."

Dmitri had jumped at this counterattack from an unsuspected source, but he recovered fast. "On the contrary, I have quite an ample idea of what he has *suffered*." Something in Jerdon's tone had taken the edge off of Dmitri, and though Dmitri was the one to look away first, it was not quite enough to blunt him completely. "...As does everyone else in Valnon." Dmitri turned on his heel, shoving roughly past Rekbah on his way out the door.

The silence in the room was fragile, obsidian-sharp, and even Ellis knew better than to break it. The least stray word could bring it all down on them, cutting them to the bone.

"It seems my reputation has preceded me," Grayson said, with strained delicacy. "I did wonder what I had done to earn his scorn, I should have guessed he already knew."

"He knows more than we do," Willim said, unable to keep the question out of his voice. It was an invitation to speak, an offer for Grayson to put forth his own testimony on the matter. But whatever confessions Grayson had made in his past, they were long behind him. His portcullis was closed, his defense silent and sovereign.

"Dmitri just feels guilty," Ellis said, at last. "He blames himself for what happened to Kestrel."

"Well, that's one thing we have in common." Grayson splayed his fingers on the dining table, considering the map his veins made around his knuckles. "But I have stretched Rouen's forgiveness far enough during our friendship. Were I to let harm fall on Dmitri, I don't think he would have any left to give me. So I will protect Dmitri for Rouen's sake, even though I'm sure Dmitri would rather I do the opposite." He sighed, and turned to Jerdon. "What should we do now?"

"I will speak to the Queen first," Jerdon said. "She must act through the council, and there is some ink-work involved, but there may be a way to intercede on a charge of High Blasphemy. Lady Milia fa Branthos--" Jerdon paused, and smiled at Willim and Ellis "--That is, Kestrel's mother--is a prominent member of the High Council, and her knowledge of city law is extensive. She will have heard of this already I expect, and will be petitioning the Regent to see Her Highness. But I can get in rather more quickly. I'm due to see her this afternoon."

"Is there nothing that can be done before we go?" Willim pleaded.

"Save your strength, Willim," Jerdon said, rising. "You'll need it before all this is done. Rekbah?"

Rekbah had been brooding on the crumpled notice; she looked up at once, grateful for distraction. "Yes?"

"After we've had some lunch, I'd like you to fetch some things from the market. Some extra clothes, and foodstuffs that travel well and stretch better. Three or so large casks would be ideal to transport our... luggage." He winked at Willim and Ellis. "You are acquiring goods for our usual winter trip to Iskarit, should anyone ask. And while you're out, make sure you chat with some people about the rumor that the Songbirds might actually be missing, spirited away by loyal allies to keep them from Raven. I think it's a good idea if you throw a little suspicion on our *acting* High Preybird."

Rekbah clasped her hands with excitement. "I think I heard someone say the Songbirds went across the Pilgrim's Passage last night at low tide, disguised as Iskati dancing-boys."

"Excellent! Exactly the sort of obvious disguise one would expect them to take, and one sure to make everyone notice them." Jerdon snorted. "If I was really trying to get you across the Passage," he confided, to Willim, "I'd turn you into such a trio of sell-swords that your own mothers wouldn't recognize you. All it takes is some dirt and a suitably ostentatious hat, and I've a ready supply of both."

12

Lunch was a subdued affair. Dmitri did not appear for it, and Grayson might as well have been absent, for all his contribution to the conversation. Jerdon kept them distracted as best as he was able, rattling off anecdotes about everything from the fees charged in Shindamiri tea houses (private sessions with courtesans were determined by the time it took to burn a coil of incense) to the more curious assassinations of Iskati Emperors (four due to squabbles over pretty cup-boys, and one in a tricky situation with cucumbers). But even his wit could not penetrate the thick blanket of despair that had fallen on his house. The notice flyer on the end of the table had somehow made Kestrel's peril tangible, and brought it into the room with them.

The most conversation Grayson offered was to ask Jerdon if there was a spare sword to be had, and he and Jerdon went off together to find it, leaving the rest of them to finish chewing their lunch in uncomfortable silence.

"I wonder if there's any weapons we could use?" Ellis asked, thoughtfully shredding his last round of bread in a kind of cairn over the sardine remains on his plate.

"Pfft," Rekbah said, stacking up dishes to take to the scullery. "You'd stab yourself in the foot before you did harm to anything else. Swords aren't for Songbirds."

"Kestrel was brilliant with that knife," Ellis argued.

"Yes," Rekbah sighed, "and look where that got him."

"Did you know him?" Willim asked, reaching over to help her with the heavy brazier, the hot coals still sizzling faintly with fish-oil.

"*Does* she know him," Ellis stressed. "He's not dead yet. I hope."

"Lord Kestrel was already a regular guest here long before I arrived," Rekbah said, her motions deft and efficient as she cleaned the table. "Jerdon met him one day in the marketplace, newly minted in blue and goggling around like a blowfish on a plank, or so Jerdon told me. They were friends at once. Kestrel would stop in to ask Jerdon about some book or another, and then stay for a glass of wine and for dinner. It was always so nice to listen to him talk, and he would sing a little with Jerdon sometimes, and he was so handsome..." She trailed off and rubbed a finger at her eye. "Was he--was he very badly hurt?" She looked hard at Willim. "Tell me the truth."

"He was injured," Willim said, with hesitation, "but I think he was feigning it to be even worse than it was. Grayson said his wounds were bad, but didn't have to be mortal. He was still standing and fighting when we escaped."

Rekbah considered this, chewing her lip. "I still say it would have been better if Grayson had never taught him to fight."

"What?" Ellis' hands clenched on his bread, unknowingly ripping it in half. "*Grayson* taught Kestrel to fight?"

"That's what Kestrel said." Rekbah's brows drew down low as she leaned in to whisper to them. "He and Jerdon went through a lot of wine that night. I don't think Kestrel remembers talking about it, and he never mentioned it again. It's none of my business--"

"Is it true what Dmitri said?" Willim pressed, even though it was obvious Rekbah was growing more and more reluctant to speak. "About the two of them?"

"Everybody in the Undercity has heard this," Rekbah said, busying herself with plates.

"We don't live in the Undercity," Ellis pressed. "Come on, Rekbah! I can't let Dmitri be a gamut ahead of me forever. Did Grayson really... I mean, he doesn't seem the sort to--well, to..."

"The sort to rape a Songbird in his colors?" Rekbah said, bluntly. "If that's what you want to ask, you should spit it out." The cutlery clashed as she threw it onto the tray. "No, he doesn't. But that's why he was thrown out of the Godswords, and out of his family, so I heard. And it was old gossip years before I came to Valnon. If you want to know about it, go ask Grayson. I've already said more than I should."

"Don't be ridiculous," Ellis said, going pale under his freckles. "You don't just march up to a man and ask--"

"I will," Willim said, standing. "I want to know the truth, whatever it is."

"Truth is a troublesome thing," Rekbah said, hefting the dishes up to her hip. "Once you've learned it, you can't console yourself with doubts."

"I'd prefer it to the doubts I've already got," Willim said. "He's my bodyguard, Rekbah. If I'm going to trust him with my life, I have to know."

"I still think it's a personal matter between the two of them."

Willim said nothing, his eyes locked on hers, and Rekbah looked away first.

"I heard the garden door a few minutes ago," she said, finally. "I think that's where he went."

"Thanks, Rekbah," Willim said. "Ellis, help her with those plates, will you?"

"Hey!" Ellis sat up, indignant. But Willim was already gone, taking the steps two at a time towards the answer to the riddle that was Nicholas Grayson.

After all this time, Grayson was amazed at how easily old wounds could sting again as though freshly inflicted. The stealthy noise of the whetstone against the edge of his borrowed sword was not enough to blot out the echoes of Dmitri's accusations, or to grind away his guilt. Jerdon had called him innocent. Grayson peered down the edge of the blade, snorted, and kept working. If only it were so.

Jerdon's so-called garden was a scrap of ancient paving-stone clinging to the sheer face of Valnon's island, little more than a half-ring of marble railing slick with sea-spray. Set into the island's bone was a sheltered alcove, which held a statue of Naime that probably had been carved in Hasafel's day. Grayson had fled for the solace beneath her chained feet, hiding under her outstretched arms and weathered face like the cooing seabirds that nested in the eaves of her shrine. The contour of the island blocked most of the wind, but it still carried a bitter, salty edge. Had Grayson been a guiltless man, he would have stayed in Jerdon's underground courtyard where it was warm.

But if Grayson was truly a guiltless man, he would not have been there at all, hiding from the sky with a blank sword in his hands.

"Could I speak with you a moment?"

Grayson looked up. The Dove of Valnon stood at the top of the stairs, the trap door open at his feet, sea wind ruffling his hair. He looked like a creature blown off the waves, gray and silver, insubstantial as a cloud. Then the light shifted and he was only Willim, squinting to see Grayson in the shadows of the alcove, eyebrows drawn down in a frown.

Grayson bent back over his work. "You should stay inside," he said. "It's cold out here, and there's less chance of anyone seeing you."

"No one's going to see me here," Willim answered, jerking his head at the cliffs above and below them. "Not unless he's a seagull." Sensing that he would not get further argument, Willim let the trap door slam shut at his feet. "I see you found a sword."

"In the broadest sense, yes. I've no idea where the Jerdon got this, but I've seen better steel in a tavern's silver drawer. If I want this thing to take an edge for me, I'll probably have to buy it a round of ale and offer to marry its sister first." Grayson lowered his whetstone. Willim was still there, his eyes searching Grayson's face, the intermittent bursts of pale sunlight rimming his hair with gold. Grayson sighed. "...You want to know if I did it, don't you?"

Willim shifted his weight, but his gaze did not relent. "Did you?"

"Maybe. What do you think?"

"I don't know what to think. That's why I thought I'd ask."

Grayson stroked the blade again with the whetstone, but his heart wasn't in it. "So I take it that unlike your Lark of Valnon, you don't believe that I simply took advantage of Rouen's friendship, and forced myself on him in a moment of brutish lust?"

Willim's mouth went back as though he was fighting off an urge to retch. "I find it highly unlikely, to say the least. Rekbah says you taught Kestrel to fight back when he was a Songbird." Willim prodded a bit of potted ivy, stubbornly clinging to the columns of Naime's alcove. "It's easy to see how you could have fallen in love with him then."

Grayson felt his face give him away. "Sometimes Songbirds can be surprisingly acute."

"So it's true, then."

"It's true that I fell in love." Grayson worried the whetstone over a stubborn notch near the hilt of the sword. Its previous owner must have used the thing to chop firewood. "Dmitri's charges are not entirely accurate, though that does not make me any less guilty of a crime. I fell in love with a Songbird, and Rouen fell in love with a prentice. When Raven was High Preybird, both those sins were unforgivable. But we weren't thinking of Raven, then. Only of each other." Grayson swallowed past a thick feeling in his throat. The memories came on as clear and sharp as a frosted morning. They burned in his lungs, too beautiful and too real to endure for long.

"I'm sorry," Willim said. "It must be hard to talk about. You say that you did not do it, and that's enough. I believe you." He turned to go, and Grayson reached out and caught him by the wrist, startling them both.

"No," he said, roughly. "No. This poison has been in the wound long enough. I would lance it, but I warn you, it will be foul."

Willim did not answer, but took a seat in the alcove across from Grayson, serene as a Songbird on his pedestal.

"We pretended at only friendship for a long time," Grayson said, the words coming slowly at first, then crowding together in a mob, eager to be free. "Rouen had ideas for when he would be a Preybird, ideas that ironically enough raised him high in Raven's affections. He thought it foolish that Preybirds were forbidden weapons even after finishing their terms as Songbirds. He thought it shameful that he could not defend himself, and was forced to rely on others. I was young, proud of my skill, and more than eager to show it off. With each other to challenge, our sword work became exceptional. My commander in the prentices commended me on my extra training, not knowing I was doing it with the Lark of Valnon. But while my skill grew, my heart was utterly lost. It would not have mattered, but for the war."

"I at least know about the war," Willim said, nodding. "It was at its worst then, was it not?"

"Yes, and I would not always be a prentice. I was soon to turn eighteen, and I would be sent south to fight the Ethnarch's forces. Even with my talents, the odds of my return were not favorable. Rouen had years yet remaining in his term, and our parting was imminent. He offered, and I did not refuse him." Pain blossomed along Grayson's palm, a surprisingly real manifestation of the sharp pangs in his heart. It took him a moment to realize he had clenched his hand against the sword.

"I think that blade is plenty sharp enough," Willim said,

cupping Grayson's hand in his own, wincing over the cut.

"My blood is not a thing for a Songbird's hands," Grayson said, but Willim had pulled a kerchief from his sleeve, and would not let him go.

"You of all people should know that we are not so precious," he said, knotting the cloth around Grayson's hand. He put his head to the side, looking at his handiwork, and made a face. "Though, I think Dmitri is better at this sort of thing than I am."

Grayson closed his fingers around the messy twist of fabric. "I think your bedside manner is far better," he said, half-smiling.

"You were going to be sent south with the other Godswords," Willim prompted, folding his hands over Grayson's. "What happened?"

Grayson remembered himself, and he pulled his hand away. "Raven happened," he said. "I think he had suspected something for a long time, and in that brief time Rouen and I were lovers, our happiness made us careless. Alexander--the Preybird Kite, as you know him--had been our confidant, but Raven forced the truth from him. And then Raven dragged the whole affair before the Preybirds. I knew Rouen would be stripped of his colors and exiled from the Temple, and I knew what a loss it would be for Valnon. It wasn't only his hair and his voice I was in love with. He made me want to be a Godsword for more than the tiresome duty of my name, he gave me something to believe in." Grayson clenched his fist around the handkerchief, feeling the folds of fabric bite down into his sliced flesh. The sting of it was sweet, and he craved it. "And so, on the day of the inquiry, I took the witness chair before Rouen could, and I confessed a lie that would save him. I said that I had extorted his kindness, and I had raped him. I knew I could be executed for the crime. But what was that to me?" Grayson's laugh was short, bitter. "Already I knew I would die for my Songbirds. That's what it means to be a Godsword, after all. It was only the manner and the timing that would be different. Raven was fully prepared to punish me as far as the law could go. Hawk protested, Osprey protested, even some of the older Preybirds stood for my sake. My name, I think, led them to believe I deserved to redeem myself on the battlefield. In the end, it was Lateran XII's direct command that spared my life, but I was still punished. I was expelled from the Godswords, and shortly after, I was disowned by my family. I was no longer Nicholas fa Grayce."

Willim said nothing, and Grayson picked up the whetstone again, and continued his work. For a long time it was the only sound, louder than the stray cries of gulls and the rustle of the sea far below, while the clouds swelled into the sky and blotted out what little amount of blue was left. Naime's shadow grew darker, the air colder. "I do not need your pity, Your Grace," Grayson said, when the silence had grown too uncomfortable.

"It is not pity, and I thought I told you to call me Willim." Willim reached out, hesitant, and laid his hand on Grayson's shoulder. It lighted there only briefly, starting away like an alarmed bird at Grayson's intake of breath. Willim twisted his hands together between his knees, as though unwilling to let them get away and be so forward again. "I--I have never been in love. I suppose I count myself fortunate that my term of service has been no burden for me, and I admit that I have been arrogant, to think myself better than Dmitri. It must be torment for him, to love Kestrel as he does and to be unable to share it. I never thought about it that way before."

"I'm sure Dmitri is a difficult man to feel compassion for," Grayson said, dredging up a smile from somewhere. "And I'm pleased you can manage it. But you should not pity him too much. Unless I'm very much mistaken, the affection is not only on his part. He has only to wait two more years, take his Preybird name, and Kestrel will be his. And I wish them both much joy in the pairing."

"But--" Willim began, confused by such a revelation hard on the heels of Grayson's story of doomed love, "what about you?"

"What about me?" Grayson countered, daring the Dove with his frank stare. "Before last week, Willim, I hadn't laid eyes on Rouen in fourteen years. We were barely men when we last saw each other, and our lives can no more meet now than the sun can share midnight with the moon." Grayson sheathed the sword, lending his words an air of finality. "Birds of the Temple are best with their own, Willim. You understand one another, you demand nothing more from each other than what you have. It's always been that way. Even had nothing happened, Rouen and I would not have lasted. Our natures are two different currents, and equally strong. We would either overrun one another, or diverge. It's best this way."

Willim's hands were taut on his knees, crumpling the pale fabric of his borrowed clothes. His color was high, and Grayson found himself unable to ignore how it flattered the shade of his eyes, how it stripped the Temple arrogance out of him, how his ordinariness made him all the more extraordinary. "If it had been me in Kestrel's place," he said, "I would have waited for you."

The silence that followed was very different than the previous one. As though suddenly realizing the full measure of his statement, Willim rose to his feet. "I'm sorry to have brought up bad memories," he said too quickly, and slammed the trap door behind him in his hurry to get back down the stairs. Grayson was left alone to contemplate the increasingly futile protests of his conscience.

Ellis was still in the dining room where Willim had left him, only in the intervening time he had somehow acquired an ancient-looking sket, its battered wood black with age and its triangular belly covered in scratches.

"Can you tell me," Willim said, the heat in his face unwilling to subside, "just when I lost my mind? Was it recent, or have I always been an idiot?"

"I thought you were always an idiot," Ellis said, gamely. "But don't let it bother you. Kite says it won't last, and just makes a young man endearing. Never mind that. Look what Jerdon gave me. He found it when he was looking for Grayson's sword."

"Ugh." Willim hurled himself into a pile of cushions, face in hands, and squinted at Ellis' new acquisition from between his fingers. "Looks like firewood to me."

"Shows what you know," Ellis said, cradling the humble instrument as though it was a lover of unimaginable charm. "Listen." His fingers sprawled across the frets, he brought his thumbnail across the strings, and a chord showered into the air like a sudden fall of rain. It was sweet enough to make Willim forget his own embarrassment for a moment.

"It plays better than it looks," Willim admitted. He was no expert on skets, but he knew a good tone when he heard it.

"She's got character," Ellis said, infatuated, and ran his string-callused fingertips over the chipped shell birds inlaid around the sound hole. "Jerdon said it's been hanging around the house for ages gathering dust. He said I could have it if I put new strings in it and tuned it up." His hand danced nimbly up the sket neck, and the first sprightly measures of Eothan's *Six of Sparrows* sparkled through the room.

"Do you know where Dmitri went?" Willim asked, rolling to his feet. "I want to talk to him."

"You never struck me as a sadist before," Ellis said, still playing. "I think I saw him headed to the library. Probably looking for some quiet. Just let him cool down. He'll be his usual frigid self again by dinner-time."

"I don't think so," Willim said. "I've never seen him break like that."

"You can't say it hasn't been building since yesterday. I'm worried about Kestrel, too, but I'm not in love with him. Still, Dmitri being an arse isn't going to help Kestrel now." Ellis stopped mid-chord, and drummed his fingers against the sket. "So! Did you find Grayson?"

"I did," Willim said, grim.

Ellis leaned forward, eager. "And?"

"And he told me what happened. It was terrible. Kestrel and Grayson were in love, and Raven found them out. Grayson threw aside his honor to protect Kestrel."

Ellis gave a low whistle. "Sounds like something out of a Canticles tale."

"Only worse, because it's true. And the more I think about it the more I think I should remember something of it, even only whispers among the older flock boys. Do you recall anything?"

"No," Ellis shook his head. "Even if I did hear something at the time, I wouldn't have known what it meant. We were only six then, Willim. We were still trying to memorize the Songbird hierarchy while Hawk was cramming a thousand measures of music into our heads every day. So I can tell you," he strummed a sing-song chord on the sket, "*'Twenty-ninth was Heron blind, he the double-sket designed; Gannet, Eagle, Shrike and then, Gull and Heron once again.'*" He sighed. "But no idea at all about what was going on right then under the Temple's own roof, of course not."

"I wish I'd been paying better attention."

"You still haven't explained why you're all pink."

"It's cold outside."

"Cold doesn't make you act like you've got a goldfish in your britches."

Willim could not meet Ellis' eyes. "...I said something foolish. To him. Grayson. I only meant to be kind to him, to apologize for being so rude to him earlier. I didn't mean--" He broke off. "It's nothing."

"Doesn't sound like it."

"It's nothing important, anyway."

"What did you say? That you wanted to take his mind off old lovers by being a new one?"

"No!" Willim sat down again, all at once. He was in no state to talk to Dmitri now, anyway. One brush with Dmitri and the Lark's parchment-thin edges would graze him with a thousand cuts, and Willim would wind up bleeding awkwardness and apology all over everything.

"You do, though, don't you?" Ellis was no longer teasing. He had gone quite serious, so that even without his copper and paints there was something of St. Thryse to him, a brilliance that would burn away any untruth like slag in a crucible.

"Yes. No. I don't know." Willim raked both hands back through his hair, making it stick up like a tuft of thistle-down.

Ellis gave a low whistle. "Damned if I ever thought I'd see the day your eye was turned by anything that wasn't in minor key."

"Oh, he's minor key all right," Willim muttered. "...Just play your bloody sket."

"Fair enough," Ellis said, and launched into his extensive repertoire of Alfiri love-songs, every one a needling variation on the themes of love and loss. They were full of complicated sket-work, designed for balladeers to impress their lovers, and they were Ellis' particular specialty.

My heart lies locked in my true love's breast,
And where she sleeps, I can't confess.

Willim had asked for it, he knew. Ellis could be downright devious when he wanted to be, and he was every bit as precise with his barbs as Dmitri. The words flew sweet and sure into the aching

146

place under Willim's breastbone. He curled around the pain they caused, and wondered if, like Kestrel, he could wait fourteen years for an errant lover.

He wondered if he could wait two.

13

Kestrel's first waking sense was one of pain. The second was the sound of gulls, close by, and the third was a rich, quiet scent, as intoxicating as the raw flesh of a torn pomegranate and as aloof as the crimson resin burnt in Temple incense. A faint breeze, salty and damp, cooled his brow. Kestrel could not open his eyes; they hurt too much, hot and throbbing. Gentle fingers laid a wet cloth over them, and the trickles of water stung in Kestrel's cuts.

"It is a dangerous game you played with Raven, Rouen. More dangerous than any you ever have before. Have I asked too much of you?"

"Your Grace?" Kestrel rasped, tilting his face a restrained fraction towards the sound. "Have they imprisoned you, as well?"

Lateran XII laughed softly. "I am no prisoner, my boy, and nor are you. Though your wounds will keep you quiet here for some time. Raven searches for what he thinks the Wing of Valnon is. He will not find me unless he knows what I truly am."

Kestrel's throat worked for a moment, but the words were more important than his own weariness. "What you truly are?"

Lateran's fingertips were cool on Kestrel's abraded flesh, and the smell of wound salve obliterated the Wing's distinct scent. "I am myself, and that is one thought that has never occurred to Raven, or to the ones in the past who were much like him. But for now, I am only Shaith, a humble Laypriest of little interest to anyone."

"Shaith," Kestrel said, and then, drunk on the dregs of his own survival, he sang softly,

Shaith na shalon ferris ti
Draith el avra jasom b'hi
Assae thasslae, Naime te m'hi.

There was a slight pause, and then the Wing's voice joined him on the translation, singing low as he tended to Kestrel's wounds.

Wander lost in endless time

Closed in shackles made of rhyme
Naime's tears her only crime.

Kestrel's tired voice broke on the last line, and he frowned. "I could never make that scan with the melody in modern Vallish."

"Translations," Lateran said scornfully, examining the bruises along Kestrel's ribs. "Like caressing your lover through a burlap sack. You get the gesture of the thing, but not the nuance, and it is overall an irritating experience." The bed creaked beneath his weight. "You have played your part too well, Rouen. Three of your ribs are broken."

"Only on the right," Kestrel said, with a terse smile. "I lift my blade with the left."

"Not for some days yet, you won't," Lateran said, rising. "I will bind them for now. But it pains me to see any Preybird of mine so wounded. Were you not so stubborn, I would have refused your request to carry a blade." He considered for a moment, leaving Kestrel to listen to the gulls. "But I cannot deny that without your skill, our situation could be far worse."

"Have I made some profit for us, then?" Kestrel heard the Wing clattering at a nearby table, the clink of salve jars and the soft crinkle of bandages. "What has become of the Songbirds? Are they safe?"

"As safe as they can be." A tiny pause, as though the Wing was unsure how much to say. "They and your friend Nicholas fa Grayce are with Jerdon, and if all goes well they will be safely out of the city by nightfall."

"Merciful Alveron!" Kestrel sank back against the pillows in relief, ignoring the protest from his body. "It's enough to give a man faith."

"I should like to think you had some of that already," Lateran answered, and there was a wry amusement in his voice that he could not fully hide.

"I have it all the more now, then. Where are we?"

"You are in my private chamber, hidden beneath the Temple, where Raven will never find you. The rooms he thought were mine were only a decoy, much as I am myself. But he will not have it out that he's misplaced you along with the Songbirds. In an attempt to flush you out, he has put it forth to the city that you and Grayson conspired in the kidnapping of the Songbirds on behalf of the Thrassin Ethnarch, and has issued a charge of High Blasphemy on you."

"*Subject to the Justice of Heaven*," Kestrel sighed, rueful. "He would not want to get the crown involved with my trial. My former house has too strong an ally in the Regent."

"All the same, I will see to it that the Queen is made aware of your situation. He would not dare carry out sentence against you yet, even if he knew where you were. He has lost the Songbirds, and until he has found them, his hold on the Temple is tenuous. He needs you to draw them out. And were the city to learn that he is the traitor, his position would become precarious."

"Not to mention that the Crown could deem Thrass' involvement an attack on the sovereignty of the nation. Raven's ploy for the city's ire might soon turn against him rather than against Thrass. What is our next course of action?"

"Yours," the Wing said, and there was no mistaking the admonishment in his voice, "is to rest, and heal. Your strength will be needed, but not now." Lateran cupped Kestrel's head in one hand, and his steady support lifted Kestrel from the pillow. "Drink this, now." The smooth lip of a pottery cup kissed Kestrel's mouth. The wine had been mixed with honey to mask the bitter herbs, and Kestrel drank it gratefully, knowing the oblivion it contained. The taste was a memory from the night he was cut for St. Lairke, when he surrendered all that was given to other men for the sake of holy song. Then, as now, the drug chased his fears away, and left his limbs pleasantly leaden.

"I will send you news as soon as I have any to give. I have two agents in the Undercity, and both of them are more than capable. Let them look after things for now, and rest easy." Lateran's fingers smoothed Kestrel's hair. The last thing Kestrel heard, as the drug pulled him down into spiraling twilight, was the sound of Lateran XII's voice singing *Naime's Lament* in Hasafeli.

In all his years in the Temple, Kestrel had never heard anything so sweet.

As the Preybird's breathing evened into sleep, Lateran XII put a shaking, ringed hand across his eyes. He had overstepped himself again, and the remnant of song inside of him would not tolerate further misuse. Already it had been stretched to the breaking point.

Surely, Lateran thought, rising from his chair and pulling up the white hood of his Laypriest's robe, *Surely it will not be much longer*.

Lateran leaned over the Preybird's sleeping form, and latched the window shut. His secret rooms were cut out of the living rock of the island; the window opened on nothing but sky and sea. The morning had turned raw and chilly as the wind changed; storm clouds racked up on the horizon like a belligerent armada. The Wing put his back to them, wondering what fresh danger filled their cloudy sails, wondering if there was strength enough in Valnon's Dove to meet it. In the most private silence inside himself, Lateran admitted to his doubts.

A coiling iron staircase led upwards to a concealed passage, and the surface level of the Temple. Lateran XII staggered halfway up the twisting path. Before he could fall, his outstretched hand was caught by another one, one tipped in the ornamental talons of the last king of Hasafel.

"You have gone too far again," Starling said. He stood inside the circle made by the stairs, grasping the Wing's hand in his own cold, clawed one, making the ruby in Lateran's ring of office flash like a shard of fire. "You have little enough to spend, to waste it so carelessly on knitting the bones of a reckless Preybird."

"I do not consider it to be wasted," Lateran answered, pulling his hand from Starling's. The sharp tips of Starling's finger ornaments raised scratches on the back of the Wing's hand, beading them with blood. "Kestrel gained his injuries in service to me; it is only just that I offer my gifts in return. I fear he will need his strength, and soon."

"I heard you singing," Starling said, his eyes much like those of the Wing, pale and ancient. They were gentled by the longing in his voice, but only barely. "It has been a long time since I heard you singing."

"I cannot risk it much these days," Lateran confessed, putting his shoulder to the railing to steady himself. Like his chamber, the stairwell was surrounded by the raw rock of the island, and Lateran pulled strength from Valnon's bones, feeding it into the cold, blue ember of song in his belly. It flared again, crimson and orange, but the heat of Noontide had never been his, and he knew the light was fading. "I could lose control. I could make a mistake again."

"You could sing for me," Starling said, and the shadows seemed to deepen around him, his own leaping and fluttering on the fractured surface of the stairs, splintering it into raven's wings. "One Evensong, one hour, one sweet requiem here for us. Then your labors and my vigil would be over."

Lateran XII shook his head, fine strands of hair clinging to the chill sweat on his cheeks. "You know I cannot. I could not do that to the others, not yet."

Starling sighed. "I know. But I will have you soon enough. Every note you sing draws that hour nearer, and I do not think you will be sorry to see it come at last." Starling turned once, with a clatter of shell-beads and dove-colored tatters, and the Wing of Valnon was alone on the staircase.

"No," Lateran said, the weight of his years bowing him until he felt as frail as Raven thought him to be. "No, I will not be sorry." Slowly, turning as the dais did on its way to ascent, he continued up the curling stairs.

The steps led to a blank wall, but the Wing touched one of the stones, and a doorway rasped open behind a rickety wine rack in the Temple's kitchen cellar. Lateran pushed it closed again, the bottles clinking gently as the rack swung back into place. He hurried up the stairs to the kitchen, and then on down the maze of corridors to the Archives.

The Temple's Archives were buried deep in the lowest parts of the Temple, far below any sounding vents and the reach of the sun. The pipes for the baths did not burrow down so far, and their steamy warmth had never been felt in those chambers. While Osprey ruled them, the Archives had been cool but bright and dry, with all the ceiling lanterns trimmed and lit, water for tea warming on a brazier far from the precious manuscripts, and a spare fur mantle on hand for any enterprising scholar unprepared for the climate.

But with those comforts removed, and a pair of prentices on guard outside the heavy oak door, the Archives had become an effective prison. The prentices were nervous, unsettled with their duty, and Lateran noted a kind of relief in their faces when he arrived to see to the captives. Obedience and reverence for all the Birds of Valnon was ingrained deep in the prentice Godswords, and they let the disguised Wing of Valnon into the Archives without question, glad that he could offer the flock mercy if they could not.

"Ferrin's got a cold," one of them said, as the other unlocked the door. "We've asked Raven to put him somewhere warmer, but he won't listen."

Poor children, Lateran thought. *Caught between warring parents and with no idea which side to choose.* Aloud, he said, "I'll see to him."

The archive door opened on meticulously-oiled hinges, and once inside Lateran heard the lock click behind him. For the moment, he was a captive as well.

The antechamber of the archives was crowded and stuffy, the polished stone floor lost under neat piles of bedding with the tea brazier doing its best in the middle. There was room enough to hold the flock boys and three Preybirds, but the thin straw pallets of the flock were not enough to keep away the floor's chill, and the brazier could not warm them all. In the adjoining room Osprey had put their captivity to good effect, setting the flock to copying deteriorating scrolls onto new parchments. The scrape of busy quills made a soft counterpoint to the sound of Kite's sket, strumming out something soothing to keep the silence away.

Hawk had been kneeling down beside one of the pallets, and he rose in one fluid motion at the sound of the opening door. The sound of the quills and the sket both stopped, but once Kite and the flock saw their visitor was only a Laypriest they began once more.

"I'd like a word with you, Shaith," Hawk said, with the brusque authority of a Preybird to Laypriest and loud enough to be heard by all. Once they were away from the group in a niche between two overflowing bookshelves, his timbre changed. "How is Rouen?" he murmured.

The Wing of Valnon lowered his white hood. "Sleeping, and with Naime's blessing, mending as well. How is everyone bearing up here?"

Hawk exhaled though his nose. He was angry, Lateran knew, and his patience was thinning. "Well enough, though poor Ferrin's miserable with fever, and I'm afraid it may pass to them all." He nodded to the place where he had been sitting, and the shivering pile of blankets on the pallet. The only sign of the flock boy himself was a shock of brown hair and muted sniffling. "It wouldn't kill a sparrow, but it would be hard on their spirits."

"And on yours as well," Lateran observed, wryly. "I can't think of a worse nursemaid."

Hawk gave him a pained look. "If you're saying I would rather take Raven apart with my bare hands than sit down here with twenty sneezing boys, then you'd be right."

"It would only lend credence to his argument that you're an uncivilized barbarian."

Hawk considered this a moment. "I could live with that," he concluded.

"Your Grace." Osprey had stepped over to join them in the stacks, his footfalls muffled by the folds of his robe of brown velvet and beaver pelt. Unlike Hawk, Osprey showed the two generations of Songbirds that had come and gone since he had sung Noontide, but he had been cut young, and at almost forty he was in his prime as a Preybird, as sharp-eyed as his namesake. His parchment skin was taut over fine bones, and his hair still had plenty of ink-black under its streaking of gray. The boys in the flock liked to say that Osprey would never die, he would simply turn into one of his own tomes and be shelved. "Please tell me you've come to give us the order to take back our Temple."

The Wing of Valnon gave him a fond smile instead. "I'm sorry, Curran," he said. "But I can see no way of doing it well. The prentices and flock would be caught in the middle, and I have enough wounded Preybirds to keep whole as it is. Besides, I would like to see Raven's plan fully unraveled before I snip that thread." He looked beyond the forty-eighth Thrush to the forty-ninth, Kite sitting in a corner with his fingers playing the sket independent of his thoughts, his gaze a thousand miles off. "How is Alexander?"

"He misses his lovers," Osprey snorted, but then grew serious. "I would like to tell him of you, Your Grace, but I did not wish to do so without your permission. It would ease his captivity to know there was a wiser hand steering affairs on our side."

Lateran made a noise of agreement, his eyes still on Kite. The former Thrush looked hollow-eyed and lost, his chestnut curls limp against his forehead, his wine-colored tunic rumpled and torn. Osprey had knocked some heads together when the prentices first corralled them in the Archives, and gotten his own knocked in turn, but he had been an Undercity orphan and was made of sterner stuff than Alexander fa Rhamel.

"Tell him all you think he needs to know," Lateran agreed. "I will have to do the same for Kestrel as well, and maybe I should have done it long ago. But Kite was not ready, and I did not wish one of them to know and not the other. It made a small divide between Raven and Falcon into a great gulf, and though Kestrel and Kite are much closer, I was content to let them wait."

Hawk and Osprey nodded in unison. They had been told early, as Raven could not be trusted and Falcon had died before his time, and they had long kept the secret of the Wing of Valnon between them.

"This is for Ferrin," the Wing continued, passing a bottle of tincture of willow to Osprey. "See he takes some, mixed with wine, at regular intervals. And mint tea with honey as often as he can stand it. I'll see to it that you have plenty of food and blankets."

"At least we'll have this winter's copying all done before time," Osprey sighed, glancing back at the flock, whose pen-work grew instantly more diligent when they realized Osprey's eyes were on them. "But I worry that if things turn for the worse we'll be trapped like mice in a bag down here."

Lateran's eyes glinted, and he put his hand to the wall between the two shelves. The walls of the archive were solid and ancient, encrusted with mosaic that was not as meticulously cleaned as the ones in the upper stories. Behind the bookcases, the tiles were dark with age and lampblack, and the wall next to him glinted only faintly in the light from the antechamber. The mosaic went well beyond the shelves on either side, full of vines and birds and flowers in an eye-height border along the wall. Across the bottom, a long line of cavorting horses pranced from right to left above a border of blue and gold tiles. The horses were all brown and riderless, except for one white horse in the middle that had a fair-haired queen astride its back.

"If the worst comes and you have warning enough," Lateran said, wiping the soot from the white flank of the horse, "Lavras fa Valos will lead you to the Palace. But only as the last resort. The passage is treacherous, and I do not know if it is even still clear." Once clean, the white tiles gleamed and the soot remained only in a thin ring around the horse, a hairline fracture indicating the hidden switch. "Even mice can chew their way out of the bag, Curran."

Osprey's mouth twitched. "Let's hope it doesn't come to that," he said. "I don't fancy leaving my books behind. Your Grace." He tilted his head at the Wing, as a Preybird could not be seen bowing to a Laypriest, and went to give Ferrin his medicine.

"Try to keep him busy," Lateran said to Hawk. "I know he rails against my seeming inaction, and would rather an open fight and be done with it."

"You think Raven has designs beyond removing Willim from the Temple?" Hawk asked.

"If that was all he wanted, he would have it now." Lateran shook his head. "But instead of closing this over, he keeps the wound open. His surgery is not yet complete."

"We will be fine down here," Hawk said, to ease the worried furrow of the Wing's countenance. "It is the safest place in the Temple."

Lateran pulled his hood back over his head. "Yes," he agreed, "but I'm afraid at the moment that's not saying much."

In the upper floors of the Temple, the prentices were on watch and the doors to the sanctuary open, but the Temple had announced that the Songbirds would not be singing hours that day, and the only music to be heard was a Laypriest singing a low chant from the sanctuary floor. Only a few patrons milled about in the atrium, most there to meet each other rather than to offer prayers. Whispers almost drowned out the music. Raven's announcement as acting High Preybird had stirred up the silt of old rumors, and the air was thick with detritus of things long settled.

Lateran bypassed the main area of the Sanctuary, ducking down into an access passage used by the flock to prepare for hours. Stepping into a niche between the prayerful statues of Gull (the forty-first Lark) and Rook (the thirty-ninth Thrush), Lateran put his mouth to a bit of marble filigree under Rook's elbow, and whistled three notes into the stonework.

Far down the sounding tunnel, there was a similar flourish of marble in one of the listening chapels in the Temple atrium. Little more than closets fitted with a bench and a rail for candles, the chapels were places for quiet mediation, where those whose burdens were heaviest could come and listen to Temple music in solitary contemplation. It was known, however, that some received echoes from the sanctuary better than the others. The sound in the chapel in the southwest corner was exceptionally bad, and it was usually empty. Its reception was in fact excellent, but only if the singer was standing between Gull and Rook in the back corridor, rather than in the sanctuary. Then, even a faint breath sounded as though it was coming from an inch away.

Lateran waited less than a measure, and then his three notes came back to him, whistled in reverse order. He smiled, grateful for the familiar warble. "I hope I haven't kept you waiting."

"Not at all." Jerdon's voice came from the chapel, and Lateran could hear the rustle of the doctor's silk Iskati tunic as he sat down near the candle-rail. "How is everything?"

"Tolerably well," Lateran answered. "One bird in the cliff nest, three wait on the wing, all the hatchlings safe. You?"

"About to migrate, as planned," Jerdon answered. "If you agree it's for the best."

"I do. Take them to the safe house in Clarie, and if things go poorly, recall the swords and bring them back here. I would rather do this without upsetting the balance on the border, but we may not have much choice." Lateran sighed heavily. "As for the three with you, tell them not to worry about their wind-hover. I have him, and he can't be caged if he can't be found."

"I'm glad to hear it. I'm leaving the butcher-bird here for you. Try to give him something to do, won't you? You know how he gets if he's idle."

"I'm not paying his gaming-debts again," Lateran answered.

"The brothels are where the real trouble lies," Jerdon said. "He usually wins at dice."

"Don't I know it," the Wing said, with feeling. "Sing a note to the wind if you get south safely. If not I'm sending him after you."

"Fair enough. But I don't much fancy leaving you two here alone."

Lateran gave an un-musical snort. "You don't fancy much of anything besides a good book and a glass of wine, and you never have."

"True enough!" The echo of Jerdon's laugh faded fast. "...Are you certain you'll be all right?"

"No," Lateran answered. "But my being all right has very little to do with anything. I haven't unearthed all of our carrion-crow's bones yet. There's something larger and meatier he's keeping away from even his prentices, and my sparrows have told me nothing. I want you right where you are, Jer. I want your claws sharp and your eyes sharper. This is bigger than I thought."

There was a pause from the other end of the vent, and for a moment nothing came to Lateran but the scent of cool, old stone.

"Starling gave him the hilt," Jerdon said.

Lateran smiled to himself. He suspected he would hear about this. "I know."

"You asked him to, didn't you."

"He may need it."

"Isn't that foolhardy?"

"No more so than most everything else I do."

Jerdon was silent again for a moment. "*F'ashi*," Jerdon said, and the term of endearment was one the Wing had not heard for many years. For some time Jerdon seemed unable to say anything else, and the silent vibration of his breath in the vent piping was full of a thousand words. "Be careful," he said, at last.

"You be *more* careful, *ashti*."

"Considering your record, there's no doubt I will be. I have to go bid farewell to Her Highness. Sing if you need us." There was the whispery fizzle of a candle wick igniting, and Jerdon's slippers scuffed on the mosaic floor as he stood. "Sing to Bring Heaven Down."

Lateran pressed his hand to the marble grate. "Once was quite enough," he said. But he knew that Jerdon had already gone.

14

A thin coil of pyre-smoke traced a wavering path to Heaven, little more than a single black thread against the gray sky. From the window of his study in the royal palace, the Regent of Valnon watched it, his face drawn with concentration as though he could read a portent in the fraying smoke. Nilan fa Erianthus was no longer young, his blond braid blanched with white, but he still had the martial bearing of a soldier, his back straight and proud beneath his saffron mantle of office.

"Rouen fa Branthos?" Nilan repeated, in tones of quiet incredulity. "I was not on intimate terms with Lord Kestrel, I admit, but I cannot imagine him capable of conspiring to harm the Songbirds."

"I regret to say that I was blinded by my affection for him, myself." Raven took a delicate sip of his wine; the flavor of the palace vintages was much more potent than that of those stocked in the Temple's cellars. "But often people surprise us for the worst. Kestrel made his move, and I was able to stop him. But it cost me." He held up his wounded hand, the palm swathed in white linen. "I dare not leave the Songbirds unprotected now. What if Kestrel had allies beyond Grayson? Indeed, I should be shocked if he did not. Thrass is behind this, Nilan. There is no doubt the very security of Valnon is at stake."

"Perhaps." Nilan did not sound entirely convinced. "But it's an appalling, underhanded tactic, even for Thrass. Songbirds of the Temple are holy innocents, unarmed and untrained in the arts of war--"

"And as such, they are the ideal hostages for the Ethnarch. Why, should he hold the Dove's life in his hands, Valnon would be his with a finger-snap. And all of the Wing's fine concessional treaties would be so many paper squibs upon our pyres." Raven contemplated his wine for a moment, watching the thin sheen of crimson cling to the golden bowl. "However, as a lesson to the Temple, as a warning, the event is not without benefit. Not to mention that no Dove has ever been a boon to Valnon."

"No Dove save Alveron," Nilan said, stern. "And as yet I fail to see how the third Dove has done Valnon any harm. We are no worse now than we were the day he was cut."

"We are no better, either."

Nilan's hand went to his hip, even though his days of wearing a Godsword's oathed blade were long behind him. "Your words would be unbecoming from any of Vallish blood, but they are even less so when spoken by one of her Preybirds."

"History is on my side here, Nilan. The second Dove did no obvious harm until Heaven's retribution came for Valnon in his last hour. Eothan should never have been cut, and it is my private opinion that Willim should not have been, either." Raven shrugged. "However, I only meant that naturally, I have more of an affinity for Larks. I'm surprised you would not say the same." With his bandaged hand, he lifted his glass in a faint, mocking toast to the painting above the Regent's desk. It featured a woman and child in a blooming garden, on a summer's day long past recall.

The Regent's lips thinned to a bitter line. "I have no cause for such attachment. The line of fa Erianthus ends with me, and no other. Demetre wished it to be so." Nilan was looking at the painting as well, not at the baby, but at his mother. Her serene face shone out of the canvas like a burning brand, even though the artist had faithfully rendered the first hints of her tragedy. The hands that cradled her child were as frail as mouse-bones, too pale for mere vanity. They were decked in heavy rings of silver and onyx: Songbird tribute she had commissioned and then bought back again from the Temple when its use was done, to further her generosity. But all her gifts to Saint Lairke the healer had not been enough to stave off the wasting sickness that had devoured her; not even her last, most precious offering. Nilan tore his gaze from that of his dead wife. "I pay no more honor to the Lark of Valnon than I do to the rest of my Songbirds."

"Would that the rest of Valnon shared your equanimity," Raven demurred. "Grayson has escaped, and the Songbirds are safe in my keeping, but only for now." Raven paused a moment, to let the full meaning of his implication sink in. "I suspect that he will strike again, to free his ally and complete his task, and this time blood most dear to you may be spilt."

Nilan closed his gray eyes. "Dmitri. It was my understanding that Kestrel doted on him. Surely he would do him no harm."

"Once I thought Kestrel the finest example of a Temple Bird

Valnon could offer," Raven said, bitterly. "The line of the last child of Queen Lavras fa Valos herself, a heritage of queens and saints, rich with the legacy of Hasafel. Many powerful Temple Birds have come from that line, and I thought Rouen capable of exceeding all of them. I thought he would be a fine successor. But in the end he proved unworthy of my faith. So much promise, only to be sullied." Raven's face was set in deep lines of old disappointment. "And with his betrayal, we are faced with a gap in power. Kite is a vain flibbertigibbet, he's no use. What the Temple needs--what Valnon needs--is a High Preybird of unswerving integrity, of cunning intelligence, and whose ties to the crown are unbreakable."

"You've already had your term as High Preybird," Nilan said, only half-teasing. "Do you honestly think the Wing will allow you to reclaim the position he revoked?"

"It's true, my retirement was sooner than I would have preferred," Raven said. "But I have no interest in taking it back. Quite the contrary. The ideal High Preybird I propose is your son."

"Dmitri?" Slowly, Nilan sank down into his chair. "But he is still in his term as Lark."

"All that would require is a dependable representative for the next two years; a regent in the position of High Preybird, if you will. Much like you are to Her Highness. For that position alone do I aspire, Nilan. No more than that, and only because I fear two more years of this madness are two years too many." Raven placed his empty cup down on the Regent's desk, its contents and his growing enthusiasm bringing a flush of color to his face. "Surely you can see the beauty of it. Dmitri, as High Preybird, would restore the uneven balance of power between Temple and Crown. Though his mother surrendered him, I know he is still loyal to the line of fa Erianthus, and to you. Always he asks me for news of you. With the Queendom united, Temple and Crown in concerted purpose, we can end this pointless dithering with Thrass, and see Valnon rise, unfettered, to its true place of glory among the nations. No longer will senile old men and cold-blooded foreigners steer Valnon's course through the waters of treachery and inaction."

"Even if I were to agree with you," Nilan said, "You forget one thing. Dmitri will never be High Preybird. That is the position intended for the highest ranking Songbird, and in this case, that destiny belongs to the third Dove."

"Ah." The sound was little more than a breath through Raven's lips. "No, I had not forgotten. But now you see, my friend, why I said it might have been better if the Ethnarch's plan had succeeded."

The Regent stared at Raven for a long moment, then down at his own knotted hands, rolling his signet around his forefinger with his thumb. "Jeske," he said, his use of the Preybird's given name a sharp reminder of their long friendship. "Tell me you had nothing to do with the attack on the Dove."

"I would never endorse any action by Thrass, or by its disgraced leader," Raven said, smoothly. "Surely, after all your years trying to convince me of the worth of lesser races, you cannot honestly believe I would ally with them? They are wholly barbarians, and as far as I'm concerned once they are swept from the hem of Valnon's train, so much the better."

"Thrass has as much right to exist as any other nation," Nilan said, and once more they were on familiar footing, an old argument, all its edges worn smooth from years of being passed between them.

Raven lifted his eyebrows. "This from the man who fought them face to face for years, who saw his dearest friend cut down by the Ethnarch's treachery?"

"I have not forgotten Josah, or any of the others," Nilan reminded Raven. "Don't misunderstand me. I want this pointless turmoil in the south over as much as anyone does. But Thrass feels its case is justified, and it's never an easy thing to subjugate a people whose faith teaches them that they are destined to subjugate everyone else."

"That so-called faith of theirs also embraces cultural extermination, defamation of old gods, and an utter contempt of mercy. And while we're at it, it forbids music and instruments as tools of sorcery." Raven pursed his lips. "You can see why I'm hardly fond of them."

"I can see, and I always have. But all the same, I'd rather we'd all got along, instead."

"Exactly the sort of weak-blooded nonsense so often purported to come from the Wing," Raven sneered. "I fear it is only so much happy fantasy. The Ethnarch will not be satisfied until Valnon is a smoking ruin beneath his standard. Naturally, I'd fight to the last breath to keep Thrass' filthy fingers off any of our Songbirds, even ones I don't much care for. And admitting that such events would play to my advantage hardly makes me the orchestrator of them. Still." He fixed Nilan with his eyes, as neatly as pinning a moth upon a card. "It goes without saying that Thrass will try again. And though I would fight, Nilan, I am a Temple Bird. My sword is no more than a surgeon's blade, my craft knitting up bodies, not taking them apart. What the Temple needs is warriors."

"Out with it, Jeske," Nilan said, his smile enough to turn blunt words into old fondness. "I should have known your visit was only the opening bid in a transaction. What do you want?"

Raven made a dismissive noise. "You needn't turn it into a haggle, Nilan. But since you offered, I might say that a few of the Queensguard would suffice."

"The Wing has only to ask if he needs more guards to support the prentices--"

"The Wing is fled, Nilan."

The regent of Valnon started with surprise. "...Fled?"

"Either that, or he never existed. Hawk's answers on the matter have proved evasive, and for the time being I feel it best to handle things myself. He and Kestrel were close, and it's entirely possible they were conspiring together. Order in the Temple--and the safety of the Songbirds--hangs by a thread, my friend, and I am that thread." Raven leaned back in his chair, relaxed once more. "Let's make this a matter of private tribute, shall we? A score of able swords, subject to my discretion, stationed about the Temple. As a temporary measure, of course, until Kestrel and Grayson are brought to justice. Surely you can spare me that much?"

Nilan's mouth was flat with displeasure. He tugged a sheet of fresh parchment out of the stack on his desk, and flipped open the lid of his inkpot. "Very well. But as a temporary measure only, Jeske. The council won't like it."

"Truly, I am grateful, Nilan."

The Regent signed his name with a series of tight, economical loops. "Don't thank me. It's not for you I do this, it's for Dmitri."

"Ah." Raven tucked his hands inside his sleeves. "And shall I tell him of his father's tribute?"

Nilan's fingers tensed on his shaker of sand. "Tell him I hope he is well," he said finally, and creased the parchment in the middle before handing it to Raven. "That's all he needs to hear. No one else is to know of this, Jeske. It's well beyond the bounds of the Crown's authority."

"Your secret is safe with me, of course." Raven tucked the paper inside his sleeve, and smiled a soft, pleased sort of smile. It was still in evidence when there was a knock on the door of the Regent' study.

"...Uncle?" The door opened, and a slender, ringed hand appeared on the frame. A young woman stood there, looking much younger than her seventeen years of age, her frost-white hair piled in careful curls around her gold circlet. Her eyes were an empty, milky blue, and sightless. "Uncle," she said again, when she got no response to her first inquiry. "Are you in here?"

"Yes, Your Highness," Nilan said, rising at once. "I'm here. What do you require?"

The Queen of Valnon stepped into the room but did not answer, her head tilted slightly in Raven's direction. "You have a guest," she said. "I apologize, I didn't know. It is of no importance, Uncle. I'll come back later."

"On the contrary, Your Highness." Raven was calm, his thin fingers smoothing the front of his robe. "The regent and I are old friends from his days in the Godswords, we were merely catching up."

Queen Reim fa Valos studied the air around Raven, as though trying to place a certain scent. "You are a Preybird," she said at last. "I can hear the music in you." She put one hand over her heart and sank into a deep bow of reverence, her gown pooling around her. "...Your Grace."

"Indeed, Highness, your senses are as remarkable as they say." A flicker of unease crossed Raven's features, but the poise of a Temple Bird's voice was not so easily shaken. Perceptive though she might be, the Queen could not read Raven's face. "I am the Preybird Raven, my dear, and I met Nilan quite some time ago, when he came to the Temple to recuperate after his injuries in the war. I was only here to discuss a few matters of trifling importance."

"I see," Reim said, distantly. "Has Jerdon arrived, Uncle? He's leaving for Iskarit tonight, and I should be sorry if I missed him before he went."

Raven blinked at her, something going opaque behind his eyes. "I expect then he sails with Captain Zeig on the *Larkspur*? To my knowledge it is the only vessel traveling for Iskarit this evening."

The queen regarded him with a cool gaze, no less potent for its sightlessness. "I'm not aware of the minutiae of his travel arrangements," she murmured.

"Nor would I expect you to be," Raven said, rallying quickly. "I only thought surely it is an inconvenience for you, Highness, to be without his assistance for the season. I hope you know if you are in need of medical counsel in his absence, I am at your disposal."

"I'm honored by your concern," Reim said, with a kind of regal warmth that left her true emotions utterly ambiguous. "Though I hope I shall have no need to call upon your services."

"As do I, my lady."

Nilan cast a swift glance at the clock on the mantelpiece, and moved away from his desk. "No doubt Jerdon's waiting for us in the Library, Highness. Allow me to escort you."

"I fear I have overstayed my visit," Raven said. "I must be on my way back to the Temple. I bid you good evening, Nilan." He took the hand the Queen held out to him, and bowed over her ring. "Your Highness."

"You should have Jerdon look at your injury," the Queen said, and Raven released her hand as though he had been burnt. He shot Nilan a look of stunned surprise, and the Regent only smiled at him, shrugging.

"You said yourself she was perceptive," Nilan reminded him. "She would not miss a bandaged hand in hers."

"Nor stiff fingers, the smell of ointment, and flesh rather hot to the touch. It is nothing remarkable." Reim reached out with her queenly fingers, and unerringly gathered up the Preybird's wounded hand in her own. Her palms were cool, careful. "But perhaps it is rude of me, to suggest you seek the aid of another physician? Forgive me. I'm certain you are more than skilled, but surely it is troublesome to treat your own wounds."

"No," Raven said, forcing a smile. "Call it rather a matter of professional disagreement, Highness. Jerdon and I have never quite seen eye-to-eye on professional matters. As for my hand, it is nothing. A careless accident with a quill."

"Ah," Reim answered, releasing him. "All the same, do take care."

"I always endeavor to do so, Madam." Raven pulled up his cowl and took his leave of them. The silver cap of his staff tapped on the parquet floors in punctuation to his steps as he departed, and while the queen's empty eyes did not watch Raven go, their still depths flickered with every hollow echo he left behind.

"Come now," Nilan said, reaching down to take the Queen's hand in his own. "Jerdon tells me you noticed the light of a candle last time. That's quite extraordinary."

"I confess, I sensed only the warmth as he moved it." Reim suffered herself to be led outside and along the corridor, though she did not need the guidance. Her step was sure and certain, the thin soles of her slippers allowing her to sense every crease in the floor and the precise width of each tread on the stairs. "But he tells me my pupils reacted, and I did not wish to discourage him. He has such high hopes of restoring my sight. I've told him how little I feel the need of it, but as queen, it would be better if I could see."

"I think you can see far better than you let on," Nilan answered, folding his other hand over hers. "And at times, better than any around you."

The queen was quiet. In Nilan's hand she felt the slight shiver of his fingers, the flicker of tension across his palm. "You're worried," she said at last. "Is something wrong in the Temple?"

"I'm afraid so, but I'm not certain I believe Raven's version of events. I will have to investigate."

"But the Songbirds are safe?" Reim pressed, her hand tightening in his.

"Raven says he has them under his protection."

"But you don't believe him." There was no question in the Queen's voice, and Nilan sighed.

"No. I don't. Which is why I hope to speak with Jerdon. He is close to Kestrel, perhaps he can tell us something."

Jerdon was indeed waiting in the Queen's private library, staring up at the pair of portraits mounted together above the fireplace. The late Queen Renne stood against a background of velvet drapes, girt as though for battle with a sword on her hip. White horses and purple doves circled each other on her shield. Her cascade of silvery hair was bound up in braids, her smile certain and stern. The painting on the other side of the landing was of her consort Josah, and his armor was not ceremonial. He wore the red collar of a high-ranking Godsword, and the assured gaze of a man who did not need titles to measure his worth. It was this painting that had the broader share of Jerdon's attention, as he peered at the face of Reim's father.

"Remarkable likeness," he said, without turning around. "Truly. I wonder that no one has made comment on it before."

"On the contrary," the Regent said, guiding the queen to a petit-point settee, "They've often been called the most accurate portraits in the palace. Sometimes I half expect them to speak."

"Portraits?" Jerdon said, and then blinked at the queen and the Regent. "Oh yes, of course, the portraits. Quite a good job on the part of your court artist. And when will he paint your investment portrait, Your Highness? During the festivities this spring to come?"

"I suppose," Reim said, with a tiny smile. "But I will have to rely on you to tell me if it's any good or not."

"Nonsense," Jerdon said, turning away and opening the latches on his medical case. "You must keep a positive frame of mind, Highness. Someday you will look on it with your own eyes."

"What has become of the Songbirds, Jerdon?"

The regent and the physician froze in place, staring at each other over the Queen's head. Nilan made a little hapless shrug. It was as though, deprived of one sense, the queen had stretched all her other ones to an uncanny extreme of perception.

"The queen does not waste time," Nilan demurred. "But I second the question. Surely you've heard things, Jerdon. You have an ear at every keyhole in the Undercity. Something is amiss in the Temple. If you know anything about this business, I'd like to hear it myself."

"Highness," Jerdon said, sinking down next to her on the settee. "How long have we been friends, now?"

The queen's mouth puckered in a little smile. "I suppose since the moment you smacked the first breath of air into my lungs at my mother's bedside," she said.

"I did, and it was quite a lot of work, at that. Most thought you wouldn't survive the day." Jerdon gathered the queen's hands in his own. "And indeed, your mother did not. That you lived was more the will of Heaven than the work of my art, I admit. Perhaps that's why I look on you as a daughter, forward of me though it may be. And as such, I must beg you to trust me."

The queen made a soft noise of impatience, one that Nilan was tempted to echo. "You know that I do, Jerdon. So tell me--"

"Highness," Jerdon interrupted. "I can tell you nothing of the events in the Temple, or the whereabouts of the Songbirds, or even my least suspicions. Nothing at all. To do so might place you in deep peril, and I will not be here to protect you."

"What's this?" Nilan started up from the arm of the settee. "Jerdon, if you know something, I insist that you tell me at once."

"Insist all you please," Jerdon said, stonily. "My orders are from a source higher than Regent or Queen. We're old friends, Nilan, and I can tell you only this: The Songbirds are safe, for the moment, but Valnon may not be. Ignorance may be the Queen's only shield. For her sake as well as your own, Nilan, not to mention the fate of the Songbirds, I must remain silent. For your part, I beseech you to bend all effort to unraveling Raven's charges against Kestrel. Throw every scrap of old city law at him that you have at your disposal, entangle him in as many snares of protocol as you can set. Anything to keep him busy, to slow him down. Lady Milia will gladly help you. I will attend to all the rest."

Reim looked through Jerdon without seeing him, and comprehension brightened her face. "You've spoken to the Wing," she said.

"Impossible," Nilan put in. "Raven said he had fled."

"Raven's word is worth less than a string of brass crescents." Jerdon shook his head. "Lateran XII would sooner slit his own throat than abandon his Temple. If Raven has misplaced him, it is only that he doesn't know what he's looking for." He reached into his bag for his magnifying glass, and held it up to the queen's eyes. "And if you'll forgive me, Majesty, I am on quite a tight schedule this evening, and had better get on with your examination."

15

Raven moved through the west gallery of the palace with measured tread, his robes reflecting dully in the mounted shields, the banners of the ruling houses motionless above him. He cocked his eye at his namesake, embroidered in sable silk upon the slate-colored arms of the house of fa Soliver, and then at the argent swan on the fa Grayces' crimson field nearby. It was, Raven had always thought, a noisy and utterly useless sort of bird. Loyal to its mate, pleasing enough to the eye, but not much else besides.

The banners rippled faintly, in a gentle sigh only they could feel, and Raven knew he was not alone. The banners went still once more, but he could smell leather, and steel, and orange blossoms, and death.

"You would not need to beg the regent for swords," said the shadows behind him, "if you had let me bring my men into the city."

"My dear young lady," Raven said, sounding bored even if he did not feel it. "I will not see your so-called men set foot in this city until absolutely necessary."

"Why?" she countered, for it was a she, somewhere in the hidden, unlit corners of the gallery. "It would have been over at the first if you had, rather than giving our swords to some fools you found to do your bidding. Do you relish losing your prey so often?"

"The Dove is not my prey," Raven answered coldly, without turning around. "And neither is the Temple."

"What is it to you, then?" She sounded bored; she didn't really care about motives. They were each of them useful tools to each other, but that was all. "Your lover, is it?"

"It is my child," Raven said, with barely-restrained emotion. "Sickly, abused, its inheritance squandered by others."

She snorted, from somewhere behind a narrow alcove. "Whatever you say, Preybird. You want things the same as any man, it just happens that our wants run along the same line."

"For now," Raven allowed. "But that does not matter. A ship sails from Valnon tonight. I think its cargo will be of interest to us. See that it does not get away uninspected."

"Very well." The banners shivered again, and Raven continued down to the Queensguard's yard, to collect Nilan fa Erianthus' tribute for his son.

"Sing something," Rekbah said, perching on a cushion at the end of the banquet table, her elbows firmly lodged among the tea plates. Grayson and Jerdon were sorting out supplies at the far end of the table, surrounded by heaps of spare cloaks, and dried figs, and casks of wine. Three large barrels were set aside in the hall beyond, but they were intended to transport a different kind of goods.

Rekbah had been at Jerdon's elbow ever since he had returned from the surface, but when the topics of travel and strategy had grown too dull, she fixed her attention on the sullen Songbirds.

"What?" Willim had been lost in unpleasant reverie over his half-eaten food, trying to reassure himself that his entire world would right itself again eventually, and not having much success believing it.

"They're not street-buskers, Rekbah," Jerdon said, without looking up from his list. "And they've had a difficult time. Don't pester them. Grayson, be so good as to hand me those gloves."

"I'm not pestering them," Rekbah argued, and turned to the Songbirds for confirmation. "Am I?"

"Yes," Ellis answered, breaking a lump of cheese into tiny chunks as though he would like to keep eating, but hadn't the stomach for it. Jerdon had insisted on a light meal before their departure, but no one had much appetite. "But to be honest, being pestered is better than siting here worrying about everything."

"Then you entertain her," Dmitri said, into the bottom of his teacup. "I'm not a minstrel to be called with a fingersnap."

"You'd never get hired as one, with that temper," Rekbah said, returning the Lark's sour look with one of her own. "Don't go into the larder with that face on, you'll curdle the milk."

"Rekbah," Jerdon said again, with a little more sternness in his voice.

Rekbah sighed, defeated, and sank down to he table, her folded arms beneath her chin. After a moment she pushed Ellis' plate out of his reach. "Don't waste food. If you aren't going to eat it, leave it alone."

"Fine," Willim said, worried a fight would erupt if Rekbah remained undistracted. "I'll sing something. What do you want to hear?"

"*The Hymn of St. Alveron*," Rekbah said, at once.

"All fifty verses of it?" Dmitri asked, wrinkling his nose. "Shall I run and fetch us a chorus of flock boys, and pipers, and drummers, and Preybirds as well? I'm so sure Raven will let us back in for our festival garb. Whyever didn't we think of that?"

"Of course I don't expect you to sing the whole thing." Rekbah said.

"Well, that's a relief," Willim said.

"Just the good parts about Alveron," Rekbah concluded.

"That *is* the whole thing." Willim put his forehead in his hand. "Haven't you heard it at festivals?"

"We're never in town for Canticles week," Rekbah explained. "Usually we go back to Iskarit for the winter. I'm from Iskarit," she added, as though her appearance had not been proof enough of that already.

"Is everyone there as noisy as you are?" Ellis grumbled, dragging his plate back to continue mutilating his leftover cheese.

"Some are worse," Rekbah said, pulling the plate away again.

"All right, fine," Willim said, defeated.

"And it's *Saint* Alveron," Dmitri corrected. "But you agreed to it, Willim, so have at it."

Willim tipped back his cup, even though there wasn't much water left. He wasn't sure why, but the notion of singing for Rekbah made him inexplicably nervous. Was it because he wasn't in the Temple? Was his faith in his abilities so tenuous? Willim shook off the clammy fingers of his doubts, and the memory of Eothan's grieving eyes, and inhaled deeply from his belly. He pulled the first four lines of the Hymn out of his lungs and the whole thing followed, spooling out of him like silk ribbon from a spindle, fine and unexpectedly strong.

O Dove of Heaven's choosing, whose song was cruelly made
By grief, by shame, by slavery, by bondage and by blade
Though years have passed like daydreams, too fleeting to
*   recall*
I see as in a mirror the moment of your fall

When king sent you to slaughter for naught but wounded pride
For claiming what was stolen, your rightful crown denied.

When glory shone around you, when music tore the sky
When all the world was broken upon your desperate cry.
The swords raised up against you, they bent like blades of
*   grass*
And down fell those who bled you, all shattered by the blast.
I never bore you hatred, I never wished you wronged,
And for that merest mercy you spared me with your song.

Willim had not sung so much as a note since the interrupted
Evensong. Not since he had been cut had he spent so long without
singing, and to his own ears his voice was startling, rough at the
edges, and fenced in by the strange acoustics of Jerdon's banquet
hall. But Rekbah's eyes had gone wide, her mouth open in
amazement. It was not every day that a Dove of Valnon launched
into song over the dinner table.

Suddenly embarrassed by his impromptu performance, Willim
fidgeted with his spoon. "That's the beginning, at least. It's usually
sung by a Preybird, since it's Grayce's lines, but I sing when it gets
to Alveron's verses. We could do the extra parts sung by the
Preybirds and the flock, but it needs a big group for the harmony."

"I don't care about that," Rekbah said, her face alight with
wonder. "That was amazing. It just came out of you. It doesn't even
sound real."

"Of course it's real," Ellis said.

"Let's hear you do it, then," Rekbah said, expectantly.

"It's not my turn," Ellis replied, prim.

"Then whose--"

Dmitri put down his teacup with an emphatic clatter, and with
half-closed eyes and no other warning, he sang:

To Saint and to my Songbird I hereby give my vow
To him who Sang Down Heaven with holy song endowed.
The wound I fail to spare you I will take twice in your stead
And twice the grief for your grief, and twice the blood you've
*   bled.*
Though death come for me swiftly, by you I will remain

With sword to guard my city, so silence shall not reign.

Dmitri's voice ended in a sigh, too quiet to be heard beyond the confines of the room and full of heartbreak. Rekbah's question died unfinished in her mouth. At the end of the table, Jerdon and Grayson had fallen silent. Grayson's face was guarded and still, he stared at the folded back of a map as though his life's secrets were printed on the empty parchment. Jerdon, for his part, was inscrutable behind the lamplight reflection in his glasses.

"It wasn't your turn either," Ellis muttered. "That's still Grayce's part. You just wanted to show off."

Dmitri shrugged, but his eyebrows gave away his smugness.

"You know, the Hymn is not quite the same story that you will find in the histories," Jerdon said, with a sudden, unquestionable gravity. "Though the bones of it are the same. I've neglected your education, Rekbah, if you don't know it. You see--" He tipped up his glasses, and took the unmistakable first breath of an expert storyteller beginning a tale. "Alveron and his two cousins had just discovered a rare metal beneath the island. No one there had ever seen platinum before, as it is the rarest metal in the world, and is found only in places where stars have fallen. Antigus would have the keeping of all of it, of course, but he had offered the boys a reward for their labor. When Alveron and Lairke and Thryse were granted audience, Alveron asked permission for his people to leave, so they might return to their homeland, saying that the platinum he had found was surely enough to buy their freedom. At first Antigus agreed, and I believe he expected to keep his word. He had thousands of slaves, and the children of Hasafel comprised only a small percentage, a few hundred or so. They were troublesome, as well, and proud. Very likely he was glad for a reason to be rid of them. Antigus was a warrior chief, and his father's father had claimed the land he ruled, and he had little patience for slaves and the tedious fussing of his household. His thoughts were better spent on war and further conquest." Jerdon spread his fingers on the table. "'*Go,*' Antigus said, '*and find this Hasafel of yours. Trouble me no more.*'"

"*And when we have found Hasafel,*" Alveron persisted, "*We may claim it as our own, never to be taken from us again?*"

"*Yes,*" Antigus said, already annoyed by terms he thought

173

futile. Hasafel never existed, and even if it had, it lay buried in the fathoms of the sea. "Take it, and damn its phantom king if he refuses your right, but get out of my sight."

From his ragged tunic Alveron withdrew a black clay flute, in the shape of a bird and banded with silver. Wrought upon it were the letters of the ancient city of Hasafel, the white island in the sea, the beautiful city of Alveron's dreams. "I have found Hasafel," Alveron said, lifting the flute in his hand. "And we stand upon it even now. In your mines, thief-king, I have found the bones of my ancestors. All that remains of Hasafel is this island, and though it is a catacomb, by your own words, you have given it to me and to my tribe."

Antigus was outraged at this trickery, and he flew into a fury. Never did he suspect that Hasafel was buried in the sea around him, and that his city was built upon its remains. He had been made to look a fool in front of those he ruled, and his wrath was terrible. At once he revoked his promise, and for their insolence Alveron and his kinsmen were castrated, so that the line of Hasafel would end there and then. But there were still those in the tunnels who bore the tainted bloodline. Rather than risk one escaping, Antigus had all his slaves dragged from their tunnels. Those that resisted were put to sword at once, and Alveron's father was among them. But the others were corralled on the high, empty place by Antigus' palace, where his warriors trained for war. There Antigus had Alveron and his kinsmen mounted on a high platform, naked and bloody, to witness the slaughter their impertinence had caused. There, Antigus ordered all his slaves to death. No one was to be spared, not the oldest grand-dame or the babe born the day before. Any who tried to flee would be herded off the cliff into the sea. Alveron and his kinsmen would be forced to watch, and they would be the last to die, not by the sword, but by slow exposure to the elements, surrounded by the rotting bodies of their people.

Antigus gave the command for his warriors to advance. But Grayce, Antigus' master of horse, refused his king's command. He and his knights threw down their blades, unwilling to cut down the helpless.

Enraged, Antigus drew his own sword, and charged his horse into the crowd. The first before his sword was Lavras, Alveron's sister, dearer to her brother than breath. As the tyrant's sword descended to cut her down, Alveron screamed out his rage and his grief, and Lairke and Thryse cried out with him. The sound was like a terrible music, and it tore apart the sky. The grass lay flat to the ground, and the sea became as smooth as glass. A wind swept down from the rent clouds, and with it came a dreadful music, beautiful and awesome and strange.

And a change came over the face of Antigus the Terrible. Terrified, he commanded his archers to kill the boys to silence them, but his knights were already dead. They lay cold and staring in their ranks, weapons still in hand. Only Grayce and his horsemen survived, as they bowed before the fear and awe of Heaven, their earlier mercy winning them mercy in turn. And yet the boys sang on. Sang away the life of any in Antigus' command, sang to spare the lives of those they loved, sang their kingdom back from the ravages of history. They Sang Heaven Down, and Heaven took back the life it had given to Antigus, leaving him as it had his cruel subjects, their corpses strewn in the grass.

Grace freed Alveron and swore his sword to him, and to whatever god Alveron called his own. His knights did likewise, and the people cried that Alveron was their new king, and Hasafel was born anew.

But Alveron wept. All that remained of Hasafel's glory was one island full of bones. Alveron's father was slain, and Antigus had murdered all the children Alveron might once have had. Rather than be king, he gave his people Lavras as their queen, and named the new city Valnon, which in the tongue of Hasafel means 'rebirth.' Where Heaven delivered them, a Temple was built, the marble dais lifting holy singers to the place where Alveron and his Kinsmen had stood that day on a rough wood platform above the field of slaughter. And for them the birds of Valnon are cut, and for them they sing, so that never for a moment will Valnon forget the moment Heaven's music came to earth, and saved us all.

In the banquet hall of Jerdon's house, there was a stunned silence. Willim felt as though a painted tableau of stiff figures had been brought, bloody and breathing, to vivid life in the room around them. Even Rekbah was at a loss for words.

"Well," Jerdon said, with a depreciating little wave of his hand. "That is how it's recorded in the old histories, anyway. You'll

175

find it that way deep down in the archives, but I expect Osprey keeps it under close watch. It's a tidier thing, in Temple song. I'm sure it squares up into verse better as it's sung now."

"Where did you hear this?" Dmitri sat at arm's length from the table, his face and tone both drenched with suspicion. "I have never read any such thing, not even in the depths of the archives." Even as doubtful as he was, Dmitri would not call Jerdon's version of the tale an outright lie. The tale was too compelling to reject without examination.

"You've seen my library, my boy," Jerdon replied, picking up a spare tunic and deftly flicking it into neat folds. "In the history of the world, six hundred years is a mere trifle, and Grayce's hymn for Alveron was not the only recording made of that day. There were plenty of other tellers. When you have time, you should have a look over the personal letters of the first Queen, or the histories of Branthos fa Valos, or even the truly interesting interpretations of the Shindamiri court historians, who weren't even there and had the whole thing by hearsay."

"We take for granted that our city is built on Hasafel's ruin," Willim said, thinking of the frescoes beneath the Temple dais. "But I wonder what St. Alveron thought when he realized what he'd found."

"I imagine it gave him a turn, and not a nice one." Jerdon put down his leather satchel with an air of finality. "Now then, Your Graces, I think it's time for us to be on our way."

16

Willim had spent the vast majority of his life unmolested by barrels, but now he was beginning to think they had long-harbored some secret grudge against him, which they were only just now in a position to act upon. The dubiousness he had shown in the face of Jerdon's plan would have been flat-out refusal, if he had only known what lay in store. As it was, an hour after clambering into it willingly, Willim emerged from the barrel shaken and bruised, and on legs that refused to hold him up in any effective way. It took him a moment to realize that the shakiness was not entirely the fault of the barrel, and had more to do with the tilting motion of the floor beneath his feet. He was standing in a small room with sharply-angled walls, ribbed in curved timbers like some of the acoustic panels in the Temple sanctuary. A lamp swayed above, revealing slanting shadows of open steps in front of the narrow end of a trade vessel's cargo hold. There was a pair of windows at the pinched-together end of the room, small round ones of thick, streaky glass. The view outside was nothing but a milky green that shivered and bubbled with each sway of the ship.

"Don't look so bothered," Rekbah said, plying a crowbar to the next barrel, and uncasking a tousled-looking Ellis. "I once spent the whole passage from Iskarit to Shindamir in a chicken crate, and it was far worse than your little trip."

"That was awful," Ellis said, hollowly. Dmitri would probably have agreed, but at the moment he was too busy being quietly sick in the corner. Willim had a moment's gratitude that, while rattled, he had at least managed to stay in possession of his dinner.

"Here," Rekbah said, plucking the Songbirds' signets from her bodice. "Jerdon said you can wear these again. The men on the ship are trustworthy, and they know who you are."

"Wonderful," Ellis said, putting his ring on, and then trying to make his hair all go in the same general direction. "They know who we are just in time to see how we look after being rolled around in a barrel for miles."

"Sorry about that," Grayson said, coming halfway down the steps and bending over to look at them through the slats. "It was really the only way to get you on board without anyone in the harbor noticing you. You all right, Dmitri? "

Dmitri waved a limp hand in Grayson's direction.

"Good," Grayson said, taking this for confirmation. "Jerdon says you three should come up and see this. It ought to be safe enough. And," he added, as Dmitri's ribs heaved again, "the air'll do you good."

The close space of the hold was pungent with the smells of tar and lamp oil and seasick Songbird, so Willim was all too glad to reach into the barrel for his cloak and follow Rekbah on deck. It took some doing to get to the stairs, as the ship seemed intent to throw him backwards in the wrong direction, but he made it to the steps and up them without getting knocked off his feet. He was feeling pretty pleased with himself until he came above and realized the tossing waves were nothing more than the gentle slosh of the harbor, and not the soaring billows of the open sea. But then he looked up over the stern, and forgot about anything save the view in front of him.

The air had changed. It no longer smelled of earth and the Undercity, it was briny and wild, and the constant cavern warmth was replaced with a dank, wintry chill. In the thin, rippling mist surrounding them, a prickly forest of bare trees was bobbing and swaying far into the twilight, lit here and there with the brightly-colored sparks of signal lanterns. The branches were the masts and turrets of vessels riding at anchor, and of some passing in or out among their larger, sleeping kin. From time to time there was the sharp call of a sailor on watch, or the shrill note of a boatswain's whistle. Their own ship glided past the waiting ships, drawn by the pull of the tide towards the harbor mouth.

It was a strange, unearthly vision, and Willim stopped to stare on the top step, unmoving until Ellis gave him a little shove from behind. He clambered the rest of the way on deck. Grayson was standing at the rail, his red cloak vivid in the fog, and he waved them forward. "You can see most of the Undercity from here, on clear evenings," he said, and a dreamy smile slid across his features. "But to be honest, I prefer it in the mist."

Willim followed Grayson's gaze, and saw a great sparkling mass of lights just beyond the line of ships at the harbor. The bright lights of the Undercity were diffused in the fog, making the whole cavern glow like a distant ribbon of stars. The ship made a slow lean around to the left, into the light of the outside world, and the mist was tinged with the vivid colors of sunset, stray beams knifing through the cavern mouth to punch shades of brilliant blue and green out of the harbor waters.

"We're coming around to the entrance," Grayson said, as a wan-looking Dmitri clambered up out of the hold to join them at the rail. "Those barrels you see floating there are filled with pitch, and are lit at nightfall to guide ships into the harbor after dark."

"That's a proper use for a barrel," Ellis said, giving Rekbah a haughty look. "Better that than for human transport."

Rekbah stuck her tongue out at him.

The ship slid out of the harbor mouth and caught a crosswind in her striped sails; they belled out and pulled the ship forward into the first real wave out of the harbor. Willim caught himself against the rail as she dove eagerly forward. They had left the mist behind inside the Undercity's walls, and the setting sun turned the water to beaten gold, the sky to a deepening, breathless blue. The whole world had been washed clean by the earlier rain.

"Here," Grayson said, pointing back behind them. "This is what I really wanted you to see."

Willim turned, looking back towards the harbor, towards Valnon. His breath caught, his blood thudded dully in his ears. For all his life, Willim had sung of Valnon, lived in it, breathed its air, but before that moment, he had never truly seen it. It was an island, that he knew, but he only knew the lie of her rooftops and towers as they looked from the Temple. From the sea, the cliffs of the city thrust upwards until they seemed to scrape the bottom step of Heaven, garnished here and there with fragments of old roads and little alcoves of gardens like Jerdon's. The white cliff walls and the city itself gleamed as though on fire, every window catching the light of sunset. The spires of the Temple rose above it all, delicate as a jeweled crown. For a centerpiece in the diadem, Willim saw the round Evensong window on the westernmost wall of the sanctuary, and knew the light of his hour was at that moment streaming into an empty sanctuary.

"It's Evensong," Willim said, thinking that at this hour the day before, his only concern had been to prove his pride to Grayson. Now, it was time for his hour, and he was standing in the wrong colors on a ship with its prow pointing away from Valnon, with the

Temple in utter disarray, his friends wounded, and the future in doubt. The beauty of the view was not dimmed, but it was tinged by Willim's own feeling of strangeness. "I would be on the dais right now."

Grayson's hand was heavy on his shoulder, but the weight and the strength of it was reassuring. "Don't think of it," Grayson advised him. "It's good luck to leave Valnon at Evensong. They say a Songbird will be singing when you return."

"I suppose that proverb doesn't have a stipulation for when the Songbirds aren't actually in the Temple to sing, does it?" Ellis looked at Grayson expectantly, but the sell-sword only lifted one shoulder in a shrug.

Willim clenched the railing as Valnon slowly shrank away from them, staring at the ring of his office, newly restored to his hand. It was sunset, and he should be singing Evensong, but he was not. Instead the words that came to his lips were those of a defeated king, the king of a city now forever lost deep in the waters beneath them.

The doves are slain, the city falls, the god reclaims his islands.
The sea that bore her comes again, to wash the blood from her
  sands.
And we are thrown upon the waves, in exile of my making,
While o'er our city, in the deep, the foaming tide is breaking.
Yet I recall her gleaming, in dreaming, in singing,
And ever will I mourn her, still yearning, unburning.

Willim was not even fully aware he was singing, not until the last word left his lips and he looked away from Valnon to see that on the ship everyone had gone silent, and even the sailors had paused in their tasks to stare at him in wonder and no little amount of fear. For a long moment there was no sound on the ship save for the creak and slap of the vessel in the waves, and the soft echo of Willim's melody echoing in the hearts of all present.

"Forgive me, Your Grace," Jerdon said, after coming down from the fo'c'sle and making a little cough into his hand, "But it is considered the utmost ill-fortune to sing any line of the *Lay of Hasafel* on a ship while she is underway."

"I thought there was nothing more fitting that he could sing,"

Grayson said, and shot a cold glare to a few of the sailors, who shook off their fascination and went muttering back to their work.

"And I thought so as well," came a voice from where Jerdon had been standing: a broad, clear voice used to cutting over the noise of storm and struggle. "And any man who considers it ill-luck to have a voyage blessed by the Dove himself had best put himself over the rail now, and spare me the trouble of doing it."

"Your Graces," Jerdon said, as the speaker thumped down the ladder towards them, "May I present Captain Zeig, our assistant in this enterprise and my very good friend."

"It is my honor, Your Graces," Zeig said, bowing to the Songbirds.

"You're a Thrassin!" Ellis blurted, before he could help himself.

Jerdon looked startled, Grayson put his face in in his hand, and Rekbah threw her arms outwards in disgust. Zeig was the color of a cup of Jerdon's tea, it was true, and his white hair was styled in thin tribal braids. But Willim would've thought Ellis had a better sense of self-preservation than to go casting aspersions on the man's heritage. For a start, he had a head in height on Grayson, who was no shirker in that quality himself. Zeig's bare shoulders could have supported half a dozen men on them lengthwise, and probably plated in lead, to boot. He wore a pair of Thrassin cutlasses on his hips, and they were well-kept and well-used. But at Ellis' comment, he only laughed.

"True enough," he said, "I am colored like my southern kinsmen. But Thrass has for centuries laid alongside Alfir, and for a long time their blood mingled in ways more pleasant than spilled together on the battlefield." Zeig gestured to Willim. "Why, even His Grace the Dove has the white hair of my people. No doubt it comes from some mixed-blood Alfiri noble in his line, much like those of my own heritage."

"What he means to say," Grayson said crisply, while Willim smoothed a self-conscious hand over the pale hair at the nape of his neck, "is that he is a highly-decorated former Godsword who once served beside the late Queen's Consort in the last war, and he took great wounds in the service of the Temple."

"Retired now," Zeig said, as though in apology, and tipped his fingers at the jeweled patch he wore over one eye. "I had enough of battle. I was lucky to call Josah my friend. In fact..." Zeig was still looking at Willim, a curious expression in his eye, but he shook his head, and turned to Dmitri instead. "I had many friends in the 'swords. I served under your father as well, my Lark, before he traded Grayce's oath for politics. He never forgave himself for High Consort Josah's death, and I fear he gave up on a promising military career as a result. But he's done well enough, I'd say!"

Dmitri looked stricken, and Willim forgot about his hair and Zeig's penetrating stare. "Dmitri's father?"

"Didn't he tell you?" Zeig looked surprised. "I thought everyone knew the Lark of Valnon's father was Nilan fa Erianthus, Regent of Valnon. He's the very image of his father. I've half my sight, but I'm not utterly blind."

Ellis' mouth gaped. "Your father is the *Regent*?"

"I am a Bird of the Temple," Dmitri snapped, staring past them at some point on the horizon far beyond the stern. "I have no father."

Zeig's expression grew thoughtful, sad. "Of course," he said, softly. "Forgive me, Your Grace, for my over-familiarity." He bowed, in respectful apology. "Please consider the *Larkspur* your home, Your Graces, and do not hesitate to ask for anything to make your voyage more comfortable. I must attend to the crew. Grayson, Master Doctor, milady Rekbah." With a nod to the others, he strode across the deck to speak with his second mate by the wheel.

"Sorry," Willim said, once he had gone. "I didn't know Hasafel was bad luck."

"My boy," Jerdon said, pitching his voice lower, "Sailors are a superstitious lot. I suspect Zeig's had to double their pay to carry a Dove still in his colors, as they have long memories in regards to your predecessor's unfortunate disaster. As for Hasafel, and Thali singing it under the sea, well. I think the reason for that particular twitch is obvious. Doves are said to have the blood of Hasal the sea-god, and while the sailors are happy enough to give their regards to his beloved Naime, they both fear and love the master of their element, and fear and love a Songbird of Evensong, with the power to lift and quell the waves with his song."

"Ridiculous," Dmitri snorted, having gotten both his color and his bad temper back. "Willim couldn't sing up the wrath of a puddle."

"Neither could you," Ellis shot back in defense.

"Of course I couldn't," Dmitri said, sweeping back his lank hair. "Because it's all a bunch of myth and nonsense. This area is prone to quakes, and both Thali and Eothan had a stroke of dramatic and tragic timing, nothing more. For the love of Lairke, there's a Songbird singing three times a day, every day, all the year long. It's hardly a shock one would be singing when the Great Quake struck. I find it hard to fathom how grown men could fear an accident of chance three centuries gone, or an old song, or the name of a city, no matter how it met its end."

Jerdon was watching Dmitri, a little smile playing around his lips. "Such stark words from a Lark of Valnon," he said. "Next you'll say the saints are equally trumped-up."

For a moment there was a light in Dmitri's eyes, and Willim could see him in his Temple paint and ceremonial blacks, plain as day. "Don't put such music into my mouth," he said, in a hushed voice. "I would not have been cut for St. Lairke if I didn't believe in him."

"Well," Jerdon said, with a dismissive air, "I'm sure he'd appreciate that."

"You mock me," Dmitri breathed, going pale in a way that Willim knew all too well was a precursor of fury.

"Nothing of the sort, my boy," Jerdon said, tapping one finger to his chin--the finger that not by chance had his tribute ring on it. "But I wouldn't go blithering about Hasafel and Eothan and saints' wrath while you're on board. I find it's better to keep the jack-tars comfortable and slightly inebriated to ensure a smooth voyage. We'll be on here for a good week or three, so it's best if we all get along."

Willim shivered, as mere mention of Eothan was enough to turn his skin to gooseflesh. He wasn't entirely sure the second Dove's misfortune was only chance, and whatever Eothan was now, it was more than myth and rumor.

The sun had set, and the sky had turned a dull purple in promise of a chilly, fine night. The ship's lamps cast a friendly yellow glow over the water, and Willim wondered if it was shameful of him to be at last excited at the prospect of the journey. For the sake of propriety, he tried to keep the eagerness in his face to a respectful minimum of mild interest as Jerdon showed them around the *Larkspur*. Willim knew very little of ships, save for the cadence of their motion and how it played into sailing ballads. Dmitri, having had quite enough of that cadence, retired to their quarters rather than tagging along for the tour. Before long Willim started to think he had the right idea. Zeig noticed the Dove yawning, and suggested the Songbirds retire.

The cabin Zeig had prepared for his guests was a close but comfortable fit for six passengers, and it was full of cunning cabinets and pegs for their belongings. Bunks were built right into the bulkhead of the stern, and the back wall had windows of tinted glass. Willim could see the lights of Valnon growing more and more faint beyond them.

"Won't anyone notice we're going the wrong way for Iskarit?" Ellis asked in some confusion, as he examined all the little niches above his berth.

"It's a bad time of year for the eastern route," Grayson explained, shedding his brigantine and sprawling in a bottom bunk with a noise of relief. "We'll need to take the currents the long way around, which works out well for us since we're going to Alfir instead. If we were really going to Iskarit, we'd have to sail downriver to Lake Clarie, and then on to Iskarit. But we won't be going that far. We'll take the river east just the same, but we'll go no further than Clarie. It should be safe enough for you there, and it's a prettier voyage this way." He gestured starboard. "As a matter of fact, at sunrise you should have a nice view of the cliffs of the Northcamp." His face went still. "I'd rather you didn't wake me for it, though. I don't care to see it."

"Zeig probably has some charts he can show you," Rekbah offered Ellis, into the uncomfortable pause. "He let me look at any I wanted on our last trip."

"And I would be grateful if you didn't pilfer any of them this time," Jerdon said in reminder, kicking his embroidered slippers into the nearest cabinet.

Rekbah pouted as she clambered into the bunk above Jerdon's. Dmitri, for his part, was already in a bunk with the blanket over his head. No one made any comment as to the early hour; sleep had been poor and in short supply for all of them. Willim took the berth just above Grayson's, and the motion of the ship lulled him into slumber in less time than it took for the dais to clear the sanctuary floor. Sleep was sudden and heavy, falling over him like the drape of a corpse upon its bier, and he dreamed.

The city was drowning while the Dove sang.

As the dais pillar rose, the sea that skirted Valnon's isle rose as well, a shimmering green wall higher than the city itself, with broken ships spinning half-capsized upon its back. For a moment the water hung above Valnon, a vast curve of terrible gravity, and then its arc shattered above the thin spires of the sanctuary dome. Beneath the crush of the blow, rooftops crumpled with the ease of a merchant's striped awning at sundown. Oak beams snapped as though they were nothing more than oat straws, their splinters washed in fragments down the rushing cataract of the market street. Whirlpools spun in the streets and fountains spewed from unshuttered windows.

There was nowhere to flee. The people of Valnon stood silent as the water swept them away, the life washing out of them as easily as dye from cheap cloth. Those in the streets were borne off into the unknown, but the others lingered behind. Like grotesque pearls in ornate coffers, the dead remained in their watery mansions, their blank faces floating past the windows.

And through it all the Dove, the sacred Dove of Valnon, could only sing. The music was a dark pressure behind his eardrums, a lingering metallic taste in his mouth. But Heaven did not intercede through him, and not a single life was spared by his singing. In the end, Valnon was drowned deep. The Dove, made impotent for his music, was impotent with it. With his Evensong's echoes still ringing in the Temple, he stepped from his dais, and broke himself on the ground below.

Still the water came. It closed cold fingers over the Dove's legs and his chest and into his open mouth, rushing into his lungs and weighting him down, swelling him like a corsair's sail. Barnacles and sea urchins blossomed between his fingers, their sharp edges bringing no blood as they burst through his skin. Crabs skittered over his breastbone; fishes burrowed into his hair. Airless music poured from his mouth, unstoppable.

The tide brought Valnon's corpses dancing to his side. They pressed their bloated faces to the high sanctuary windows, their ruined jaws pouring forth a parody of Evensong. Soft, white hands clutched at his own. Terror at last brought a sound out of the Dove that was not music, his song breaking. Unable to scream with his dead, waterlogged lungs, the Dove could only drown until the waves tore him away, out of the sea--and he woke.

Willim sucked in a raw gasp of air, not of salt water, and let it out again in merciful silence, not song. He was not the Dove he had dreamed of, the dark-haired one futile before the rising sea, the one shattered and bloody at the base of the dais pillar, buoyed upon a sinister tide. He was not Eothan. He was Willim, and he had not fallen.

The cabin was dark, but faint moonlight trickled through the window. Willim swung his head out of the berth and saw Ellis' hand hanging over the bunk above, his Thrush's ring glinting as he twitched in his sleep. Dmitri didn't seem to have moved since Willim had gone to bed, and Rekbah was snoring faintly. Jerdon's berth was empty, and so, too, was Grayson's. Willim slipped out of his berth and plopped softly to the floor, gathering his cloak around him and padding out onto the deck. Sleep would not be an option, he knew, for some while.

Willim had thought a ship at night to be much like the Temple at night: hushed and pensive. In truth it had more of the bustle of Gemsplit Close. The sailors on watch were engaged in small knots of conversation as they worked, someone far up in the fore was playing a flute. The gentle creaking of the ship could not mask the three voices above Willim, though Willim suspected he was the only one close enough to hear the actual words. He moved under the shadow of the ladder to listen.

"You could have warned me, Jer," Zeig was saying, and Willim could hear the captain bring his hand down against the ladder rail in emphasis. "The boy nearly startled me out of what I've got left of my wits. And that after singing of the old city; I confess I called on the saints before I got the better grip of things."

"Forgive me, my friend," Jerdon answered, with what sounded like utter sincerity. "It slipped my mind. I have got more than a few cakes in the oven at the moment, you know."

"I had no idea," Grayson mused. "Does Willim know any of this?"

"Nothing," Jerdon said, firmly. "If a boy does not already

186

know his origins before coming to the Temple, he is not to be told of them until the end of his service. One cannot risk the split loyalty of a Songbird whose heart is not wholly the Temple's. Willim will be told all when he becomes a Preybird, and not a moment before."

"Surely Raven knows," Zeig said, in disbelief. "He has only to look at the Dove's face."

"Oh, he knows," Jerdon snorted. "Rather, he thinks he knows. His suspicions are sordid, and I'm sure you can well imagine their nature. Few alive know the truth, and now you are two more of them. I must implore you to utter silence, on your honor, or on whatever else you hold suitably dear. Should word get out, it would double the danger Willim faces, and I'm having enough trouble keeping him whole as it is."

Willim's blood was loud in his ears. Should word of what get out? What was it that Jerdon knew, and Raven suspected?

"...What are you doing?"

Willim nearly came out of his own skin, bashing his head against the underside of the step. "Ellis!"

"We saw you sneak out," Ellis explained, as though this justified creeping up on an eavesdropping friend and scaring five years off his epitaph. "So we snuck out."

"Ellis snuck out," Dmitri yawned, pulling the cabin door to behind him. "It's more effort for him to be quiet. I just walked."

"Well, both of you be quiet," Willim hissed, straining to hear anything further from above. "I'm trying to listen." The next voice, however, was a sharp cry from the sailor on night watch in the rigging, and it brought a stampede of footsteps after it.

"Distress lamps off starboard, Captain!"

"What's that mean?" Ellis asked, but Dmitri was pulling up the ladder past him, and Willim was hard on his heels. Zeig was at the aft rail, his good eye to his glass, Jerdon and Grayson close by. A good many of the ship's crew were also peering through the dark. Willim could see pinpricks of light, but could not judge their source or distance.

"What do you see?" Grayson asked Zeig. He cast a quick glance at the Songbirds, and it seemed to Willim that his gaze lingered a little longer on him than on Ellis and Dmitri, but the moment had passed before Willim could pin it down.

"Vallish, by her line," Zeig said, collapsing his glass against his hip. "She's caught on the rocks off the point. Looks like she nipped too close to the cliffs, caught a back-wave and swamped. The tides here can be deadly without warning, even to seamen who know them." He turned to Willim, an expectant light in his eye. "By the code of the merchant navy, we're obliged to offer our assistance. However, I'm aware of the need to protect our passengers. It is up to you, Your Grace."

"Of course we should help them," Willim said, immediately. He thought he detected a note of approval in Grayson's nod.

"I agree," Grayson said. "If they prove untrustworthy, we will deal with it, but I've no heart to turn my back on our own in danger. "

"Nor I. Send out the longboats!" Zeig called, to his men. "Check for any survivors or any salvage, and see if you can find her name. We can log the loss for the owner, if nothing else."

Willim very quickly found himself in the way, but no one ordered him back to their quarters. He found a place up on the fo'c'sle where the Songbirds could watch the rescue operation without being underfoot. Grayson, though a landsman, had spent plenty of time aboard ship and lent a hand lowering the boats and casting them off. Had it not been for his charges, Willim was sure he would have volunteered to go with the rescue party.

"What's going on?" Rekbah asked, yawning. Her hair was fraying out of its braid, and she laced her bodice as she came up the aft ladder. "Why have we slowed?"

"A ship foundered near the cliffs. Zeig's crew is looking for survivors." Ellis took a glance at Rekbah's vest, sighed, and batted her sleepy hands away. "You've got all your eyelets wrong," he said.

"Heaven forbid I turn up sloppily dressed for a shipwreck," Rekbah said, but she let Ellis redo her trussing, and Willim thought he detected a flushed tinge to her brown cheeks. Unlike the other two, Ellis had responded well to being dressed in plainer clothes, and it gave him a comfortable appeal that was most often quashed under his Temple finery. The results had not been overlooked by Rekbah. Dmitri, on the other hand, looked like an orchid trying to bloom amid inhospitable conditions. When Jerdon called his name, the Lark of Valnon started as though braced for some new, grueling indignity.

"Dmitri!" Jerdon came halfway up the ladder, and rested his knee against the edge of the deck. "Am I correct in remembering that you studied medicine under Raven's tutelage?"

Dmitri drew himself up. "I did, and I certainly hope that's not some censure against my knowledge."

Jerdon shook his head. "Of course not, my dear boy. The man is a consummate surgeon. Unfortunately he's also a reprehensible bastard, but that's hardly here nor there. Odds are good we may have some patching-up to do, and I can use another set of skilled hands if you're willing. Rekbah, if you would be so good as to stop making cow-eyes at the Thrush of Valnon, and fetch my case."

Rekbah turned entirely crimson at this, and fled down the ladder like a quail flushed from underbrush. Dmitri, on the other hand, followed with a more dignified haste, pleased to find himself both needed and respected.

"Glad to see them getting along," Ellis muttered to Willim. "I didn't want to spend this whole trip with Dmitri going prickly whenever Jerdon came around."

"Dmitri does not forget an insult," Willim said, and added, "Which is why, should we have the chance to face up against Raven again, I plan to wind Dmitri up and throw him at him."

Ellis' expression had grown serious. "Do you think we will? Face Raven, I mean. Seems to me we're going in the wrong direction for that."

Willim frowned, but he had no answer. The lights from the longboats had once more turned for the *Larkspur*, and Ellis went down to watch them approach.

"Don't like running away, do you?"

Willim started. Grayson had come up the ladder as Ellis went down, and Willim had not heard him approach.

"Does anyone?" Willim asked, exasperated.

"I've known a few." Grayson rested his arms on railing, peering out at the bobbing points of light on the water. "I've done it often enough in my time."

Kestrel, Willim thought, glancing down at Grayson's sword belt. Raven had not only wronged the Songbirds. If it weren't for him, Grayson would be a Godsword, with wings on his hilt and a crimson gorget at his throat.

Willim blinked. There *was* a winged hilt at Grayson's belt, but it was a hilt only, and seemed to be made of stone. It had been on the table when they arrived at Jerdon's house. "What is that thing, anyway?"

Grayson followed Willim's gaze, and his mouth twisted in a way that was not a smile. "A souvenir of my trip through the catacombs. It came from Grayce's tomb."

"Your ancestor?"

Grayson shrugged. "I hardly think he'd claim me, now." His voice grew soft, as though he had forgotten Willim was listening. "Too much running away."

"Grayson," Willim began, cautiously. "I heard you talking to Jerdon and Zeig." Grayson stilled, as though he had forgotten to breathe, but Willim pressed on. "What were you--" he continued, but there was a thump from the hull of the ship, and one of the sailors called out that the rescue party had returned. Zeig strode over to the starboard rail, and there was a moment's conference, followed by noises of consternation.

"They didn't sail back by themselves," Zeig hissed, over the din.

Willim leaned over the edge of the fo'c'sle and waved at Ellis, below on deck. "What's going on?"

"The longboats are empty," Ellis said.

"Empty?" Grayson began, and within a single measure he had pressed Willim behind him and drawn his sword, as all at once every lamp on the *Larkspur* was extinguished.

The darkness came alive all around them. The moon was only a sliver on the horizon, and by its grudging light Willim could see that every shadow on the deck had come undone from its proper place. Shrieks and cries came from the deck, followed by other, wetter noises whose origins did not bear examination. One of the shadows slid up the ladder, and Willim had a glimpse of pale eyes, and a dark face swathed in even darker fabric. Grayson swept his sword down, and the figure toppled from the rail.

"What are they?" Willim asked, thinking for a moment that some of Eothan's undead kin had come to find them.

"Shadowhands!" Grayson spat. "They knew we were coming! Get down behind that rigging!"

Willim tried, but the dark ship suddenly had arms and legs of its own, and they caught him and held fast. There was a clang of steel, and then Grayson swore. Willim struggled and writhed to get close to him, but the grip on him was like iron, and so was the strident voice that rang out in his ear.

"Hold! Lights!"

As quickly as they had gone out, the ships lanterns were lit again. The deck was strewn with bodies, some moving, more not. The Shadowhands swarmed over every surface of the vessel like ants upon a crumb of cake, their black clothes making them all seem one and the same. Two stood on either side of Grayson, with curved glaives to hold him at bay. His sword had been kicked to the far side of the deck.

For a fleeting, shameful second, Willim thought that Zeig might have held true to his coloring, and betrayed them. But then he saw the captain lying limp and still by the mast, with Jerdon leaning over him. It seemed an eternity before anyone spoke, and the Shadowhand holding Willim was first to break the silence.

"A good catch, friends." His captor was a woman, Willim realized, though he could not see her face. Never before had he heard a true Thrassin accent. It was all curled r's and warm vowels, and Willim thought it unfair that the beauty of it was not lessened by the cruelty of the speaker. "We had thought to find a Kestrel, and instead we have caught a Dove!" She jerked her arm tighter around Willim's neck, lifting his hand so that his ring caught the light, and Grayson tensed, only to be edged back by his watchers. "What else have we found?"

Two Shadowhands stepped forward, one holding Dmitri by the neck, one with Ellis collared as Willim was. Dmitri had caught a blow to the temple, and he swayed on his feet.

"And two other birds, with him!" She laughed. "Fear not, little birds. You will live to sing another day. Had we found the Kestrel, we were to take him back, but now I think..." She paused, considering. Willim struggled to breathe steadily, his lungs full of the orange blossom and leather scent of his captor. Her clothes were drenched with seawater, and Willim realized how they had seemed to come from everywhere at once, slipping out of the boats and climbing up the ship. The fate of the rescue party was certain. Willim felt the cold grasp of fear breaking through the haze of action, as his captor considered what to do with her prize.

"I think our true master will have a better use for you," she said, to muted agreement from her men. "His holiness the Ethnarch will have many questions for you, little bird." She stroked a gloved hand over Willim's cheek, and then thrust him forward towards the ladder. "Throw the birds into the hold," she said. "Kill everyone else."

A Shadowhand started up the stairs for Willim; the two guarding Grayson moved in for the kill. Willim was too far, but he ran for Grayson anyway, though everything in Grayson's face told Willim to go the other way. The leader of the Shadowhands would have nothing of it, and she caught Grayson's sword up in her fist, moving in to enforce her orders and herd Willim back to the steps. She had not taken a full step when something crashed on her from above. Rekbah had crept up on them from the rigging, silent as any Shadowhand. She clung to the Shadowhand like a determined spider, clawing at the woman's masked face with her fingernails.

"Don't stand there like a lemon!" she shrieked at Willim. "Go help Grayson!"

Willim sprinted for Grayson. He had made some space for himself in the distraction, but was hard pressed to defend against the advances of the Shadowhands. Unarmed, he had only his speed on his side, and struggled to get up in the rigging before they could catch up. On the deck, the battle had begun anew.

Grayson looked up, saw Willim running towards him, and flung an arm out to ward him back. "Willim, get off the ship!"

Willim stopped as though rooted to the spot by this seemingly impossible command. "*What?*"

Grayson kicked one of his pursuers in the face. "Jump, for Naime's sake! Get in one of the longboats!"

Without pause to consider, Willim turned to do as he was told. He had one leg over the rail before he realized that he was running again, as he had when Boren was killed, as he had when the Temple had fallen. He put his back to the rail instead of going over it. Twice was enough. He would not run another time.

The leader of the Shadowhands had at last gotten free of Rekbah. She flung the snipe off her shoulders and Rekbah rolled down the ladder to land on the deck below. Hood torn back to reveal her crown of white braids, snarl twisting her blood-streaked face, the Shadowhand advanced on Willim like a hungry lioness on a tethered kid goat.

Willim's only option was retreat over the side, but he was frozen in place. A boot-step sounded on the rail, and Grayson jumped down on the deck in front of Willim. "I told you to go over the side!"

"I'm not running away!" Willim shouted back.

"The hell you aren't!" The waves tipped the boat, and Grayson fisted his hand in the front of Willim's tunic. "Jump, now! While the drop is clear!"

"I'm not leaving you!" Willim had meant to say, *I'm not leaving everyone behind*, but the words did not come out as intended.

Grayson turned to Willim, and there was something in his eyes that Willim could not identify. He started to speak, either to answer Willim or order him to flee, but he never finished. He got no further than the first syllable of Willim's name before the point of his own sword ripped through his breast, and his blood scattered in a fine mist across Willim's face like a mockery of Temple-paint.

For an instant, everything was still. Willim saw Grayson's eyes lose their focus, saw the glint of blood at the corner of his mouth. Then the Shadowhand withdrew her stolen sword, and Grayson's body tumbled forward into Willim's arms. He went to his knees from the weight, and felt the heat of Grayson's blood as it spilled from the gaping wound in his chest over Willim's hands, his arms, his legs. Grayson's face had fallen onto Willim's shoulder, in some obscene parody of a lover's embrace.

The Shadowhand was saying something. She was smiling, triumphant; she spun Grayson's sword in her hand. Beyond her, the fight continued, and the cries of the living and the dying pierced the night. Willim heard none of it. There was some terrible vibration in his ears, some note beyond the range of his hearing, like a mighty voice from beneath the sea. It thrummed in the cage of Willim's ribs, it roared in his ears like the tide. Something inside Willim was tearing loose from its restraints, something he could not control, something he could not care enough to fear. It was only when he saw the Shadowhand turn to him in horror that he realized he was the one making the sound, that his mouth was open and his lungs were straining. Willim thought he was screaming, but he was singing, singing one single, growing note to tear the sea from its very foundations.

The Shadowhand staggered back, her hands to her ears, her face contorted in pain. The waves had gone flat, as before a tidal wave, and the Larkspur sat on the mirror-smooth surface like a toy vessel affixed to a glass plate. And still Willim sang, singing out his rage and his grief and his loss and his fear, and the ship began to buckle beneath the strain. Ropes snapped, timbers splintered, and then the whole ship cracked as though struck amidships by some giant, invisible fist. The sea rushed in to fill the void, washing blood and bodies from the wildly tilting halves of the deck. Willim's song ripped through the vessel and through him until the foaming water rushed over him, pulling ship, Shadowhands, and Songbirds all down into swirling darkness.

17

In the hidden depths of the Temple of Valnon, Lateran XII started awake, his hand to his breast, his eyes wide. For a moment it was all he could do to steady his breathing, lest the sound of it wake Kestrel, sound asleep in the bed. Lateran's ears rang with a dreadful echo, and he rose from his chair by the brazier.

Without a moment's pause, he snatched up his hooded mantle, and flitted up the stairs with the silent urgency of a ghost on his appointed rounds. Down the still corridors of the Temple, through muted gardens with autumn's last glory edged in a feathery rime of frost, through tower and colonnade and gallery he ran, until at last he made his way to the humble back gate of the Laypriests' kitchen garden. A lone prentice stood there on watch, his head nodding over his halberd.

Lateran put a hand to the drowsy boy's shoulder, and Alder Haverty started awake, a shout of alarm half-started in his mouth.

"Peace, Alder," the Wing breathed, putting fingertips to his lips. "It's me. I've a task for you."

Alder shook off his sleepiness, and blinked at Lateran. "Is everything all right, Your Grace?"

Lateran's lips went taut. "I pray so," he murmured. "If you go out into the Godswords' training yards, you'll find a man sleeping in the stables there. Give him this for me."

Alder's face was clouded with confusion. The Wing had placed a small object into Alder's hand, something oblong and dark, lightweight for its size. "I don't understand--" he began.

"Nor do I expect you to. But he will. Tell him the melody has begun anew, but the descant has gone silent."

"Melody new, descant silent," Alder repeated. He tilted his cupped hand to the light of the nearest lantern, and the shape in his hand became a bird fashioned crudely of black-fired clay, punctured with holes here and there to make a little whistle. "But what does that--" Alder stopped, staring at the corridor. It was empty.

Alder Haverty was in many ways an unremarkable young man. He came from an average family of merchants, whose name commanded a middling amount of respect in the city. He was one of several children, and little depended on him save for him to find a way to earn his own keep in the world. He was a decent soldier, not so good as to attract notice, not so poor as to do so either. In many ways, Alder's utterly nondescript existence was what made him what he was: an extraordinary spy.

For six months he had been the confidant of the Wing, or at least, of the man who said he was the Wing. Alder's experience with the underside of Temple politics had made him a man of suspicious nature; he had wondered, more than once, if the Wing was a decoy placed in the position by Hawk. It would be a simple ruse, a warm body to fill the position while Hawk held the reins, leaving the High Preybird free to do as he wished in the Wing's name. Surely Raven thought that to be the case. And yet, while those theories came on fast and thick in solitary contemplation, they fled like gulls before a hurricane whenever he was in Lateran XII's actual presence.

It was through Alder that the Wing had learned of Raven's impending betrayal, but at a stage almost too late to be of any service. Alder had thought himself securely in possession of Petrine Tolver's heart, but that did not mean he had her complete confidence. When word came of her sisters' deaths, she closed up like a cuisse. Alder was left sniffing for scraps to take to his master, and he had the sneaking feeling that nothing he brought to Lateran's attention was new.

But a spy is only as good as his work, and Alder was glad for some. He lacked the temperament for outright war, and held in his heart a quiet, unabashed affection for the Temple, its music and its myth and its law. And then of course, there was Petrine. If by stealing through the night on strange errands for men who may or may not be the true Wing of Valnon was of any use in keeping Petrine from rushing off to die like her sisters had, then he would do so.

The Godswords' training grounds were deserted. With the prentices firmly under Raven's control, and the invested Godswords gone south to reinforce the border, the grounds were unlikely to see much activity until new recruits arrived in the spring. Which was why the lone figure, stepping suddenly out from the row of target dummies, gave him such a turn.

"What do you think you're doing?" Petrine hissed. "You're supposed to be on watch!"

Alder sagged with relief. "Thryseblood, Trine, you scared me."

"And I should!" Petrine strode across the yard, and jabbed one finger in the middle of Alder's chest. "I should report you to Raven!"

"Raven has enough on his mind right now," Alder said, reasonably. "And how much guarding does the kitchen garden need, anyway? Are we in danger of sabotage by an invading army of turnips?"

"That's no excuse," Petrine began, but Alder could tell her fire was faltering. She had been expecting far worse, he realized, than a truant prentice in the yard.

"Come on," Alder cajoled. "Raven doesn't need us now, he's got the whole Temple blanketed with those Queensguard he bought off of the Crown. They're enough to handle any trouble. Besides, what are we trying to keep out? The Songbirds are gone, they're not coming back here. We've only to make it look like we're protecting them." Alder straightened up, and looked at the sky. "I'm just going for a walk to get my blood moving," he explained. "I was falling asleep on watch, and that's worse than stretching my legs for five minutes." Petrine seemed to consider this for a moment, and Alder brushed his fingertips against her cheek. "What are you doing out here yourself?"

"I thought I heard something down in the stables," she said, pushing his hand away, but gently, as though she only felt it wasn't the time for such gestures, not that they were entirely unwelcome. "But it was only one of the off-duty Queensguard asleep down there; I suppose Raven doesn't want them in the Pilgrims' rooms or the barracks."

Alder tallied the obvious sum with a speed that would have made his shopkeeper mother proud. "Listen," he said. "Go back to the garden door and wait for me, and I'll make sure this fellow isn't skipping his duties."

"Like you are, you mean?" Petrine asked, her eyes glinting at him in a faint smile.

"You're diligent enough for both of us," Alder said. "It's why Raven counts on you so much, isn't it?"

Petrine's smile faltered. "Yes," she said, as though to herself. "But..."

She trailed off, and Alder took a step closer. "Tell me the truth, Trine," he murmured into her hair. "You don't like the turn this has taken."

"I did not think he would harm the Songbirds," Petrine admitted, clenching her gloved hands together inside her cloak. "But if what he says about the Dove is true--"

"And what," Alder broke in, "if it isn't?"

Petrine's face grew still and hard. "He is a Preybird of Valnon," she said, quietly. "Surely he does what he does for the best of the Temple. The second Dove brought disaster--"

"The second Dove died three hundred years ago," Alder countered. "I'm talking about the current Dove. The one alive now. The one you swore fealty to when you got your spear."

Petrine stiffened, and she took a step away from Alder's warmth. "I swore my fealty to all the Temple Birds," she said. "And that means Raven, too. I cannot discount his truths without discounting all the Temple's truths. Eothan brought ruin on Valnon, and Willim has not brought the peace St. Alveron promised his heir would bring. My sisters swore to him as well, and it only brought them to their pyres." She jerked her head towards the stables. "Go and root that Queensguard out if he's slacking," she said, "and then you return to your post. I have rounds to make."

Her salute was like a slap to the face, and Alder stood alone in the courtyard, cursing his haste. Once, she would have listened to him. Once, when her sisters still lived. The wind picked up, making the training dummies stir like living things, and Alder pressed on through the dark to the strawy confines of the stables, shivering.

In spring the stables had been full of horses, those belonging to the Godswords billeted in the Temple or those passing through before or after their leave. Now only two sleepy donkeys remained, with a small congress of doves roosting in the eaves. The man sleeping in the straw under their crooning perch didn't look much like a Queensguard, with a broad-rimmed feathered hat pulled down over his face, and the green jacket of his office--at least two sizes too big--used for a blanket. He was tall, but rangy, and looked like one of the practice dummies deemed too scrawny to even serve as a scarecrow.

But whether this really was Lateran XII's other spy remained to be determined. Alder kicked the man's boot to rouse him, and was rewarded with one windmilling arm, a grunt of profanity, and a further continuation of snores. Alder's next kick was more forceful.

"Wake up, dammit!"

The feathered hat slid up a few inches, revealing bright green eyes, a thin mouth, and the stark line of an old scar, all arrayed into a put-upon expression. "Look," the hat's owner said, "I've had a long day, and all I want is a decent night's sleep, and to be shat on by these birds as little as possible in the process. Nowhere do you enter into that equation. Now toddle along and go prentice something that wants prenticing."

"Found this out in the garden," Alder said, holding up the bird whistle. "Thought you could tell me who it belongs to. If you don't know, by all means, carry on with your nap."

Something changed in the man's face, and Alder hurried to reassess his opinion. If this man looked like the worst of the Queensguard, it was his intent, and very likely he was the best of something else. Without moving an inch, the sleepy, surly layabout was suddenly gone. The stranger was now as taut as a sket string, his eyes intent, jaw tense. "What did he tell you?" Even the man's voice had changed, the roughness scoured out of it to leave something sharp and burnished behind. Alder swallowed, unsure why his throat had just gone dry.

"The melody has begun anew," Alder said.

"And the descant?" the man pressed.

"Has gone silent," Alder said.

The man closed his eyes, as though this was the gravest of news. When he opened them again, he held out his hand to Alder. "Give it to me," he said.

Alder, bemused, did as he was told. The man put his mouth to the bird's tail, as though to sound the whistle, but no note came out of it. After a long moment, he passed the trinket to Alder again. "Give it back to the one that owns it," he said, and rose to his feet. He pulled a sword belt out of the hay, and slung it around his narrow hips. Though it was blackened with age, and most of the enameling had been knocked from the metalwork, there was no mistaking the shape of wings spreading protectively over the hilt.

"Who are you?" Alder asked, in wonder.

The man pulled his cockaded hat over his flame-red hair, and flashed a rakish wink at the prentice. "I am the harmony," he said, and in a swirl of motion he was over the gate and gone, swallowed up in the night.

18

Grayson's first thought, on waking, was that he didn't remember drinking near enough wine to merit the thunder rolling around inside his skull. The second thought was that he hadn't drunk any wine at all, and the third and fourth thoughts mainly consisted of profanity. None of it made it into words; the only thing coming out of his mouth at the moment was a copious amount of seawater.

Belly-down in the wet sand, with the tide tugging at his ankles, Grayson shoved himself up to his elbows and retched up water until his body shivered from the strain. Spent, he collapsed into the sand, and it was a long time before he moved again.

His memories were jumbled, as though the brine had seeped in through the cracks and spoiled them. He remembered the ambush by the Shadowhands, he remembered fighting, he remembered the cold intrusion of steel through his chest. With one hand, he groped at the front of his brigantine. The leather was torn as though from a direct blow, the raw edges of the metal plates inside the padding scraped at Grayson's hand. But though the skin underneath was clammy and wet, it was whole. Grayson prodded it until he gave himself a bruise, bewildered. He had been struck from behind, he knew it, and knew the blow was mortal. He had seen his own death in Willim's face.

Willim.

Grayson staggered to his feet and stood there a moment, scanning up and down the beach. He had fetched up on a forlorn strand, little more than a narrow strip of sand and pebbles beneath the towering limestone cliffs of the Northcamp. From the angle of the light, it was not yet noon. The beach was littered with storm-wrack, but Grayson saw no sign of the shipwreck. The *Larkspur* had wrecked, surely. Yet he remembered no storm, no swelling wave. Nothing but a profound stillness, and a single ringing note whose faint echo lingered in his mouth like the bitterness of salt water.

With no other guide, Grayson staggered down the beach towards a clutch of petrels and gulls gathered on the shore. If there were casualties of the wreck, the scavengers would be there to inspect whatever washed ashore. Heart heavy with dread, Grayson tried to see what had the birds' attention. They were clustered in a tight group, with more swirling above like a signal. Their calls ricocheted from the cliffs, but there was none of the usual squabbling over a meal. Grayson was close enough to see that they were huddled around a limp figure half-buried in the sand, his back to Grayson. The breeze stirred hair the color of the gulls' wings, and Grayson forced his waterlogged legs into a run.

Startled by his approach, the birds took off in a fluttering wave. For a moment Grayson was blinded by their beating wings, then they were gone, their prize left unguarded. He went to his knees. Willim lay there in the sand, his clothing beaten to tatters by the waves, his eyes shut, his face still. Yet his ribs moved with his even breathing, and as far as Grayson could see, there was not the least scratch on his skin. The birds had not been pecking at him, as they would at a corpse or anything close enough to one, and for a six-foot circumference around Willim the sand was unmarked, though the prints of the gulls clustered thickly at the edge of that perimeter.

The echo of music was stronger around Willim, and even Grayson, without the canniness of a bird, could sense it. The sea-god knew his own blood, and had borne Willim on some gentler swell than the one Grayson had ridden ashore. It took some nerve to reach across that space, to touch the Dove's shoulder. It was warm under Grayson's hand, and Willim rolled over at Grayson's gentle tug, but did not wake. For a while Grayson simply sat with him, letting the sun and wind dry them, as he summoned his last reserve of strength. When he could manage it, Grayson pulled Willim up into his arms, and set off in search of a way up the cliffs.

Willim stood in an empty courtyard overrun with hibiscus vines, the white marble gleaming beneath their vibrant mantle, glossy leaves fluttering in a warm, salty breeze. The sun that beat down on Willim's shoulders had all the heat of midsummer, while the sky above him arched fathomless and blue into an unknown distance. Music swelled all around him, a buoyant chorus that rushed through Willim's blood like undiluted wine. It was the Evensong, but never as Willim had heard it before, sung by so

202

many voices. Threaded through the melody was the Noontide in harmony, and the slow reverence of Dawning served as a descant. Until that moment, Willim had never considered what the songs of all three Songbirds would be like combined. They formed a whole of unspeakable beauty, and standing there listening, Willim lost all sense of time, of urgency, of past or future. There was only the music; it was all there ever had been and all there ever would be again.

Compelled by the song, Willim wandered the streets that unfolded beneath his feet. The city was ancient beyond measure, with avenues lined in trees whose roots had buckled the paving-stones, and the benevolent faces of the statues softened with the steady caress of wind and rain. Every stone and step of the city was carved deep with inscrutable symbols. They made cool places in the hot stone beneath Willim's feet, they glinted with a faint blue light in the blowing leaf-shadows. Willim understood somehow that they were the notes of the song, even though the fluid sigils looked nothing like the simple note-shapes used by the Temple.

He followed the song at last to its source, and emerged in a vacant city square. Effusive fountains made a watery counterpoint to the song, and the black shadow of a mighty figure stretched out over the stones. Gulls swooped and dove around the head and shoulders of a colossus in the square, his winged crown bright with silver-leaf against the sky, his feet placed firm at the bottom steps of his Temple.

Willim turned to follow his gaze, and saw below him the tiled rooftops and arched bridges of a city whose boundaries he could not perceive. Whenever he thought it must end, another island's peaks stood up out of the sea, connected to the others with the thin threads of bridges and gates, crowned with pillars and palaces. Somewhere, at the very edges of vision, sea became sky in a smudged blue line, somewhere only the eyes of the statue could reach.

At the bottom of the Temple steps, the chorus had risen to a roar. It drummed against Willim's breastbone like the hammering of the tide, enough to pull the dead from their graves and the living into theirs. All around the empty city, the music trembled in every leaf, every carved sigil, every stone. Willim was engulfed by it, lifted on the rising notes, the shivering harmonies. When the song was shattered by a single, piercing scream, Willim thought his heart would stop. He jolted awake, the scream still ringing in his ears.

He was in a room, the only room in a cottage that was little more than a stone shed, long and low and windowless. The roof was thatch, in need of repair. The bare eaves were warped with age and the weight of their burdens: saddles, bits of armor, burlap sacks, bundles of herbs, papery onions, ponderous hams. The only light came from a small fire on a low hearth, sputtering and smoking on its block of peat. Willim lay on a makeshift bed of straw, covered with a few woolen blankets that smelled of horse.

The door of the cottage was open, but the view was blocked by a tall figure standing there, his face to the twilight. Willim made a sound, of recognition or alarm, and Grayson turned around.

"Are you awake?"

Willim tried to speak, but his throat felt like it had been lined in broken glass. He nodded.

Grayson sat down on the end of the bed, straw crunching beneath him. It was hard to tell in the dim light, but there was a kind of reservation in his face, something Willim might have called fear, had it been on anyone else.

"How?" Willim rasped, hoping it would serve for all the questions he wanted to ask. He lifted one hand to touch the front of Grayson's shirt, a roughly-made one that fit him poorly.

For answer, Grayson lifted the shirt for Willim to see. His chest bore the marks of his trade, scars in dull white and faded pink crisscrossed over his skin, one jagged one near his hip even bore the pinprick dots of costly silver suture pins. But where Willim had seen the blade jutting from his ribs, there was nothing. Only supple muscle and unmarked skin.

"I was hoping," Grayson said as he lowered his shirt again, "that *you* could tell *me*."

"How would *I* know?" The look was on Grayson's face again, and Willim realized it was awe. He wasn't sure what to make of such an expression. It was one thing to get that when he was decked out in his armor and paints, and quite another when he was only himself. Willim struggled to swallow past his sore throat. It was as raw as though he'd sung all of Canticles at one go. "You don't think that I..." Willim trailed off, and blinked away whatever

204

argument he was going to make. "Where is everyone?" He looked around the hut, but there was no evidence of other occupants. "Ellis? Dmitri?"

"I've searched the shoreline, but found no trace of the *Larkspur* or her crew." Grayson gestured to their humble shelter. "Only this scavenger's hut, and what was left of the owner. I suspect he was too close to the Shadowhands' so-called distress ship for their plans. He had certain tell-tale marks of their handiwork." Grayson tipped his head to the door. "I buried him just behind the stable. As for the ship we stopped to rescue, it's gone. Either the Shadowhands left some crew behind to escape with her, or she sank when you--" Grayson broke off, not looking at Willim. "At any rate, they might have picked up any survivors. We lived, there's no reason to think the others did not."

Willim put his hand to his breastbone. There was a strange ache there, under his ribs. "I... did something, didn't I? On the ship that night. Something... unnatural."

"It's not for me to say what is natural and what isn't," Grayson replied, with care. "I'm fairly certain I was dead at the time."

Willim shuddered, the memory vivid in his mind, a single note echoing between them. For a long moment they stared at each other, until Grayson rose, clearing his throat, and busied himself at the hearth. "Our late host was a man of humble means, but he left us with a decent supply of food. Not to mention the interesting hoard of things he's picked up off the beach." Grayson nodded to the side of the hearth. A wooden hatch, looking like something scavenged of the side of a ship, was nestled in the smooth dirt floor. There was a pitted, black iron ring in its center. "I already helped myself to his spare clothes; there should be something down there to do for you as well."

Belatedly, Willim realized he was wearing only his linen clout, and a few bits of jewelry only meant to keep his piercings from closing. He drew the blanket tighter around his hips, but it was so holey it did little enough good, and Grayson no doubt had seen plenty already.

"We should be comfortable enough here until you're feeling rested enough to travel." Grayson returned to Willim's side and passed him a chipped crockery bowl of stew. "Here."

"Travel to where?" Willim prodded at the stew; it was mostly broth with some onions and stringy bits of meat, far rougher fare than what he was accustomed to getting. Nevertheless, the smell reminded him that he was ravenous. He bolted it down as though it was his favorite lobster pastry from the Temple's kitchens, burning his tongue and not caring. "Back to Valnon?"

"We'll continue to Clarie, in Alfir, as we had planned to do from the start. If the others have made it safely to some shore, they'll do their best to get there as well." Grayson offered Willim an encouraging smile, as the Dove of Valnon hesitated over his next bite of stew, his face clouding. "Bear up, Willim. We must proceed as we can, and assure ourselves that they are in Heaven's hands, if not ours."

"...I Sang Down Heaven," Willim said, his voice hushed. It felt somehow better to admit it, but once the words were out, there was no getting them back. "Didn't I."

"I could not say for sure," Grayson said, equally quiet. "Such a thing has not been done since St. Alveron's time. But if I had to say what that would be like, what you did on the *Larkspur* would be my best guess."

"It must have been. I couldn't control it, I couldn't stop it. You were dying, we were all lost, and I..." Willim pushed away his empty bowl, its contents now sitting uneasily in his belly. "...How are we going to get to Clarie?" he asked. It was easier to talk about practical things than what had happened the night they were attacked. "We can't walk there."

"We'll head northwest from here," Grayson said, and picked up Willim's bowl, dropping it in the bucket of water by the hearth. "We'll cut off the long edge of the coast and go to Memwater. It's the shipbuilding port of the Northcamp, and should be little more than a day's ride. There's regular travel south from there; we can book passage for little enough, I think." He looked at Willim, and offered up a reassuring smile. "You still look tired. Lie back, it's almost dark. I was about to close up for the night."

Willim didn't really want to sleep more, but his head was still heavy. He lay back on the bed, drifting into a light doze as Grayson sat by the fire, mending the two holes in his armor from the wound he no longer had.

The next morning, Willim felt as well as he expected he

would, and they set about preparing for the trip north to Memwater. The storage cellar was crammed full of treasure and junk in equal measure, all piled together in some higgledy-piggledy order known only to the hut's former occupant. Anything that had washed up on the beach had been stored in case of need: chests of silver coins as well as ancient, sand-clotted pottery and stringless bows. Grayson pulled out clothing for them both, and boots for Willim, who had lost his in the wreck. He found a sword for himself, a magnificent hand-and-a-half thing, with the hilt wrapped with gilt wire in extravagant patterns, a carved glass gem in the pommel, and (so Grayson said) absolutely wretched balance.

"Beggars can't be choosers," Grayson sighed, sheathing it. "Though I'd rather something less ostentatious." He buckled the weapon around his hips, and Willim noted that Grayce's sword-hilt had somehow survived the wreck. The lump of masonry was still tucked into the back of Grayson's belt. Willim was about to ask about it, when he noticed that Grayson had brought up an extra sword. This one was plainer, but shorter as well, less suited to the reach of Grayson's fighting style. Grayson saw the question in Willim's face, and picked up the spare blade.

"Only because you'll look suspicious without one," he said, with resignation, and passed the sword and belt to Willim. "Any man of your age would wear one in the Northcamp. Don't try to do anything with it. Just keep it on you."

Willim looked down at the weapon in his hands, the first one he had ever held. It wasn't as heavy as he thought it would be, and the blade, inched out of its sheath, reflected one uneasy eye. "What if we're attacked, and I need to defend myself?"

"You've got me to defend you," Grayson said, gruffly. "And if something should happen to me--" He broke off, putting his fingers to the mended slit in his brigantine, "Forgive me Willim, but in that case, I don't think you'll need a sword."

Willim wasn't sure what to say to that, so he pulled on his new boots while Grayson gathered the rest of the supplies. The boots were a little big, and water-stained, and Willim tried not to think about what had happened to their previous owner.

Beside the hut was a little lean-to of a stable, occupied at the moment by an old, placid wall of a cart-horse, and a high-strung roan gelding. Neither of them were restrained in any way; they wandered along the grassy cliff to graze during the day, trotting back home again at night for the water trough and a little speck of grain. According to Grayson, they were hardly paragons of their species, but they were sturdy enough.

In the stable were also five saddles in various states of repair, some without stirrups, some whose covers had rotted away, and between them Grayson had spliced together two that would service. Willim, who knew about as much horses as he did swords, eyed the two beasts warily.

"This one's more to my liking," Grayson said, slapping the broad shoulder of the larger horse, his tan coat marked with white from the wear of a harness. "But since you're a novice, I think it's better if you take him." He grunted as he tightened the girth on the saddle. "The other fellow will need a firmer hand than you have, and I wouldn't want him to bolt with you. Go on, up you get. Easy as climbing a fence."

Willim and the horse both eyed each other askance. It wasn't exactly a reunion of soulmates. Willim had to credit the fellow for his patience, however, standing stock still and looking put-upon as Willim clambered gracelessly up onto his back. It was like sitting astride one of the Temple pillars, and the ground seemed much further away than it had when Willim was standing on it.

"I feel a bit like we're stealing them," Willim said, when he was mostly sure he would not fall off his mount. It wasn't entirely out of conscience that he said it; he would have been much happier walking.

"Better than abandoning them there," Grayson said, mounting the roan with enviable ease. "We're simply making do with what we found, which no doubt was the credo of their former owner. We'll sell them in Memwater, and it should be enough to pay for passage south, and they can go on to another home." Grayson looked back over his shoulder at Willim, and had the self-possession to refrain from laughter at the sight. Instead he urged his own mount over until they were side-by side, and nudged Willim's knee with his own. "Put your back straight," he suggested, "and tuck your knees in a little. But don't squeeze--"

It was too late. Willim tightened his thighs and his sedate mount was startled into a half-trot, taking him down the track at what Willim felt was an appalling speed. The brown grass blurred by his massive hooves, the horizon jolted up and down, and Willim sloshed around in the saddle like a particularly inebriated bag of grain, swearing and praying by turns. By the time the horse slowed down of his own accord, the cottage and the humble grave by the sea were long gone.

Grayson soon caught up with Willim, laughing as he caught the other horse's bridle. Grayson straightened up at Willim's pained look, and was careful to preface his further suggestions with what Willim should *not* do, rather than what he should, just in case. Willim's feelings towards horses were not warmed by the incident. They did their best to ignore each other for the rest of the morning.

Fortunately for Willim, there was plenty to distract him from his moving seat. The track they followed veered away from the cliffs and the sound of the sea, carrying them inland to a dirt road so old that the ground rose high on either side. Scrub and low brambles slowly turned into the overhanging branches of oak and ash, and the sky was a patchwork of blue between their turning leaves. The shadows had autumn's chill in their damp breath, and Willim looped his arms through his reins and folded his hands under his cloak. By midmorning they crested a rise in the road and were looking down into a wooded valley, dappled with the crimson and yellow of the fading year. In a distant cleft between far hills, Willim could see the faint haze of smoke, and the rooftops of a small town. The air smelled of leaf-mold and smoke and apples lost in yellow grass, and Willim felt as though he had just woken from some long, uneasy slumber. Never had the world felt so clear.

"I didn't know the Northcamp was so beautiful," he said, but one look at Grayson's face kept him from any further enthusiasm. Grayson was staring at the woods and the hills with the stark grief of a bereaved man at his beloved's pyre, and he twitched his gelding's head to the west, away from the cozy village in the distance.

For some time there was nothing said, as the horses' hooves thudded dully on the dirt track, and a mockingbird ran, shrill and careless, through its repertoire.

"You haven't been back here, have you?" Willim asked.

Grayson's hands tensed on his reins, leather gauntlets creaking. "No," he said, at last. "Not since I was seventeen."

"Don't you miss it?"

Grayson swallowed, staring at the packed earth road between his mount's ears. "As much as Thali of Hasafel missed his city," he said, and flashed Willim a weak smile, "but with considerably less talent at expressing it."

"*Still yearning, unburning,*" Willim murmured. He was thinking of the way the light tilted through the Songbirds' solar on just such an autumn day, turning Dmitri's hair the color of old ivory as he read beside the fountain, while Ellis strummed some thoughtless chords on his sket. His eyes burned.

"Don't," Grayson breathed, eyes closed. "I can't bear that song right now. Sing something cheerful instead."

"I can't think of a single note," Willim said, and for the first time since he had been cut for a Dove, it was true. They rode on in silence, each heartsick, each one alone.

19

When they dismounted for the last time that day, Willim swung one leg down off the horse and it folded underneath him at once, sending him flat on his back in the grass with one foot still in the stirrup. His horse snorted, as if it had expected such an outcome, and made a little sidestep to shake Willim out of the stirrup, as though the Dove was no more than a bit of manure clinging to his hoof. Grayson bent down over Willim, shaking his head.

"Have I pushed you too hard today, Your Grace?" The stress on the last word was none too subtle, and had very little to do with formal titles.

"You can take my grace and bugger off with it," Willim grumbled, sorting out his feet and his cloak and his sword, which he found to be an awkward, dragging thing at his hip. He didn't know how anyone could stand to wear one all the time. "I don't want it. I want a bed and some food and a roof, and for that beast to mind his distance from me for at least eight hours."

"Food, we have," Grayson said. "Bed and a roof, not so much. And your mount needs looking over before you can call yourself done with him. He's carried you all this way, the least you can do is make sure he's comfortable."

"*I'm* not comfortable," Willim said sulkily, rubbing at his tailbone. His legs felt like loose harp strings, his shoulders ached, his backside was numb. But in spite of that Willim listened as Grayson talked him through the process of unsaddling his mount, checking over its hooves and coat, and getting it settled for the evening. Under Grayson's hands, even the skittish roan calmed, and Willim could see how much affection Grayson had for the beasts. There was, Willim considered, no accounting for taste.

"You have a horse in the city?" Willim asked, as Grayson pushed the roan's head away from his hair for the tenth time.

"They're too expensive to keep in the Undercity," Grayson said, with obvious regret. "At least, too expensive for a man of my means." He patted the roan's flank, the horse deciding at last that grass was tastier than his rider's hair. "But I trained for cavalry when I was a prentice--shock cavalry."

Willim blinked. "What's that? Different from regular cavalry?"

Grayson looked pleased to be asked. "That's the mounted knights you send in to break the enemy's line. Not as fast as your light horse, but heavy, powerful. They are your army's fist, made to strike the first blow." He pulled a burr from the roan's mane, and slapped him in apology for the discomfort he had caused. "When I was a prentice we would go over the Pilgrim's passage to train on the salt fields across the channel, thundering back and forth at each other until the tide changed and we had to come back."

"I've never heard you talk about your past like that," Willim said, reaching up a hand to stroke the roan's warm cheek. The sun was tilting to the west, Evensong tingled in Willim's blood, and the night was coming on cold around them. Willim found he could even be fond of horses, for Grayson's sake. "Like something pleasant."

"You shouldn't think my life has been one tragedy cycle from beginning to end," Grayson answered, with a shrug. "It's been a life, with low notes and high ones, much like any other."

Willim shuddered, and not from the cold. "Don't," he said. "You make it sound like you're done with it."

Grayson eyed him across the roan's back. "Well," he said, softly, "if we manage to get through this all alive, and the Wing remembers to pay me for my services, I may be done with part of it." He winked at Willim. "But only part. Now! Something tells me you've never been obliged to dig a latrine trench before."

Willim groaned.

The night was full of noises, the fire chuckled to itself as it sank into embers, and Willim could not sleep. Grayson was sprawled next to him, one hand on his sword, head on his saddle, snoring as though he was in the Temple's finest velvet-curtained bed. Willim, in spite of careful searching to find a patch of grass that wasn't on an anthill or didn't send the blood rushing to his head, had still managed to find a root that dug painfully into his hip. But in spite of roots and crickets he had thought himself exhausted enough to sleep as easily as Grayson. Instead his thoughts returned again and again to Ellis and Dmitri, and the Temple, and Kestrel, and to the strange power that had coursed through him on the *Larkspur*. If he had such a skill, would it come to him again? And if so, why had it not manifested when Boren was attacked, or when Raven took over the Temple? Was it really to be trusted, if it was so capricious? Or would it come again in his moment of need? And (this was the one thought that kept him tossing and turning) had his song caused the death of everyone on the *Larkspur*, including his dearest friends?

Stomach twisting with guilt, Willim squirmed around in his cloak and tried to get comfortable in both body and mind. Eventually he curled up against Grayson's back to steal his warmth, and rested one cheek on his bodyguard's shoulder. The cadence of Grayson's breathing was soothing, he smelled like leather and horse and sunlight, and sleep found Willim at last.

It felt like only seconds later when Grayson's voice woke him. It was still dark; the fire was cold, the sky was pierced with stars and there was no sign of dawn. Willim started to ask why they were rising so early when Grayson spoke again, but not to Willim.

"...broken through to the south mines," Grayson breathed, and then fell to muttering, and Willim could only catch stray words. Grayson shuddered in his sleep, his hand tore into the flattened grass, and Willim understood. Grayson was fighting a battle again in his dreams, and it was not the pretty pageant of cavalry in the sunlight. The few broken phrases Willim could parse made his skin crawl, painting an image of bloody desperation somewhere far from Willim's understanding.

"Grayson," Willim whispered, putting his mouth to the curve of his ear. "Grayson, wake up. You're dreaming."

His bodyguard did not wake, but tensed at the new voice as though it was a sudden enemy. Willim could feel the strain running through him, the vibration of a drum-skin about to tear. Shaking Grayson out of the nightmare might only get Willim a blackened eye for his trouble. Willim thought of his own dreams, and their horrors, and wondered what would be best for a soldier to hear. He didn't even know who Grayson was fighting.

"It's all right, Grayson," Willim said. "They're retreating. They've..." Willim wracked his brain for the words of one of Ellis' battle-ballads. "They've fallen back beyond the wall. It's over. We've won."

For a moment he did not think it would work. Then Grayson went limp against Willim's chest with a choked sound of relief.

Willim swept his fingertips over Grayson's damp hair, and if there were tears mingled in with the sweat, Grayson would never hear about it from Willim. The Dove of Valnon wrapped both arms around his bodyguard and hummed some idle notes until Grayson's breath was steady once more. Feeling strangely protective of a man intended to protect him instead, Willim let Grayson's quieted dreaming lull him once more into sleep.

"Grayson," Willim asked the next morning, as he fed tinder to the rebuilt fire, and Grayson prodded a few hard sausages around on a hot rock, "...What are the south mines?"

Grayson's head came up quickly, he opened his mouth in something Willim thought would be a short retort, then closed it again. He said nothing until one of the sausages popped a moment later.

"Talking in my sleep, was I?"

Willim shrugged, making a deliberate ritual of each twig he put on the coals. "You don't have to tell me."

Grayson considered this. "I don't have to do lots of things," he admitted, with a little smile. He took a deep breath and then left breakfast alone to cook itself, twisting his hands together before his bent knees. "The south mines," he announced, "were a series of tunnels and earthworks beneath the fort of Kassiel, on the border. They were dug by Thrassin forces and Vallish ones as the fort changed hands over the course of the war, and are a veritable warren of passages, most so small you cannot even stand upright in them." His face paled a little, and he swallowed twice before continuing. "When Kassiel was in our hands, Thrass attempted to take the outpost back by sending slaves under the fort to gas out the defenders with sulfur lamps. I was part of the team assigned to keep them out. By the time the siege was over, I was one of only two survivors from the initial defense of the mines."

Willim's throat ached as though he could taste the pressing closeness of the dirt. "How long was the siege?"

"Four months, one week, three days," Grayson said, without a pause to calculate the number. "The slaves who asphyxiated from their lamps or were killed by our troops were left to rot, to block the way for further advances." He flipped the sausages over. "For forty days I was buried alive in the dark, and every breath full of the stench of the dead. Light meant an enemy lamp to poison the air, or a fire that could sweep through and kill us all. I went without seeing the sky for days at a time. When it was over, it took another month to bring out our dead and fill in the Tunnels for good."

Willim had been holding the same twig to the fire for the last full minute; he finally remembered it when the flame crept up to his fingertips and burned him. In all the horrors he had witnessed lately, he had not even conceived of something so awful. And yet for Grayson, it had been his life, day in and day out, all for the sake of a Temple and City that had wronged him. "*Grayson*," Willim said, and found that it was all he could say.

"So," Grayson said, and speared one of the sausages neatly on an iron fork, "sorry if I woke you. Hungry?"

Willim started to protest that he could not be hungry after such a tale, but something in Grayson's expression warned him from expanding on the subject. Grayson had told it matter-of-factly, but the fork shivered ever so slightly in his hand as he reached across to proffer it to Willim. Willim choked back his words, accepted the food, and murmured his thanks.

Some things were not meant for extraction in the light of day.

They reached Memwater by noon. It sat along a long cleft of harbor that bit deep into the heart of the Northcamp, with the deep-green wall of the timber forests on the other side. There were easily four times as many boats as there were houses, and the harbor could have been crossed by stepping from deck to deck without ever getting one's feet wet. Willim could see why the -*water* part of the name was stressed, as there was very little of note in Mem itself. The dirt road led right through the center of the town, where it became cobbled with an indifferent spattering of stones, and a clutch of inns and taverns huddled around a market square. It was infested in equal measure by dogs, children, sailors, and the smell of fish guts.

"Charming," Willim breathed.

"Not every city is Valnon," Grayson answered, with a little shrug. "Mem is hardly a shining jewel of culture and grace, but it'll do for our needs. And it'll do you good to realize that the Queendom is not only Valnon's island. You sing for the blessing of these people just as much."

Willim had had little occasion to sing for anyone's blessing lately, but he refrained from pointing that out, as Grayson led them to a neat little whitewashed inn by the name of the Seal and Sextant. Willim waited in the doorway, watching the colorful panoply of figureheads jostling for space at the nearest wharf, while Grayson paid to have their horses stabled and then went inside to negotiate rooms. Now that he was used to the smell, and with the pleasant breeze coming off the water, Memwater could be considered picturesque, if nothing else. But Willim's heart still yearned for home. He scoured the faces of the passing sailors, wondering if any of them had picked up the *Larkspur*'s castaways. For once in his life he wanted nothing more than to see Dmitri coming up out of the crowd, with his scowl and his scorn in full evidence. But though he saw Iskati and Shindamiri and even a few Thrassin sailors, no one in the marketplace looked like a Songbird of any sort. Willim realized too late he had been looking for Ellis and Dmitri by the colors of their titles, which they would not even be wearing.

Grayson's boot-step behind him startled him out of his reverie. "There's room for us in the snug above the cellar, but if they're going to be honest, they should call it a *cramped*, not a *snug*. There's hardly enough room to change your mind."

"As long as it has a bed, I don't care," Willim said, fervently.

"It does, and I'll take it over sleeping rough. Let's hope it's only for one night." Grayson tucked his purse back into his belt. "Come on. A nice walk down to the wharf will feel good on your legs after all that riding, and we'll see who's going south on the morning tide. And this time, don't bring up Hasafel."

"Believe me," Willim said, bitterly, "I've had enough of that tune."

Grayson caught Willim by the elbow and led him along the cobbles, his face tilted up into the salty breeze. His spirits seemed improved by their progress and by being in his boyhood country. Either that or his negotiation for their lodgings had included a pint of ale. Willim suspected the latter.

"You can note a ship's usual cargo by its figurehead," Grayson said, pointing out a few of the more colorful ones. "That one with the stag on it is a timber-ship or a furrier, probably both. Most with ladies of some sort are merchant vessels from various ports, look at what they're wearing and holding to see the trade that paid for them. That one's indigo, that one's woolens, that one's probably spices, hard to tell. Mer-tails mean they make their living by the sea--that fellow there's probably a whaler, look at the harpoons along the rail. And that--" Grayson's gaze fell on a slim vessel with crimson sails and clean lines, and his face went white. The figurehead was a woman holding a silver swan out before her, its wings outstretched, a sprig of wheat in its beak. Willim could not see what about it could inspire such terror, but Grayson wheeled them both around to stare at a ribbon-monger's fluttering wares.

"What?" Willim breathed. "What is it? Shadowhands?"

"Worse." A muscle in Grayson's jaw twitched. "It's my sister."

"Your sister?" Willim craned around to see who among the crowd might do as Grayson's sister. "I didn't even know you had one. Maybe she can help us--"

Grayson yanked Willim back around. "Isbell wouldn't help me to kick the stool if I wanted to hang myself, much less help us out of this." His words were as bitter as lemon-rind. "And I don't want her to see me. The *Swan* is our family vessel. She's inspecting it before it goes south." His mouth twisted. "Let me know when she's gone."

"But I don't even know what she looks like--" Willim began, and then he said, "Oh." The woman who appeared at the rail of the ship could not be anyone but Isbell fa Grayce, no matter that Willim had only learned of her seconds before. Isbell was at least forty, but she wore it well, her golden hair braided in a crown around her head like a circlet of autumn wheat. She was tall, well-built, and the collar of her modest black gown pushed her chin high. Willim thought her head probably would have been high even without the help. There was something steely and unyielding in her aspect; a battering ram would have called her formidable. Willim could not hear what she was saying to the crew, but he knew their expressions and her gestures, and was forcibly reminded of Hawk telling off a passel of flock boys for being flat.

"She's... quite a composition," Willim said to Grayson, delicately.

Grayson made a pained noise in his throat. "It's time for the autumn ales to go off, and she sees to that personally. The palace orders several casks from that run, and she won't leave so much as a peg out of place on their shipment." He sighed through his nose. "Damnation! Another half a week and we would have missed each other. It'll be tricky work trying to avoid her now."

"Surely she would *want* to see you," Willim tried, thinking that the fa Grayce vessel looked comfortable, comfort that they would otherwise be unable to afford, even after selling the horses. "It's been years since she saw you, hasn't it?"

"She stripped me of my inheritance, Willim," Grayson countered, in a low voice. "True, she had no choice, what with our family standing. But she made it clear at the time what she thought of me. I don't think the years have warmed her heart towards me."

"You're her brother--"

"She has other brothers."

Grayson's tone left no room for argument. He was done, and Willim stopped pressing. Nevertheless, he marked Isbell's progress across the market, and saw her sable mantle sweep through the door of a house two doors down from their inn. "She's gone," Willim said.

"Let's try the south dock," Grayson said, hurrying past the befuddled ribbon-seller. "Some of the *Swan's* crew might recognize me here."

Willim followed, but he had seen the hollow, aching look on Grayson's face, and it caused an echoing pain in his heart. He did not need Ellis there with his sket and his Alfiri love-ballads to tell him what it meant.

218

20

Hours later they returned to the Seal and Sextant, exhausted and thwarted. Bad weather was gathering up in the west, and most ships planned to lie in harbor until it had passed. Those that were going out were not the sort Grayson wanted to hire, as only illicit business risked hurricane. Back at the inn, they paid a copper crescent for the use of a wooden tub of hot soapy water in the inn's bathhouse, where Grayson stood guard while Willim tended to his ablutions in private. The landlord gave them a funny look; it was far cheaper to share a tub in one of the public bathhouses, but certain quirks of Willim's anatomy would raise too many questions.

Willim fumbled back into his breeches as Grayson made use of the water, and he tried not to ogle his bodyguard. Willim had been casual enough with his fellow Songbirds, but he couldn't deny a natural curiosity about ordinary men in general and Grayson in particular. The scars on Grayson's skin, however, implied a certain kind of privacy, and Willim turned away, his stomach knotting up as though he was about to sing without knowing the melody.

"Will the storm keep Isbell in Memwater, too?" Willim asked, staring up at the steam-warped rafters as Grayson swizzled his borrowed razor in the tub.

"I don't know," Grayson admitted, and Willim heard him navigating the tricky area under his nose. "She usually stays in town a few days for business, or at least she used to. Our holdings are far east of here, in the lake country. She'll probably wait for the storm to pass before pressing on."

Good, Willim thought. Aloud, he said, "I suppose we'll have to take care to avoid her."

Grayson surged up out of the tub, stripping water from his limbs. "I know her haunts. If we can avoid her on the docks, we'll be in the clear. Hand me my shirt, will you?"

Willim tried to keep his eyes to himself, but he failed at it thoroughly. Grayson, catching his stare, smiled wryly.

"Impressive, isn't it?"

"What?" Willim blurted, blood rushing to his face in a burning wave.

Grayson ran a fingertip along the thick scar over his hip, a white rope of tissue that stretched from his groin to the curve of his waist. "The worst one I've ever taken, and I didn't even come by it in battle. Twenty-six pins. Took me months to pay Aeric back for them."

Willim let his breath out all at once. Grayson was talking about his *scar*. Which *was* impressive, it was true, but perhaps not so much as other things.

"How did you get it?" Willim asked, relieved as Grayson climbed into his shirt, and it was safe to look at him again.

"From a seven-year old girl, in the marketplace of an occupied village on the border of Alfir and Thrass." Grayson sloshed out of the tub, and shook his fingers through his wet hair. "She threw a water-pot at me, shouting that Godswords had killed her father and we were all-- well, I'm sure you can imagine. The worst of it was, I wasn't even a Godsword, I was just escorting some of them at the time. I'd gone on a supply run with Aeric, my commander, and Dessa fa Ransey, a friend of ours from the infantry."

"What did you do?"

"Me?" Grayson laughed. "I fell down on poor Dessa and started bleeding all over her, what do you think I did? Girl nearly took my leg off. But Aeric gave the girl some money and food, and Dessa asked if she had anywhere to sleep." Grayson fingered the scar thoughtfully through his shirt. "She threw the money in the dirt and ran away. They're an ancient people, and proud. Only in the last century or so have they become so aggressive. Religious zealots gained the ear of the Ethnarch after several years of poor weather and worse harvests, and overturned the more moderate forces in the country. It's a complicated situation, and one that can't be solved by brutality or by kindness. This scar reminds me of that." Grayson twisted the corner of the towel in his ear.

Willim looked down at himself thoughtfully, at his carefully placed rings of platinum and his white, unmarked flesh. Compared to Grayson, he looked like something *made*, something false without any useful function besides decoration. "Do you know, the way Songbirds are cut, we don't even have a scar to show for it?"

"I knew," Grayson said, shooting Willim a loaded look. Willim felt himself blushing again. He had almost forgotten about the details of Grayson's disgrace.

"I meant," Willim said, plunging ahead, "It's how the boundaries of a Songbird's term are marked. At the start, we're cut. It's only a tiny incision, not a very complicated surgery and much kinder than what happened to Alveron and his kinsmen. These are done at the same time." He put fingertips to his earrings, and then to the small hoops in his nipples and navel. "After that, we're Songbirds, and no knives are brought near us again, not even to cut food. Only a dull scraper to clean parchment or a tiny blade for trimming quills. We're not supposed to bleed again while we're Songbirds. Then on the last night of our term, we're given our final ring by our predecessor in the title."

"Ah, Rouen mentioned that," Grayson said, with a wry little smile. "You can imagine I thought it intimidating, to say the least."

Willim shrugged. "Kite says it's not so bad, only inconvenient while it heals, and he rather liked the look of his. I expect his lovers do, too. But that's supposed to be the next time we bleed, twelve years later after we're cut and when our term is done. We're no longer Songbirds, no longer avatars of the saints. We're mortal again. Something like that. With that second bloodshed, we are done." Willim hugged himself, his fingers touching the scabbed line on his arm where Raven's dart had grazed him so many days ago. It felt like it had been decades, and it was not so fresh as the other, invisible wounds that stung Willim's heart. "But I feel bled already, forced out of my term before my time."

Grayson rubbed his freshly-shaved jaw, as though considering his words. But instead of speaking, he took Willim by the wrists and held out his arms, as though inspecting the wingspan of a hunting hawk before choosing it.

"What are you doing?" Willim asked, startled out of his reverie. "What--what are you looking at?"

"You look fine to me," Grayson said, shrugging as he let him go. "I would say you are still whole, and still Dove of Valnon, unmarked."

"And what about this?" Willim asked, pointing to the cut on his arm.

Grayson reached out and closed his hand over Willim's arm, running his thumb just beneath the healing cut. "A wound I should have taken in your place. I was clumsy in my rescue, Willim, and that scar should be mine." His eyes flicked beyond Willim, thoughtfully. "It's an oversight I plan to remedy." Grayson walked over to the bench, where Kestrel's knife lay beside his armor. The blade was of the finest patterned steel, and it parted Grayson's sleeve and his skin with equal indifference. Two cuts, one above the other, just under the curve of his shoulder, each no more than an arrow's graze. More than enough to sting, and just enough to scar. Grayson's blood raced through the damp weave of his shirt fabric, spreading in a crimson blossom like an unfolding rose. He had only a moment to smile at it before Willim caught up with him, wrenched the knife out of his hand, and flung it away across the stone floor.

"You cut yourself enough by accident, do you have to do it on purpose, too?" Willim clamped his hand over the parallel cuts. "Is this some sort of natural idiocy of yours, or is it common to all swordsmen?"

"I will take twofold the wound I fail to spare you," Grayson said, putting his hand over Willim's. Willim went still in recognition of the phrase, and he remained so, blood trickling out of his fingertips, as Grayson continued. "For my saints and my city, I lay down my life. As Grayce to Alveron, so I to my Songbirds, so never will silence reign beneath the wings of Heaven."

Willim's throat worked for a moment as he fought for his words. "Grayson, that's--"

"The Godsword's oath, yes." It was the vow Grayson had never before been given the chance to say, the oath of a prentice on receiving his wing-hilted blade with Grace's words engraved along the steel. "By rights, I'm violating the terms of my punishment for even saying it. You could have me charged with blasphemy."

Willim's fingers twitched on Grayson's cut arm. "Don't be ridiculous," he breathed. "You know I would never--"

"Your Grace," Grayson interrupted, before Willim could protest further, "Someone once asked me which Songbird I would choose to serve. At the time, I thought I didn't know, but my choice had been made the moment we met. I would be your Godsword, Third Dove of Valnon, Heir of Alveron, Bird of Evensong, if you would have me. Will you?"

Willim looked down at his hand, with Grayson's blood welling up in the engraved wings on his Dove's ring. His answer came all at once, in an embrace as sure and certain as any note he had ever sung, and as powerful. He threaded his hands in Grayson's hair, pressed their mouths together, and spoke his yes in a grateful sigh against Grayson's lips. For a moment they stood there, heartbeat to heartbeat in the drafty bathhouse, but then Grayson shuddered like a grounded ship lifted free by the tide, and he gently pushed Willim away.

"No, Willim," he said. There was no rebuke in his tone, no mockery, only apology. "I'm foolish enough to be flattered, Your Grace, but not fool enough to make the same mistake twice."

Willim bit back his lips, and curled his shaking hands together. "I'm sorry," he breathed. "I don't know anything about... I'm sorry." Then everything else he was going to say got clotted up in his throat, and he could manage nothing else.

Grayson cupped the Dove's chin in his hand, and his smile was heartbreaking. "Not near so much as I am, Willim. Sorry for wanting it, sorry for welcoming it. I have not been kind to you to lead you so." He lifted Willim's face until their eyes met. "But you are a Songbird. Never bow your head to me. Not for this, or for anything else. You have my sword and my oath and my heart already, Dove of Valnon. It must be enough for now."

Willim felt then a flicker of the power that had coursed through him when the Shadowhands attacked, he heard the melancholy echo of Eothan's last song. For a moment it had been only the two of them there, but now a thousand years of destiny and song crowded into the space between them, and Willim felt not Grayson's kiss, but the song of Heaven burning on his lips. "I understand," he said.

"Good." Grayson took a deep breath, raked back his hair, and looked around the bathhouse with a feverish gleam in his eye. "Now stop standing there looking at me like that, put on your shirt for God's sake, and help me find my trousers before I take it all back."

"Oh?" Willim blinked down between them, and his eyes widened a bit. "Oh! Yes. Well." He looked around desperately, but a funny kind of haze had come over his vision and it was hard to pick out shapes. He happened upon the pile of clothes mostly by chance, and thrust Grayson's breeches at him as best he could without looking in his direction at all. "...I thought you said you didn't want--"

"Bugger what I said," Grayson said, getting into his breeches with some difficulty. "Mother of Naime, Willim, I'm just a man."

"Yes," Willim said, yanking open the bathhouse door, hoping the shock of cold sea air would do them both some good. "I noticed."

The storm arrived in Memwater shortly before midnight. Willim woke from dreams of drowned friends and rising seas to find that the creaking noise of his nightmares was not ships shattering before the wave, but the Seal and Sextant settling down in the face of a howling wind. The inn's snug had no windows, but the bed was wedged in against the chimney, and the air sang in the shaft like Valnon's waterlogged dead. Willim mopped a hand over his damp hair, and spent a minute trying to calm the clamor of his pulse.

Grayson was snoring gently on his side with his back to Willim, as it had been when they had climbed into bed together and tried to pretend the press of their bodies together in the small bed was a commonplace thing, and nothing to set the blood burning in their veins. Willim made sure of Grayson's sleep for several minutes, counting his bodyguard's breaths before slithering out of the bed and reaching for his boots. The tavern was still lively below in the common room, and the sound of conversation and the howling wind drowned out the squeaking of the floor. Willim inched into his boots, gathered up his cloak, and slipped out of the door.

He fastened his cloak around his throat as he hurried down the narrow stairs. The tavern was busy, all the sailors glad for a safe harbor and a good flagon of ale. The rafters rang with sea-chants and the scraping of a fiddle somewhere near the fire, and Willim stepped out into the cool dark of Memwater unimpeded, his heart hammering against his ribs. It was one thing to undertake danger for himself, as he had done when he went through the Undercity with Ellis and Dmitri. It was quite another to do it for someone dear. He only hoped that if Grayson woke, he would think Willim had gone down to the privy, and would not worry.

Willim walked through the stormy darkness of Memwater with his cloak whipped flat against his legs, the wind knifing in through the opening of his cloak and cutting away at his warmth and resolve with every stroke. It had only just begun to rain in small, hard drops of almost-ice when he turned up a neat stone path from the marketplace, and knocked urgently on the door where Isbell fa Grayce had gone that morning. He had only the vaguest hope that she would actually be lodging there, and if not he was disturbing a stranger. After a few seconds, which felt much longer to Willim, the door opened a grudging crack and a stripe of candlelight fell across his face.

"Who are you?" an old woman asked, her face suspicious under her black lace cap. "What do you want at this hour?"

Willim pulled his hood away from his face. "My name is Willim, and I'm here to see Isbell fa Grayce." The maid's face remained stony, and Willim saw at once that it was not going to be enough.

"Her ladyship has retired for the evening. Come back at an hour fit for the saints--"

Willim wedged his boot in the door before she could snap it shut. "Please," he breathed, hoping his plea would find some crack in the woman's heart, and have a better time of it than his foot, which was being pinched by her continuing efforts to close the door. "It's important. It's about... It's about Nicholas. Her brother, do you know him?"

"Of course I know Nicholas!" the woman cried, clutching at the front of her shawl with a withered hand. She cast a swift glance behind her, and then continued in a loud whisper. "How could I not, when I bounced him on my knee as a babe! And if you know what's good for you, you'll say naught about him in front of my lady. She only just heard today about this new business going on in the capital, and it's brought shame on her afresh. If I've seen one tear from her I've seen a thousand, and I've no more wish to cause her pain than to--"

"Nicholas fa Grayce is innocent," Willim said, taking advantage of the maid's distraction to get his hand around the door as well. "Both of his former crime and his current one, and if you'll let me see Lady Isbell, more than one heart may be mended tonight. To say nothing of saving the Temple itself."

The old woman stared at him in patent disbelief. "Ha! You'd have to be Saint Alveron himself to convince me of that."

"I am no saint," Willim breathed, and held up the hand that he had pushed through the door. "But I have sung for him. Please, lady. *Please*."

The maid's eyes went from Willim's to the Dove curled around the amethyst on his signet, and to the numeral etched between the tips of its wings. Her face went as gray as her hair, her toothless mouth sagged. She hoisted it up a few times in a vain effort to say something, and finally turned and rushed away from the door, taking the light with her.

Willim stood waiting on the doorstep, the wind buffeting his back as he shivered with cold and nerves. He wondered if the maid would come back, or if she was off having a tipple of spirits in the scullery. But after a few minutes she returned, and wordlessly pulled the door wide to let Willim in.

"Thank you," Willim said, coming in out of the storm. The maid bolted the door as though there were wolves on the other side, and creaked up the stairs. Willim, without any other instruction, followed her. She came to a stop along the landing, opened a door onto a well-lit bedchamber, and dropped into a curtsey.

"Thank you, Ella," said a woman's voice, low and reserved. "You should go back to bed now."

"Yes'm," Ella whispered, and with one last fearful look at Willim, fled. Willim was alone with Grayson's sister.

She must have been roused from her sleep; the coverlets of the bed behind her were rumpled, her thick hair was bound in a simple braid, and she was dressed in a plain wrap. But she sat in her chair by the fire like a queen upon her throne, and her eyes went right through Willim and back again. Close up, the resemblance to her brother was striking. The bone structure that made Grayson's face handsome made hers a little too strong to be beautiful, even had she been younger, but she was grave and clear-eyed and elegant, and her hands were lovely.

"You do not look like a Dove of Valnon," Isbell said curtly, after her examination was complete. "More like a vagabond in threadbare wools. Perhaps Ella was mistaken."

"She wasn't," Willim said. "But I'm not here about me. It's about Nicholas."

Isbell's eyes flickered. "Should that name have some meaning to me?"

Willim had to bite back on his shout of frustration. Isbell was like Grayson in more ways than appearance, each as stubborn as granite. "Surely you have heard word from the capital," Willim said, choosing to continue as though she had not spoken. "Raven has charged him with high blasphemy--"

"The *Temple* has charged him with High Blasphemy--" Isbell began, then broke off with a little sharp gasp, as though she had not intended to speak. She sank back into her chair, eyes glittering. "I don't tend to keep track of idle gossip from Valnon," she said, inspecting her fingernail. "Nor of the further transgressions of sell-swords--"

"He's here," Willim said, shortly. "In the Seal and Sextant in Memwater, now."

Isbell raised an eyebrow. "And you're telling me this why? Would it not be better to go to the watch, so he could be arrested?"

"I'm telling you this," Willim grated out, "because he's your *brother*, no matter what else you both might try and pretend."

"What Nicholas is and is not is no concern of mine," Isbell said, rising. "Nor is where he sleeps, whom he consorts with, or what he does. And if he has paid you to come here and pretend at being Dove of Valnon only to seek my aid, he has sunk lower than I ever dared believe."

"I *am* Dove of Valnon," Willim said quietly, and something else crept into his voice, something he could not quite place. It was a note, or a timbre, or a shiver of sound in his words, and it made Isbell grow pale. "I am Willim, third of that title after Alveron and Eothan, singer of Evensong, and I come here by the demands of my own heart, and no other. Grayson--Nicholas--does not even want you to know he's here. He practically fled from you today at the harbor. He seeks neither your aid nor your forgiveness. But I have come to tell you that his disgrace is nothing but a ruse, and as he is dear to me, I cannot allow him to continue under the burden of such an undeserved shame."

Slowly, Isbell sank back into her chair. For a long moment she said nothing, lips pursed, hands twisted tightly together in her lap. She raked him over with her eyes, and looked pointedly at the sword Willim wore at his hip.

"It's only for my disguise," Willim explained. "I haven't the faintest what to do with it."

"That's the first thing you've said that I believe." Isbell mulled Willim over for several measures more. "Sing something," she said, at last. "If you are indeed Dove of Valnon, then your song will be the proof of it."

Willim's belly seized up with fear. He had not sung a note since the disaster on board the *Larkspur*, and for a moment he had the terrible vision of the house and most of Memwater sliding into the harbor at the sound of his scales. "I am out of practice," he admitted.

"Hm," Isbell said, unconvinced, and Willim saw he was not going to get out of it. He wracked his brain for the best scrap of melody to give her, something not too demanding on his disused voice, and anything but the *Lay of Hasafel*. He fumbled over a line from the *Hymn of Saint Alveron*. Willim had drawn in a breath to start singing even before he'd fully decided on the choice of song.

> *I give to you, o sister, a crown of only grass,*
> *That grows upon this island, still fairer than that passed*
> *From tyrant's hand, here fallen. Of homeland now restored*
> *I am no king, nor shall be; I am not prince nor lord.*
> *For me, my line is ended, for I am robbed of sons,*
> *Our father lies unburied, my kinsmen like undone.*
>
> *Mourn not for me, my people, for love of you I fought*
> *And fine and rich the country my sacrifice has bought.*
> *Take up, my queen and sister, your spear and burnished shield*
> *May peace and Heaven's wisdom be always yours to wield.*
> *Throw down the servant's bondage, throw down the fettered*
>   *chain*
> *For Valnon and her Queendom forever shall you reign.*

The house did not crumble, but neither was Willim's song mere music. He wanted to persuade her with it, to remind her of the bond between her and her brother. The force of his conviction pressed the sound of his voice around them, seeking the crevices made by old pain, smoothing them over. Willim had become something more than Songbird, his voice something more than sound.

"Enough," Isbell said, before Willim could start the refrain. She slumped in her chair as though exhausted, her shoulders shivering. "Enough, Your Grace. You have convinced me who you are. However." She lifted her head and looked at him sharply, but sideways, like a hawk, her face still to the fire. Her eyes were bright, and she swept one hand beneath her lashes. "I have yet to be convinced about Nicholas. Sit down, and let's have your story."

Willim eased down into the chair across from her, collected his thoughts for a moment, and began. He spoke of Boren's death in the garden, he spoke of his flight from his captors, he spoke of Grayson's rescue in the rain. He did not spare his own pride or suspicions, he laid his heart bare before her as though he was a penitent in a listening chapel. Raven's betrayal, Kestrel's wounds, their escape from the Temple and then from Valnon, even the unanswered questions of Lateran XII's face and his own visions of Eothan were revealed. When he told her the truth of Grayson's past, she listened with her face closed and impassive, her pulse fluttering in her white neck. He stumbled only when he described what happened on board the *Larkspur*. Isbell's hands went bloodless as she clutched the arms of her chair, and Willim stammered over the memory of Grayson impaled on his own sword. He told her of their arrival in Memwater, and Grayson's vow, and was just wondering how to handle the subject of his own spurned advances when Isbell lifted one hand to quiet him.

"Stop," she said. "You must have known that only by concealing nothing would I believe you." She stood up, clutching her robe around her, and stared into the glowing coals in the grate. "Indeed, there is far more that you have not said, but you have told me all the same. My brother was ever ruled by his heart and not his head. It is the sort of thing that he would do, all of it. Foolhardy, rash. I had hoped his years had given him some measure of wisdom." She gave Willim an appraising look, but it was a very different sort than she had before, and it warmed his blood. "At least he has chosen company with it."

"Not so, lady," Willim wet his dry lips. "I am hardly wise, and I suspect the Wing of Valnon chose us for each other long before we had the sense to see it ourselves."

"*As Grayce to Alveron*," Isbell murmured. Then, with the direct motion of one who has made a long-postponed decision, she crossed over to her writing desk in three brisk strides, and flipped up the top of the inkwell.

"You must understand," she said, writing out her note while still standing. "It will not do for me to meet with Nicholas while this business is ongoing, nor for me to take any action. I must wait and let the Wing handle things before I can make any obvious move."

"Of course, I understand," Willim said, as his heart swelled with hope within him.

"However," Isbell continued briskly, blowing into her seal before pressing it into the letter's wax. "I can make some subtle moves. You have answered many questions for me this evening, Your Grace, and not all of them about my brother. My ship sails the moment the weather is clear." She rose, and placed the letter deliberately on the mantle. "It will take you straight back to Valnon."

"Valnon? But no, I told you, we're going to Clarie, in Alfir--"

"But it is to Valnon you need to go, Your Grace. If what you have told me is true, then Valnon is in great danger." Content with her letter, she poured a cup of wine from the ewer, and passed it to Willim. "Are you familiar with the name fa Soliver?" she asked, pouring another for herself.

Willim sipped his wine out of both thirst and politeness, but it was far stronger than what he was used to, and it took him a moment to get his tongue working again. "One of the twelve houses, isn't it?"

"Even more, it is the house to which Jeske fa Soliver, now the Preybird Raven, once belonged. And it is a house which in the past year has commissioned no less than twenty ships to be laid down at the shipyards here, and then to be sent south, presumably to Alfir. But I suspect they are in truth a gift for the Ethnarch, and as we speak they will be sailing to Valnon in order to strike at the moment of the city's vulnerability. Thrass has no real sea power, but with this, it will have an armada. And the Godswords will not be there to stop them."

Willim spluttered on his wine. "You mean--"

"I mean that not only has Raven conspired to start this war, he has planned to *lose* it."

"Why?" Willim breathed. "Lose to Thrass? Why would he do

that?"

"Because Valnon will be his when the treaty is dry. He has always had a loathing for the crown--the late queen was particularly cold to him, and he made no secret of his dislike of her. The regent is in his sleeves--no doubt Raven has some choice bit of blackmail over him, and Queen Reim as yet is powerless. But to have the Temple's rule absolute over Valnon, with the Crown out of the way? This is only his first step. Thrass seeks dominion over the four nations, but it stretches itself too far. Should it try to strive for Shindamir, the might of that nation will break it. Raven has seen this, and I have cause to know that he has made inroads in that nation, as well. The name fa Soliver is not unknown in the royal enclosure of Shindamir, and the Shindamiri prince's army stands tens of thousands strong. Roused, they will be unbeatable, even should the other three nations fight them together. Thrass will be obliged to withdraw, perhaps mortally wounded, and Valnon will be left to its own devices, queenless, with the Temple above all. Raven will be free to press Valnon's advantage, and conquer what is left of Thrass."

"Neither Temple nor Crown is to rule over the other," Willim said. "That was St. Alveron's first law."

"A law Raven has chosen to overlook," Isbell said, and polished off the contents of her glass. "I leave it to you to dispose of him. If what happened on the *Larkspur* is true, I've no doubt you're capable." She flashed Willim a smile, and the transformative effect it had on her face was marvelous. "And anyone who can give Nicholas a serving of his own draught is worthy by my account. I will send my letter to the inn in the morning."

Impulsively, Willim took her hand in his, and kissed it. "Thank you," he said. "Thank you, Isbell."

Isbell colored faintly, as a white rose touched by the light of dawn. "Willim," she said, her fingers tightening in his, "make sure he doesn't do anything foolish. And for the love of Lairke, get him to teach you how to use that sword." She let off an impatient little sigh. "If he's tumbling you, he can't use your vows as an excuse."

Willim blushed to the roots of his hair, "He is not tumbling me," he said, and at Isbell's dubious eyebrow, he stammered out, "...not for my want of trying."

"Well, well," Isbell said, and there was something like

mischief in her eyes. "I don't know if that makes him wiser than I recall, or more foolish. But either way, you had better get back to him before he notices you're missing."

The storm was in full force the next morning, and Willim and Grayson had their breakfast in a main room that still needed lamplight. The hail beat a percussion on the bull's-eye glass of the inn windows, and Willim said a silent prayer of thanks that they were not at sea, or even still on the road.

The landlord brought a folded and sealed parchment note over to their table along with the porridge. Willim, who had been expecting it, watched intently as Grayson studied the seal and the handwriting, his expression guarded. Grayson skimmed the letter, and his eyes flicked up to Willim. "I suspect you had something to do with this," he said, tossing the letter down between their trenchers. It was a writ of passage for the *Swan*, to allow the bearer and his companion passage to Valnon, with utmost courtesy, by order of Isbell fa Grayce. The captain was to provide them with a handsome sum from the ship's coffers, for any supplies they might need. "You spent a long time in the privy last night."

Willim blinked his innocence. "I don't know what you're talking about."

"And you're an awful liar," Grayson said, but he was smiling.

"What do you expect?" Willim asked, cheerfully brandishing his spoon. "I'm a Songbird."

21

Ellis was trapped in a kind of nightmare from which he could not wake. From the moment the Shadowhands attacked the *Larkspur*, his life had become a lurid chain of random terrors, lurching from fear to fear until he had lost all concept of time. For a while he had drifted among broken timbers and wreckage; vaguely he recalled the shadow of a long black ship looming above him, its garish figurehead a red lion with fangs bared. He had been pulled from the water, but it was not in salvation. Stripped to nothing, chained hand and foot, he was flung into the stinking belly of the ship. There were others there, men, women, children, and gray-haired elders deserving of better dignity, all jumbled together in the hold like so much cargo.

Ellis had been found by an Iskati slaver vessel, and the only mercy was that they did not seem know the meaning of the Thrush's ring they took from him. For a long time Ellis simply lay where they had thrown him, his face against the clammy boards. Too numb to even sob, Ellis' only consolation was that Willim and Dmitri were surely dead, and therefore spared similar hardship.

There was a rattle of chains near his ear; a hand gripped his shoulder.

"Sit up, brother," A voice whispered to him, hushed and urgent, the accent strange. "If they think you sickly, they'll throw you to the sharks so you don't spread it among the other wares."

Ellis blinked up at the speaker. He saw a jagged corona of black hair, and one bright eye gleamed in light from the cracks in the deck. The rest was in shadow. A rough wooden cup was put to his mouth. The contents were stale and musty, but it was water, and Ellis drank it down.

"Who are you?" he gasped, when he finished.

"Better to say who I was. Once, I was Sarin, prince of the Reni clan in the Draramir lands south of Alfir. But Thrassin raiders attacked my village, killed most of us, and sold off the survivors to the Iskati. Now I am a slave, like you." Sarin refilled the cup from a skin hanging on a nearby peg, and pressed it once more into Ellis' hands. "Drink a little more. They give us enough water, at least."

Ellis did as he was told, and felt his head clear a little. He scooted himself upright against the hull of the ship, and got a better look at his fellow captive. With his eyes growing used to the gloom, he could see that Sarin was his age or slightly younger, and one narrow whiplike braid hung over his shoulder, strung with beads. Ellis recognized the style as one worn by the Draramir: nomad tribes of Alfiri's southeastern highlands. They had long lived in the mountains between the borders of Thrass and Alfir and the Iskati Empire, and though rightly part of the Queendom, they did not recognize Valnon's authority, or the in fact any government beyond their loose collection of tribes. They were a rare sight in the city, and Sarin's bare skin still bore traces of the elaborate ink dyes used by his people. But the novelty was forgotten as Ellis looked past Sarin to see a pale figure lying alongside him, seemingly asleep, his white-blond hair clotted with blood, and his manacled wrists in his lap.

"Dmitri!"

Sarin blinked at the Thrush of Valnon, and then tipped his head at the Lark. "They brought him down a few minutes before you. You know him?"

"He's my--" Ellis began, and then hesitated, not sure how much to say. "That is, we're... friends. My name's Ellis."

Sarin nodded, knowingly. "I know who you are. You were both made eunuchs some time ago, and you are pierced for jewels. This must be a great hardship for such creatures as you."

Ellis stared at him, dumbfounded. Some words were never used in front of Songbirds. Even the gelded horses of the Godswords were described as being *cut*, rather than blunter terms. More than all the other mistreatment, it was Sarin's words that shocked Ellis the most. "You... know who we are?"

"Of course." Sarin shrugged, as though it was no great secret. "The pleasure-house ateliers of Shindamir always match up their wares in pairs," he went on, not aware of Ellis' relief at his misapprehension. "The better to train them. And you are both too fine to be from the Thrassin trade, those are little more than monsters bred for the arena. Did your master tire of you? Or was he forced to sell?"

"He..." Ellis scrambled around to reinforce the alias that Sarin had provided him. "He was on our ship when it wrecked."

"I see." Sarin settled his shoulders back against a bit of the

234

ship's ribbing. "You have had a difficult time, then."

"No more difficult than you," Ellis said, eager to get the conversation away from himself. Dmitri seemed to be roughed up at the edges, but otherwise whole, and his sleep looked natural enough. "You know a lot about this. Have you been a slave a long time?"

"A month," Sarin said, grimly. "But I'm familiar with the trade. Don't worry, you'll likely go to a noble house and be well-treated. You're an expensive sort. Not so me." He gave Ellis a sharp smile. "Draramir slaves tend to murder their masters and escape. My mother did so three times."

Ellis made a nervous little laugh. "Do you know where we're going?"

"Traderstaak, to be sold. It's the only place where slave-trade is legal in these waters."

Ellis nodded. Traderstaak was a small cluster of islands several miles off the western coast of Alfir, an independent state supposedly governed by Iskarit, leftover from the ancient days when the Iskati Empire had covered most of the known world. Slavery was outlawed in Valnon and its territories, but Traderstaak was a bastion of commerce outside the law of any one country. Ellis had heard that anything could be bought there, if one was willing to pay enough. He slumped back against the hull, defeated. They might as well have agreed to Raven's treaty, and spared themselves a lot of bother to be in the exact same place.

Next to Sarin, Dmitri stirred, groaning. Sarin hurried to pour him a cup of water, and Ellis sent a grateful prayer to St. Thryse that they had been granted a kind friend in their hour of need.

"Dmitri," he whispered, behind Sarin's back as the former prince was preoccupied with the water skin. "This is Sarin, he thinks we're pleasure-slaves from a Shindamiri house and our master died in the shipwreck. We're going to Traderstaak to be sold. Play along, will you?"

The Lark of Valnon gave Ellis a baleful look. "Of course I will, idiot!" he hissed. "I've been awake this whole time." He wriggled in his chains a little, and his expression softened. "...Are you all right?"

"Oh, fine," Ellis shrugged. "Never better."

"From what I can tell, no one else from the *Larkspur* is on this ship," Dmitri whispered urgently. "But keep your eye out once we make landfall. Lots of vessels come through the channel, and the others might have been picked up by another ship."

"...You think Willim's still alive?" Ellis asked, his throat tightening with worry.

"He better be," Dmitri answered, frostily. "Because when I see him, I'm going to kill him myself. If he could Sing Down Heaven, why in Lairke's name didn't he do it sooner?"

Ellis felt his jaw come unhinged. "Sing down-- You mean when that-- Willim actually---"

"Dmitri, is it?" Sarin asked, scooting back and proffering the cup to the Lark. "You're both lucky to be alive, you know."

"The saints are merciful," Dmitri said, and shot a warning glance at Ellis as he drank deeply from the cup.

Ellis looked down at the rough hinges of his manacles, and wondered how many of his friends were equally lucky. Willim Singing Down Heaven? Perhaps that's what Ellis had felt, a moment before the ship capsized, tugging at his heart as though it was a kite striving in a high wind. But even if it had been, Ellis could not see that it had saved any of them, much less Willim himself. When he put his face down on his knees, he pretended to be dozing, but the tears coursed hot and unimpeded down his face. Sarin gave his shoulder a sympathetic squeeze, but let him have what little privacy the hold could offer.

By the time they landed in Traderstaak a day later, Ellis was weak with hunger and exhaustion, sick with the reek of the hold. They had been given some bread, but it was tenanted by too many weevils for Ellis' taste. Sarin picked his out as though they were no more offensive than pips in a fig.

On land, even if Ellis had had the strength to escape, he could not have. The slaves were washed down with buckets of shockingly cold sea-water on the ship's deck, hooked into a long chain by their wrist manacles, and then marched onto the docks in a line. Ellis could not flee unless all the rest of the captives took to their heels in unison.

Shivering, blinking salt water from his eyes, and blinded by the first sight of the sun in two days, Ellis stumbled down the gangplank and along the cobbled street without looking at his surroundings. Traderstaak stank of too many animals and people crammed into a tight place; the city streets were pitted with age and disrepair. Ellis plodded through the filth of trampled orange peels and manure, trying to dodge the worst of it with his bare feet. His only hope was that he and Dmitri might be sold together, as Sarin had implied they might. For the moment, all he wanted was to lie down and sleep. But as miserable as he was, he kept his face in check. He was still the Thrush of Valnon, and though the humblest of the Songbirds, it was pride enough for an Undercity foundling with no name save the one the Temple had given him. He pushed past his weariness, and tried to lift his shoulders.

"That's good," he heard Sarin whisper, behind him. "Bear up. The sale will be the worst, but then it will be over."

Ellis started to reply, but the slave in front of him came to a sudden halt, and Ellis crashed into him before he realized they had stopped. He lifted his head, and gave the crowded street a bleary eye. There was a disturbance ahead on the line. Looking towards the source of the shouting, he was hit with a jolt of recognition that roused him even more than the shock of cold water. Arguing with the head slaver was a red-haired man with a cockaded hat and a scar down one cheek. As Ellis' heart lurched into his throat, the man turned and pointed down the line of slaves, directly at Ellis and Dmitri. Ellis could not understand what was being said. Though it was loud, it was entirely in Iskati.

"He says you belong to him," Sarin said, leaning forward to murmur to Ellis. "You and Dmitri. He does not seem the sort to be able to afford a Shindamiri pair like you two. Do you know him? Is he your old master?"

"We've met," Ellis said, remembering the flight through the Undercity to Jerdon's house, and the man who had pursued them from the Swallowtail. Clearly, he had survived having a cart full of barrels shot at him.

"You speak Iskati?" Dmitri asked Sarin, from behind him in the line.

Sarin shrugged with a rattle of chains. "I speak enough." He paused, listening intently. The red-haired man and the slaver were both doing a lot of shouting and gesturing.

"He says he can prove he owns you, that you both should have had a certain kind of ring. The boss says he doesn't know about any rings--of course not, he wants to sell them--and if the man wants you he will have to bid for you at the auction like anyone else."

"Delightful," Dmitri muttered. "I wouldn't want to miss that treat."

"Wait." Sarin squinted. "The man with the scar has offered to buy you outright."

"Can he do that?" Ellis asked, turning around to look at Sarin, and then turning right back again as one of the guards flicked the end of his whip in Ellis' direction.

"If he pays enough." Sarin tilted his head to hear better, now that the two men were no longer shouting. The crowd, bored now, began to mill past them again. "Ah, they're bartering." He gave Ellis a sad smile. "It looks as though this is farewell for us, brother."

Ellis realized, with a jolt, that he would very likely never see Sarin again. He sought desperately for something to say, to thank him for his kindness, but it was too late. The head slaver spat into the street in a conclusive sort of way, the red-haired man followed suit, and Ellis and Dmitri were roughly unshackled from the line.

"I hope you get back to your people," Ellis said to Sarin, before they were pulled apart. "And may St. Thryse keep you safe."

Sarin lifted his head to look at Ellis, and the wind ruffled his jagged hair. For a moment, his chains and nakedness aside, Ellis could believe he was a prince of the mountains, once content with his clan in their trackless forests. "And to you, Ellis," Sarin said, with a quiet gravity. "...Thrush of Valnon."

Ellis' eyes went wide. Sarin was pulled away into the crowd and lost along the line, his knowing smile echoing in Ellis' mind. Ellis was yanked to the side of the street by his manacles, forced to turn away and face his new owner.

"Merciful Naime, I'm so glad you're both safe," the red-haired man said in loud relief, and unexpectedly swept Ellis and Dmitri into a hug, one arm around each of them, his head between theirs. "Try anything and you'll make us all sorry," he hissed in a lower voice, his fingers digging into their shoulders. "If you want to live, you'll play along and answer my questions straight. Where's Willim?"

"Not here, obviously," Dmitri answered, tense but obedient for the moment.

"Grayson?"

"How do you know--?" Ellis began.

"No," Dmitri said. "We were the only ones on board."

"Damn." The man stepped back, eyeing them as though to make sure they were both in decent shape. "Come on, then." He gave their chains a sharp little tug, and they were obliged to trot after him through the crowd.

Alert now in spite of his exhaustion, Ellis tried to get his bearings as the city went by. It seemed to consist of endless merchant stalls wedged up against crumbling, ancient architecture, their colorful tarps a sharp contrast to the old sandstone walls. No one so much as blinked at the stranger with his scar and his vivid ponytail, towing two naked slaves behind him as though they were a pair of goats. People of every color and creed mixed in the streets, and the air was a jumble of scents and shouts, hawkers crying their wares in a dozen languages. Ellis saw jewelers, alchemists, and wicker cages filled with strange animals. Buskers and jugglers turned the fountains into impromptu fairs, beggars tugged at the cloak-hems of passersby, and the wealthy floated above the crowd in gilt litters carried on the massive shoulders of their slaves. Horses screamed, whips snapped, and a trio of courtesans eyed Ellis and Dmitri with a kind of undisguised calculation that made Ellis feel like a leg of mutton hanging from the butcher's stall.

"I don't suppose," Dmitri said, as their guide and owner pulled them down yet another alley in the unending maze, "it's worth it to ask your name, and what you intend to do with us?"

"No," the man said, cheerfully. "Not at the moment, it isn't."

"I thought not," Ellis sighed. "What's bad," he muttered to Dmitri, "is I don't even care, so long as he gives us some food and a pair of breeches."

"When you've got them, you'll care about what comes after," Dmitri said, in ominous tones. "Believe me."

This did not make Ellis feel better in the least.

The squalor and splendor of the market proper was soon left behind them, and they made their way now through narrow streets with painted doors and latticed windows, and the air was sweeter.

There were no more hawkers or beggars, only servants scurrying past, intent on their own errands. Ellis caught glimpses of houses like heaps of colonnades piled one atop the other, their round balconies overlooking quaint little courtyards and burbling fountains.

The red-haired man came to a stop at a slice of steps set deep between two walls, leading up to a gate set with circles of glass in such a dark shade of blue they were almost black. He said nothing as he unlocked it, pulling the two Songbirds in after him, and locked it once more. He brought them through a low, plaster-walled walkway, down more steps, and finally into one of the private courtyards, this one a squareish affair with a sunburst-shaped fountain in the middle.

A small figure sat by the fountain, prodding morosely at the lilies, but she started up with a cry when she saw them. There was a wild pattering of sandals, and Ellis' arms were suddenly full of Rekbah, hugging him like a long-lost brother and sobbing with relief.

"You're alive!" she hiccupped, pulling away to look at Ellis, then flinging her bangled arms around his waist again. "Oh, thank all the gods! All I could think of was how I'd hidden your clothes, and called you names, and I'm so sorry, Ellis, I'm so sorry!"

"Come on now," Ellis said, his own hardship suddenly secondary in the face of Rekbah's tears. He gave her a bracing pat on the back, which was awkward with his bound hands. "We're all right. Probably did us good, to be honest. Nobody can say we're still pampered Songbirds, anyway."

"So," Dmitri said to their guide, his gray eyes cold with pride, "Rekbah's your prisoner too?"

"Ha!" the red-haired man said, taking off his hat. "You couldn't pay me enough for the keeping of *that* one."

Rekbah smoothed her hands over her hair, trying to pretend she had not been crying, and stuck out her tongue at him. "And I wouldn't have *you* either."

"You know him?" Ellis boggled. "Have you known him all this time?"

"Of course I know him," Rekbah said. "Haven't you told them who you are, Aeric?"

Aeric shrugged, pulling a ring of keys from his belt, and

240

working one of the slab-toothed bits of iron in Ellis' manacles. "Well, I haven't really had time--" he began, hunching up a little as Rekbah slapped him on the shoulder. "Ow!"

"How could you? After all they've been through!"

"I couldn't really announce myself right in the middle of the market, Rekbah." Ellis' manacles fell off with a clank, and Aeric started working on Dmitri's. Rekbah's shrill abuse of Aeric brought another familiar figure out of the house, and Jerdon came down the steps to meet them, arms outstretched.

"You've found them!" he chirped, as though Dmitri and Ellis were mislaid hairbrushes, and clasped Dmitri's hands, which Aeric was still trying to get loose.

"Thryseblood!" Ellis swore, massaging his aching wrists. "Will someone just tell me what in hell is going on?"

"Ellis, Dmitri," Jerdon said, with a formal little flourish, "May I present Captain Aeric the Shrike, personal spy of His Grace Lateran XII, famed among Godswords as the butcher-bird of Kassiel, and my very dear friend."

"Hello," Aeric grunted, without looking up from his work.

"Godsword." Dmitri said, and looked a little bit like he would throttle Aeric the very moment his hands were free. "You're a *Godsword.*"

"Why didn't you tell us?" Ellis exclaimed, exasperated.

"Exactly what I was saying!" Rekbah agreed.

"Perhaps," Aeric answered, giving them all a sharp look, "because you're been too busy running away from me, and throwing barrels at me, and costing me a pretty bit of coin just now, I might add."

"You can hardly blame them," Jerdon said, mildly. "You don't look like a Godsword, even when you're in your gorget."

"Then you look like you robbed the armor off a Godsword's corpse," Rekbah observed, with some sagacity. "I'd've thrown a barrel at you too, quite honestly."

"And another thing," Aeric said, jabbing his key at Jerdon in exasperation, "Enough with this "Shrike" business. That regiment of Shadowhands impaled *themselves* on Kassiel's walls; in truth I had very little to do with it."

"Besides blowing up their powder stores," Rekbah put in.

"Yes, well," Aeric considered, as he finally freed Dmitri from his leg-shackles, "I suppose that did improve their velocity somewhat."

"Enough of that for now!" Jerdon said, waving Aeric away, and beaming at the Songbirds with undisguised affection. "We have you both back safe, and you give me hope that Willim and Grayson will turn up eventually as well. Meanwhile, I expect you'll both want a bath, and some food, and to sleep the clock round."

"And some clothes," Rekbah added.

"Yes," Dmitri said, in scalding tones. "That would be nice."

Ellis had almost forgotten that; he folded his hands in front of him in what was most assuredly a lost cause, and they all followed Jerdon into the house.

"Baths first, though," Rekbah said to Ellis, in a loud whisper. "Don't misunderstand me, I'm happy to see you both! But you do smell a bit like a cattle-pen."

22

The house in Traderstaak was one Jerdon owned--according to Rekbah, he had houses in several cities--and Dmitri and Ellis were granted the run of it so long as they didn't go beyond the gate. Ellis wouldn't have wanted to, anyway. There was nothing in Traderstaak to tempt him more than the hot baths, curried scallops, and feather cushions on offer in Jerdon's home. He fell asleep halfway through his second melon sherbet at lunch and did not wake up again until well after noon the next day.

Lying in bed, dressed in the vermillion silks Jerdon had given him, and the sun casting stripes over the mosaics, Ellis felt a little twinge of guilt at how comfortable he was. Heaven only knew where Willim and Grayson were at that moment, or if they were alive at all. Aeric had fished Jerdon and Rekbah out of the sea, and he had found a good quantity of dead Shadowhands, but no trace of the Dove or his bodyguard. Zeig was missing as well, but he had taken a blow for Ellis during the struggle, and Ellis suspected he lay in Hasafel now, both in the literal and figurative sense.

When this is over, Ellis thought, *I'll write him a song. And Willim will help me, because he's better at minor key, and because he's out there alive somewhere with Grayson to look after him.* Then Ellis thought of Sarin, and his heart sank again. Good mood dampened, he went looking for some breakfast.

Rekbah was just finishing her own tea and honeycakes among the pillows in the main room of the villa, a columned chamber that served as both dining room and library. She fetched more for Ellis and had another breakfast to keep him company while he ate his.

"What's the long face about?" Rekbah asked, sucking honey off her little finger.

"One of the slaves with us," Ellis said, rolling his honeycake around on the plate, picking up and losing any number of sticky sesame seeds. "I was just wondering what would become of him. He spoke pretty easily about escaping, but I think it was only to keep my spirits up. I don't think he really knew how he would get back home."

"Where was home?" Rekbah asked in a distracted fashion, while meddling about with the teapot.

"He was a prince of the Draramir tribes, in the Alfiri mountains. The Reni, I think he said his clan was."

"Prince? Pfft!" Rekbah dropped the lid back on the teapot with a clatter. "Of those savages? What noble qualities did he have? Could he read and walk upright?"

"He could read, speak three languages, and knew I was Thrush of Valnon without giving me away," Ellis said, rather coldly.

"Huh," Rekbah chewed on her honeycake. "Probably adopted."

"Now see here--" Ellis began, rising up from his cushion.

"Don't bother," Aeric said, from the doorway. "It's a lost cause. The Draramir tribes and Iskati have always hated one another, back since the days of the empire. This friend of yours would probably say Rekbah's a greedy, conniving jackal who would sell you your own mother's corpse if she could."

"And it would be true," Rekbah said, downing her tea. "Don't know where she is, do you, Aeric? I could use some money."

"*Pistak'ki,*" he said to her.

"*Naalafak tak zurin,*" she retorted, gamely.

This settled, Aeric sat down to have some tea himself.

"I missed that last bit," Ellis commented.

"You don't speak Iskati?" Aeric clicked his tongue in disappointment. "I'll have to have a word with Osprey about his lessons for Songbirds. They should be passable in all four nations, and old Alfiri, and be able to read Hasafeli backwards."

"I can *sing* in all of those," Ellis said, acerbic. "But high Iskati is hardly the same as marketplace slang."

"There's some very good songs in marketplace slang," Aeric pointed out. "Of course," he paused to chew noisily for a moment, "I don't think the Temple would want Songbirds singing those."

Rekbah made an impatient noise. "He called me a bitch fox, and I called him a meal a maggot would refuse. Both good, useful insults that will get you pretty far for their value. You should remember them." She pointed at Ellis' honeycake. "Are you going to eat that, or do you plan on marrying it?"

Ellis sighed, plunking his uneaten honeycake down on Rekbah's plate, and Dmitri came yawning into the room with Jerdon not far behind him.

"Ah, good," Jerdon said, surveying the room. "You're all

together. I spent some time yesterday evening rooting through the marketplace, and I've turned up a few articles you might find of interest." From the inside of his coat Jerdon withdrew two small bundles wrapped in scraps of silk, which, when untied, revealed Ellis and Dmitri's rings of office as well as most of their other jewelry. They had only been wearing the bare minimum when they were captured, but it had been taken, and Ellis had not been looking forward to having to reopen all his holes if they grew together. It would make getting into St. Thryse's jewels a lot more pinchy, provided he had the opportunity to sing Noontide again. But it was his ring he had truly missed. The white band around his index finger where it had been was a painful reminder of all that he had lost since the Temple's fall. Sliding the delicate copper band with its carved carnelian signet back into place, Ellis felt as though he had found a missing piece of his soul.

"I can't believe you found these," Dmitri breathed, placing his ring back on his finger and closing his fist around it.

"This is Traderstaak, my boy," Jerdon said, pulling a large bundle off his shoulder. "You can find anything if you pay enough. Though I do admit, *this* was a bit of a surprise."

Ellis bit back on a cry of delighted surprise as Jerdon pulled away the wrapping to reveal a water-stained sket-case. The padding had kept it afloat and dry, and inside, the sket Jerdon had given him lay as safe and serene as a babe in the cradle.

"That old thing!" Aeric exclaimed. "What was it doing here?"

"I gave it to Ellis," Jerdon said, folding the wrapping up. "And if that bothers you, you should stop leaving your junk in my house. It's not a closet for hire, you know."

"This was yours?" Ellis asked, stroking the neck of the instrument. "Sorry, if it's important to you--"

"No, no," Aeric said, holding out both hands as though to keep Ellis from handing it back, which Ellis was having some trouble working up the will to do anyway. "Glad to see it getting some use. I haven't played it in years. But don't go losing it again, and that goes for your rings as well."

"Don't worry," Ellis breathed, hugging the sket. "Nothing could make me part with either of these."

"Now!" Jerdon said briskly, rising again, "I must confess this house is woefully under-supplied to keep us all clothed and fed,

245

and if we are to progress on to Clarie--where I hope our missing friends are waiting--we're going to need to do some business in the market. I think it'll be safe enough here for our two Songbirds if they're with us, and you deserve to see Traderstaak from the position of buyers, not the wares. I don't expect anyone is looking for you here, but to be on the safe side, don't go flashing those rings around."

Flashing his ring was the least of Ellis' worries once they were out in the marketplace. His needs had always been provided for by the Temple, and though luxuries were plenty, they were all tribute from the city merchant guilds or doting nobles. Never before had he had money of his own to spend as he wished, but Jerdon had provided him with a string of gold-hearted crescents and told him to purchase whatever he might need for the coming days.

"And before you ask," Aeric reminded them, "It's not enough to buy a decent weapon and everything else you'd need as well. So nothing pointy. You're still Songbirds."

Even with that prohibition, there was plenty to choose from. They were hardly allowed to run loose; Jerdon and Aeric were never more than a few steps away. But for Ellis, it was a glorious freedom. Jerdon had taken them to a much better section of the bazaar than the one they had gone through as slaves, and the stalls were full of dazzling glassware, bolts of jewel-toned fabrics, somber leather-bound books, perfumes and spices and sweets and wines. Ellis didn't need anything more than spare clothes and some basic toiletries, and in spite of Rekbah pointing out everything from trained pet mice to clockwork birds, he restrained himself as best he could and negotiated the purchase of his necessities first. Still, he could not resist a set of copper finger-picks for his sket, and he and Dmitri went in together on a rare volume of Shindamiri epic poems, many of which were set to music. The journey would be long, and it seemed like a good investment to pass the time.

Dmitri was examining tiny glass pots of kohl when a dull roar of crowd noise rose up from the far side of the square. Several of the people nearby--mostly the rough, unoccupied idler sorts-- brightened like hounds at the sound of a scraped plate, and rushed off in the direction of the commotion.

"What's going on?" Ellis asked Rekbah, who was helping

herself to some caramel nuts from the booth next to the apothecary.

"Sounds like they've caught a runaway slave," she shrugged.

Ellis felt his mouth go dry. *There but for the grace of Heaven I go*, he thought. Aloud, he asked, "What do they usually do when they catch them?"

"Depends." Rekbah didn't seem too entranced by what was clearly a commonplace occurrence. "If he's worth a lot, they might just whip him in public and call it enough. If he's cheap or troublesome they might castrate him, or stone him, or hang him up for the birds to peck at till he dies, or do all three in a row. It's really up to the owner, and how offended he feels--"

Rekbah broke off. Ellis was no longer there to listen. He had run off into the crowd, a heavy and certain foreboding like a ball of lead in his belly.

The crowd thickened the closer he got to the noise. But with a persistent use of shoving and stepping on toes, and the advantage of his height, Ellis soon spied the edge of a rough wooden platform where the punishment was taking place. There, a burly Thrassin with two equally thick attendants lorded over a large rack of hooks and chains. A squat brazier glowed through a smoldering mouthful of hot brands. A weedy-looking man in garish velvets watched the proceedings with a vengeful gleam. And chained up to a large turnstile in pride of place, gagged with an iron bit, his skin laced with cuts and his blue eyes hot with hatred, was Sarin.

Ellis shouted in recognition, but his voice was lost among the violent noise of the crowd. The torturer spent some time deliberating over his assortment of knives, while one assistant rolled the brands around in an offhanded way. His fellow smeared pitch over Sarin's eyes, yanking his hand back as Sarin tried to bite him in spite of his gag. The crowd guffawed with laughter.

"Bet he squeals more over his tackle than he does his eyes," said a filthy boy not far from Ellis, an eager light in his face.

"Naw," argued his companion, an old beggar with three missing fingers. "These mountain savages is proud. They always holds up till they run one up their arse."

The torturer made his selection, the red-hot iron was ready, and Sarin was daubed with pitch in places where the sustained burning would cause the most pain. Blinded by the gobs of it across his eyes, he tilted his head towards the scent of the smoking brand, and Ellis saw his ribs heaving in barely-controlled terror.

Blocking out the noise of the crowd and his own horror, Ellis put both hands on the edge of the platform and vaulted up on it. It was his voice demanding that they stop, his hands reaching out as though to wrest pokers and knives from men twice his size. And yet there was something of it that was not him, something fearless and hot inside his breast, something he had only ever felt before when his lungs were full of song and Noontide's light beat down upon St. Thryse's copper armor.

He was the Thrush of Valnon, and he would not stand for this.

"Get down!" The weedy merchant rushed over at Ellis with his arms flailing, as though shooing a cat from his doorstep.

"I will not," Ellis said, shooting a glare in the man's direction. "This man is my friend, and you have done harm enough."

"Harm!" The man shrieked. "This worthless bit of flesh nearly destroyed my house when he tried to leave it! Broke a priceless vase--said to be fished up from Hasafel itself--incredibly valuable-- cut at me with the shards! Look!" He brandished one arm at Ellis, revealing a cut almost as ugly as its owner. "And by my father's blood I will have my revenge for it! I was a fool to buy a Draramir slave, might as well throw my money in the sea, but he's mine to kill if I please! Now get down!"

The crowd by now was shouting this as well, some loudly hoping the tormentors would give Ellis a taste of their skill for equal measure.

"I'll buy him from you," Ellis said, and did not pause to consider how. Already his ring was off his finger, its brilliant stone glittering as he held it out. "If you kill him, you profit nothing. Give him to me, and you come out the better for it. Your choice."

The merchant wavered, clearly tempted. His eyes flicked from Sarin to the ring and back again, and he twisted his hands together. "Well, now," he began. "That is, he *is* quite a specimen, lively I grant you, but very strong, and I couldn't part with him for more than--"

"The ring," Ellis said, flatly, "or nothing."

The man's eyes devoured the ring, and it seemed to Ellis that the stone caught the light and refracted it a thousand times, burning like a miniature sun in Ellis' hand. Until that instant, he had not realized the placement of the sun in the sky. It was noon.

"Done!" the man said, and the crowd hooted their disappointment. The man holding the brand thrust it back into the brazier with a guttural curse, and Ellis felt his knees go to water. He swayed with relief, but there was a thump of boots on the platform behind him, and Aeric caught him.

"Come on, my boy," Aeric said, through a tight smile, "How many times have I told you not to buy your stock off the block? My little brother," he said, to the merchant, "--Always one with an eye for a bargain! One of these days it'll be trouble, I tell you! Nothing for it, though, a deal is a deal." He turned to the Thrassin and said something to them in their own tongue that made them laugh. They roughly unhooked Sarin and let him fall to the platform, still gagged and chained. Aeric pulled him up by the arm.

"Let's go," he muttered to Ellis. "I don't like the mood of this crowd."

One of the Thrassin torturers shoved a rough tin plate into Ellis' hands, the metal struck with letters to indicate Ellis' ownership of his new property. Aeric hustled them both off the stage as fast as he could manage, with Sarin still blinded by pitch and stumbling with exhaustion.

"Of all the stupid, foolhardy, arse-fronted things to do!" Aeric fumed, steering his charges away from the crowd and into a small alcove, where Jerdon was waiting with Dmitri. "What part of *lie low* means marching up in front of half the town and waving your ring around? Might as well have sung them Noontide while you were at it!"

"Right," Ellis shot back, writhing out of Aeric's grip. "I suppose I should have stood by and let him be murdered in front of me!"

"I *suppose* you should have stopped to think for five damn seconds before jumping up there!" Aeric retorted, his face flushing so that his scar lay white against his face. "I don't think you realize the danger you're in, the danger it would be to all your other friends--to Willim, to Dmitri, to your Preybirds, to *Valnon*--if you were caught. You are the Thrush of Valnon and--"

"I am the Thrush of Valnon," Ellis retorted, "Yes. But I am also Ellis, and I value my friends over trinkets and titles." He curled his ringless hands into fists. "Would you have me leave him there to die? Where would my saint be, if Grayce had not cut him and his kinsmen free when they hung dying and shamed before Antigus? Have you forgotten that they were slaves before they were saints, and faced the same death as Sarin?" Ellis tossed his hair out of his face, his eyes burning, his voice shaking. "Who are you to tell me how to serve my saint? Thryse would rather a saved life than an hour of safety, or a Songbird's useless bauble!"

All the color had gone out of Aeric's face. Jerdon had put a hand over his mouth, as though he was trying to hold back words or laughter with it. He met Aeric's eyes for a long moment, and finally Aeric, with a noise of disgust, tossed Sarin's chains at Ellis.

"Fine, then," he said, defeated. "But you're taking care of him."

Ellis was already trying to wipe the pitch from Sarin's eyes. His hands were trembling harder now than they had ever been in front of the crowd. Rekbah joined them just then, looking pleased with herself. No one asked where she had been, and she didn't volunteer the information, eyeing Sarin with interest.

"It *was* pretty stupid, Ellis," Dmitri began.

"Shut up," Ellis retorted, unlatching the bit and flinging it away onto the ground. "You know you would have done the same."

Dmitri made a face. "That's beside the point."

"Songbird?" Sarin rasped, working his aching jaw and trying to get a look at Ellis through his gummed-up eyelids. "Is it truly you?"

"It's true, Sarin. Just hold on a moment longer, this tar is everywhere--"

Sarin clutched Ellis's arms, his expression intense. "There's no time for that now."

"That's probably true," Ellis said, sending Sarin's wrist shackles after the gag. "Better to do this back at the house. Ugh, these have rubbed your skin raw. I'll have to clean them up for you."

Sarin shook his head. "Your city is in great danger. Come with me, I have to show you--"

"What's this?" Aeric asked, breaking away from a silent conversation of expressions with Jerdon. "What about Valnon?"

Sarin drew himself up at Aeric's approach, meeting his gaze

through reddened, pitch-sticky eyes. "I knew when Ellis and Dmitri were brought on board that they were Songbirds, and when I saw you I knew by your sword that you were a Godsword. I saw it when you pulled back your cloak to pay the slave master, and knew they would go to safety. I thought all would be well with them. But then I was sold, and the man who bought me was a harbormaster from one of the smaller islands. When I learned of his business, I knew Ellis and Dmitri had to be told. When I ran, it was in hopes of finding you, to warn you."

"Warn us of what?" Aeric pressed.

Sarin peered around them at the rooftops. "We should be able to see if we get high enough." Ignoring his wounds and his nakedness, Sarin took Ellis by the hand and pulled him along the street. The others followed, Aeric cutting ahead of Sarin, something in his face making Ellis think he had gleaned some idea about Sarin's news.

"You can see most of the west islands from the crest of the next street," he said. "This way."

The road turned into a bridge leading over the steep side of the old fortress walls, streets falling away below in tiers of rooftops and gardens. It was easy to see the outlying islands dotted here and there around Traderstaak's ragged skirts, and Sarin pointed to a medium-sized, crescent-shaped one.

"My former master's guests," Sarin said, grimly. "I heard them talking over wine last night. Once they are fully supplied and given word, they will sail for Valnon."

Riding at anchor between the tines of the island's arms were twenty heavy battleships of Vallish make, their ramming prows glinting just below the waterline, and their masts hung with pointed, crimson-edged standards bearing the black hand of the Ethnarch's Shadowhands.

"Well," Jerdon said, after a stunned pause. "I suppose we're not going to Clarie, after all."

Rekbah sighed, and Ellis started as she took his wrist. "In that case," she said, placing something small and warm into his hand, "You'll need this back. You're lucky that merchant has easy pockets."

Ellis looked down in surprise, and the carnelian stone of his Thrush's ring winked up at him from his pitch-streaked palm.

23

Rekbah had declared in no-quarter terms that Sarin would have to wash in the fountain outside, and even then with a bucket, before there was to be talk of getting in the actual baths.

"I'm not cleaning pitch out of the drains before we leave," she said, shoving bucket and sponges and ointment at Ellis. "He's a savage, he should be grateful to bathe like a horse. It's more than most of his kinsmen do."

"She doesn't mean anything by it," Ellis said to Sarin, trying to put everything down in order, without dropping the salve.

"The hell I don't!" Rekbah called back, from the cool shadows inside the house.

Sarin caught the jar before Ellis could drop it. "I've heard enough real insults to know the difference," he said, his pitch-smeared smile wan. "She is proud and spirited, like all her countrymen, but if she meant me true malice I think I would know." He pulled the cork from the jar, and made a noise of approval at the contents. "This will do it."

"Oh, good." Ellis tried to come up with anything more than that, but could not. Sarin slathered yellow globs of ointment over his tarry skin, and the noises of Traderstaak's residential quarter doggedly continued the accompaniment while the singer floundered, mute. "You need some help with that?" Ellis managed, far too late.

"I think I have it now," Sarin said, massaging salve over his feet. "It will need to sit a while before it can be scraped off, though. The Iskati girl is right to have me do it here. Cold water will make the tar easier to remove. It would stick if it was warm."

"Really? Never knew that." Ellis flopped around a little more, and then sat down on the fountain to have something to do. Sarin was one of those people perfectly content with silence, but it made Ellis squirm. And rightly so, he thought. How on earth is one expected to speak with someone he just bought? If there was such a protocol, it had never reached Ellis' ears. The evening shadows of the city grew long, oozing in purple and gold stripes across the paved courtyard.

"You will be returning to Valnon at once, I should think?"

Ellis started. The fountain's burbling and the birds in the hibiscus bush had lulled him into a kind of trance. "You're welcome to come with us," he said. "It will be easier for you to go to Alfir, or... or wherever you want to go, really."

Sarin worked his thumb at a black smear between his knuckles, contemplative. "I am not free to make such choices for myself."

"Of course you are!" Ellis waved at Sarin in mild consternation. "You don't really think... I'm not going to *keep* you, for God's sake. You're free to do what you like. Go home with a light heart."

Sarin looked up at Ellis for the first time. "I have no home," he said. "It is burned, and my people are slain or scattered. But even if it was not so, I am not free. I owe you a great debt, Thrush of Valnon. And to my people a debt is a chain as surely as one made of iron."

"You were kind to me, and to Dmitri," Ellis said. "You nearly got yourself killed so you could tell us about the ships. You owe me nothing."

Sarin dipped a hand in the pool, and scraped away the pitch and ointment on his face, leaving clean tracks through the grime. "I do not see it that way," he said. "And so I cannot go with you to Valnon."

"Where will you go, then?" Ellis asked. "You can't stay here, it's far too dangerous."

"Were you alone, I would stay to protect you. But your Aeric and Jerdon are more than enough for that." Sarin squinted at a lit window above them, where Jerdon and Dmitri were discussing the best route back to Valnon. Their shadows were black against the lattice, their voices low and worried. "And so I will go where I can be of most service. The Thrass are not a seafaring people, you see. Apart from a few traders, they fear the ocean. This Raven of yours may have given them boats, but not the means to sail them. They will hire local sailors for that. I heard their leader speak to the man who bought me, to ask where to get them."

Ellis' heart grew heavy and cold inside him. "Sarin--" he began. But the Draramir tribesman held up one hand to silence him.

"In truth, I know ponies better than I know the sea. But I can get on board, sure enough. And then once they are underway to Valnon it will fall to me to stop them, or slow them, however I might manage."

"You'll be killed," Ellis breathed.

Sarin shrugged. "Perhaps. If so, I will be in good company."

"You're a fool."

Ellis looked up in surprise. Rekbah stood there, a bundle in her arms and her face hot with anger. "This is why I cannot abide you savages. After all Ellis has done for you! You would go off and kill yourself for some oath or honor or debt or whatnot. Can't you see how it would hurt him?"

"Rekbah, please," Ellis began. "Sarin's not mine. He can do as he likes."

Rekbah turned from Sarin's serene face to Ellis' worried one, her small shoulders shivering with barely-contained fury. "Well!" she said, when she could not come up with anything withering enough, "if you haven't the sense to stop him I suppose it's on your head. Here." She dumped her bundle down on the edge of the fountain: clothes for Sarin, a satchel of supplies, sturdy sandals. "And take this," she added, hesitating only a moment before pulling out one of the two slim knives she wore at the small of her back. "The handle is fox bone, it will make you quiet and clever. Which any Draramir oaf must need. Don't die. I'll want it back." With that, she turned and marched back into the house, one knife short.

"...I think she's warming up to you," Ellis whispered, when he deemed Rekbah was out of earshot.

Sarin arched a brow at him. "Songbird," he said gently, "If she is kind to me, it is not for my sake, but for yours."

Ellis felt the blood go up into his face, and he swallowed a bit without getting anywhere. Sarin let him sit there gulping, while he made short work of washing off both ointment and tar together.

"May I ask you something, Thrush?"

"Of course. And it's Ellis. Calling me Ellis is fine."

Sarin mused on the rusty heap of his discarded ankle chains by the fountain. "The thing that is done to Songbirds, it is something done to prisoners and to slaves. If it had been done to me, or to a brother, I would kill the one responsible. But it is not so with you."

Ellis let out a breath, and smiled. This was a subject more

familiar. "No," he said. "It's not the same. When I sang at the trials, I was chosen to be a Songbird, and asked if I would be willing to be cut. It is a very great honor."

Sarin frowned. "I know a little about Valnon," he said. "But I don't understand Valnon. You say it is an honor, but you risked your life to keep something like it from happening to me today."

"That's different." Ellis' brow furrowed. "That's how it was done to Saint Alveron, and his kinsmen Lairke and Thryse. It wasn't a choice for them, it was done to humiliate them. Antigus the Terrible meant to make them watch as he massacred their people, and he castrated them so they would know that they were utterly the last of their kin. But it's not done that way to us. It's a small cut and hurts only a little."

"A little hurt to honor your saints?"

Ellis shook his head. "Not just that. A little hurt to give them our voices. No one but a Songbird can sing like a Songbird. You see," Ellis took a deep breath and settled down on the fountain, tucking one knee to his chest. "Six hundred years ago, Alveron's people were slaves. Alveron went to the king with his two kinsmen to request the freedom for his people. They had served Antigus for long years and mined many riches for him, and Alveron had learned the island was theirs by ancient right. But they were betrayed, and imprisoned, and castrated. The slaves were all captured, and Antigus meant to wipe out Alveron's people, but instead Alveron and Thryse and Lairke Sang Down Heaven, and Antigus and his warriors fell down dead where they stood. Alveron's people were freed, and the island was theirs, and Alveron named it Valnon. He made his sister Lavras the queen, and it's her descendant Reim that is queen of Valnon now. But because the saints could have no children, Valnon gives up some of her children to be theirs. When I say I am of the line of Thryse, I mean it--I took on his wound and became his heir. When we ride the stone dais during our hour and sing for our saints, we honor what they did for us. We open a door in Heaven and bring them down to sing for us again."

Sarin thought over this for a long while, slowly lacing up the shirt Rekbah had given him. Ellis could tell he was having trouble getting his head around the notion. "There was a boy in my tribe who could see visions and spirits, but that is the only thing like that

I know. But even he spoke in awe of Songbirds. I had thought them strange creatures, not like us. And then I saw you and the Lark, and you were hurt and lost, and I realized you were just human, and what you do to yourselves became all the more incredible. And I still do not understand."

Ellis inhaled to answer and then stopped, letting the breath out in silence. Words were not the answer for Sarin. When he drew in air again, he let it go all the way down inside him, filling the powerful chest and lungs he had bought with the lives of all his children, his body swelling with fiery promise like molten glass on a blower's pipe. And then he sang:

> *O light of Heaven*
> *O gilded sun*
> *O burning heart of all undone*
> *The Second saint*
> *Of brightest blood*
> *The open hand against the flood*
> *The fearless thrush*
> *With burnished breast*
> *The sun stands still at your behest*
> *A flaming tongue*
> *A steadfast heart*
> *My light of Noontide in the dark.*

When Ellis was finished, it was fully dark. Sarin said nothing. He bent down, caught both of Ellis' hands in his, and pressed them to his face for a long moment. Then he picked up the knife Rekbah had given him and slipped out of the gate and into the night.

Ellis stared after him, but Sarin did not return.

"You know," Aeric's voice came from the veranda above, where he sat on the railing smoking a long pipe, "if you really cared about being hidden, you probably wouldn't sing Eothan's *Hymn to Thryse* loud enough for the saints themselves to hear."

Ellis whirled around on the edge of the fountain, and shot Aeric a hot glare from his too bright eyes. "If they don't want to hear," he snapped, his voice thick, "then they can cover their goddamn ears." With that, he got up and went inside, leaving Aeric to look out over an empty courtyard.

"I never said they wouldn't want to hear," Aeric said, but the only thing there to listen was the ember of his pipe, and it had gone out long before.

Getting on board one of the Thrassin ships was far easier than Sarin could have hoped. In fact, it was only a matter of going up to the quay next to the largest vessel, and requesting a place in the crew. The harbormaster who had bought him would have nothing to do with so menial a detail as the hired hands, and the important people from Thrass did not know Sarin's face. He was a young man looking for work in a city full of the same, and the mate on duty looked him over, made an approving grunt at Sarin's arms, and thrust over a rough paper contract to sign.

"Green pips like you get the night watch," the old sailor said. "You'll be paid when the voyage is over." He stuffed Sarin's contract in a tin box filled with others much like it, and whistled up to the railing of the flagship. "Here! One-eye! Another one for your keeping!"

A towering, white-haired Thrassin peered down at Sarin, his one eye impassive, the other twisted shut from some old wound. He said nothing to the mate or to Sarin, but waved for Sarin to come up and join him on deck.

Simple as walking into a rabbit snare, Sarin thought, with grim pleasure. *It's getting out that will prove difficult.*

Up close, the Thrassin was even bigger than Sarin had thought. He was one of his rare seagoing countrymen, his stance made for gales and his arms like iron. "You're small," he said, and Sarin thought that if the man used himself as a measure, most would come up wanting.

"I'm strong," Sarin countered. "And light on my feet."

One-eye considered this, and a mirthless smile spread over his features. "Take the nest," he said. "And don't fall out and make a mess of the deck. The Ethnarch won't be pleased."

Sarin's breath caught. "The Ethnarch is on board this ship?"

One-eye's open palm caught Sarin just under his ear, setting his head ringing. "It's no concern of yours who is and who isn't here," he growled. "Get your ass up in the rigging before I throw it overboard."

Sarin shook his spinning head and turned to mount the ropes, getting only two steps up before One-eye's hand closed on his leg, pinning him in place.

"Wait," he said, and yanked Rekbah's fox-bone knife from its sheath before Sarin, his fingers tangled in the ropes, could stop him. "...How did you come by this knife, boy?"

His one remaining eye had changed its shape, narrow in the man's dark face. There was something sharper in his voice, and his thick Thrassin slur was less apparent. Sarin stared at him a long moment, knowing that if he made a scene over the knife, he was likely to lose it.

"From a junk vendor in the marketplace," he said. "The sort as picks through wrack for anything. I'd lost my old one, but I'll sell that one to you if you want it." He shrugged. "I can always come by another just as serviceable."

One-eye knew Sarin was lying. It was as obvious between them as the knife's curved blade, glinting in the light of the ship's lanterns.

"There is only one other like this," One-eye said, and after a troubling pause he slid the knife back into its sheath at Sarin's hip. "Up in the nest with you," he said, all gruff and Thrassin once more, cuffing the back of Sarin's head again for emphasis. "We sail for Valnon before the week is out."

Sarin did not dare hesitate or ask any questions, but scrambled up the ropes and into the rough wooden bucket of the nest. From there he had a clear view of the ships, the rooftops of Traderstaak, and his former master's mansion. Sarin had not been in the nest a full hour when a dotted line of torchlight unraveled from the gates of the quaymaster's house. Though they moved quietly, Sarin could hear the tramp of armored feet, the jingle of mail. A runner pounded up the dock in advance of the party, and the deck of the ship suddenly became an ant-hive of activity. Sarin watched as the deck was cleared of work and clutter, and One-eye's white braid whipped through the dark like sentient lighting. By the time the torches reached the quay, every sailor stood alert, every lamp was trimmed, every rope shone.

Four Shadowhands marched up the gangway, two and two and swathed in black, torches raised. Another set of four followed behind, and in their midst was a Thrassin man in his forties, with a proud and handsome face. He was dressed all in white from his gloves to his boots, his silver armor chased with threads of gold. His pale hair he wore braided in an elaborate milky crown around his dark brow, the braid-tips sheathed like daggers. One-eye bowed low as the Ethnarch of Thrass stepped aboard, his personal guard of Shadowhands fanned in a protective semicircle around him. Sarin could not hear what was said, but the Ethnarch nodded, and he seemed pleased. With a benevolent gesture to One-eye the Ethnarch vanished into the ship's main cabin with six of his guard, the other two stood at the door.

The men on the ship seemed to exhale as one, and slowly the activity on the deck went back to normal. But the Shadowhands were like cold ghosts outside a tomb, and more than one sailor went up and around the stairs rather than pass under their gaze. Sarin studied their stance, alert but relaxed, unspeakably dangerous. He wondered if he would need to kill all six of them before he could sink the fox-handled knife into the Ethnarch's throat. For surely that would slow the armada, and Sarin could be of use to his Songbird.

It grew cold up in the nest as the stars wheeled slowly by, and Sarin hugged his arms around his chest and tried to remember the words of Ellis' song.

24

The silence in the Temple of Valnon ate at Raven's nerves, much like the dull pain in his injured hand. While he struggled to maintain a sense of normal activity, the absence of both Songbirds and Preybirds had caused quite a stir in Valnon, as had Milia fa Branthos' rumor-mongering among the nobility.

Raven had been obliged to keep the Laypriests chanting hours, spelled by a few members of the flock too young to cause trouble, as he could not risk letting the Preybirds out to sing. They were openly rebellious, and only Raven's threat to retaliate their actions on the flock had kept them in check. Hawk was especially prideful, and his silence smarted. Raven had locked them in the archives, kept them well-guarded by the prentices, and tried to focus on other things. He had neither Songbirds nor scapegoats, but he still had plenty of pieces in play, and one he thought lost had just returned.

"A woman of Thrass, you say?"

Petrine's discipline wavered just enough for her distaste to flit over her face. "Yes, Your Grace," she said. "She arrived at the Temple a few moments ago, and asked to see you. She will not give her reason for coming, or her name, only that she is expected." Petrine's pause was slight and unhappy; and Raven felt a rare twinge of remorse. She was a good soldier, and loyal, but he could not trust all his plans to her.

Raven rose up from his desk, reaching out a hand for his staff. "See our guest to the portrait room," he said. "I will meet with her there. And once you have done that, go and find that useless Laypriest for me. I need more thyme oil for my hand, and the Temple's stores are nearly spent."

Petrine bowed and exited with a jangle of mail. She was young, Raven knew, and time would make her wiser. When all was done, she would see the full nuance of the song, and understand that sharps and flats were needed in order to make the melody sweeter. That decided, Raven put Petrine out of his mind as he made his way down to the portrait room.

Apart from her striking coloring, the woman waiting for Raven in the portrait room might have been a member of a well-ranked Vallish house. She was dressed impeccably in a gown that enclosed her throat but bared her shoulders, suitable for a visit to the Temple in the middle of the day. Her hair was arranged in a single, artful coil of braid, with two ornaments to hold it atop her head. A casual observer would have thought the pins mimicked black wings, and taken her for a devotee of St. Lairke. Raven, on the other hand, knew the stylized black hands for what they were, and that the beautiful woman was the highest ranked of the order of the Ethnarch's Shadowhands, and one of the deadliest creatures under the sun.

"My Lady Jacind," Raven said, closing the door behind him. "What a pleasant surprise."

"No doubt," she said, dryly. "I expect you thought me lost along with my ill-fated mission."

"And of course I'm delighted to learn otherwise." Raven settled himself in the chair beneath St. Alveron's portrait; a deliberate placement beneath the saint's gesture of command. "I hope your visit means you've some information for me?"

Jacind snorted with disdain. "Only that had I known you set me on the path of demons, I would have demanded more pay."

Raven's fingertips went still on the arm of his chair. "...Demons?"

Jacind's eyes flicked up to the painting, then quickly away again. It discomfited her, Raven could tell, but it was not only a general unease. There was a recognition, there. Jacind was no southern heathen, she was well-educated about her foes, and had been taught much of Valnon's history and myth. No doubt she knew St. Alveron's story as well as Raven himself did. "I never thought it true," she said, "that your eunuch saint sang up curses from hell."

"From Heaven, my dear," Raven said, in gentle correction. "I take it something has changed your mind?"

"We set upon the vessel as agreed, but it was no Preybird we found there. Your missing Songbirds were on it instead."

Raven grasped the arms of his chair, the pain of his wound sending knives of unnoticed pain up to his shoulder. "And?"

"Nicholas Grayson I ran through with his own sword." Jacind closed her hands into fists, and leveled an unwavering gaze at Raven. "And then your soft, helpless little Dove made a sound that tore the ship to splinters, and dragged it and all my men to the bottom of the sea."

For a moment Raven was too stunned to speak. Jacind, if choosing to lie, would select a more credible tale than this. Her voice was grim with truth, and Raven's mind reeled with the implications of it. Surely it was not possible that Willim was a true Dove, with the power to have last been wielded by Alveron. It was true that his blood bore the holy tinge of Hasal the sea-god, and of Naime his bride, passed through the kings of Hasafel to Alveron and Queen Lavras fa Valos, and to all her line to follow. But it was a stolen birthright, one born out of shame, one the late queen had hoped to hide by foisting the him on the Laypriestess' mercy at his birth. It was dilute, tainted, as the Temple's power was. Having the power of Alveron did not mean Willim had the blessing of Heaven, Raven reasoned. No, if nothing else, it made his blasphemy all the more perverse.

"Did they survive?" he asked, at last. "The Songbirds?"

"My spies in Alfir have not reported seeing them. But that does not mean they are truly dead." Jacind made an impatient gesture. "My lord father will wonder if perhaps this was betrayal, Raven. He will not be pleased."

"Never once have I implied I would not give him his due," Raven retorted, stiffly. "If he does not trust me, perhaps I should revoke my gift to him."

Jacind's white smile flashed in her dark face. "The Ethnarch of Thrass trusts no one, Preybird. I have enough dead brothers and sisters to be the proof of that. As for your gifts, they so far are nothing but boats and promises. He desires more. He is through with your delays. It is time for the hammer to fall upon the iron, before it grows too cold for the forging."

Raven's mind worked frantically. Willim had become more than an idle piece to be moved at whim, but even if he was alive, he was alone, shipwrecked, helpless. How much could he really do? The full power of Singing Down Heaven had never been measured, but if Willim was stranded miles from Valnon, it was unlikely he could bring it to bear on Raven. And if he had truly controlled it, he would not have lashed out at friend and foe alike. Jacind would not have lived to make her way back to the city. No, Willim's act had been one like Thali's. The last King of Hasafel plunged his city beneath the sea to keep it from its enemies, and in doing so cursed his people to a life of wandering and slavery for thousands of years. It was a miracle of the desperate, not of the calculating.

"Very well," Raven said, rising. "We will proceed as planned. However, I require a task of you here, Jacind. The queen has proven to be less malleable than desired. She has been too much in contact with that fa Branthos harpy, and all her brood on the High Council. I fear now she will not concede to any treaty put before her. And Nilan fa Erianthus, though a friend, has laid down his coin on the wrong side of the table. I doubt he would agree to side with me now." He paused by the window, looking out over the city to the palace in the distance. "When the battle begins, you must kill them both."

Jacind smiled warmly. "With pleasure."

"You sent for me, Your Grace?"

Raven started. The fair-haired Laypriest stood in the doorway of the portrait room, peering at them from the rumpled shadows of his hood. Raven had not heard the door open, and his nerves still quivered.

"I did," Raven snapped, hoping a scolding would blot out the memory of anything the boy might have overheard, "and it took you long enough to get here. Are your legs made of lead?"

The Laypriest doubled over in his bow, as though his obeisance was brought on by an unexpectedly intense pain in his belly. "Forgive me, Your Grace. One of the flock boys has a fever, and I was tending to him."

"If you're going to be late because you're dithering over runny noses," Raven retorted, "then at least have the manners to knock." He turned back to Jacind, as though the Laypriest was not there. "If there's nothing else, you may go."

Jacind tilted her head towards him at a mocking angle; it was not obedience. "Until our next meeting, Preybird," she said, and stepped around the Laypriest as though he was no more than a bit of rubbish in her path.

"You," Raven said to the Laypriest when she had gone, "Shaith, wasn't it? The stocks are low in the medical stores. We're nearly out of oil of thyme, and all the wound salve. You haven't been overdosing some idle sneezer with precious medicines, have you?"

The Laypriest murmured something apologetic and unintelligible, still in his bow. Raven reached over to yank back his hood, unleashing tousled strands of pale hair. "And stand up, for the love of the saints. I can't hear anything if you insist on muttering it into the carpet."

"Forgive me," Shaith said, upright now but with his eyes still on the floor. "I was clumsy, and when fetching medicines, they spilled--"

"Then you will have the chore of procuring more from the Apothecary's guild," Raven answered, cutting him off. "And from your own pockets, boy, not the Temple's coffers. Valnon should not have to pay for your thick fingers. Should this wound in my hand turn for the worse, I'll have yours in payment, is that clear?"

The Laypriest's body jerked as he fought off the urge to bow again. "Y-yes, Your Grace."

Raven nodded curtly. "Now get out."

The Laypriest backed up to the door, still half-bent. Raven ignored him and turned to the desk, staring down at the maps there. The Ethnarch's fleet was swift, and Raven had built it to be so. It was only a matter of days, now. The music had begun; the notes could not be unsung. They were not as he had laid them down on the page, but they would do. They would have to.

"You never could improvise, Jeske. Not even when you were a Lark."

Raven whirled, in fury and shock at a Laypriest addressing a Preybird by his common name, but the room was already empty. His neck prickled, and he looked up at the painting, half-expecting to find Alveron's gaze upon him, the stern line of his mouth parted for further scolding. But Alveron remained as he had always been, stiff and aloof, his crimson robes billowing and his blunt-cut fair hair just so against his jaw; his eyes centuries too old for his handsome, stern, and strangely familiar face.

The room pitched around Raven like a yawing boat, he clutched for the table to brace himself as his heart stuttered in shock. He blinked, and the illusion was gone. Alveron was a collection of oils streaked upon a canvas, and his resemblance to the Laypriest was nothing more than a trick of light and Raven's exhaustion. Raven put a shaking hand to his face, and felt his wound burning with fever even through the bandages. Next time he needed private council, he decided he would do it in his rooms, far beyond the reach of the first Dove's painted eyes.

Grayson had bartered his gaudy sword for something more serviceable, but through the days of the journey south again to Valnon, it was Grayce's hilt that came more frequently to his hand. He could not find reason for his strange preoccupation, save that through all his misadventure--and the loss of two other blades--the chunk of his ancestor's effigy seemed determined to stay by him. Grayson had gone over Starling's words in his mind dozens of times, wondering uselessly how he came by his knowledge and his prophecy, but in the end he had only what he held: a stone hilt from a grave, given to him by a madman.

There was no other sword like it. The winged guard was reversed from the usual Godsword's weapon, not back towards the grip to protect the wielder's hand, but forward, to snap the blades of those that crossed it. Grayson had dreamed of that sword as a boy, when a stake from the family hops vines served his imagination in its place, as he warded off foes for the sake of his Songbirds. Now, Grayson thought he would be better off with his old vine-stake instead of the dirty bit of marble he'd been given.

"Two hundred repetitions," Willim announced, flopping down on the *Swan*'s deck beside him. His hair clung to his flushed cheeks, his shirt was drenched with sweat even though the day was cold with coming winter, with a thin blue sky and a chilly wind. Willim rolled his right shoulder gingerly, and sheathed his sword. "Tell me, when exactly does learning swordsmanship branch beyond the standing-in-place-doing-drills part?"

"When you can do those drills in your sleep, or in a flash when someone strikes at you." Grayson tucked the hilt back into his belt. "You're the one that wanted to learn, and I protested, if you recall."

"It was Isbell's idea." Willim fell back against the rail, mopping his hair away from his forehead and looking pleased with himself. "And you promised I'd get to actually cross blades with you at some point," Willim said, tapping the point of his sword against the deck. "So we'd better do it now before we get back to the Temple and I'm obliged to hand in my steel."

Grayson sighed, but he rose to meet his Songbird's challenge.

He had disarmed Willim twice and was on the verge of doing so a third time when a call from the lookout halted most of the activity on the deck. Willim tensed as though he expected another attack, but the sailors had only paused to lean over the port rail for a moment before returning to their tasks. Most of them dropped something over the side: copper coins or buttons, a lock of hair tied with ribbon, a morsel of honey candy. A few had wrapped their trinkets in scraps of paper, or murmured a silent prayer. While some gave in a fashion that was little more than perfunctory, a few lingered reverently over the task.

"What are they doing?" Willim asked, bewildered.

"Ah," Grayson said, sheathing his sword. "We're passing over Hasal's grave." He waved Willim over with two fingers. "You should have a look. You would not have seen it on the way out. It was dark, and we were angled too far south in the channel."

Willim leaned over the rail, his eyes searching the water below. Grayson had seen the sight many times, and he watched Willim's face instead, waiting for the moment of understanding. The water was calm, and clear for fathoms down. Willim watched a sea turtle glide up over a smooth flank of rock and did not realize what he was seeing until the turtle sailed serenely between the vast stone fingers of a colossus.

Toppled on the floor of the channel was a giant. His lower half was lost in gently swaying fans of coral and weeds, claimed centuries ago by the ocean. Only his upper torso was clear, the rest sunk deep in the murk beyond human sight or reach. He rested on his back among the fishes and anemones with his hand lifted to the sky. It was hard to fathom his size, only that he was massive beyond comprehension. His other arm lay broken some distance away, and its outstretched palm could have cradled the *Swan* as though it was an egg.

The ship slowly passed over the fallen titan, and Willim stared deep into eyes that had looked on the sky for eons. His face was clear and noble, untroubled by his submergence. The sea floor had dressed him in fine raiment of coral and sea-fan, as though sympathetic to his lost glory, and his crown was festooned with starfish.

"Hasal," Willim murmured, his eyes standing out starkly in a face gone the color of cream. "God-king of Hasafel, who formed it

266

out of the ocean for Naime in time beyond anyone's reckoning."

Grayson spoke quietly, as there were still sailors at the rail, making their petitions. "When Thali Sang Down Heaven, Hasal fell with his city, and sailors who come this way still offer tribute for their safe passage."

"I dreamed of him, as he looked in Hasafel, standing before the Temple of Doves. I did not know he could be seen."

Grayson pointed downwards past the *Swan*'s prow, as Hasal was enfolded in the silent blue of the sea as they passed him. "He can, in good weather, and if you're lucky you can see more besides. Look there. I've never seen the ruins so well as this. It's a good omen."

At first the reef only looked more varied in its shapes and sizes. Then the smooth curves along the bottom were revealed as the remains of roads, deliberate and planed smooth by the hand of man. Arches rose up from the sea floor at crazed angles. Everything was blanketed in a coat of sea life, but the regular lines of doors and windows were unmistakable, and one dome hovered mostly-intact on its pillars, bits of crimson tile flashing beneath the grime. From there Willim saw the broken teeth of columns, jutting in a crown above sunken stairs. Foundations remained where houses were long gone, blocky patches of anemones bloomed in ancient gardens. Schools of fishes made fleeting shadows over the ruin, as clouds had once done over land.

Willim did not have long enough to look all he wanted. After that fleeting glimpse, the sea floor plunged down again, the water became opaque, and the last idlers drifted away from the ship's rail. The rest of Hasafel belonged to its founder, and he would share no more of it with mortals.

Willim curled his knuckles against the railing, staring down into a sea that gave back only foam, and the color of the sky. "It's strange," he murmured. "Once I hardly believed that Hasafel was real, or at least, real as sung in the Temple. Valnon is only the last of many cities in this same place, or so I thought. What harm was it in believing one of those old cities was Hasafel? It makes the island dearer to us, it makes for good music. That was enough for me."

"I daresay that you've changed your mind now."

Willim made a noise of bewildered dissent. "I don't know that

·I have. Songs are powerful, but they don't just happen. They're written, and writers can't be trusted, even if they say they're historians. I supposed that Alveron needed a firm claim to Antigus' lands, so why not call it Hasafel? Why should his enslaved people not believe they were taking back their sovereign home?" Willim turned his back on the sea, and lifted his head to the sky. The sails rippled and belled, and Willim sighed. "Somehow, everything that's happened has only served to open my eyes to a thousand more possibilities. There are things I had never considered before, and I'm afraid I'm only skimming the top of it. The singing, and the dreaming, and Eothan... It's like Hasafel under us. I can see it only when the light is just so, and never clearly. It was easier to be a Dove, and stand on the Dais, and sing because I was good at singing. I didn't have to believe in anything, be anything, except that. I never knew what was underneath me, underneath the city, underneath the sea. I never really cared."

"And yet--" Grayson began, and made a slight gesture to his chest, to the tidy mending holding his torn armor together. "This..."

Willim shook his head. "It only confounds me more. It only makes me more afraid."

Grayson's hand closed in an empty fist over his heart, turning the gesture into a salute. "In the Northcamp, there's a saying: *Faith and Bravery come easiest to the Ignorant.*"

Willim's laugh hit hard on his teeth, wry. "Then it's no wonder the Temple strives to keep her Songbirds ignorant."

"And her prentices," Grayson added. "But the time always comes when prentices must be Godswords, and Songbirds change their colors. None of us are children forever, not even in the Temple. Fear and understanding create a different kind of faith, one that is stronger in some ways, but more meager, more dear."

"Can you spare me a little of yours?" Willim asked, only half joking. "I've been coming up short of late."

"You're cruel to ask a beggar for his only coin." Grayson smiled. "But what I have is yours, and rightly so. It all came from you, after all."

It was a long while before Sarin was able to do anything to further his plans. One-eye's namesake was on him constantly, making sure Sarin's hands were never idle. He could sleep only

during the day, in a hammock in the hold surrounded by other sleeping crew. Two Shadowhands stood always outside the Ethnarch's door, but it was impossible to tell them apart and Sarin never saw them change shifts. Instead he peeled tubers, and mended sails, and scrubbed the deck with seawater. None of the other sailors were inclined to make friends, and most of them were Iskati mercenaries, who wanted nothing to do with a Draramir tribesman. Sarin grew used to their spitting and sneering in his direction, and found himself missing Rekbah's almost kindly abuse
.

"Don't make a lot of friends, do you?" One-eye said to him one evening, while Sarin ate his biscuit and oranges up on the foredeck, away from the stares of the other hired crew.

"Iskati have no love for my people," Sarin answered, with indifference.

"And Draramir princelings have no love for Thrass," One-eye said, leaning down low. "Perhaps they are too stupid to know the meaning behind that braid of yours, but I am not, and the Ethnarch is not."

Sarin felt a cold chill, but resolutely continued to peel his orange. "My people are long dead, and I must earn my own way in the world. I am not interested in revenge or old grudges."

"You could have taken crew in any ship in Traderstaak. Yet you chose this one, with your enemies, going to war and not to profitable trade. You are not a common mercenary, though you may try to pretend so."

Sarin flung the orange peel into the churning waves below, and took his time picking pith from the fruit before he answered. "What's it to you what I am?"

"What you are is a terrible excuse for a spy." One-eye put his hand over Sarin's, pushing the orange away from his mouth. "And as I am a very good spy," he said, "I want to thank you for being so goddamned obvious that no one has looked my way twice on this voyage."

Sarin stared at him. "I don't know what you're--"

"I was there the day Jerdon gave those knives to Rekbah," One-eye hissed. "And the Thrush of Valnon bought your life in the marketplace in Traderstaak. If I had not lost you both in the crowd I could have spared you the trouble of coming on board, but as you're here, I want you to know to stay out of my way."

"Who are you?" Sarin asked, still guarded.

One-eye's hand tightened painfully on Sarin's wrist. "I am Captain Zeig of Her Majesty's navy, former commander of the *Larkspur* and once a Godsword oathed to fight by the side of the late High Consort. And through hell and shipwreck I have made it this far, and you will not bar my way."

"If you mean to kill the Ethnarch," Sarin said, dropping his voice to a bare whisper, "I could help you."

"Kill him?" Zeig shot back. "Now? Don't be a fool. Those Shadowhands of his are all his sons, and each one of them ready to rule at the flick of an assassin's blade. There's three more on each vessel sailing with us. We'd have to kill them all to undo this voyage, and that's to say nothing of the sons and daughters he has left behind in his country. We'd have to wipe them out at once, undiscovered, and likely take ourselves with them."

"I'm not afraid to die--" Sarin began.

"Lairkeblood, boy, I am," Zeig retorted. "And I'm not throwing my life away without some care for how I leave it. Have you been on the gun deck?"

Sarin blinked at the sudden change of subject. "No. You've kept me on deck or in the hold."

"Then you'd better come with me."

Zeig stood up and strode over to the hatch without waiting for Sarin to follow. He took the steps down into the gun deck two at a time, and Sarin hurried after.

"Thrass has some skill with powder," Zeig said, stooping to walk in the low-ceilinged level, sandwiched as it was between the hold and the topside. "Small bombs, smoke flares for the mines, things like that. They have been hard-put for supplies since their largest mine was destroyed years ago. And the Temple of Valnon does not encourage war with powder. It is too barbaric, too imprecise. And Iskarit uses it only for alchemy and diversion."

Sarin squinted at the dim gun deck. Each port had a shrouded object before it, long and low and sinister. "So these..."

Zeig reached out and pulled the canvas away from the nearest gun. Its barrel was twice the width of Sarin's own body, and the gaping iron muzzle was covered in writhing brass dragons. Sarin looked on them in confusion, and then in horrified understanding.

"These are Shindamiri guns!"

"Yes," Zeig said. "Raven the betrayer has been betrayed in turn. Shindamir has been waiting years for a clear victor in this conflict, so it will only have to conquer one of them to rule near all the world. For a time it seemed Valnon would succeed, but now Shindamir favors a different gamble. Raven gave the Ethnarch ships, but Shindamir gave him guns and powder enough to blow Valnon right to the bottom of the sea."

Sarin stared at the gleaming weapon. He had not planned for anything so disastrous. He had not planned for anything, actually; he was not one inclined to strategy. His only real thought was to stab whomever was in charge, set fire to the ship, and ram it into the rest of the armada. He had neither intention or hope that he would survive, only that he would make the best of his death that he could. But he had not bargained on the Ethnarch, six Shadowhands, and the deadliest guns under Heaven. "What are we going to do?"

"We're going to do what we can, lad, and no more." Zeig let the canvas fall back over the cannon. "I admit, it would please me to at least see the Ethnarch safe off to hell before we follow him, but I was confounded on how to do that before you arrived." His good eye gleamed with dangerous pleasure. "But now that you're here, I think I might have a solution."

25

Willim and Grayson had traveled openly on Isbell's ship, without bothering to hide their faces. The crew of the *Swan* was small and intensely loyal to Isbell fa Grayce; they asked no questions about their passengers and had been well-paid by their employer not to answer any, either. If they recognized the set of Grayson's features, or the telling signs of Willim's long build, they pretended not to. But it would be a different matter in Valnon.

Numerous disguises had been discussed and discarded, but in the end Willim and Grayson had decided that Jerdon's notions of subterfuge were fairly sound, barrels notwithstanding. Shortly after she docked, two sell-swords disembarked from the hold of the *Swan*, their faces shielded by broad-brimmed feathered hats, their belts flashing with the gaudy trinkets hanging from their swords, and neither one of them too well-washed. They stepped into the crowd on the docks, and instantly vanished into a crowd of similar cloaks and hats.

"Where are we going?" Willim whispered, as they sidled past a heap of lobster traps, their live contents clicking in dismay. "Is there anywhere safe?"

"My old rooms above the Silver Pearl won't do," Grayson said, eyeing the street from under his hat. "They'll be watched. Jerdon's house is too public. Maybe we could take shelter in one of the tombs, or go under in Fishmarket..."

Willim paused at the end of the quay, letting the market patrons surge past him on their business. There was music coming from somewhere. No one else seemed to have noticed it, or they simply didn't care, and the noise of the docks and the slosh of the waves would blot out the song from time to time. But it crept along the back of Willim's neck like an invisible hand, pulling him towards the source.

"What is it?" Grayson was looking at Willim with a perplexed expression. "What's wrong?"

"Don't you hear it?" The melody wafted towards Willim again, and he tugged at Grayson's sleeve. "Someone's playing music."

"I don't hear anything," Grayson began, but then had to run after Willim, who had plunged into the crowd in search of the melody.

Willim did not know the song; every time he thought he had placed it, the notes veered off into another direction to begin another melody, equally familiar, equally unknown. It was as though he had heard the song in his cradle, or half-recalled from a dream, and it stirred a strange longing in his breast. He had to find its source, and he forgot all else in pursuit.

Three streets away from the harbor, a gated but unlocked alley opened out into a small courtyard, overlooked by the backs of the houses and shops situated at the edge of the block. It was home to a public well, a broken-down wagon, and a clutch of ill-tempered geese. It was the last place in Valnon Willim would have thought to find a busker, but there he was, seated on the edge of the well, wrapped up in his patchwork cloak, a humble clay flute at his lips. He lowered the flute as Willim came into the courtyard, his eyes alight with affection and relief as Willim goggled at him in disbelief.

"Took you long enough," said the Wing of Valnon, tucking the flute back down inside his shirt. "I was about to give up."

"Your Gr--!" Willim started, then clicked his teeth shut, looking warily around them.

Lateran XII laughed. "Don't worry," he said. "Only the geese can hear us, and they've no interest in spilling our secrets. That said, perhaps it would be better to move to more comfortable surroundings."

"I don't understand," Grayson said, in considerable confusion. "I didn't hear anything. How did you find him, Willim?"

"Forgive me," Lateran said, sliding off the edge of the well, "but I knew wherever Willim went you would follow, and it was an easier thing to bait my line for him." The Wing's hood was a ridiculously long thing of colorful mismatched scraps and tassels, but he wore it as regally his crimson robes of office. He pulled it up over his face, and his features were lost in the shadowy folds. "No doubt you've had quite a journey, but if you'll suffer to walk with me a bit, it'll spare us all the trouble of telling things twice."

Willim shot a look at Grayson, who shrugged helplessly and waved in the Wing's direction. Lateran led them out through the other side of the courtyard, across streets and alleys and under bridges, without the slightest pause to consider the direction.

Willim and Grayson trailed at the hem of his belling cloak of motley patches, afraid that if they lost sight of him, he would turn a sudden corner and vanish. Willim was so intent on the Wing's back that they were smack in the middle of Saint's Walk before he knew where he was.

Earlier in the day, the district had quite a different feel. The brothels and gaming-houses were not yet open, shutters closed, lanterns dark. The street-performers and musicians idled about under the lamp-posts, eating fish dumplings and exchanging gossip. The courtesans strolled down the empty streets, clad in plain work-a-day clothes to do their errands before work began for the evening. The air had a strangely comfortable feeling to Willim, the same expectant relaxation as the back halls of the Temple between hours. The gilt and the glamor were put aside, and the living wonders and temptations of Saint's Walk were glad, for a little while, to be perfectly ordinary with one another until the time came to dazzle the patrons once more.

Until that moment Willim had never stopped to consider the parallels between his own life and that of the lowest juggler on an Undercity curb, but they struck him now, and hard enough to make up for lost time. Lateran was no help in creating a distinction between a holy singer and lowly sket-scraper, as he was hailed familiarly by many of the locals, offered food and news, and generally looked on as one of their own. His companions were eyed with more curiosity, but Willim detected no malice in it. If their eyes lingered too long on Willim and Grayson, Lateran would lift the little flute to his mouth, sound a note or two, and the three of them would pass by, no more noticed than a breeze.

"Heaven's song is one thing," Grayson murmured to Willim, "But that smacks a bit of enchantment, and I'm not one to hold with such things."

"Your incredulity does you credit," Lateran said, before Willim could open his mouth to reply. "I admit, I have little respect for the gullible, but I have less for those who cling to weak explanations when something is plainly of the divine." He smiled back at the two of them over his shoulder, Grayson looking a bit flushed at having been overheard. "I'm glad to see you strike a nice balance between the two."

"So it *is* magic, then?" Willim asked. It didn't look like his idea of a magical instrument, being only a black clay whistle shaped like a bird, rather plainly made.

"I dislike the word," Lateran admitted, pausing to return the wave of some acrobats doing their warm-ups in the alley. "I prefer to think of it as something merely beyond our understanding, as much as life and death itself is. But as for the flute, no. It is not magic. It is simply a reservoir of something I no longer sufficiently have within myself."

"Well," Grayson breathed to Willim. "That makes it completely clear, doesn't it?"

"Just like a brick wall," Willim answered. They stopped as the Wing did, beneath the ornate porch-posts of a large house. To his surprise, Lateran had not led them through Saint's Walk, but to the heart of it. They stood beneath the ornate sign of the Swallowtail brothel, and it was the madam that opened the door to the Wing of Valnon's knock.

She too was dressed in simple day clothes, but her beauty was not dimmed by her practical dress and unadorned hair. She greeted Lateran with the familiar welcome due an old friend, and her face lit up at the sight of Willim and Grayson behind him.

"You've room for two more I hope, Benetrice?" Lateran asked, lowering his hood as he stepped inside.

"Of course." Benetrice pulled the door wide, and waved them towards the dim, velvety interior of the brothel. "This way, gentlemen."

Willim was slightly mollified that Grayson looked at least as discomfited as Willim himself felt, and they followed the Wing of the Temple into the best brothel in all of Valnon.

Willim wasn't sure what he expected, but it was something less tasteful than what he found. The main room of the brothel was full of plush couches and low tables, all clustered around warm braziers to keep the Undercity's damp chill away. The stone walls were draped with thick hangings in rich, jeweled colors, lit with a glowing rainbow of multicolored lamps. It was empty now, but it had a patient air of expectation. It was a comfortable place, for relaxing, pleasant conversation, good company. True, the statuary holding the lamps was rather suggestive, and there was a desk with a thick ledger of appointments, but other than that it could have been any well-to-do Undercity salon. Like Jerdon's house, a single stair rose up at the back of the main room and split to follow a landing lined in gilt railings. Numerous doors opened off from the balcony, but Benetrice led them around it to the door directly above the entrance. When she opened it, Willim found that he was in a spacious chamber, luxuriously appointed, with balconies overlooking the street and the front of the brothel. It was from there that Benetrice had hailed the Songbirds the night they passed through Saint's Walk.

The room was not unoccupied. Two elegantly-dressed courtesans, both young men, were entertaining a pair of older male clients with a performance on sket and flute. It was only when the sket-player looked up and utterly missed his next chord that Willim recognized Ellis.

The Thrush of Valnon started up with a cry of surprise, Dmitri threw aside his flute, and Willim forgot all else as he rushed forward to meet them. For a moment the sounds of music were replaced by excited questions from all parties all at once, none of which were clearly answered. Even Dmitri caught Willim up in an embrace, though he let go fairly quickly and something about his face discouraged Willim from making mention of the event again. Ellis had no such reservations, pounding Willim on the back in enthusiastic greeting until Willim began to wonder if he was going to keep his spine in place. He was so busy with Ellis and Dmitri and the numerous *merciful-Alveron-you're-alives* that he did not realize that his was not the only reunion taking place.

Grayson had clasped the arm of one of the two patrons--the one, Willim concluded, that was not Jerdon. Not that the other was a total stranger, as Grayson was greeting the red-haired man who had been in that very room the night the Temple was overthrown, and Willim had last seen him on the wrong end of a tumbrel-full of barrels.

"Aeric!" Grayson exclaimed, with genuine delight. "You're not dead yet?"

"Not yet," Aeric replied, looking pleased with his continued viability. "But I keep trying. And so do you, I hear! We've not been in Valnon a full day yet, and here you two are already. I'll take that as a sign of Heaven's favor."

His name sounded a familiar note in the back of Willim's mind. "*You're* Aeric?" he asked, dumbfounded. "The one who chased us in the Undercity? The same Godsword that was with Grayson when he got that scar across his hip?"

"How do *you* know him?" Dmitri wondered aloud.

"More importantly," Ellis said, coyly, "how do you know about Grayson's *hips*?"

"There are many questions to which we all want answers," the Wing said, with something suspiciously like a wink, mercifully sparing Willim from further teasing. "And it will take some time to get it sorted out, so I suggest we get down to it."

"Benetrice, my dear," Jerdon said, settling back down onto his cushion, "If you could send up Rekbah with some refreshments once she's back from her errands, I'd be much obliged."

"It will be my pleasure," Benetrice said, dropping into a curtsey. "I'll be downstairs if you need me, Your Graces." She closed the door behind her, and Willim stared after her in some confusion.

"So, she knows who we are?"

"Of course!" Jerdon looked surprised that Willim had asked. "In addition to being one of the best informants in the Undercity--"

"As well as the best at several other things," Aeric put in, with a fond look on his face.

"--Benetrice was once first lady-in-waiting to Her Late Highness Queen Renne fa Valos, and now serves both Crown and Temple as a fine pair of eyes in the Undercity."

"And a fine pair of--" Aeric began, but Jerdon shot him a look, and he shut up.

"Jerdon's bad choice of words aside," Lateran continued, sounding slightly less indulgent than before, "Benetrice has very kindly offered us refuge in her house for the duration of our need, at no small personal risk and inconvenience to her."

"She's not charging us by the hour, to start," Aeric muttered to Ellis, who put a hand over his mouth to stifle a snort of laughter. Willim couldn't blame him for being giggly. Finding his friends whole and alive had ripped an invisible weight off his shoulders; only Lateran's grave expression kept him from floating right up to the rafters out of pure relief.

"The first order of business," Lateran said, ignoring them both, "is to assure one another that we're all alive and safe, which it seems we have done, and the details of that, I fear, are less pressing than other concerns. Jerdon and Aeric arrived only yesterday, with two Songbirds and far too much ill news for my liking. I should however let you know that the Temple and its inhabitants, while inconvenienced and uncomfortable, are safe for the moment. Kestrel I have tended in secret, though Raven did take note of the loss of medicines, and it's that I have to thank for the ease of me getting out into the city today. As I have already told the others, Kestrel is still injured, needs a good month of bed rest to be himself again, and he has taken to insulting my parentage whenever I tell him to stay in bed and quit pacing."

Willim caught Dmitri's expression out of the corner of his eye, and saw the fleeting shine of gratitude in his eyes. No wonder the Lark of Valnon had greeted Willim with such good cheer. Knowing Kestrel was safe must have put him high enough to sing harmony to Heaven.

"But that is all we can spend on those matters. You are all here," Lateran said, "because Valnon stands oblivious and unguarded in what may be her darkest hour, and we alone are able to save it."

His words wiped the humor out of everyone's face, even Aeric's, who was now as grave as shrouded Death standing over a sick-bed.

"In a matter of days," the Wing continued, "ships in the command of the Ethnarch of Thrass will reach the city. Already they make north for the channel."

"We have word of this," Willim broke in, eager to share what they had discovered. "In the Northcamp I spoke personally with Isbell fa Grayce, who saw them built by Raven's order."

"And we've seen them complete," Dmitri put in, grim. "They were lying in wait in Traderstaak while we were there, stuffed to the sails with Shadowhands."

"What were you doing in *Traderstaak*?" Willim asked.

"Being sold," Dmitri answered, shortly.

Willim supposed it was his own fault for asking, and turned back to the Wing. "Isbell said Raven plans to lose Valnon to Thrass, so that Thrass will overreach itself when it tries for Shindamir, destroying itself."

Lateran nodded. "Very likely this is the case. He has been waiting patiently for his contacts in the Imperial Enclosure in

Shindamir to bear fruit, and now sees a way for Valnon to rid itself of its greatest adversary and grant solitary rule to the Temple in one step. For that, the city will be sacrificed in order to be built anew to his liking."

Willim shivered at the prospect of Valnon pressed into a mold of Raven's making. "Are there no Godswords left to help us?"

"A few in the Garrison," Aeric answered, and Willim wondered how the lighthearted grin had even fit onto his face before, it was so utterly absent now. "Swords who are too old, too young, or too injured to be fighting in the south, where all the rest of them are. All they would be able to do for us in a direct attack is to die nobly. And while I've no doubt they're willing, I won't make such waste. We need something more effective than sword-dullers."

Ellis broke in, excited to be a part of the plans. "But Sarin's on the Thrassin ships, and he'll do what he can to help. Although," Ellis' face grew gray for a moment, "I'm not sure what he can manage alone."

"Who's Sarin?" Willim asked, trying to sound less exasperated than he felt.

Dmitri looked a little put-upon as he answered Willim, as though he begrudged being the only reliable source of information. "A prince of the Draramir tribes. Ellis bought him at the slave market."

"You *bought*--"

"I set him free!" Ellis exclaimed to Dmitri, as though he was not in the habit of buying people and then keeping them. "He offered to be our spy--"

"Because he owes Ellis some kind of eternal debt for saving his life," Dmitri grumbled, clearly disapproving of life-debts involving Ellis.

Willim was starting to feel a little bit lightheaded; he shed his heavy sell-sword's cloak and reached for the water ewer. "Will they get here in time?" he asked the Wing, in what was very nearly a plea. Later, he would have the story out of Ellis and Dmitri in the proper order, but right now it was like having two different songs sung at him at once.

"Sarin's aid is invaluable," Lateran continued, "And I'm grateful for it. But as Ellis says, we cannot depend on him alone to stop an entire armada. Which leaves Valnon woefully ill-prepared to defend itself, even if the Temple and Crown were firmly allied against them. But with the Temple under siege, and an assassin lying in wait for the Regent and the Queen, it will take all our effort to keep the Ethnarch's banner from rising above the Temple's spire."

There was a pause, and for the first time, it was not broken by pent-up information.

"What are we going to do?" Willim asked, at last. "We can't just sit here, and I'm not about to turn and run. Not again. Not anymore."

Lateran smiled at him, and Willim had the feeling that he had just been given a trial more subtle than the one in which he earned his title, and had passed it far better. "That, Willim," he said, "is up to you."

Willim felt the bottom drop out of his stomach. "Up to me?" he repeated, dumbfounded. "But I don't know anything about war, or strategy, or fighting--"

"Nice sword you're wearing, by the way," Ellis said, dryly.

Thus reminded, Willim fumbled his blade off his hip and avoided the Wing's eyes. "For my disguise," he muttered, as he threw it in the cushions. "I don't really know how to do anything with it--"

"You've started on him with Gerod's defensive technique, I expect?" Aeric asked Grayson in a knowing voice. "It's the best for his build."

Grayson tilted his head down a fraction, in the barest indication of a nod.

"Which only means I can get disarmed with remarkable speed," Willim said to Aeric, in exasperated accusation. "I'm still only a Songbird--"

"Songbirds," Lateran said, in a level voice, "are the only ones who have ever been able to save Valnon in her moment of need. You have shown already that you have the voice, and Heaven has deemed you a worthy vessel for its will. I know my own song when I hear it."

Willim's heart slammed once against his ribs, like an angry beast ramming its cage, and then seemed to go suddenly silent. He looked to Dmitri and Ellis, but from the blank expressions on their

280

faces, they were as shocked as he was. "What do you mean," Willim whispered, "your *own* song?"

"Just as I said," Lateran answered, simply. "The song of a Dove of Valnon, sung in the fullness of his power, without the dulling of age and waste. I have been waiting a long time to hear it again, Willim."

The whole room caught its breath, and held it. The idea had blossomed in all of them at once, as though something had been pulled away to let the light shine on it, drawing it leafy and eager out of the soil and into full, undeniable bloom. It was not only about the Wing, but the two men on either side of him, sitting with the easy familiarity of old friends, with the warm space between them that spoke of a kinship and love that needed no plain gestures or loud protestations. Willim felt for the first time in his life, his sight was clear. Lateran, the Wing of the Temple; Jerdon, the Queen's Physician; Aeric, a rough soldier. And yet, they were not those people, and they never had been. Willim took in the Wing's plain bird whistle, Jerdon's heavy onyx ring, and the battered copper hoop in Aeric's ear, and saw them, and their owners, for what they were.

"...My god," Willim whispered.

"Hardly." It was Alveron who smiled at Willim, Alveron sitting there in a busker's motley, Alveron who had been Lateran XII and all of the Laterans before. "We are saints only, and to be honest with you, I'm not very fond of that, either. It implies a certain amount of heavenly ordination, which is too much consideration to be given to a mere instrument."

"Which you must understand," said Lairke, who had been Jerdon, "is all that we are. Vessels, my boys, made to hold something, and then to pour it out bit by bit until it is gone."

"And it very nearly is," Thryse finished, and Willim marveled that he had not heard the music in Aeric's voice before, as it was so plainly there, in all three of them. "Six centuries is a long time."

"You--" Dmitri began, but his voice dried up, and he had to give up on it as a lost cause. Willim thought it more than he could have managed. He could only stare at Alveron in undisguised wonder, as his thoughts vainly tried to gather themselves up for another go at the impossibility in front of him. Speech was a few steps beyond that.

Ellis nevertheless beat him to it, falling forward on his knees with his face in his hands, his voice pitching up to a mortified groan. "Oh, *no*," he said, and continued on in that vein for some time. "No no no no no no *no*."

"What?" Willim asked, shaken out of his reverie. "What is it?"

"He's thinking about Traderstaak," Dmitri said, in a strained voice. He had gone white as alabaster, but was at least still upright. "He...er... said some rather pointed things to Aeric--Thryse--about what was and was not becoming of his saint."

"Not to worry, Ellis," Aeric said, brightly. "You put me in my place better than I've been in centuries."

"And you deserved it, you know," Jerdon muttered. "After he did just what you would have done."

This wasn't much help. Ellis made a little defeated moan.

"As I recall," Grayson said, looking no small amount shaken himself, his voice rough, "You were rather forward yourself in Jerdon's house that first night, Dmitri."

"Yes, thank you," Dmitri answered crisply, two bright pink spots appearing on his cheeks. "I haven't forgotten and I'm quite well aware of it, now please be quiet."

"Let's just say," Alveron said, smiling, "that your offenses are summarily dismissed. You saw what you were meant to see, and that was all. My disguise is the weakest of the lot, I admit, as I no longer have the strength for its upkeep."

"That and you keep that bloody massive portrait in the Temple," Aeric drawled. "Though it would look more like you if Rey had given you any other expression besides that scowl."

"But *how*?" Ellis asked, his wonder winning out over his embarrassment. "You don't look six hundred years old, but you're no immortal boy saints, either. When they--you--Sang Down Heaven, you couldn't have been older than the oldest flock Boy is now."

"A curious development that has been quite helpful to us," Jerdon said. "For certainly, when we looked like saints, we were hampered by it. We had to build a Temple full of secret rooms and passages, to concoct false names for ourselves, and for a time even leave Valnon altogether. But it would seem that in taking so many lives that day, we have kept them, aging with a strange slowness. In six centuries we have been given a few decades. Perhaps in a thousand years we would even grow old, and spend our last centuries in a decrepit old age."

"Or maybe not," Aeric countered, with a kind of forced brightness. The talk of endless years of feebleness and stolen lives had made his face go a bit gray. "Maybe it is like they said of the children of Naime and Hasal, who had long life like that of the gods, and became mortal only when their father returned to the sea. But one thing is certain," he added, drawing a fingertip over the scar on his face, "we still can bleed as readily as any men, and like as not die the same, as well."

"A theory you have come far too close to proving too many times, *ashti*," Jerdon said, with fond exasperation. "I've sewn you up more than enough for all my lifetimes."

"Explains how you always had enough wound pins to share," Grayson said, the most he had managed so far. "And it also explains that frankly unlikely story about an Iskati princess castrating you after catching you in bed with her lover."

"Well it sounded better than saying I'd fallen on a rake when I was a boy," Aeric answered. "And though I grant you it's not very credible, that princess was mad enough to do it if I hadn't already had it done. Lucky thing I got out of the window in time."

The questions died for a moment as they all looked at each other in slow acceptance, letting all the lies fall away from them, leaving only the old echo of a miracle.

"If you are St. Alveron," Willim said, finding his voice at last, "Then why ask me how to defend Valnon? Why ask me anything?" Willim felt a hot surge of emotion, harsh and metallic at the back of his throat. From some great distance, he knew that he was angry. "Why could you not stop Raven before this even started? Why didn't you sing to spare Boren's life, or Kestrel's wounds? Why have you even let Valnon reach this point of desperation? Why are the Godswords at war at all? Have you stood by all this time and done nothing, as you did when Eothan died? Don't you even *care*?"

In the ringing silence, Willim realized he had been shouting. Alveron sat and endured his abuse with a kind of fragile dignity, and when Aeric leaned forward, flush-faced and ready to retaliate, Alveron waved him down.

"No," he said. "They're honest questions, Thryse. And I don't begrudge Willim the asking of them." He leveled his gaze at Willim, and the third Dove, noticing he had risen up on his haunches during his tirade, meekly retracted. "We are not divine, Willim. Nor do we possess any wisdom more than that gained by a few centuries' continued existence, and we are not immune to mistakes." Alveron closed his eyes for a moment. When he opened them again, they were as clear and hard and as blue as those of the second Dove's ghost, and saying his name was a clear effort. "Eothan is my gravest failure, my abiding regret, and a loss more bitter than I can convey. But he was also as human as any other man, with the same passions, same loves and hates and longings as anyone. He was a musical genius beyond anything I have ever witnessed, a song and a power that I thought worthy of Heaven. Hoping he meant the end of my term, I sought to mold him into something he was not. But, in the end, Eothan's gifts were born of the fleeting brilliance of his mortality. Heaven refused to move through him, and his last song, in the hour of disaster, was only human. Realizing that the power I coerced him to expect was not his to claim, he chose his death. And in my arrogance, I strove to deny him that choice. I poured all my power into the effort of saving his life, and only succeeded in keeping from him the peaceful oblivion he so desperately sought. I failed him, and Valnon, in ways I cannot begin to relate." For a long measure Alveron's throat worked without managing words, to swallow back a grief still fresh after three centuries. "I made Eothan into the nightmare he is now, Willim. Because I thought I knew better than Heaven how best to use my song, because I refused to accept that some things cannot be changed and cannot be undone. And so I squandered what I was given to make the man I loved into a creature of vengeance, and for three hundred years I have tried to remember Eothan as what he was, instead of what I created. With my power spent, since then I have been forced to rely on what can be borrowed from my fellow singers. I have enough to keep myself alive, little more. The gift Heaven gave me to protect this city was squandered out of grief and guilt. But we are not here to dwell upon my sins and missteps, thank Naime. If so, we would be here many a long year, and we are already pressed for time. So that is my confession to you. And if you wish to hate me for that--" He lifted one thin shoulder in a shrug, "Well, I can't blame you. But you will have a hard task in front of you if you wish to hate me for it more than I have hated myself."

Willim struggled to swallow, but his throat felt too thick. "No," he said. "I have seen enough of Eothan to understand."

"And by now you should know, even having sung it once, that the will of Heaven is not ours to command." Alveron's smile was knowing, bitter. "You ask me why I saved this life but not the other, why I did nothing on this occasion but unleashed the full might of Heaven on this other one. But these are the same questions you have asked yourself before, are they not?"

Ashamed, Willim hung his head. "...Yes."

"And you will ask them again, over and over again, as long as you live." Alveron reached across the space between them, and lifted Willim's face with his hand. His voice was full of compassion, his eyes held a sad understanding multiplied by all his long years. "I wish I could answer you, Willim. I do not know why Heaven chose the three of us, that day six hundred years ago, when we should have died by Antigus' command. I do not know why we were given the lifetimes we took from him and his men with our song. Nor I do not know why it refused to give Eothan the least mercy," he swallowed, his face hardening with old pain, "Or why on that day of so many deaths all our singing could not spare even one life. Even after all this time I have only scratched the surface of the truth we carry. All I know is how little I know. You are an instrument, Willim, and you must have faith in the wind that sounds you." Alveron's expression was kind; he swept one thumb over Willim's cheek to catch a tear before Willim knew he was weeping. The gesture broke some last restraint in Willim's heart, and he surged up into his saint's embrace. Larks and Thrushes all had Preybirds to look to, to be fathers in their titles and friends when their terms were done. But until that moment Willim had been an orphaned heir, with only a ghost's echo and painted saint to guide him. Alveron was real and warm and solid, and he pressed his cheek to Willim's hair like the prodigal father of a faithful son.

"Forgive me, Willim," Alveron murmured. "I could not make the same mistake with you as I did with Eothan, and I dared not inflict the burden of my hopes on you. As a result, I fear you have been very much alone in your term. I hope you know that though you have been deprived the presence of your saint, you have not been without his love, nor his pride."

Willim nodded into the folds of Alveron's robe. Though it was the garb of an Undercity entertainer, it smelled like the Temple, and Willim was nearly overwhelmed with yearning. It took all of Willim's resolve not to cling to him and sob to be taken back home. Suddenly aware of the others around them, Willim slid out of Alveron's arms and back into his place. He was not the only one to rub at his eyes, and Ellis sniffled audibly.

"Well," Willim said at last, hoping his voice sounded more steady than he felt, "since we can't rely on Heaven to save us, we'll have to do the best we can on our own." He took a deep breath, and curled his hands on his knees. "Where do we start?"

"And just what is it we're expected to start?" Grayson put in. "We've no swords, no ships, the Godswords are mired in the south and word will never reach them before Thrass arrives."

"You said the Regent was in danger, as well," Dmitri added, as though the Regent was not his father. "He must be warned."

"I have seen to the Regent's protection," Alveron assured him. "And the Queen's. You need have no fear for them. Raven and his men in the Temple are our first concern. I believe we can win back our Temple, and our prentices, and once we have done so Valnon can endure a siege for a while. The gates to the harbor can be closed, the walls of the city are thick, and no one will be coming over the Pilgrim's Passage this time of year. I have sent a message by bird to Captain Ransey in the southlands, and he will bring back his men to our aid. With a force of Godswords by land and by sea, Thrass will be forced to surrender. They have planned this attack for speed and surprise, and their surprise is already lost."

"The question remains, of course, how to get into the Temple to do anything." Jerdon rubbed his jaw in thoughtful contemplation. "The dais pillar passage is open only for fleeting periods; it would be risky to try to get us all through there at one go. And once you did, you're hardly in an ideal place to attack. You'd have to split up to take on a far larger force, and all with no escape route behind you."

"There's the bath vents and the sounding tunnels, I suppose," Aeric added. "But we'd be crawling on our faces for hours to get through them, and I don't know if they're in good shape. You can't even stand in the steam vents, and most of the sounding flues wouldn't hold a cat."

Willim was staring up at the elaborate lantern hanging from its chain in the middle of the room, its tongue of flame sending up a transparent distortion of air as it burned. His brain worked feverishly in the hopes of some solution. Aeric's words woke a memory in Willim, and a plan flashed across his mind with all the speed of divinity. He remembered another crackling fire, and Grayson's voice telling him of a distant fortress, and earthen passages, and smoking lanterns. "What if we didn't need to get through the Temple passages?" Willim mused. "What if something could come *out* of them, instead? Something to do our work for us?"

The others looked at Willim blankly, but Grayson made a noise, and Willim looked over to see both the understanding and fear in Grayson's face. "Willim, no," he said. "Nearly every slave sent in to gas Kassiel through the mines died in the attempt--"

"A Thrassin slave doesn't have a Songbird's lungs." Willim pressed on, excited. "And we wouldn't have to do more than knock them out. The prentices Raven's convinced to his side don't deserve to die simply because a Preybird that they trusted twisted their loyalty to his own ends. Surely Jerdon can make a lamp that's not deadly. Then if we could see to it that all of Raven's men were in one place, somewhere with a large concentration of sounding vents--"

"The main narthex of the Temple," Dmitri said, understanding. "If we could fake a main attack on the Temple doors, say with those Godswords in the garrison, then the three of us could set sulfur lamps in the proper sounding vents and knock them out without landing a single blow. They would be fish already netted. We open the doors, and in comes Aeric and Jerdon to mop up the mess."

"We'd need to find a way to shut off the vents to get the air currents going right," Ellis put in. "Someone on the inside before we got there. I suppose one of the Preybirds could do it..."

"Or me," Alveron said quietly. "With Kestrel's help, I think we can do that quite handily."

In the heat of inspiration, Willim had almost forgotten they were there. Alveron's expression was inscrutable, but Willim could tell he was thinking hard.

"Your Grace!" Grayson said, pained. "Surely you're not considering this plan? It puts the Songbirds in terrible danger."

"On the contrary, it makes full use of their abilities while keeping them out of the immediate fray." Alveron fixed Grayson with a sharp eye. "Willim has suggested a plan that involves little bloodshed, and does not even violate a Songbird's terms by making him fight with steel--which I would rather they not do, even if they had enough skills to risk outright combat. It overwhelms a large force with few, evening our odds, and allows our better fighters-- namely you--to remain in reserve until a clear path to victory presents itself. Have you a better idea?"

Grayson scowled, disarmed. "No," he admitted. "It's a sound plan." His eyes flicked to Willim, then to the Wing of Valnon, then to the carpet. "...To my regret."

"Very well," Alveron said, as though they had only agreed upon the best wine to compliment dinner. "Thryse, you know how I hate to bring them into this, but if you would be so kind as to have Civalle pick six or ten of her best women to join you, as many as she can arm like Godswords. They are skilled enough to be a suitable distraction force for you."

Aeric nodded. "They should have enough armor in their smithy for that."

Ellis brightened. "Of course! The Laypriestesses make all the Temple armor, they must have piles of it. Dress them up like Godswords, and Raven won't be able to tell the difference!"

"And you can garnish them with whatever remaining Godswords you can find at the Garrison, but choose carefully. We're not so rich in allies that we can be spendthrift with their lives. Lairke, how long will it take you to come up with some gas lanterns for our third Dove?"

"A week would be ideal," Jerdon said, wistfully.

"You have eight hours," Alveron countered. "I want the Songbirds and Grayson waiting at the dais passage before Evensong tonight. They'll have an hour to place the lamps and then you and Thryse will lead our Godswords to the gate under cover of full dark. Make us some flares for our distraction, lots of flash and noise but minimal destruction. I have no desire to build the Temple of Valnon again. With luck we will have the Temple back in our hands by midnight, and by Dawning we will be ready for the

Ethnarch's attack. We can only hope to hold out against them until reserves arrive." Alveron paused, looking at each one of them in turn. He came to Grayson, and stopped. "You look like you have a question, Nicholas fa Grayce."

"Only one," Grayson said. "You charged me with the protection of the Songbirds, and the Dove in particular. I cannot very well do that if I'm focused on hunting down Raven."

Alveron smiled a quiet little smile. "You have already given Willim everything he needs to fight for himself as well as any man, and it is all I had hoped for. I leave the rest up to him, and to Heaven."

26

The queen of Valnon had no fear of the dark. Her only fear, and it was a potent one, was of fire. As a child learning to move through her strange terrain, she had constantly upset the lamps and candles left by her nursemaids. She remembered the horrible flare of heat as a toppled lamp once spread fire across one of the carpets, catching at the hem of her skirts. When the flames were trampled out, the shrieks of alarm turned to clucks of dismay. Reim was not scolded, but the pity of her nurses was suffocating. She was a such a poor thing, she could not help being clumsy, she could hurt herself so easily.

Even at seven years old, Reim's retort had been scathing. She could navigate around her rooms perfectly well, if only her minders were not so foolish as to leave their lights in her path, always in a different place. She had learned to walk without the aid of light, she had no need of such dangerous tools. If sight required light to function, she thought it was the least efficient of the senses. She was content with her four that required nothing more than her own body. It was no wonder the palace servants were so handicapped, she had said, relying on only one of their senses all the time, and it the weakest of the lot.

From that point on, there were never any lamps left for the queen when she was alone, and those brought by her servants were required to be placed in certain precise locations every time. Darkness was no danger for Reim, and it held far less fear for her than fire did. So while tales of the catacombs had terrified other children, Reim had found them comforting. There, the advantage was hers. There were no fire-bowls or braziers there, no smell of burning to stifle the other, more delicate scents she used to define the world around her. The natural question, of course, was how to get down to such a wonderful place. She managed it as she managed everything: with observation and patience.

There was a door in her study that no one ever used, or mentioned, or displayed any knowledge of at all. She could smell it while they could not: a dry, cool, earthy sort of smell that lingered like a shy ghost behind her desk. She was eleven before she was strong enough to shift the offending bit of furniture; she was twelve before she could reach the hidden latch, cunningly disguised as a knot in the wood. It might have deceived the sighted, but never the queen's fingers.

Once she had found it, the panel of wood slid back to reveal its splintery backside, and the cold, hard flags of stairs cut deep into the island's own flesh. The secret world of Valnon unraveled at her feet.

At first she feared becoming lost, and only traveled a short distance each day, using a coil of embroidery floss to mark her path. In those hollow galleries and narrow corridors of stone she found a natural cathedral, one that transformed her least whisper into a choir. She sang in the tunnels for the pure pleasure of her own voice, and sometimes wished she had been a Songbird, and not a Queen. Soon, the thread was left behind. Reim learned to find her way through each peculiar echo, singing a note into the dark and waiting for it to come back, listening to the exact sound of each path. The black labyrinth of the tombs became nothing more than a pleasantly engaging puzzle, and no one ever knew.

No one, of course, with the exception of her Physician.

"I would advise you to take care, Your Highness," Jerdon had said one afternoon during her routine examination, when she was fourteen. "As I have it on good report that the Hall of the Heavens has suffered from a cave-in, and you will not be able to follow your usual route to the pool."

Reim stiffened, furious and betrayed. "I fear I haven't the slightest what you mean."

"Now my dear. Let's not play that game, we've been friends for far too long." The clasps of Jerdon's case made their own music, a businesslike click-click. "I only wanted to let you know of the blockage, not to hinder you. If you take the left-hand path, you will come to the water more swiftly, though I should caution you about the cliffs, there. And should you take the center passage, and travel until the path becomes steep upwards, you will find a small dead-end tunnel. There is a secret door there on the left; I've no doubt you can find it. It leads to a house in the Undercity. Mine, in point of fact. Should you ever need to, you can find me there."

"You will not stop me?" Reim asked, wondering.

"Highness." Jerdon's voice was soft and sweet, and Reim wished she had known the sound of her father's. "Have I ever stopped you from doing anything?"

The memory made her eyes burn. Reim had always had a girl's heartache for him, for his understanding and his cleverness and his deft hands, but he was far too old for her. Her lady-maids said he could be no more than thirty-five, and that was a tolerable gap, but Reim knew better. Age was more than a smooth face and quick step; those things could deceive. Jerdon knew more, was more, than she could define. Should she live to a hundred and eight, she would still feel a child beside him.

But she had no heart to linger over memories now. Her song in the dark was quick, and she was impatient for the echoes. She was dressed in her simplest stockings and shirt, her thin leather slippers sending up a clear map of every pit in the stone floor, every discarded stone. Beneath her outstretched fingers, rough limestone with its diminutive bones gave way to the smooth intrusion of unpolished marble. Valnon was a violent island, she knew. It had been forged by time, by fire, by pressure, and it had shifted often in its watery bed. It was gloriously easy for her to find her way on a path so variously marked, and soon her fingernails caught in a crack that was not made by nature. A breeze as thin as frost trickled between her fingers. It smelled of lamp-oil and lemons and the earthy odor of the leaves packed in bolts of Shindamiri silk. It smelled like Jerdon, but it was cold, and Reim's heart sank. He was not there to open the door for her, as he so often had when she needed his counsel at any hour, with his warm voice and his loose hair brushing the back of her hand as he kissed her ring.

He would not be there today, or ever again. Word had reached Valnon that the *Larkspur* had not come into port anywhere along the channel as scheduled, nor had it been seen by any other ships. Her battered figurehead had been found washed ashore in Alfir, and she and all aboard her were presumed lost.

Reim pressed her cheek to the stone, and the cold rock grew hot with her tears. "Why have you left me, now when I need you most?" The queen of Valnon sank down to her knees, as the faint thread of hope that had carried her so far disintegrated. Jerdon was gone forever, down to the depths where Hasafel lay. Until that moment, she had not permitted herself to believe it.

Reim could not weep in her palace, within hearing of her maids. She would not do so even in the arms of her adopted Uncle

Nilan, as she had when she was a child. Reim was Queen, and Queens could not mourn as mortals did. Her fears and her grief belonged to the silent places beneath her city, so she curled up against the untended door to Jerdon's house, and sobbed into her knees. She cried until her ribs ached with it, until her eyes burned and the cuffs of her shirt were soggy. Bereft of father and mother and sight all before her first breath, and now fate saw fit to revoke something else dear. Never before had Reim pitied herself.

She let herself fall to the floor, and her outstretched hand touched something that was neither rock nor bone. Surprise made a sob catch in her throat, as her fingers closed on velvet. Her first thought was that she had found a body, but she did not smell flesh, either alive or dead. The fabric was as soft as a kitten, beaded with pearls, and had not been there long. At the bottom edge, it had been torn roughly away. Reim's fingers wondered at the loose threads, the straggling remnants of what had been lush embroidery. Who would discard something so rich, here in a forgotten corner of the Undercity? She dragged it closer to smell it, and jumped as something made a loud metallic clatter on the stone. What she thought was only fabric was bound firmly to a piece of armor.

A half-moon shape, gem-studded, connected to a matching back piece and more velvet by delicate, jeweled chains. Reim was baffled, her fascination overtaking her grief. She groped gently over the floor, and found a smooth, hollow cylinder of metal, also jeweled, and a strange prickly thing hung with jewels. Only when her hand glided over the massive pearl on a broad collar of metal did Reim begin to understand what she had found. Not a forgotten wrap from a noblewoman's tryst, not the mortal remains of one of her citizens. A Songbird's armor was here, discarded in a heap, smelling of censer smoke and blood and ink.

Which one, though? Reim wondered. And why? The Songbirds were safe in the Temple, guarded by Raven, to protect them from those outside who would do them harm.... were they not? Reim clutched the Songbird's collar to her breast, as a chill sweat broke out on her face. Once shaken, the Preybird's lies fell away like sand through a sieve, leaving the truth there upon the mesh for her to see. If the Songbirds were in the Temple, there would be no armor here, battered and discarded. And if the Songbirds were not in the Temple, then Raven had lied, and if

Raven had lied--

Reim was already on her feet and running, the armor scooped up into her arms, her voice lifting to sing her way home. Jerdon might be lost to her, but she would not lose another.

She had been singing her path for nearly half an hour when something changed in the space around her. A volume that had been empty a moment ago was suddenly filled and solid, the pressure against her ears shifted with the sound of displaced air, as faint as an intake of breath. It was not as though someone had walked up and approached her, or as though she had turned a corner and come upon him. A second before, she had been alone in the tunnel, and a second later, she was not.

"Who's there?" Reim was too well-trained to let her fear show. Hers was a voice of command, and it was used to obedience for answer. "Name yourself, and your purpose."

"...I will not hurt you."

Reim stiffened, clutching the Songbird's armor closer. He was nearer than she had thought, closing the distance between them with soundless, inexplicable speed. "Who are you?"

"The only other soul in Valnon who moves in these tunnels like you do." Something fluttered in Reim's hair, a cold butterfly that smelled of metal and age. "I have heard you singing your way through my realm, Queen of Valnon. Only one other voice could wake me from my dreaming, and though the blood between you is dim with distance, I can see it. Though sightless, you have his eyes. Though untrained, you have his music. Your beauty, though, is your own. I marvel at you, Highness. Had I a heart, I might lose it to you."

Reim swallowed down past her panic. Half-remembered tales surfaced in her mind, rumors of the phantom of the Undercity tombs. "I cannot tarry for this. I must--"

A hand caught her by the wrist, solid enough flesh, but the only warmth in it was stolen from her. The Songbird's armor fell around her in a clamor that echoed all around her, blinding her with the overload of sound. The ends of his fingers were clad in metal, sharper than her embroidery needles. His voice swallowed up all the echoes around her. "Did I not tell you I would not hurt you? Do not be afraid. You have stumbled into my bedchamber unawares. Tarry with me a while, daughter of Lavras fa Valos, first queen of Valnon. Sing with me a while."

Reim felt him move around her in a slow circle, the brush of his clothing against her legs, the cobwebby drift of his hair on her burning cheek. "I must return to the Palace. Valnon is in danger, and I must be there."

"No, my queen. You are the one in danger if you return. Stay here with me. I will keep you safe." He took both her hands in his, and pulled her a step forward. "It is a promise I'm keeping, to protect you. I keep all my promises, you know. There's a song like that." His voice was sweet, but wild as the sea in high storm. *"When the moon falls spear'd on Temple spire, when dogs bay ballads and cats a choir, only then call me a liar.* Lovely thing. Do you know it?"

"No," Reim said, towed along after him and helpless to resist.

"Alas, many have forgotten it. It was written by a fool, long ago. I will teach it to you. It needs a duet, as all good riddle-songs do. Mind your step, Highness."

At his word, she stumbled. Something rolled and snapped beneath her feet and she fell forward into his embrace. He caught her up against him, and her fear blossomed into terror. He had no scent, only dust and empty time, like the passages. Beneath her hands, his chest was bare, his nipples hung with a Songbird's metal hoops. His skin was as smooth and cool as the marble flesh of a soul-maker, and as mute. Her captor had no heartbeat.

"Let me go!" Reim screamed, panic winning out over her queenly reserve. She pushed herself away from him, she whirled. There was a door just behind her, she could hear the open air beyond it. But she had gone no further than a step before the presence of the doorway was obliterated in her senses, overwhelmed by a musical hum in the air, the vibration of a hundred phantom voices. Reim tripped, she fell onto a heap of smooth, round stones. When her fingers fumbled over their sinister contours, she let out a tiny cry. She was lying atop a pile of countless skulls.

"Ah, you have woken my bedfellows," he said over her, unconcerned. "Perhaps they will give us a performance. It's a pity they're usually so silent. Can't be helped, really." She could hear him shrug. "Most are missing their jawbones. And they can't enunciate at all. No lips. Their resonance is quite good, though."

"I know who you are," Reim gasped, pressing her back to the pile of skulls. It was a better comfort than having him behind her, even as she tried to force out the overwhelming sensation that the music was coming from them. "You're Starling."

"I have been called so," he answered, sounding not displeased. "Would you like to know who I really am?" His hands closed around her shoulders; effortlessly he pulled her to her feet. "Come here, my dear, and meet your host." With one arm around her waist, he steered her back deeper into the chamber. "Stretch out your hand, lady, and flatter your paramour with a touch."

Reim's hands were shaking too hard to obey. Starling lifted her wrist and guided it forward, down to a strange landscape of textures. Leather, Reim decided. A belt, cracked and dry. Once upon a time, it had been tooled in ornate patterns. Her fingertips brushed over something smoother, cold: the buckle. She outlined the shape of a bird in flight, the opposite side of the clasp held in its beak.

"A Temple Bird lies here," she breathed. Somehow, for no reason she could explain, her fear was fading. Even with her brief inspection, she knew the identity of the horrible object before her, the empty container of a soul. And yet she could only feel pity.

"He does, lady." He pressed his cheek to hers, his breath fanned her temple. "The very last laid sleeping here. He trembles at your touch."

Reim's hand floated over crumbling fabric, once silk. It had decayed to almost nothing, leaving only the metalwork embroidery behind.

"Lovely, isn't it?" her captor asked. "A pity you cannot see the colors. Let me tell you of them, as you can imagine them in your perfect darkness. They are the gray of polished stone: a marble bench in the garden in the depths of winter, the color of the cold that creeps along your legs when you sit on it. They are purple: the color of my lady's majesty, the color of a deep-blossoming bruise, the color of heartache, of the sky when the sun has gone."

A row of buttons flickered under her fingers, and then she touched the unmistakable angles of a jawbone. Pearls had given way to teeth, to the high ridge of a cheekbone, to the empty bowl of an eye socket. His laugh, so close, lifted the hairs at the back of her neck.

"Ah, such a sweet caress. But you don't know yet, do you? Let me help." He moved her hand back down again, over the collapsed breast, down to the fragile cage of finger bones folded together. There was a weight on one, an object of twisted metal. A ring, Reim thought. A curled bird of filigree wrapped around a gem, a pearl for its eye, a number etched in the embrace of its wings.

Two.

It was no longer just Reim's hand that was shaking. She was trembling all over, and the hum of voices around her had risen to a distant roar like the sound of rising water. Starling turned her to face him, his clawed hands buried themselves deep into her braided hair. "Tell me, my queen. Whisper my name to me. It has been so long since I have heard it, and the world has gone so cold while I have been waiting."

His mouth closed over hers, swallowing the sound of the name she said, drinking it like wine. The voices in Reim's ears had risen to a deafening crescendo, an otherworldly chord that drowned her deep. Her lone heartbeat in that desolate vault beat hard and fast like a captured bird, her lover sang a single low note into her parted lips, and she knew nothing more.

"Peril," Ellis said, tipping his consort across the board they'd borrowed from Benetrice. Rekbah had returned with the thyme oil and wound salve Alveron was supposed to be getting for Raven, and then she had promptly been sent out again for materials to assemble the chemical lamps. Jerdon had requisitioned Dmitri to help him with the construction, and now the three of them were smelling up Benetrice's scullery with their efforts. Aeric had gone to recruit their diversionary forces from Darkmarket Garrison, Alveron had returned to hiding in the Temple to prepare for the assault. Grayson had sequestered himself on one of the secluded couches in the corner and was working his sword over with a whetstone--a task, Willim had learned, that was more meditation than necessity. Suddenly at loose ends, Ellis and Willim had looked at each other, prepared to talk for hours about their experiences, and both found they were unable to have anything like a normal conversation. Too much had happened; too much still hung in the balance. In the end, Ellis had suggested the old comfort of queensperil, and Willim fell upon it with gratitude.

Six moves in, however, and his attention was straying.

"Peril," Ellis said again, when Willim did not respond to the first notice, and had no better luck the second time. "Queensperil," Ellis tried, even though it wasn't. "Queensperil and you have three measures to make your move. Queensperil and I'll eat your pieces if you don't. Queensperil and did I mention Dmitri proposed marriage to me this morning?"

"Hmm?" Willim had the niggling feeling that Ellis was saying something to him. "What was that?" He shook himself, took his eyes from the narrowing gleam on the edge of Grayson's sword, and blinked down at the board. "Peril?"

"About four hours ago," Ellis said, exasperated. "Forget it. My heart's not in it, either." He raked his hair out of his eyes. "Though it's worth mentioning that I was winning."

"Sorry, Ellis." Willim sighed, falling back against his pile of cushions. "This waiting around is going to kill me."

"Too many other people are trying to kill you first. The waiting will have to get in line if it wants a chance at you." Ellis, setting the pieces back into their case, paused. His cleverness had not roused so much as a blink out of Willim--who was staring at Grayson again--and he exhaled in a little impatient explosion. "For the love of god, why don't you just go talk to him?"

"Because he is a sell-sword, and I'm the Dove of Valnon," Willim said, with a matter-of-factness that he wished he believed.

Ellis rolled his eyes. "And both of you are dolts. I'm going to go see if I can help with those lamps, and you better take care of things here." Ellis gave Willim a look of affectionate warning. "Because if the worst happens, I don't want to listen to your bellyaching all through the afterlife."

The Thrush of Valnon closed the door after him, and Willim nursed the silence for a second before rising.

"...You wish I hadn't thought of this plan, don't you?"

Grayson tapped the tang of his sword, making the metal chime. "It's a good plan, Willim. And like any good strategist, you're willing to take the greatest risk yourself to see it through. It's admirable."

"Only you think I'll need you to protect me the whole time, is that it?"

Grayson looked up at him in surprise, but it softened into a smile. "On the contrary. I look forward to seeing you in action." He pulled his empty scabbard off the sleeping couch behind him, and patted the pillows. "Here. You'll be up all night, and there's no telling when we might have another chance for a rest. Get some sleep if you can."

Willim sank down into the blankets. The Swallowtail did not scrimp on its furnishings, especially not something so central to the business as bedclothes. The bed was soft and sweet-smelling, the silk cool under his cheekbone. But it was not enough to make Willim sleepy. He nuzzled his face into the pillow, wishing for the supple angle of Grayson's arm beneath him instead. Grayson sheathed his newly-sharpened sword, and between that and the room's lissome statuary, Willim could not help being reminded of other things. "...Why do you think Alveron chose to throw us together as he did?"

Grayson shrugged, propping his weapon against the wall. "It's not for me to say, but I suspect it was more than my name. He says he knows little of his power, but he knows the impetus for it. He sang freedom for his people, life for his kinsmen, and then broke himself for the sake of a life Heaven denied him." Grayson swept his fingertips over the fall of Willim's hair. "Faith and Love can lead a man to his lowest depths, and to his highest pinnacles, and Alveron has seen them both. I doubt we would ever get him to say he threw us together for that very purpose, but I think it was not only my skills with a sword that led him to select me as your guard."

Willim reached up to tangle Grayson's fingers with his own. He did not want to think about Alveron's long life, or the terrible burdens of his losses. "We may never have another time like this."

Grayson's mouth twisted. "Considering what Benetrice charges for this room, that may very well be true."

"*Grayson.*" Willim wasn't sure if he wanted to laugh or burst into tears. The tight feeling in his belly was somewhere between.

"I know," Grayson said, leaning over Willim, and cupping the Dove's face in his hands. "Believe me, Willim. I know." His mouth closed over Willim's, Willim's long fingers sank into the soft gold velvet of Grayson's hair, and together they shoved away the future as far as it could go.

There was desperation between the two of them, and neither

one would deny it. The surroundings urged languor, and slow care between lovers. But more than the cost of the lodgings, that luxury of time was what they could least afford. It was a matter of hours, not of days or years, and the parting at the end was inevitable. At best, it would be the two years remaining in Willim's term, at worst it would be forever. Willim tried to burn every sensation into his memory, to hoard it all up against potential famine. But in the end, being a miser was not he wanted, and between them they gave everything away to each other.

Willim closed his eyes, his limbs heavy with sweet exhaustion, his body cradled in Grayson's. When he opened them again, he stood in Hasafel.

He knew the courtyard, and the white Temple, and Hasal's colossus. But unlike his dream before, everything was silent. The emptiness of the city was no longer inviting, but foreboding; the shadows did not stay still. Willim spun around, unwilling to let the black doorways see his back. The hush at last was broken by a familiar clinking sound, metal chiming on stone. Willim looked towards the sound, at the top of the stairs, and saw something bright rolling towards him. It bounced on each step with a peal like a little bell, and at last came to a stop by Willim's toe. He knelt to pick it up, curious. It was a Songbird's cuff, worked in plain silver, and it fell from Willim's numb hand as he saw its owner.

The Temple singer was a young girl, and she lay on the top step with one arm outstretched towards her lost cuff, her hair a merciful veil over her face. A fresh wound yawned in the flesh between her bared breasts, precise and fatal. As Willim stood, frozen in horror, her blood pooled in the time-worn depression in the step just below her, and a crimson cascade of tiny rivulets overflowed the edge and traced lines of red lace over the white marble.

Willim ran to her. He mounted the steps two at a time to draw her up into his arms, her blood staining his knees. She was long beyond his help, her eyes already dulling, her mouth smeared with her rouge and the brighter stain of her blood. Willim passed his hand over her staring eyes to close them. He murmured a prayer as he laid her back down, smoothing her simple drape, folding her hands beneath her collar to cover the wound. Then he entered the gaping mouth of the Temple, knowing already what he would find.

The incense was still burning, thin threads of smoke unraveling from the censers, their sweet breath not enough to blot out the stench of blood. The sanctuary was a vast chamber of soaring arches, a majesty echoed faintly in Valnon's more humble Temple, and Willim barely took note of it. The ornate mosaic floor was covered in a carpet of broken bodies. They were Temple singers, all of them, young men and women in Songbird paints and armor, their skin streaked with blood and ash. Willim could not count them, their faces faded into a whole too heartbreaking to endure singly. Scattered among them were the butchered gray forms of countless doves, as though the singers were no more than birds shot for sport. Their blood mingled with the singers', turning the floor slippery beneath Willim's bare feet. A faint breeze stirred the smoke, lifting soft gray feathers in a filmy shroud around the dead.

Willim's breath shuddered in his lungs, his eyes blurred with tears. So great was his heartbreak that it was a long time before he realized he was not the only person still standing in the sanctuary. A young man was there, little more than a boy, his dark hair drawn back into ornate braids, his head bowed over the one body that was not a Songbird's. A warrior lay at his feet, sword in hand, as though in death he still sought to defend those no longer in any need of it. Willim blinked back his tears. He knew the face of the boy, the boy with no weapon save the birdlike silver points on his hands.

Myth and song collided in Willim's memory, as the boy turned his face to Willim. Willim knew his name, knew the tragedy he witnessed, and he knew the depth of Thali's grief. The Evensong arched upwards, freed from the ribs that caged it, and music and water rose all around them in a towering wave of destruction. Hasafel's last king sang his city into the sea, and Willim opened his arms to the flood, letting it wash everything away.

The waves came, and the song did not end. It continued in a different voice, one whose sorrow was tempered with the distance of time. When the water receded, Willim stood in the same Temple, ruined now with age, the pillars tilting. Water lapped at their bases, the tide wearing away the engraved letters, filling the deeper ones with sand. In the middle of the sanctuary where Thali had stood was another figure. Water rippled around his ankles and his bare back was turned on his visitor, and his was the voice that was singing Evensong.

"You're the one that's been showing me these things," Willim said. "Eothan."

Only then did the melody stop, and the second Dove tilted his head in Willim's direction, his profile lost in shadow. For a split second it was not darkness that concealed his features, but a black web of kohl, its patterns the complex mesh of a Songbird's last hour, gleaming wet. It was gone by the time Willim sucked in a breath, but that did not change that it had been there.

"No," Willim breathed, his heart fluttering. "No, you are not merely Eothan."

"It would be more accurate to say that Eothan is not merely what I am," he answered. "What you call Eothan is a lost soul bound to a song that it never had any right to." The ghost turned, and in the milky light of the water he wavered between his forms: the Evensong phantom in his baleful paints, the echo of Thali with his knotted hair and armored fingers, the ragged guardian of the catacombs. Only his eyes remained the same, and in them Willim saw all of his predecessor's mortality, his pain, his humanity.

"What are you, then?" Willim asked, wondering if he should be more afraid.

Eothan spread his hands, and the claws on them flickered in and out of existence like distant lighting. "What am I? I am the Evensong. I am Heaven's rage, Thali's vengeance, Alveron's heartbreak. I am holy song given life separate from my singer, poured out of Alveron in his grief and bound to Eothan's soul. I am the Evensong as it was first sung by Thali of Hasafel when his city was wrested from him. I am his destruction and I am my rebirth, and when the final note of Alveron's life is sung, I will be yours to wield fully."

"Mine?" Willim repeated. "But--no. I don't want that kind of power."

"Don't you?" Eothan's smile was swift, knowing. "You cannot lie to me, Willim. I'm too much a part of you. Already I am in your lungs, and you have only to sing the note. You cannot stand silent, though you may try. More than any blade, I am the weapon made for you. When you take me as your own, Alveron will at last will be free. As will I."

"You will be dead, you mean."

"Death does not mean to us what it means to you." Eothan moved closer to Willim, and the water around his ankles was not disturbed by his motion. "The Evensong belongs in a living Dove, Willim. One chosen by Heaven to sing it. I am not either of those things, and the burden crushes me. You are my salvation, and I have waited a long time for you, to give you the song that should be yours." He unfolded his hands around Willim's face, claws glittering, his face full of a wholly human longing. "For long enough have I been custodian of it. This paint, these claws, this rage--this is Thali's will made into music, the power of Hasal the sea-god and Naime's music, the justice of Heaven given full-throated voice. Their blood is in your veins, their song in your flesh. Your very veins are an instrument, Willim, and I am the song made to sound on you. Thali's song sits ill on a soul not made for it. I can only use it for destruction."

"I'm sorry," Willim said, his heart moved to more pity than fear. "I'm sorry I can't help you. But I'm no saint, no child of prophecy."

"So says every saint, and every child of prophecy. But those that know better already know you. Look, how Hasafel hails its prince, its salvation." Eothan swept his arm out towards the lake beyond the walls of the submerged Temple. As Willim watched, transfixed, the cloudy water cleared until it was as transparent as a bell's note. Fathoms deep in the sea, the rest of the Temple lay in silent repose, the statues and columns still standing. In the center stood the great pillar of a dais, like a Songbird's, lording over a vast chamber with its roof open, the faint echo of the Temple above. And from the depths Willim could hear voices, a chorus of song without beginning or end. The song that had haunted his dreaming, the song of the slaughtered Doves of Hasafel, the song that had pulled a city from the sea, and back into it again.

"What do they want?" Willim breathed, awed. "I can't save them. I can barely save myself."

"What you can save remains to be seen, but for certain, it will be more than I ever could." Eothan drew close to Willim, resting one hand in the other Dove's hair. "But for now, I can give you one thing, as poor a gift as it is from your predecessor. Sleep, Dove of Valnon. You have had enough dreams."

At once oblivion rose up and swallowed Willim, empty and encompassing, and he tumbled into a deep sleep without the faintest footfall of nightmare.

27

The infirmary of the Temple was sunlit and empty when Alveron stole into it during what should have been Noontide. The sounding vents carried only the spindly notes of a single sket; Kite was filling in for his absent successor, and grudgingly so, with armed prentices to see him back to his imprisoned fellows when he was done. Only Hawk's urging had gotten Kite to play at all. The High Preybird thought it best to show some slight signs of capitulation to Raven, the better to soften up their adversaries.

Still, Kite was not serving his role without irony. For the hour he had chosen one of the songs from his saint's primary song-cycle, a melody sung by Thryse when he and his kinsmen were captured by Antigus and awaited their death at sunset. Saint Thryse's song was one to fill hearts with courage in the face of adversity, to go to destiny with one's eyes open, to be brave, to have faith, to be unafraid of the coming dark.

And, Alveron had cause to know, it was nothing so pretty as what his cousin had said at the time, when they lay chained together in Antigus' stinking dungeon, child-figureheads of a slave rebellion and doomed to die. If Alveron remembered correctly, Thryse's comment had been that it had been fun while it lasted. But he knew as well as the next Temple Bird that such truths didn't make for the best songs.

The music was haunting in the stone confines of the infirmary, thin-noted and eerie as Alveron slipped into the herb cupboard. He was just nudging the last jar back into place when the silver-shod butt of a staff cracked on the stone flags like thunder. His heart fluttered for a moment, and then he slid the mask of his Laypriest alter-ego over his face, letting his eyes become dull, and the line of his mouth soft and uncertain. It was hardly the elaborate distraction hummed over the truth by his fellow saints, but it served well enough to insure that the oblivious remained so.

"So!" Raven said, as Alveron shuffled out of the cupboard, his hands fisted in the sleeves of his robe and his head bowed. "You're back, are you?"

"Yes, Your Grace," Alveron demurred.

Raven did not move, standing between Alveron and the door

to the passage, his staff like the iron bar of a gate.

"Replaced everything you spilled in here, have you?"

Alveron's blood sang with warning as he answered Raven's question with an affirmative murmur. Raven did not initiate conversation--certainly not with a low-ranked Laypriest--unless he wanted something.

"What a thorough job you've done of it," Raven purred, with a sniff, "Not a wisp of scent remains. You know of course, how pungent such medicines are. When they've been spilt before by a clumsy flock boy, the stench would hang in the air for days."

Alveron's blood went cold.

"Pity, of course," Raven continued, "that you had to go to the Apothecary guild for supplies. Normally we raise enough in the herb gardens for our own use, but there was such trouble with the beetles this year."

Is he trying to trap me? Alveron wondered. Everything Raven had said so far was true. They did normally raise their own medicines, and it had been a dismal year for beetles, forcing the Temple to purchase supplies they would normally stock themselves. Raven had not stated a deliberate lie, as though trying to convince Alveron to agree with him and reveal himself as a false Laypriest. But he was laying barbed lines, all the same. Alveron's back was to the shelves, and the smooth belly of a clay pot met his searching fingers.

"Still, I thought we might have some hidden away somewhere, and you were so tardy in your return I didn't wish to wait for you to come back before I could treat my injury. So I went down to speak to old Wyn in the kitchens, and he was quite happy to oblige me with some wound salve from his personal stores. And he told me something rather curious." Raven was now directly in Alveron's path, sneering down at the saint's white hood. "...There is no Laypriest in the Temple by your description, and none by your name. So," he went on, in chilly courtesy, "just who exactly are you, my boy?"

Alveron's fingers tightened on the jar behind him, and he knew the time for deception was done. "I am the Melody," he said, "and I have suffered your insolence enough." With that, he hurled the jar into Raven's face. It caught Raven squarely on the chin, struck the doorframe of the cupboard, and shattered in a blinding

306

flutter of glazed shards and chamomile blossoms. Raven flung up a hand to protect his eyes, and Alveron shoved past him to reach the door of the infirmary. He had almost made it when there was a sound of tearing air behind him, and Raven's staff clipped him smartly on the back of his head, sending him sprawling.

"How--how dare you," Raven wheezed, towering over him with his staff at the ready. "You aren't even a Temple Bird, not even a true Laypriest, nothing but a filthy spy of Hawk's--"

"I am who I have always been," Alveron said, and looking up at Raven, he let his disguise fall away. "I am the song's beginning and its ending. I am the time between daylight and Darkness, when all the doors open. I am Alveron, Wing of the Temple, and I always have been." For a moment Alveron did indeed look like his painting, stern and cold and blazing with a quiet power beyond that of mortals, even on the floor, even in a Laypriest's robe. Slowly he rose to his feet, and shook the wrinkles from his sleeves. "I will ask this only once, Jeske. End this. Now. I give you your life and your freedom; only exile will be your punishment, the same as you offered the Songbirds. You will be free to go wherever you wish. But you will return Valnon to me."

Raven did not take a step back, though he curled his hand around his staff, his knuckles blanching with the desperation in his grip. His face was white, his breath ragged, but his eyes burned with a terrible light. "...I think not, Your Grace," Raven said at last, thin lips twisting back in a painful semblance of a smile. "I think if you could have wrested the Temple from me already you would have done so. Saint? Perhaps. But if that is so, I think you are old inside that smooth skin of yours, and as fragile as a plaster cast." Raven took a step forward, and another, and Alveron did not retreat. "I think you are powerless."

"I think you have no concept of what my power is." Alveron answered, evenly.

"Oh, I suspect I might," Raven said, steadier now. "Some capricious whim of Heaven breathed its magic through you, and you feed on it still, like a sea-worm slowly devouring a whale's carcass. Your power, *Saint* Alveron, is in your name and your myth, one you have carefully groomed and maintained over the centuries, one keeping this Temple and the whole city in thrall. It matters not to you who suffers for it, the corpses heaped up in the name of your legend, even Eothan singing to his death in the vain hopes of pleasing a saint not even dead--"

"I have endured enough from you, Jeske, but I will not have Eothan suffer your insult as well!" Alveron's voice cracked in the room like the report of a cannon; the glass window-panes trembled in their lattices of ornate leading. "You, who have bloodied your Temple Birds in every way save that one ordained by their office, you with the arrogance of the ignorant and unimaginative, you traitor to every note you ever sang in service to Heaven, rendering you no better than a whore to your own ambitions. You have defiled Valnon a thousand times more in your willful arrogance than Eothan ever did in his affection, and I will have no more of it!"

Raven's staff clanged to the floor, as its owner put his hands to the cold, steel-tipped ones that had suddenly wound around his neck. He took one breath, but no more, and it rasped in his constricting throat as the grip tightened. His eyes were wide in shock and disbelief. His attacker was not Alveron, and the room had only one door. His assailant had appeared without a single footfall, and latched his fingers around Raven's neck.

"He will have no more of it, he says," Starling breathed into Raven's reddening ear, as his hands, cold of flesh and steel alike, slowly wrung the Preybird's throat. "And so we shall have no more of you."

"Wait," Alveron said. He clutched the back of a chair for support, one hand to his heart, as though he was the one being throttled. "Stop. I won't let you."

"Let me," Starling countered, eyes blazing at Alveron through the tangled mass of his hair, "and let us have done with this. It would have been over long since if you gave me freedom to work my will. I will end it. I will end *him*."

"It is not your will you are made to work, and you will do nothing you are not told to do!" Alveron pinned Starling with his gaze. "Dammit, Eothan," he breathed, his fair lashes spiky with tears, his voice a plea, "Have I not sullied you enough?"

Starling glared at Alveron a moment longer, and then he flung Raven to the floor with a noise of disgust. "This sort makes their own end," he said, with a scornful look at Raven, and a toss of his beaded hair. "But I wonder why you hold me back, when I could make it quicker." The air stirred, as with breath before singing, and Starling stepped through the wall and vanished.

Alveron took a step closer to the prone figure on the flagstones. Raven groped for his staff and struggled to rise, and for a moment it was no longer clear who was the captor, and who the captive. "I have warned you once, Jeske, and spared you once. It is the last such mercy you will have from me and mine. You desired a war? Well you shall have one. No longer does your office spare you the horrors of battle. From this hour, you are a bird of Valnon no longer."

By the time Raven swept his silver hair from his face and looked up, Alveron was gone as though he, too, was little more than a ghost himself.

When Willim saw the curved wall of the dais emerge out of the darkness, he felt as though time had become so compressed that he and his companions would shortly meet themselves on the way out. His days away from the Temple, and all that had befallen him, seemed like a mere breath between notes. It had not escaped his notice that they were returning for Evensong, as Grayson had predicted on the *Larkspur*'s departure.

Their journey through the Undercity--from the Swallowtail, to Jerdon's house, and at last through the tombs back to the underside of the Temple--had been even more fleeting. There was nothing in Willim but a kind of cold dread tempered with resignation, and the bracing comfort of Grayson at his back could do little to alleviate it. Even Ellis was somber. Dmitri had the clear-eyed determination of a Godsword on holy crusade, and Willim could well picture the number of times Kestrel had been rescued in the Lark of Valnon's imagination. Or perhaps they had only died gloriously in each other's arms. Willim suspected either way would elicit much the same expression from Dmitri.

They passed through the Undercity and the tombs like ghosts on an appointed round, and stood patiently by the dais pillar's base, waiting. Willim shivered. They had only one lamp, to keep the gas flares from being lit by accident, and the night of the tombs pressed in close around them. Glass-flecked eyes glared at them from the figures on the walls, their painted frowns grim and silent.

"Anyone have a guess how long we have?" Ellis asked, his

voice startling in the dark.

"Less than an hour, by my thinking," Grayson said. "Our saints cut things close to the seam."

"Aeric and Jerdon should be in place by now," Willim said, finding it better to talk about the others than to continually roll his own plans over and over in his head. "I wonder how many are with them?"

Grayson shifted the weight of the pack on his shoulder. Jerdon had been obliged to make their gas flares in clay pots, and they were heavy. "We'll have to focus on our own task for now. The rest is out of our hands." He tilted his head to the shining curve of the dais as it stirred in its socket. "It's time."

The Songbirds of Valnon returned to their Temple in silence, like thieves, and the dais pillar slowly spun closed behind them as they hurried up the dank passage beyond. It was only when they reached the backside of the Dovecote that Willim realized there was no latch obvious from the tunnel side. He knocked softly on the wall and waited, but there was no response.

"We're dead in the water if Alveron doesn't come," Dmitri said, voicing a thought Willim had been reluctant to admit.

"He'll come," Willim said, with a firmness of voice, if nothing else. "It's just a matter of time."

"So long as it gives you long enough to set these bombs before Aeric launches the feint on the front gate." Grayson loosened his sword in its sheath, and gave the doorway a wary look.

"I hope nothing's happened to him," Ellis said.

Me too, Willim thought, and then let out his breath in relief as the stone door rasped open, letting in dim candlelight and the smell of the Temple, throwing Alveron's shadow over them like a coverlet.

"I apologize for my tardiness," Alveron said, waving them into the Dovecote. "I had a few delays."

Willim caught a glimpse of the back of his head, his fine hair streaked with dried blood. "You're wounded!"

"A minor issue," Alveron said, dismissively. Now that they were out of the passage, Willim could see that his white Laypriest's robes were muddied and torn, his knuckles scraped. "I fear Raven is aware of my presence, and he has roused his forces, which hampered my movements somewhat. The sooner we get them all

310

over to the main gate, the better for our plans. The flock is safely concealed in the Laypriests' garden with the Preybirds, and all is set for our singing. You have the lamps?"

"Here," Grayson said, passing him the satchel. "He only had enough materials for half a dozen."

"It'll be enough." Alveron slung the satchel over his arm, and stole a glance out into the empty corridor. "Grayson, a friend waits for you by the mosaic of the Seven Larks near the Preybird's tower stairs. I was assured you would know the place."

A kind of stillness settled on Grayson's features, as though he already reclined on his bier. "I do."

"Hide down the northwest passage by the Laypriests' atrium, and do not be seen," Alveron stressed. "It is empty for the moment, and distraction is the only concealment I can offer to you. When the battle begins, make for the Preybirds' tower. Know that Jeske fa Soliver has been turned out of his colors and has forfeit his right to the name of Raven. I do not expect you will hesitate as you would to a Preybird." Alveron studied him carefully. "Am I clear?"

Grayson bowed, fist to his chest in a Godsword's salute. "Yes, my Saint."

"Then go," Alveron said, and added, "and know that Grayce would have been proud to stand beside you."

A shiver crossed Grayson's fingers; he put his hand to the carved hand of his ancestor, both of them curled around the stone hilt in his belt. "Thank you."

The moment Willim had been dreading most came and went before he even had a chance to wince over it. The parting from Grayson was as swift as a merciful death, and it was no time or place for demonstrations of affection, to linger for what might be the last time. A fleeting glance at Willim, an almost-smile, and Grayson was gone.

Willim took a deep breath, surrendering all his hopes and fears into the vacant place by his side, and turned to face his saint. "We're ready," he said. "Tell us what to do."

"I really must beg your forgiveness, my dear," Jerdon said, looking quite unlike himself in a Godsword's borrowed armor, his features disguised further by the shadows of the surface alleyway. He had taken off his spectacles, and may as well have been a stranger. "I would really rather you waited this out in the safety of the Undercity."

Rekbah put a hand to her head, gingerly. The Laypriestesses in the Undercity forged no armor small enough for her, and her helm was padded with an old towel. "Of course you know I'd rather be here with you."

"I've gotten you in danger enough over the past years," Jerdon mused, as though to himself. "And I've been far too indulgent. Anything is better than the life you had before, of course, but I can't help thinking how selfish I've been..." He rested his hand on the top of her head. "How grateful I've been for you, and how lonely I would be without you. Remember that if you are tempted to try anything foolish tonight. If there is danger, flee. At the worst, shed this disguise and mourn me at a safe distance. The house in the Undercity is to be yours, and you'll find all the required papers in--"

"Stop," Rekbah choked, punching the alley wall for emphasis. Her eyes were too bright, though Jerdon had never once seen her weep. "Stop it, Lairke."

Jerdon's breath caught, but as Rekbah struggled to get her face back in order, the surprise slowly melted into chagrin. "...How long have you known?"

Rekbah shot him a disgusted look through her blurring vision. "How could I be your snipe, and *not* know? You charged me with ferreting out the secrets of the Undercity; you should have known the first ones I would find out would be yours."

Jerdon swept a hand over her cheek. "Then you should know just how dear to me you are, my daughter-that-never-was. In six centuries there have been few I loved so well as you."

Rekbah choked back a full-throated sob, forcing it to come out in a hiccup. "And of all of them, I'm the one who gets shorted on my time with you--I'll never let you hear the end of it!" She jabbed him in his belt buckle. "Understand?"

Jerdon smiled, but it was such a wan, faded thing that Rekbah flung her bony arms around his middle and squeezed, as though forcing water from the lungs of a man already drowned.

"Don't you dare leave me," Rekbah whispered fiercely. "Don't you *dare*!"

"I long ago learned the perils of running afoul of your temper, and I don't wish to do so tonight," Jerdon said, and then made a little gasp. "But I fear if you don't let go, I'll asphyxiate before I have the chance to die any other way."

"Good," Rekbah grunted, giving him one last squeeze before letting go.

There was a rustle of armor beyond the alley, and Aeric stepped inside. He gave them a businesslike glance, and nodded. "Probably the shortest and the tallest Godswords I've ever seen, but you'll do well enough. Remember this is a feint, after all." He eyed Rekbah sharply. "That means no heroics, missy."

"Only if you don't try to pull any heroics yourself," Rekbah retorted. "Are we ready?"

Aeric nodded. "The others are scattered around and will move in at the signal. We're set."

"Glad one of us thinks so," Jerdon muttered, reaching up to make sure his cloak was secure. "Beastly thing, this. I look dreadful in red."

28

More than once Willim wished for Eothan's ability to come and go at will, to melt through walls and materialize whenever he pleased. The Temple was swarming with green-coated Queensguard under Raven's command, outnumbering the prentices three to one.

"There certainly are a lot of them," Ellis said, in breathy exasperation as Alveron and the Songbirds were forced to take cover yet again to let a patrol pass them by. The Queensguard were hard-faced men, an eager rumble in their voices. Willim doubted they would hesitate when faced with a Songbird, as the prentices had.

"Raven has been feeding mercenaries into the Queensguard for quite some time, paying them extra from his family's coffers to stay there." Alveron pressed his cheek to the stonework as he watched the men retreat. "It gave him a large pool of swords at his disposal, hidden in plain sight. He knew he had only to ask the Regent for them when the time came. Nilan fa Erianthus' reputation is too dear to him to refuse any request from Raven."

"The regent?" Willim asked, and felt Dmitri stir beside him, attentive. "Raven is blackmailing him?"

"Only with a rumor, but it is a potent one. It could do considerable damage to the Regent if unleashed."

"What rumor?" Dmitri demanded, but Alveron moved past them into the hall.

"The next patrol will be here in less than ten measures. Hurry."

Their questions unanswered, the Songbirds hurried to follow the saint through the thick air of the muffled corridors. Only when they reached the back access corridor to the sanctuary did the atmosphere feel normal once more, and that only because Alveron had opened the vents there. The Wing of Valnon pressed a hand to his lips to indicate the need for complete quiet. With no one now singing in the Sanctuary, and the vents open to channel the gas fumes, even the least sneeze could give them away.

With grueling slowness they unpacked the bombs: two rough clay bowls inverted one on top of the other into a flattened sphere, the seam sealed with waxed cord, a hole drilled in the top for the fuse. Once lit, it would drop down into the sticky paste of chemicals inside, and smolder while it sent up plumes of tainted smoke. They placed them one at a time beneath the grates leading to the sanctuary, and waited for Aeric's feint to begin.

Raven strode down the corridors of the Temple, his robes boiling around him in his haste, his face set in cold lines of fury. Had Petrine dared to study his features more closely (which she did not) she would have seen fear beneath his stony countenance, a fear that, like sand, rendered unsound every heavy construct placed on top of it.

"I don't want so much as a mouse-hole overlooked," Raven said, the latest in a sharp volley of orders that he had been firing at her since she had reported to his side. "Tell your prentices this is a war, and I expect a fitting response from them."

"But--" Petrine dared, in some confusion. "Who is it, exactly, we are at war against?"

"I already told you," Raven snarled, turning on her so fast that his sleeves flared out ahead of him, still trying to keep up with the pace of their wearer. "That sniveling Laypriest is nothing but a spy, and he has escaped. See to it that he does not return, and that any friends of his stay well beyond the walls."

Petrine had only begun to nod when Raven clutched her upper arm, a cunning light coming into his eyes. "As a matter of fact," he said, "I believe it was Haverty that picked that Laypriest for you."

Petrine's throat closed around a sudden lump of fear. "Alder?" she said, in a bare whisper. "I'm sure he had no idea--"

"You might be sure, but I'm far from it." Raven's hand tightened on her arm. "Bring him to me. I want a few words with him."

Petrine had barely taken two steps away from Raven when the first explosion came. It rattled down the Temple corridor like an invisible behemoth ramming the walls, sending the hanging lamps swirling on their chains, shaking down a fine rain of dust and mortar from the ceiling.

"What in the name of Grayce--" Petrine began, twirling her spear to readiness.

Raven's staff scraped over the floor as he turned, a knowing light in his eyes, a thin frost of fear and disbelief across his features. "They're charging the very Temple doors!"

"They will never even cross the threshold," Petrine swore, and whistled to the rest of Raven's escort of prentices to follow her. They clattered down to the Ave with a bright jingle of mail, spears blazing in the tremulous lamplight.

Raven, rather than following, had other concerns. He knew the outcome of the struggle was really irrelevant; the Ethnarch's armada would be arriving well before dawn. He had only to let things play out, and nudge things here and there into the proper places. If he were to be killed or detained before the siege began, however, that could prove most inconvenient.

Unwilling to let his limp slow him more than the slightest fraction, Raven hurried back towards the Preybirds' tower in search of a judicious retreat.

What he found, instead, was a Preybird and a Sellsword waiting for him, weapons drawn, the grim pleasure of revenge in their faces.

"Why so much haste, Raven?" Grayson asked, in a low voice. "Does the song in the Sanctuary not suit your tastes?"

"He only likes destruction's melody when he is the sole orchestrator of it," Kestrel added, a longknife once more in his hand, glinting and eager. "But now we will carry the tune to our own end, and I don't think you'll like the conclusion."

"You should be dead," Raven gasped, more unsettled by the sight of them than he had been by Alveron. After all, his offense to the saint was an indifferent thing, on a scale more grand and impersonal than the scar that was now ripped open between the three of them, seething and raw as though newly-made. "Both of you."

"If I live, it is only because Heaven moved through the Dove to save me," Grayson said, raising his sword in mocking salute. "And by His Grace and the command of his saint, I will have your life."

Raven knew he could not outrun them; his leg would not permit it and they blocked his escape. But he leveled his staff at them, a carrion bird still sharp of claw and beak, ready to rip and tear at his enemies. Another distant explosion rocked the Temple's walls, as Kestrel and Grayson rushed forward as one to strike down the destructor of their boyhood dreams.

The first explosion startled Willim badly. After so long in the oppressive quiet, hardly daring to breathe, the sudden calamity made him jump. His hands were still shaking as he pulled the cowl of his cloak up over his face, and the other two Songbirds hurried to do the same. Once protected, they snatched up their waiting candles, took as deep a breath as they could hold, and put flame to the fuses.

Willim's first bomb lit with a blinding fizzle, and he shoved it quickly into the sounding vent. It cast a wan light down the channel as it went down it in a wobbling roll, sending up an acrid cloud of fumes. Even with the fabric across his face, and his own capacious lungs, Willim fought to keep from inhaling the gas. Eyes watering, he bent down into the cleaner air by his feet and lit his second bomb, shooting it down the next vent over.

Ellis staggered back from the wall with a racking cough, one arm over his face. Dmitri, eyes streaming, finally got his second flare lit and shoved it on its way.

"That's it!" Alveron called to them, yanking the passage door wide. "Quickly, go!"

They rushed out into the corridor and fell forward with their hands on their knees, gasping for clear air. Whatever Jerdon had packed into the bombs, it was potent. Willim's eyes burned, his ears rang with a tinny echo, and the world swam around him in a lurching circle. After a few ragged gulps of cold winter air, the symptoms began to fade.

"Well done," Alveron said, locking the door behind them. His eyes were red-rimmed as well, and he tugged the cowl of his robe away from his nose and mouth. "But we can't stay here. If we can catch up with Grayson, we may be able to force Raven to a surrender and halt further bloodshed." Another muffled explosion came from the sanctuary, and with it followed the sounds of combat, the clash of spears and swords, uncomfortably close. Alveron caught Willim under one armpit, and helped the Dove of Valnon to stand upright again. "On your feet, Willim."

"I'm fine," Willim said, glad to find it was true. The burning in his throat had eased. He looked over at Dmitri and Ellis, glad to see them leaning on one another, their breathing evening again.

"You two all right?"

Ellis dragged a sleeve across his eyes. "We're ready," he said, and then shook his head a little to clear out the last of the fumes. "Phew! But I don't envy those Queensguard!"

"The Queensguard here aren't even worthy of the name," Dmitri put in, bitterly. He shrugged off Ellis' arm, standing upright. "Let's go. I want to see Raven's end with my own eyes." With their bloodthirsty Lark at the lead, they raced down the corridor away from the sounds of the battle, deep into the sleeping, silent heart of the Temple of Valnon.

Raven's first charge had not been entirely without success. Though he took wounds to the arms for it, plunging directly between Grayson and Kestrel at the start had cost him little more than the sleeves of his robe, torn away as Raven shrugged out of his outer mantle in order to break free. In return, he gained the high ground of the stairs to the Preybirds' tower, and was that much closer to his escape.

Grayson's sword bit at his heels as he hurried up the spiraling stairs to the upper corridor. Only Raven's staff gave him the distance he needed, as he thrust it behind him to trip up his pursuers, forcing them to dodge. Though he had no formal training in the arts of war, he had a savage desperation that was far more deadly than the cool precision of a soldier. He was a cornered animal, and it only fueled his rage and his speed. Even with his game leg, Kestrel and Grayson could not travel up the stairs together as quickly as Raven could alone. Kestrel was hardly knitted whole from his earlier wounds, and Grayson's armor slowed him. It was the barest shaving of an advantage, but it was Raven's, and he wrung it for all it was worth.

He flung himself on the door of the upper passage, and hurried through the bookshelf-lined corridor of the Preybirds' tower, tipping furniture behind him to slow his pursuers. It was not enough for a complete escape. Grayson's sword tore through the air and splinters of ironwood burst from the staff as Raven hastily blocked the strike.

"You should have stayed in the sewers with the rest of the rats," Raven spat, swinging the head of his staff towards Grayson's face. Grayson had tasted the bite of the staff's ornament before, and had no interest in a second helping. He parried the blow, but barely, and reeled off-balance into a bookcase. Scrolls and manuscripts tumbled down in a papery avalanche.

Kestrel sprang forward to block Raven from pressing his attack on Grayson, slamming his shoulder into the opposite bookcase and sending it into Raven's path with a tremendous crash. "Better a rat than a carrion bird eating his own kin," Kestrel hissed, his knife cutting a long gash in the back of Raven's robe as Raven fled back, sending a sprinkling of the Preybird's milk-white hair down among the toppled books.

"What, Willim?" Raven paused long enough to gloat, as Kestrel and Grayson had to now get over the blockage they had made in the corridor. "He's no kin of mine."

"If you knew whose kin he was, you might have thought the better of it." Grayson kicked books away from his path, his advance inexorable. Raven had reached the end of the corridor, and there was no escape.

"Oh, I know what he is." Raven's eyes glinted. "Product of the late queen's shame and indiscretion with the man who now calls himself the Regent. Nilan fa Erianthus confessed to me his love of her, his jealousy of her Consort, when he lay wounded in the Temple years ago. Willim is their bastard, and a poorly-concealed one at that."

"That's not how I heard it," Grayson growled, and Raven could not quite block his strike. His sword had grazed the Preybird's side, and not only fabric had been cut this time. The wound flowered with blood, shallow but stinging. "Jerdon was in attendance when Willim was born, serving in the office of Queen's physician. He took Willim to the Laypriestesses, he told them he was a foundling meant for the Temple."

Raven snorted. "Why would a Queen hide her firstborn in the Temple, save out of shame?"

"Out of faith, then," Kestrel said, white with pain from his injuries, but unflagging. "The war was endless, the Queen's beloved consort facing death every day on the front line. Willim could never rule Valnon, he was a male child. But as a Dove, he might save it. Those of us who knew could never speak of it, and fools like you were free to make your own erroneous conclusions."

"If Nilan fa Erianthus once loved Queen Renne," Grayson

added, "He loved her unspoken, and untouching. Willim is of the line of fa Valos, and of Alveron, and there is no shame in his pedigree. You have struck out against the very blood of Hasafel."

Raven inhaled as though to deny Grayson's words, but then his eyes darted beyond Grayson, and a smile twisted his features. "No shame, perhaps," he said sweetly. "Save that you did not tell him."

Grayson turned. Willim stood at the end of the corridor, his shout of defiance dead on his lips, his face gray with shock. Behind him, Alveron and the other two Songbirds had likewise come to a halt. Dmitri's eyes were wide, Ellis' mouth gaped with surprise, but Alveron's face was dark with fury.

"Unwilling to cut your ordained Songbirds, striking out at them in violence, and now revealing birthrights to a bird still in his colors. I wonder, Jeske, if there's any law of the Temple you have not flaunted."

"Only this one," Raven said, thrusting his staff at the window behind him, and shattering the stained glass. He fled through the bright shards onto the Temple's ramparts.

"Willim--" Grayson began.

"Not now!" Willim shouted, shaking off his momentary amazement. "You'll let him get away!" Willim clambered over the bookcases and snatched up a toppled light stand, using it to knock away loose glass still clinging to the leading. "If he gets down the far side of the wall, we've lost him!"

"Yes, Your Grace!" Grayson plunged through the window after his Dove, saints and Temple Birds at his heels.

Sarin was not overly blessed with patience, and what little he had was long since spent. The ships Raven had given the Ethnarch were the fastest of their line, but even so the days had dragged at Sarin like the chains he had left behind. Zeig, once more a mercenary sailor, had treated Sarin with the same aloof scorn he gave the other crew, and bowed obeisance to the Ethnarch as though killing him was the furthest thought from his mind. His plan put them both in considerable danger, and Sarin had as little hope as any that it would succeed.

But now, at last, the ships had shuttered their lanterns and put aside all attempts to masquerade as common merchant vessels. The gun-ports yawned open in every hull, the Ethnarch stood at the prow with his gilded breastplate gleaming, and Sarin waited in the rigging with Rekbah's knife clenched in his hand. In a matter of moments the assault would begin, and Sarin's only chance had come. One of the Ethnarch's Shadowhand escort stepped just slightly aside to make a landing place on the deck, and Sarin vaulted down from the lines with Rekbah's bared dagger lunching for the Ethnarch's throat.

It never reached its target, and Sarin had not expected that it would. He was only meant as a distraction, after all. He didn't deny it would have been a certain satisfaction to kill the Ethnarch, in spite of all Zeig's planning. But he had not yet landed when there was the twanging of dart-bows all around him, and five poisoned needles sank deep into his flesh. Sarin landed on the deck in a boneless heap, his limbs numb and twitching, the fox-bone knife tumbling from his hand.

I suppose, Sarin thought with chagrin, *it didn't really make me fast or sly after all.*

"My dear young man," the Ethnarch said, as though Sarin had only bumped into him on the street. "That was a very foolish thing to do."

Sarin would have answered, but his tongue was thick and useless in his mouth. One dart from a Shadowhand's bow was enough to incapacitate a grown man, five left Sarin barely able to hold his eyes open. The Shadowhands had put aside their bows and drew their cutlasses: wicked-looking things of serrated steel.

"I suppose it's some kind of honor grudge," the Ethnarch continued, bending down to pick up the knife. "Your style of braid... it's the Reni clan's, is it not? I passed through your mountains once, you know. Beautiful country, the Draramir clan lands. Happy children, good sturdy ponies. A shame they had to aid our enemies." He turned the knife over in his immaculate gloves, his brow creased with something like sorrow. "You would have been better off burning with the rest of them."

Sarin roused himself for a curse, but he could not work it past his lips. He spat, instead, at the Thrassin ruler's boots.

The Ethnarch shook his crown of white braids. "A shameful thing to happen on the eve of our victory." He held the knife up to the sky, examining the shape it made against the emblem on his sail. "I will remember you both in my daily prayers." And then he turned and rammed Rekbah's knife deep into the belly of the Shadowhand standing behind him.

Sarin could not even scream. He lay on the deck in helpless horror as the Ethnarch ripped the black Shadowhand's cowl from Zeig's head.

"One of *my* sons," The Ethnarch hissed, twisting the knife further into Zeig's belly, "would not have *missed*."

Zeig meant to speak, his one eye fierce as he glared at the Ethnarch, but nothing came out of his mouth but a froth of blood. His dark skin had gone the color of cold ashes.

"Though I suppose," the Ethnarch continued, "you have rid me of a weakling son. For that, you have my gratitude." He released the fox bone handle of the knife and Zeig's body tumbled to the deck. Sarin saw the weapon shudder once in Zeig's ribs and then go still, his eye staring emptily into eternity.

We've failed, he thought, bleakly. *Forgive me, Ellis.*

"And now, my little would-be-assassin," the Ethnarch said, pulling off his bloodied gauntlet, "What shall I do with you?"

29

The rooftops of the Temple would have been a treacherous terrain in broad daylight and at a cautious pace; in the dark and at a flat run, slick with ice, they were nothing short of insane. Willim spared it not a thought. He ran after Raven because he had to, because the concept of Raven escaping judgment for his crimes was a thing so foreign to Willim's mind that there was no room for fear. Nor was there room to comprehend the provenance of his birth, though he felt the idea beating its wings against the back of his mind, longing to break free. One thing he understood fully: if his blood was of the line of Hasafel, of Thali, then his need to bring Raven to justice was doubled.

Behind him in the dark, he could hear Grayson close on his heels, the scrape of his boots on the slate. The others were surely following, but at a slower pace; the path from the Preybirds' tower to the buttresses above the western Temple wall was nothing but a narrow thread of stone trimmed in a lacework of marble and curling iron. It was a straight drop down to either side, past the white crown of the island, past her shoulders and her skirts, all the way to the invisible ocean so far below that its very waves were silent. The only way to follow was in single-file, and the low-hanging clouds offered only a grudging filter of moonlight.

It was barely enough to see ahead, but Willim could perceive the darker, bluer shadow against the sky that was Raven. It came to the end of the narrow bridge of roof and then vanished around one of the massive pinnacles lining the western wall. Willim hurtled after him without slowing, ignoring Grayson's cry of warning. Whether it was to wait, or to be careful, or to let him go first, Willim didn't know. What he did know was that he whirled around the towering pinnacle with one hand on the stone to keep him from flying clear off the wall, and came directly into the path of Raven's staff.

Willim heard his ribs crack as Raven's staff connected with his side, and pain jolted him out of his single-minded rage. Willim's breath rushed out of his lungs as he collapsed at Raven's feet, his head spinning. Raven's staff whistled through the air again, and a brief explosion of light burst in Willim's vision before darkness blotted out the world.

Rekbah had hoped for a glorious fight, to show Jerdon her skills and perhaps even save his life once or twice. She was sorely disappointed. Once they had forced open the Temple doors, there was no one left to fight, only heaps of insensate Queensguard and a handful of swooning prentices. She stepped away from the doors, choking and gagging until the cold fresh air cleared out the fumes. Her only comfort was that the others with them were just as overcome.

Aeric and Jerdon recovered the fastest, Aeric shoving past the splintered doors and snatching up the first prentice he found, dragging her out onto the steps. She was not much older than Rekbah herself, and she gasped like a floundering fish.

"Tell me where Raven is," Aeric demanded. "Now, girl! That's an order!"

"Let her breathe, Aeric," Jerdon said, and his face brightened as he got a good look at her. "Ah, Petrine, isn't it? Now please. We can all end this tonight if you'll just cooperate, all right?"

Petrine Tolliver blinked in slow recognition at Jerdon. "You're that doctor friend of Kestrel's. Word in the city is that you're dead."

"This isn't a tea social." Aeric gave Petrine a little shake, and held up his sword before her face. "You know what this is, I trust."

"Yes, sir," Petrine rasped. "You're a Godsword."

"Good. Now tell me where that bastard Preybird is."

Petrine closed her eyes and turned her face away. "I can't let you kill him," she said. Her eyes were streaming, and not from the fumes. "He's a Temple Bird, I can't--"

"Petrine," Jerdon said, and the air around him seemed to vibrate as though from some kind of impact. There was more than mere sound in his words; it was a coercive force, like the inexorable push of the tide. "He's not worth protecting."

Petrine slumped against Aeric as though her strings had been cut. She staggered upright, and blinked at Jerdon in mingled horror and awe. "What--what *are* you?"

"He's a saint," Rekbah said, lurching away from the pillars. "And that outranks a Preybird, so do as he says!"

"Saint--" Petrine began, and then shook her head. "In the hallway there," she said. "We left Raven by the stairs to the archives."

"And he's long gone now." Alder Haverty emerged from the wreckage of the doors, a broken spear in his hand, his face shining with sweat. "They've gone up to the roof with Kestrel and that sell-sword, and the Wing and Dove with him."

At this, Aeric tore past Alder with a murderous gleam in his eye, and Alder was left to catch Petrine.

"You'd best look after her," Jerdon said, and rushed after his fellow saint. Rekbah was on his heels in a flash, her lone knife in her hand. There might be another chance for valor, though she began to get the feeling that Jerdon really didn't need protecting.

"Stop!" Raven shouted, and Grayson felt his limbs instinctively obey, but not because of the command. The Preybird stood over the Dove's body, his staff raised. "One more step, from any of you, and I'll spatter the Dove's brains all over this parapet." His smile was slow, calculating, as he saw he had at last gained the upper hand. Behind him, Grayson heard Kestrel skidding to a halt, the quick breathing of Alveron and the other two Songbirds.

"You wouldn't dare--" Grayson began, but Raven cut him off with a little wave of his staff.

"I would, and you know it full well. Don't think I don't know the weak point in a man's skull, and don't think I will miss." His eyes flicked to Grayson's drawn sword, and then to Kestrel's knife. "I'd drop those, if you want your Dove to remain breathing. Over the side. Now."

Grayson bit his lip, his muscles straining to rush forward and bludgeon Raven with his own staff, but the sight of Willim's limp body held him in restraint. He spared a glance back to Alveron, who gave a barely-perceptible nod.

"Do as he says," Alveron said tersely. "I'd sooner let him go than risk Willim's life."

Grayson held his arm out over the steeply-sloped roof on the side of the parapet, and let go of his weapon. He heard it clang as it hit the slates, then it scraped down the roof to land at last in the greenery far below. A skittering noise behind him, and Raven's triumphant face, told him that Kestrel's knife had followed suit.

"Flee now, if it pleases you," Grayson said, in a low growl. "But know that I will hunt you down to the very edges of the horizon."

Raven let out a single bark of laughter. "Flee?" he spat. "Had I wished to flee, I could have done so a thousand times over. What is it to me if my prentices and blades are defeated? I can make them over again, given a little time. I would rather that than leave Valnon in the hands of such as you." He looked each one of them in the face, growing more disgusted with each one. "And what are you? An honorless sell-sword, a whore of a Preybird, a pair of foolish boys." His face hardened as he looked at Alveron. "And a powerless saint with his Queen's bastard of a Dove." He scuffed the toe of his boot towards Willim's outstretched hand. "No, it ends here, and it should have done so long since." With that, he raised his staff over his head, and brought it hurtling down towards the Dove of Valnon's still face.

Grayson had no thought in him, only the pure urgency of the moment. When he charged forward, he did not know if it was to tackle Raven, to fling his own body over Willim's, or something else entirely. He was spurred by instinct and emotion, not thought. It was instinct that prompted his hand to his belt, instinct that folded his fingers around the sword hilt that they found. But what happened after that was nothing but music.

It came from behind him and was all around him at once, like the rush of an incoming wave at tide's turning. It was a single note, as beautiful as a dying sun, and so brief that Grayson had barely heard it before it was over. When reason again took hold of Grayson, he found that he was standing over Willim, with Raven impaled through the heart upon the gleaming, impossible blade of Grayce's sword.

It could be no other. The wings were swept forward, the oath upon the blade was scribed in the letters of Antigus' tribe, filling rapidly now with Raven's blood. Grayson looked down past the blade into Willim's eyes, and they stared at each other in mute amazement until a drop of blood fell down onto the Dove's cheek, and the whole world began moving once more.

Grayson stepped back, withdrawing the sword, and Raven's body tumbled down, his staff rolling away from his nerveless fingers. Willim gained his feet unsteadily, clinging to Grayson's arm. For a second they looked at each other, at the sword, at Raven. And then comprehension dawned on Willim's face. He ran past his knight, back along the rooftop, to where Alveron lay lifeless upon the stones.

"No," Willim breathed, taking up one cold hand in both his own, and clinging to it as though it would undo the trade Alveron had made. "No, no you can't!"

There was a transparency to Alveron, the thinness of something waned into near-invisibility. He smiled fondly up at Willim, and at Ellis and Dmitri over his shoulders. "I may have been off-key," he admitted. "It has been such a long time." He tilted his head over to get a better look at Willim, uncurling one finger to brush at a tear, streaked with Raven's blood, as it slid down Willim's face. "It felt good," he sighed, closing his eyes, "to sing like that again."

And he died.

Willim stared down at his saint, his face blank with disbelief. Ellis and Dmitri held on to Willim as he slumped down, too stunned for tears, at Alveron's side. Kestrel staggered back against a parapet, one hand across his eyes, and choked on an inarticulate noise of grief. Grayson could only stand by and watch, like a patron at a Canticles play, holding in his hand the bloody miracle that had cost the first Dove of Valnon his life.

The silence was unbroken until some measures later, when shouts and footsteps came from inside the tower. Aeric appeared at the broken window, his blood-streaked face white as chalk. When he saw what had happened, a resigned kind of grief settled over his features. He already knew the fate of his kinsman, and when he was joined by Jerdon, Jerdon's face told a similar story. Jerdon put his face in his hands and leaned into Aeric's shoulder, briefly overcome, and only then did Grayson see Aeric's calm demeanor shudder for a moment.

"Why?" Willim gasped, having found language at last, and emerging, red-eyed, from his fellow Birds' embrace.

"Because he was done," Jerdon said, and stepped out onto the parapet. He seemed to have aged years in a matter of hours. His brown hair showed streaks of gray, the lines at his eyes had grown deeper. "To be honest, he had been done for years. Ever since he lost Eothan."

"I had so much more to ask you," Willim said, looking down at Alveron's serene face. "For a few hours I knew what it was to have a Preybird of my own, but now I must be a Dove alone, again."

He folded Alveron's hands over his breast, and would not let Dmitri and Ellis help him to his feet. Grayson watched him stand, and then straighten, and though they all stood around him Willim was in that moment utterly alone on the icy parapet, his face lifted to the sky in mute bereavement. He was dressed in the wrong colors, he wore no paint and no jewels, and yet never had he looked more like the Dove of Valnon than he did at that moment.

A song worth my life, Grayson thought. *A Dove of Valnon.*

They were all of them lost in their own heartbreak, and none of them heard the deadly whine in the air until it was almost too late. Aeric lifted his head sharply, his face drawn and pale, his eyes blazing.

"Get down!" he shouted, reaching out and throwing Rekbah and Ellis to the rooftop. "Get down now!"

"Willim!" Grayson reached out for his Dove, but the whine ended in a deafening explosion of rock and a swelling plume of fire, and the world collapsed all around them.

30

The Regent of Valnon rapped gently on the door of Reim's private study, and waited for an answer. There was no light beneath the door, but that meant only that the queen was alone. Her dinner had been sent back untouched, her puzzled waiting-maid told Nilan that the Queen refused to answer her knock.

"Reim," Nilan said, putting formality aside, and resting his hand on the door latch. "May I come in?"

Silence. Nilan sighed. She had taken the news of the *Larkspur's* loss with admirable serenity, but then had sent off all her servants and shut the door to her rooms. As queen she was rich in all things but privacy, and Nilan was loath to intrude on her meager supply. But she had been alone now for hours, and it was well after dark. He didn't like the idea of her sitting up all night. He pressed his hand more firmly on the latch, but it was locked from within.

"Reim, please," the Regent said, in more pleading tones. "Don't do this to yourself. Talk to me." Another minute crawled by without a response, and Nilan's scalp prickled with a new fear. What if she was hurt, or ill? Worse, what if she had done some harm to herself? Despite her justified pride in her abilities, she still had a considerable handicap. It would only be a matter of a chair leg angled the wrong way by accident to make her fall and hit her head. Presented with a vivid image of the queen bleeding unconscious on the carpet, Nilan thumbed a key from the ring at his belt, and thrust it into the lock.

The Queen's study was not wholly dark. The drapes were open wide, Reim's maid had done so that morning. Cloudy moonlight revealed the queen's empty chair by a hearth filled with cold ashes. In her adjacent chamber, her bed hangings were still tied back, the quilts smooth.

"Reim!" Nilan called out, though he knew she was not there to answer. Where she was, he had no idea. As he stood staring at her vacant rooms, the gray landscape beyond her window was illuminated by a dazzling burst of red and gold. Nilan blinked away afterimages, and a second later the report of the explosion reached the palace, faint but distinct. Reim's tapestries rippled, and the ceiling lamps swayed. Nilan staggered back from the window. He inhaled to shout again, to call for steel and for horses, but a shadow blossomed behind him and a thin wire bit deep into his throat.

"My apologies, Regent." A woman's voice, with a southlander's accents. "Raven insisted that I not kill you in the usual fashion of my people. A knife would be more proper for a nobleman. But there are so many details to attend to, when one is starting a war."

Nilan scrabbled for purchase on her, on anything. He staggered back into the window in the hopes of shaking off his assailant, but though the panes cracked with the impact of their bodies, the garrote only tightened. Nilan's lungs began to burn, and fire licked along his neck. From somewhere far away, another cannon report cracked along his city's towers.

"I am Jacind, Daughter of the Ethnarch of Thrass," she said to him. "And we will have conquered your island before dawn comes. At the least, Regent, you will know who it is who has killed you."

Nilan's knees gave way, but the wire was unrelenting. Images floated in before his eyes like afterimages of light, the faces of his wife, his son, of beloved friends long gone. He wondered if this woman had already killed Reim, and the grief stole the fight from him. He had never loved war, had never wanted war. But he had been obliged to fight one all his life. It had cost him his dearest friend, and his Queen. Queen Renne had died on her child-bed, with her hand in Nilan's own, Josah's name on her lips. Nilan could not bear the death of another queen he loved. He closed his eyes, and waited to hear the song of Heaven.

The music came over him almost at once, full of a strange, sinister joy. It was Evensong, Nilan realized, but Evensong as he had never heard it, cold and vengeful and heartless. He had hoped for better comfort.

"Stop it," Jacind hissed into his ear, and her powerful hands were shaking. "Whatever it is you're doing, stop it now!"

But Nilan could make no noise at all, much less that one. He fell unconscious to the carpet as the wire unraveled from Jacind's hands. The moonlight flared on silver claws and tumbling white hair, it caught in a queen's sightless eyes that blazed with the deadly blue of a ghost's rage. The flare of a Shindamiri gun turned

330

a Dove's armor to crimson, it made fresh blood stark and black on Reim's white skin. Nilan did not wake, or even stir, as the song rose relentless and beautiful over the sound of Jacind's dying screams.

"Nicholas!"

Grayson came back to his senses with a jolt, and groaned with the pain lancing through his arm. It was twisted awkwardly, and as he tried to free it, he heard Kestrel's answering sound of agony above him.

"Don't pull me down, you idiot!"

Grayson's world righted itself, and his stomach plummeted. Between his boot-toes he could see nothing but empty darkness, and only Kestrel's grip on his arm kept him from tumbling down into it. Kestrel lay on a jagged plateau of what had been the rooftop, now tilted crazily down onto the wall. Pained sweat stood out on his face, and he panted with the effort of holding Grayson up.

"Rouen!" Grayson said, and his boots found purchase on a crumbling arch of buttress. "Hang on, I've almost--" There was a moment of desperate scrambling, and Grayson got a leg up on the ledge. They rolled up to safety and Kestrel curled up on his side, clutching his ribs.

"If Raven wasn't already dead I'd kill him again," he moaned, and spat blood onto the buckled stones.

"Where are the others?"

Kestrel dragged a torn and bloody sleeve across his forehead. "I don't know. It's too dark to see. They could be in the ocean, or crushed under the rock."

Another missile sliced through the air above them, detonating on the far side of the wall and illuminating the night for a brief glimpse of the surroundings. The Preybird's tower lay across an impossible chasm of rubble and rock, the place where Willim had been standing was nothing but empty air. Grayson feverishly scanned the rubble, but the flare of the cannon fire passed, and he was blind again. In his brief glimpse, he had seen nothing but destruction.

There was another explosion, more distant, and the night was torn by screaming.

"Those are no southlander's guns," Grayson said, bitterly.

"No," Kestrel agreed, propping himself up on the wall. "Shindamiri, I'd have to say. Thrass has been playing both sides. And if they keep this up, there will be no Valnon left for them to conquer."

"You're wounded," Grayson said, creeping close enough to Kestrel to mop at the blood on his forehead.

"Leave it, Nicholas," Kestrel sighed. "We've been outmaneuvered, and Alveron is dead. The others too, most likely." He leaned his head down to rest on Grayson's shoulder. "Though it was sweet to fight Raven beside you. A fine finish, Nicholas, for all that it bought us. It will have to do."

"No." Grayson looked out into the darkness, where sparks in the distance forewarned other cannon blasts, hammering down upon the previously unassailable walls of the city. "It's not over yet. Willim is not dead. He's the Dove."

Kestrel stirred a little. "You believe in him?"

Grayson drew Grayce's sword from his belt, and lay the blade across his knees. The oath engraved there glittered as though it had been carved yesterday.

"Yes," Grayson said. "I do."

The Dove of Valnon was falling. Whether it was from the dais and by his own will, or careening wildly through a landslide of rock and rooftop through the open air, for a second he could not be sure. But he was not Eothan, he knew. He had not stepped from the dais out of guilt and grief. He had fallen once before, when he was singing Evensong, and Grayson had caught him.

He was not there to catch him this time.

Willim opened his eyes. Everything around him had slowed to a crawl, even his own plummet down to the sea. Though it was dark, the world was bathed in a strange glow that illuminated every stone, every tree branch, the ridge of every wave far below. In the distance he could see the Thrassin ships like toys on a pond, their flanks flashing with cannon fire. Above him, the Temple's wall had crumbled. Ellis and Dmitri lay one atop the other, unmoving. Grayson dangled from Kestrel's hand, and Aeric frantically shoved rocks aside to free Jerdon and Rekbah.

The air screamed by Willim's ears as he fell, and it was with a sudden wonder that he realized he was screaming with it. No, not screaming. He was singing. Singing like the end of the world, singing as he fell towards Hasafel and his death, singing as Thrass rained down fire and destruction on his city. But as he was not Eothan, nor was he Thali. He was Willim fa Valos, and the Evensong was his and his alone.

The song began low in his belly, a purely physical push of diaphragm and lungs and air and vocal cords all working in unison to produce sound. It was as plain a mechanism as a water-wheel, and yet the result was nothing of earth. The song inside Willim was a burning brand, a star's course, a surging wave. When it broke free of him, it fused everything he was into a single chord of pure music, and Willim was borne up on its rising swell.

Willim, as a man, had ceased to exist. There was only the music, a music so vast and faceted that his voice was nothing but a tinny echo by comparison. It poured forth from the brightening sky, it rumbled deep in the haunted canyons of the sea. Willim was aware of everything the music permeated, as the whole world became saturated with sound. This was no wild, unpredictable cry, as the one that had brought down the *Larkspur*. It was not even the vengeance and heartbreak of Alveron and his kin that day on a bleak field, when his song wiped the life from Antigus and thousands of his men. This was the Song of Heaven, as had been sung in Hasafel, and Willim went with it out into the air.

From his vantage point outside himself, Willim saw all of it. In the old tunnels of the Undercity, the vibration of sound shook eons of dust from old sigils, and the Hall of the Heavens glowed pale blue with their light. In the deep watery places of the city, in the stillness of wells and the dark pits below the harbor's surface, something was waking. All around Valnon, the sea was suffused with a faint light, growing stronger with the coming dawn. On the enemy ships, Thrassin soldiers grew nervous, muttering in their unease. They made signs against evil and whispered about the sorcery of the demon eunuchs worshiped by the northern barbarians. But the Ethnarch was at their head, garbed for battle in armor of white steel, and they pressed on through the luminous waves.

Willim had already lost all sense of everything but the music. He did not control it, he was an instrument to be played by a will beyond his own. It was an ecstasy of the soul, the chaos of human emotion beaten out into pure light, and as the sun cracked a fissure of fire along the eastern horizon, it coalesced into a single, heartbreaking note.

The light in the sea had become blinding. The men on the ships flung their hands before their eyes. Water surged up around the lead ship, and a great spear of stone thrust upwards from the waves, splintering the ship in two.

The ships were flung upwards by the rush of the city being born beneath them. Spires and bridges broke free of the waves, tossing the vessels aside like leaves, leaving them to crash down upon the surfacing streets. One after another, the islands of the old city burst forth into the air once more. In the dazzling light of her song, gulls screamed and dove through the open windows of the reborn houses, and a great empty city stretched from horizon to horizon over the sea.

Heaven looked on Hasafel for the first time in a thousand years. The Thrass armada was broken to pieces on her shoulders, and the echoes in the sky began to die away. Willim was caught in the cupped hands of a rising statue, where he fell back into the deafening silence of his own body, and knew nothing more.

31

When Willim woke again he was in his own bedchamber, dressed in his own sleeping clothes, his hair damp and fragrant from a recent bath. For one dizzying moment, Willim thought everything had been a dream. But the restrained hum of holy song under his breastbone was no illusion, and he sat up quickly, blinking away sleep. His windows were bright with sunlight, the sounding vents were open and the Temple rustled with the noise of life, if not full song. Without pausing to soak in the comfortable peace of familiar surroundings, Willim pulled on the fresh clothing laid across the end of his bed and went out.

The broken furniture was still in the solar, heaped up in one corner. Dmitri and Ellis' beds were recently slept-in, but empty. Willim's fingers fumbled the dove-shaped buckle of his belt, managed to get it around his hips, and hurried down the stairs and into the corridor.

In the ave, late morning light streamed through the windows on a scene of somber industry. prentices still recovering from the effects of Jerdon's smoke bombs were laid on pallets of blankets, while the Queensguard loyal to Raven, conscious or not, were nowhere to be seen. Jerdon was tending to a few wounded prentices in one of the listening chapels, with Rekbah attending, wearing her arm in a sling like a pennant of valor. Aeric, not far off, was orchestrating the cleanup of the ave. Both of the saints had a kind of restrained grief in their faces, but Willim did not think he was mistaken in seeing some relief there, as well.

All in all, it was remarkably organized. Outside, a large crowd of citizens had gathered for news, and Kestrel was busy telling them that the Temple would be open again for Hours as soon as possible. Wyn, from the kitchens, was distributing honeycakes and tea to anyone who needed it, and he had roped Kite and Osprey in for assistance. The crowd was mostly hushed, thoughtful. They had come to the Temple not out of fear or need for aid, but because they wished to be together in one place, to contemplate the miracle of which they had unknowingly been part. Ellis, Dmitri, and Grayson were nowhere to be seen.

Willim found a nervous-looking prentice standing by the

corridor doors, and tapped him on the shoulder. "Where are the others?" he asked.

The prentice looked at him in something not unlike terror. He had been one of the ones following Petrine, and he clearly expected to be punished for it. "The--the Songbirds are in the Sanctuary, Your Grace."

"Thanks," Willim said, and sidestepped the crowd to reach the sanctuary doors, trying to ignore the sudden hush that happened wherever he passed.

The doors to the sanctuary were closed, but not barred. Willim put his fingers against the silver-banded wood and pushed it open to slip inside. The vast chamber was quiet, echoing. One section of the roof gaped wide to the bright winter sky, but the rubble had been cleared away, and all the stained glass was intact.

At the center of the room, near the covered dais pit, Alveron's body lay upon an ebony bier. He had been dressed in fresh robes of crimson velvet, the Wing of Valnon once more. Ellis' sket lay across his feet with its strings removed, as befitting the death of a Bird of Valnon. Willim expected a surge of grief, but at the sight of Alveron's tranquil face, he felt only a kind of aching peace.

A discreet distance away lay another body, this one completely draped in a Lark's sable. Dmitri was just putting a flute at Raven's feet, its sound-holes stoppered with cloth, as Ellis stood by.

"I thought you said you'd piss in his pyre one day," Ellis said.

Dmitri shrugged. "His pyre is not until tonight. I might yet."

"I doubt it," Ellis huffed. "It's a bit too much honor for a traitor, if you ask me."

Dmitri adjusted the angle of the muted flute. "Jerdon asked me to do it," he answered, quietly. "Out of respect for what he once was, if not for what he became. And since Jerdon's his saint, I think it's best to heed his wishes."

"Jerdon is right," Willim said, striding across the sanctuary to meet them. "It is better to remember his services to the Temple, rather than his crimes. I won't pretend I'm not relieved, but there's no reason to be disrespectful about it."

Ellis started, rushed over to Willim as though to embrace him, and then stopped short. There was still enough of the Song hanging over Willim to make him uncanny, and Ellis fidgeted, uneasily.

"Hasafel is already sinking again," Dmitri said, before Willim could ask. "Only a few of the tallest spires are still above the water, and Grayson went out with Hawk to look for any trace of the Thrassin or their ships." He shrugged. "They didn't find anything."

"No," Willim said, remembering the crush of water, the merciless sea-god for whom Hasafel was named. "No, I expect they didn't."

"You won't believe who they did find, though," Ellis said, beaming. "Sarin, cupped right in the palm of Hasal's statue. The Ethnarch had wrapped him in chains and thrown him in the sea, but somehow you managed to save him, too." His expression drooped, he twisted his ring on his hand. "He was with Captain Zeig on the Ethnarch's ship. But Zeig was killed before the battle began. He died trying to kill the Ethnarch, to slow down the armada."

Willim walked over to Alveron's side, and stared down into the face of his saint. "How many others have died?"

"We don't know," Dmitri answered. "The guns hit the harbor the hardest, but the cave itself kept most of the houses safe. There is plenty of damage to the Temple, but all the flock and Laypriests are accounted for, and all the Preybirds. If Raven had not had them all corralled down in the archives, many of them would surely have been killed. The Preybird's tower is practically a ruin, and I don't think there'll be any hope for our garden. But the sanctuary is mostly whole, at any rate. We'll make do."

"Do you think he knew all this would happen?" Ellis asked, nodding his head towards Alveron's still form.

"I think he knew he would not see the end of it," Willim admitted. "But beyond that, no. He was only human, like we are, like Eothan was."

Behind Willim, Ellis gasped faintly, and Dmitri said, in a strangled kind of voice, "Are you sure about that?"

Willim looked up. The doors to the sanctuary were wide open, and beyond them, all industry had grated to a halt. Standing in the doorway of the Sanctuary, his outline haloed in uneven light, was Eothan. He cradled a young woman's body in his arms, and strode into the Sanctuary with an echoless tread. For only a second, Willim glimpsed the tattered trappings of Starling, just before they bled away forever. Then Eothan was wholly himself, in his gleaming Temple garb and his labyrinthine eye-paints, and a smile that none there had ever seen.

"This is yours, Third of Doves," Eothan said, and laid the girl at Willim's feet. Her hair was the same colorless shade as Willim's, and Willim, with a jolt, saw in her face the same lines as his own. She was dressed in Willim's own discarded armor, her hands heavy with the claws that Eothan no longer wore. They were black with blood that was not her own. "Your sister, your queen, and my last command," Eothan explained, kissing the Queen's forehead before rising. "She is a Dove in all but the cutting, truly. I kept her safe, as Alveron wished."

"Is that why you came?" Willim asked, trying to read his predecessor's expression behind his paints. "To bring her back?"

Eothan's eyes thinned as he strode past the Songbirds, to the bier. "I came for what is mine, Dove of Valnon." In one motion he knelt down and swept Alveron's body into his embrace. "The Evensong is yours, but Alveron has always been mine." There was a whirl of motion all around him, the tumultuous beat of a thousand fluttering doves. In an instant, they swirled out of the gap in the arching roof of the sanctuary, and vanished. Eothan and Alveron were gone.

Reim stirred, her eyes opening with a soft noise of confusion. Willim shook off his wonder to kneel at her side, and catch her hand up in his.

"I dreamt of music," she said. "Where am I?"

"You are in the Temple," Willim said.

Reim studied him a moment, with her sightless eyes. "I know your voice," she said. "You are the Dove of Valnon."

"Yes," Willim answered, and the truth of that burned through him, as pure as the first note of Evensong. "I am."

"I assume there's a good reason for you dragging me all the way out here," Grayson said, trudging along after Kestrel through the empty prentices' training yard. "I want to talk to Willim, and you should be resting."

"You'll have more interesting things to report once I'm done with you," Kestrel answered, mischief dancing in his eyes. He wore his bandages like favors from fair lovers, and all Grayson's fussing could not have kept him in the infirmary.

338

Grayson eyed him askance. "I'm not sure I like the sound of that."

"Oh?" Kestrel would have said more, but a sound broke across the training yard. It was not the usual Temple music, but it was music to Grayson: the bright, trumpeting whinny of a stallion. "What about the sound of that?"

"Rouen--" Grayson began, but Kestrel waved him silent. Across the training yard, the gate to the stables opened, and Hawk emerged, once more resplendent in green. Following him was Alder Haverty, clutching the halter of a vast gray-dappled war-horse, easily eighteen hands high, and built like a fortress. It tossed its head lightly as it stepped into the sunshine, danced sideways a little with its back legs, and then went still, only a faint shiver to show its impatience.

"Per your original agreement," Hawk announced, allowing himself a little smile at Grayson's expression. "The finest horse in Valnon."

"Though I should admit," Kestrel said, in a murmur, "He's probably the finest horse in several places."

"I know this line," Grayson said, holding out his glove for the horse to investigate, nostrils quivering. "This is one of fa Ransey's grays."

"It is," Kestrel said, his grin utterly unrestrained. "His name is Shalefarrow, and he has been spoiling for a fight down in Darkmarket Garrison. You'll find his pedigree in the saddlebag. His blood's bluer than mine."

"As for the rest of your reward," Hawk went on, "I feel there is no sword we can give you more worthy than the one you already wear. However." He waved his hand, and Alder went into the stable to retrieve a chest, which he set down on the brown grass near Grayson. "I think you will find these of use."

Grayson was not prepared for the sudden clamor of his heart. He drew back the bolt on the chest, and the lid creaked open to reveal a cloak of fine wool in blazing crimson, a cuisse of black brigantine, and the burnished collar of an officer of the Godswords, trimmed in scarlet leather.

"The Wing of Valnon," Hawk said, presenting Grayson with a scroll whose heavy wax seals nearly overwhelmed its ribbon, "had already prepared the commissioning papers. Until the Dove finishes his Term, I fear I must act in the Wing's place. Therefore." Hawk let his smile show for the first time, as Grayson slowly unrolled the document of his investiture. "Welcome to the Godswords, Captain fa Grayce. It is the Temple's honor to have your service."

"And," Kestrel added, "about damn time, too."

The portrait room was an island of peace in the midst of chaos, and the queen of Valnon savored it like a hermit would her seclusion. At first the chamber had been a cacophony of new smells and textures, but now she knew its fragrance of wood polish and old linseed oil, she had learned the smooth wood and plush velvet of the heavy furniture. Temperature told her about the warm glow of the fireplace and the chilly frost laying on the windows. The faint notes of Dawning outlined the shape of the door in her mind. The rest of the Temple lay beyond it, where the scents changed, where the music grew stronger. Celebration and mourning were moving together there, swirling like a whirlpool at the changing of the tides. To most of them, everything was over. But Reim knew the subtle catalysts of change. What was happening to the Temple, and to its Dove, and to her, was only beginning.

There was the click of an oiled latch, a brief swelling of the Lark's melody, and then it diminished again. The queen was no longer alone.

"I wondered how long it would be before you came to see me, Dove of Valnon," she said, and smiled to hear his breath catch. She was turned away from the door, and he had thought to surprise her.

"You knew it was me?"

It was Willim's voice, and Reim shivered. They had not yet spoken together in private, to fill in the shapes that had been outlined between them by others. There had been no time. By the time Reim had fully recovered from her dreaming, Hasafel had sunk again, Raven was on his pyre, and the Dove of Valnon was once more established in his colors. There could be no meeting of them but here, at the border of the Temple's authority. Willim was her brother, born in secret, surrendered in secret. And yet he was not her brother. His blood was the Temple's, and would be forever. He had his vows, and his wound, and his song. Reim had her crown, and her darkness, and her destiny. Their lives would not be joined now simply because they knew of each other. And yet Reim was not sad. Some loose, rattling bead inside of her had at last found its stringing.

"I knew it was not Jerdon," Reim explained. "His sashes have a certain rustle, his tread a certain weight. His hair-ribbon makes a sound as it moves over his shoulder. You are wearing a Songbird's tunic with suspended sleeves, your hair is cut short, your stride is equal in his to length but you are younger, your boots are lighter. You are wearing bracelets that clink together, your earrings have bells with pearls for clappers. You took a bath in rose-scented water recently, but you used a soap of cassia and frankincense that is made especially for you by the perfumers' guild as Tribute. Your clothes smell of beeswax tapers and silk and the cedar-wood clothes-press you keep them in." She paused, smiling, drinking in his astonished silence. "Even if I was not expecting you, Your Grace, I would know you for a Songbird."

"How?" Willim wondered aloud, though she had just told him that. "How can you know so much without seeing me?"

She arched a brow in his direction, her smile puckering into a scolding pout. "How can you sing a melody without hearing it anywhere, but by looking at little marks on a paper?"

She startled an exhalation out of him, not quite a laugh. "I suppose, Your Highness, that your handicap is nothing of the sort."

"No more than yours is," Reim answered, pointedly.

"Ah," Willim said, with understanding. There was a pause, as he shifted his weight in the doorway. "Did you know?" he asked, at last. "About me?"

Reim twisted her hands in the folds of her skirt. "No," she said. "Like you, I was not to be told until your term was finished. Nilan tells me that my parents wished it to be so, in order that neither of us would strive from our places until we had grown into them fully. As fully-invested Queen and Wing of Valnon, we would be powerful together, but our loyalty to each other must never exceed the loyalty to our places."

"I had no idea," Willim said, in a bewildered tone. "The Temple deliberately avoids any attachments to our old families. I had assumed I was a bastard like Ellis, picked up by the Laypriestess in the Undercity, sent on to the Temple when I showed an aptitude for music. I hardly gave it a thought that I would have parents... a sister."

"Alveron dared not tell you. It would give weight to your position as Dove, and place an even greater burden on you than the one under which Eothan failed."

She heard his head come up, his earrings jangle. "You knew? About Alveron?"

"Willim," Reim said, saying his name for the first time. "Everything that happened here, I saw. I saw your face when Raven revealed your bloodline, I felt the passing of Alveron's last breath, I shivered in fear as your song wrenched Hasafel from the sea. Alveron himself ordered Eothan to watch over me, but I think he knew that in doing so, I would learn more than I ever would by being in the thick of battle." She rose from her seat, following her senses unerringly until she stood in front of him. His hand was warm in hers, their rings clinked together. "And even if he didn't plan it, even if it was pure chance and the capricious will of a ghost, I'm not sorry. Eothan and Alveron were both generous men, in spite of everything that had been taken from them. Because of them I was able to save Nilan, and you were able to save Valnon. You are a true Dove."

"I had thought to surrender my colors," Willim admitted, in a rush. "When we had the Temple back, and everything was done. I've done so much... things a Songbird should never do. I've been bloodied and I've taken a lover and I've broken so many of my vows I lost track of them. But when I mentioned that to Hawk, he nearly took my head off. Told me that he'd never heard anything so selfish. I am Dove of Valnon, I'd sung down Heaven's will, and with Alveron's death they will need me to be Wing of Valnon when my term is through. He said he didn't care what I'd done or with whom, that I had Heaven's blessing, and that was good enough for him."

"And," Reim said firmly, "it is good enough for me, and good enough for Valnon. In fact I think you'll be quite busy. My investiture festivities are going to be utterly eclipsed now, you know."

His other hand came near her braided crown of hair, but did not quite touch it. "What now?" he asked. "We are strangers, and our lives are as divided as they ever were. It's not as though we can suddenly be a family, you and I. What is to be gained by it?"

"Gained?" Reim repeated. "More than either of us know or yet suspect, Dove of Valnon." She brought his hand to her cheek, pressed her lips to the curved dove on his signet. "But know that if you ever need me, as a Queen or as a sister, I will be there."

"You know you don't have to rush into this tonight," Ellis said, settling the winged coronet on Willim's hair. "Everyone will understand if you want to let things settle, first."

"Most of Valnon is out in that Sanctuary, Ellis," Willim reminded him. "And the ones that don't fit are spilling out into the street. They've been waiting all day, and I'm not about to let them down."

"Well," Ellis said, "As long as you're sure."

Willim was looking for his other earring. He had not been gone from the Temple all that long, and yet it seemed like it was taking him twice as long to prepare for the dais. He turned up the errant jewel, at last, under the lid of his kohl. "Of course I'm sure. One doesn't just sing up Hasafel and then skip out on Evensong."

"Sarin's very excited," Ellis said, clipping Willim's mantle to his collar. "Me too, actually. I mean, it's pretty exciting."

"Well, I'm as nervous as I was for my debut." Willim reached for his cuff but fumbled it, and landed on the floor with a clatter, somewhere towards the end of his freshly-mended drape. "Ugh, saintsblood! Get that on me, will you, Ellis?"

Preoccupied with his mirror, and with a strand of pearls that seemed insistent on going directly into his eye, Willim held out his arm. The platinum cuff clicked around his wrist with surprising gentleness, and warm lips brushed the top of Willim's ring of office.

"Yes, Your Grace."

Willim's cry of surprise died unvoiced. Ellis, astutely, had abandoned the premises. Standing in Willim's chamber was a Godsword in black and red, his gorget gleaming in martial echo of Willim's own, Grayce's sword resting patiently against his hip. Willim tried for words, and fumbled them. It was as though he was meeting the man again for the first time, and his familiar bodyguard and lover was only a pale shadow of the holy knight now before him.

"I take that to mean," Grayson said, his smile dispelling the glamor somewhat, "that it suits me?"

"Yes," Willim managed. "It does." He let out a breath, with a little shudder. "For an instant I wondered if I even knew you."

"That's fair," Grayson said. "Now you know how I feel, seeing you in all this." He summed up Willim's priceless garb with a gesture. "They've done a good job with the repairs."

"It'll do," Willim said, tracing a finger along a mend in his drape. "I suppose I should get used to calling you Nicholas fa Grayce, now."

Grayson laughed. "Not quite. My family is not so quick to forgive as the Temple. It might take them another fifteen years to accept my name back, if they ever do."

"I don't see how they couldn't. You bear Grayce's sword, given to you by Alveron himself."

"A trifling fact that is unlikely to sway Isbell. Besides, I've grown fond of being Grayson. It lacks a certain arrogance that I always found a burden. Then again," he flashed a wink at Willim, "I think a certain Songbird has a way of getting on Isbell's soft side. Perhaps I will leave that task to him."

They looked at each other until the stillness became awkward, both of them acutely aware of their positions. Once more in their proper trappings, they were caged by everything they stood for.

"I came to tell you how much I have enjoyed my time in your service," Grayson said, a little stiffly now. The light in Willim's windows was quickly yellowing with the approach of sundown.

Willim's breath caught. "You're leaving?"

"Only if you are willing to accept my resignation as your bodyguard," Grayson said, looking away. "Thrass has been caught off-guard, Willim, and badly. They are leaderless, and ill-prepared. Hawk and the Regent agree that if we can press for a new treaty with the Ethnarch's heir, it might quell the turmoil on the border at last. I hope to go south to meet fa Ransey's troops, and with Heaven's will, we can finish this. I should like to be a part of it. Perhaps my service to the Temple will not come too late, after all."

Willim turned around on his stool, staring at the jumble of jewels and paint-pots until they became a glittering blur. "I should have known," he murmured. "I should have known long since. You tried to tell me, already."

"Please, Willim," Grayson said, and then, meeting Willim's eyes in the mirror, said nothing else.

Willim smoothed his features, rose up from his seat. "Ellis has deserted me, it seems," he said, gathering up his train. "Will you help me down to the dais?"

Grayson brought his fist to his chest, then held out his arm for Willim to lean on. "It will be my honor."

They descended the stairs together in silence, barely touching, faces still. It was only once they had passed the Dovecote and started down the shadowy dais passage that Willim slid his hand down Grayson's arm, and twined their fingers tightly together.

"You have two years," Willim said, without turning to look at him.

"Two years?" Grayson echoed.

"Two years, until my term is done," Willim said, stepping up onto the lowered dais. Above them, the sound of Valnon was like the shush of the tide. "And in that time, Nicholas fa Grayce," Willim went on, turning to look down at his Godsword, "I expect you to win this war for me."

Understanding blossomed on Grayson's face. He knelt down at his Songbird's feet, his sheathed sword to his forehead. "Yes, my Dove."

Willim reached down for Grayson, and pulled him to his feet. Their lips met in a kiss that would have to last them through all the days to come, through darkness and battle and hundreds of sunsets. They held onto each other until the dais trembled to life beneath Willim, slowly pulling him out of Grayson's arms. Willim let Grayson's fingers slip through his, as the first note of Evensong replaced Grayson's warmth upon his lips, as the dais lifted him up into the sanctuary where Valnon was waiting for him.

* * *

Leah S. Baird is a native of Kentucky and a graduate of Berea College with a degree in Theater. She has been by turns a weaver, a costume designer, a tour guide, an animal handler, a jewelry maker, an actor, a switchboard operator, a corporate drone, and a cash register jockey. She has been telling stories all her life, including the one when she was seven about how it was totally someone else that drew on her jeans with magic marker. She's been getting into trouble over her stories ever since, up to and including getting married because of them. Currently she lives in Maryland with her partner, Joy, their cat, Tseng, and their action figure collection, Legion. She is a dragon-year Cancer, a believer in mountain folk magic, a player of video games and a baker of cookies. She is not the famous silent film star you will find when you google her name. She enjoys dressing up as other people and talking about herself in the third person. Her hair is often pink. You've probably read some of her fanfic.

For more about the world of Valnon, visit her official webpage at http://www.valnon.org

Made in the USA
Charleston, SC
28 June 2013